A. McNeill

TO THE WOOD NO MORE

BOOKS BY ERNEST RAYMOND

Novels :

A LONDON GALLERY *comprising*

WE, THE ACCUSED
THE MARSH
GENTLE GREAVES
THE WITNESS OF CANON WELCOME
A CHORUS ENDING
THE KILBURN TALE
CHILD OF NORMAN'S END
FOR THEM THAT TRESPASS
WAS THERE LOVE ONCE ?
THE CORPORAL OF THE GUARD
A SONG OF THE TIDE
THE CHALICE AND THE SWORD

OTHER NOVELS :

TELL ENGLAND
A FAMILY THAT WAS
THE JESTING ARMY
MARY LEITH
MORRIS IN THE DANCE
THE OLD TREE BLOSSOMED
DON JOHN'S MOUNTAIN HOME
THE FIVE SONS OF LE FABER
THE LAST TO REST
NEWTIMBER LANE
THE MIRACLE OF BREAN
ROSSENAL
DAMASCUS GATE
WANDERLIGHT
DAPHNE BRUNO I
DAPHNE BRUNO II

Biographies:

TWO GENTLEMEN OF ROME
    (The Story of Keats and Shelley)
IN THE STEPS OF ST. FRANCIS
IN THE STEPS OF THE BRONTËS

Essays, etc.:

THE SHOUT OF THE KING
BACK TO HUMANITY (*with Patrick Raymond*)

Plays:

THE BERG
THE MULTABELLO ROAD

TO THE WOOD
NO MORE

A NOVEL

by
ERNEST RAYMOND

THE BOOK CLUB
121, Charing Cross Road,
London, W.C.2

FOR

EDYTHE BLAINE

Nous n'irons plus aux bois, les lauriers sont coupés

MADE AND PRINTED IN GREAT BRITAIN BY
WYMAN & SONS LIMITED, LONDON, READING AND FAKENHAM

CONTENTS

CHAPTER ONE

THE PARSON OF MOSGROVE

ONE should be shocked when a brother dies by his own hand, and especially so if one is a clergyman in the Church of England; and the Reverend Albany Grahame, Rector of Mosgrove-St. Neots, strove to be properly shocked. And certainly to appear so. " It is terrible," he said to his wife and daughter in the hallway of the Rectory, when he was returned from a visit to the place of disaster. " Terrible. There can be no doubt about it : he shot himself in a beechwood on his estate. His gun was beside him." And, shaking his head sadly, he hoped he looked as shocked, if not as white, as they did. He passed by them, hurrying to his study door, with his mouth set tight and square, and he couldn't stop the thought, " If they think I'm clamping back the tears, why, so much the better."

Once in the study, with the door shut, he said again, " Yes, it's terrible," because he really desired to be shocked.

But if that shot far away, ninety miles away, meant a trans-figuration of one's whole life, if the sudden death of an elder brother, seldom seen and never approved of, changed one from a comparatively poor man with a stipend of four hundred pounds and a huge, decaying, flaking rectory into a compara-tively rich man with a capital of forty thousand, if, above all, it changed him, an exceptionally tall and handsome man (one had no need to affect modesty behind a closed study door) from " The Reverend Albany Grahame " into " Sir Albany Grahame, Baronet," if, in a sentence, that shot in the far distance flung open his prison doors—if, not unlike the Last Trump, it opened one's grave and summoned one to arise and live—well, it was not easy to sustain grief. But he did not abandon at once the effort to be unhappy. Rather did he say again and again, " It is terrible," and " I am a lot shaken."

He walked to the window. The afternoon sunlight lay upon his garden and upon the pastures beyond where the cattle browsed. It hung on the bare trees and on the flanks of the far-off hills. " I must go out for a walk," he thought. " Alone. It has shaken me a lot, this. I feel I want to get the air on my brow."

The Reverend Albany Grahame, whenever he was possessed by thoughts of sadness or by thoughts of joy—or, as on this occasion by both, with the joy predominating—felt driven to take them out of his house and walk with them under the sky. And so this afternoon he walked quickly from his study, drew his handsome ebony walking stick from the hatstand, and passed out into the garden. In the garden he swung the stick in a lovely circle, and then remembered not to. Wife or daughter, not wishing to worry him with their questions at this stage, might be glancing at him from a window and thinking, " This has shaken him a lot. We shall have to try later to comfort him." So he held the stick in a firm control until he was through the gate and out of their sight. Some effort of the will was necessary to control it, because this handsome black stick, the companion of his walks, always seemed to have a life of its own, a gay life and irrepressible, as if it were filled from crook to ferrule with *joie-de-vivre*.

Perhaps its inward gaiety was little suited to its appearance, for with its sleek black polish and deep silver neckband, it had something of an ecclesiastical look, almost, you might say, an archidiaconal look. It was extraordinarily like the Archdeacon of Johannesburg, Albany would say, when he was feeling as gay as the stick. It was long ; it had a black sheen, and it wore that round clerical collar, the silver band, just like that good-looking archdeacon, the Venerable Michael Furse. For this reason the Rector always called the stick " Michael."

Imprisoned how long ? Twenty-seven years. Twenty-seven years in Mosgrove——

But poor old Vick. Poor blithe old Vick. To think that he should have done this desperate thing. And he the very picture and statue of a successful man ! Vick who always seemed a man without a care, ever jovial, ever jesting, ever feasting and making merry with his friends ! Vick who was said to be the most popular ' savage ' in the Savage Club ! And he barely sixty when he went with his gun into the beechwood, only five years older than himself, the new baronet, Sir Albany ! Poor, poor, lonely, secretly despairing old Vick. The Rector swung the ebony cane in lively circles as he expressed compassion for poor old Vick. One's heart did bleed for him—but, " You won't come far short of fifty thousand, Albany, old cock," he had said five or six years ago after he'd heard of his only son's death in the Transvaal, fighting the Boers. " I must leave you enough to support the old title. Good God, it cost me enough to get it, one way and another. And forty thousand or so won't be a quarter of what I shall be able to leave, my dear fellow, so don't worry about that." Vick had always been rather vulgarly purse-proud, so his brother thought, who disapproved of purse-pride, having never achieved more than four hundred a year.

Forty thousand at, say, an average of five per cent. Two thousand a year.

The Rector of Mosgrove walked along his lanes between hedgerows newly starred with primroses and daisies and dandelions. A chiff-chaff, newly arrived, tossed his double note at him, tossed it twenty times, from the top of a tree ; chaffinches saluted the sunlight and the warm, earth-scented air with their defiant and saucy trill ; the sun had the whole clean sky to itself and, delighted with this monopoly, gave of its bounty to every hedge, field, gate and lane ; and this sunlight upon the world was sister to the glow in his heart.

He was very happy ; yes, very happy ; and ashamed that he should be so. Ashamed, because he had a heart that was soft in places and a conscience trained by his calling and his cloth to be tender all over. But nevertheless nothing could suppress the leaping joy in his heart as he walked onward into the delightful afternoon. Buried how long ? Twenty-seven years. Twenty-seven years in Mosgrove. And full thirty-two years since, as a not very intelligent young man of twenty-three (or so it seemed now) he had made himself, with some pride and more doubts, into a parson and shut upon himself, without perceiving it at the time, the prison-doors of Holy Orders. Very secret thoughts, these. No one, and certainly not Delia, his wife, and Susannah, his daughter, must ever know of them. And now this day, he was free of the prison——

But Vick dead ! *Dead !* Looking far back into the past, he saw Vick and himself as boys together ; and he watched their ways diverging : Vick going one way, to become a man of money and power and position ; and Albany taking another and quieter road, to become, and, alas, to remain, the rector of this little hidden parish through whose bright lanes he was walking.

There they were, those two boys, in their small London home : Victor Pemberton Grahame and Gerald Albany Grahame. Their father, Major Alastair Grahame, young, tall, stately and somewhat pompous, had insisted on giving each boy a family surname for his second name, and Gerald had always been grateful to him for ' Albany '—as soon as possible he had dropped the ' Gerald ' altogether. ' The Reverend Albany ' had sounded well ; and now what could sound better than ' Sir Albany Grahame ' ? That young, stately Major had died all too early, just as he was about to get a deputy governorship in the Prison Service, and thenceforward the London home of their childhood had been in a leafy street of small, quiet, decorous houses on the east of Richmond Hill. In the little grey houses dwelt other widows of half-pay officers and little clerkly persons from banks, insurance offices and counting-houses, and a big whiskered curate with a worn little wife and a string of babies, and a modest young doctor with a long square beard—all very genteel and striving, and some, like the Major's widow, very near to poverty.

Vick from the first had been a boy with more talent for being noisy and larky in school, and for fiddling profitable deals with his fellows, than for passing exams, but this constancy in failure didn't worry him at all, since he had early announced that he wasn't going into any ill-paid ' gentleman's profession ' but was going to make a pile of money as quickly as possible, and to hell with all gentlemanliness—Vick was given to language like that. Albany, on the other hand, a shyer boy but not less ambitious in his own way, had a strong determination never to sit on a high stool in bank or insurance office, but to be beyond question a gentleman ; and since in those days, even as now, the easiest path for a poor boy to a gentleman's profession was the path to Holy Orders by way of a theological college, he turned his eyes that way, not without enthusiastic and rather overwhelming encouragement from the big whiskered curate. When he told his mother that he " thought p'raps he'd be a parson," she, a pious lady and unremitting churchgoer, was overjoyed and praised God in her prayers and strengthened the boy's will to this purpose, day after day, year after year, till at last, almost without his full consent, almost as if he were powerless flotsam on this enthusiastic tide, it was settled that Albany was ' going into the Church.' And so he had become a curate at twenty-three, and four years later married Delia Freestone-Hay, the admiral and churchwarden's daughter, eight years older than he but one of a staunch churchgoing family which had a country living in its gift ; and after only five years as a curate, he was inducted into this incumbency, which was the incumbency of Mosgrove-St. Neots. He and he only knew that when he married Delia Freestone-Hay he was deliberately marrying also the reversion of this living; but he could tell himself that he was driven to this expediency, not only by a desire to advance as soon as possible from curate to rector but also by a craving to escape from the hard London pavements and to bask in the calm and beauty of broad meadows, quiet streams, and gentle tree-capped hills. No such longing for the peace and beauty of rural scenes showed itself for many a day in Vick, that other town-bred boy. London for two score years was his pasture and his hill, and his bright, sparkling stream.

Somehow, Albany never knew how, Vick had arrived on the board of Prince's Music Halls Ltd. and though he never rose to be captain of that enterprise, for old Isidor Prince was always the titular president, he quickly became the real power in its battle-headquarters. He had had the fortune, or the flair, to get into the music hall trade just when that form of entertainment was conquering the tired, the semi-literate, or the lazy-minded multitudes, just as the cinema was to do a generation later; and soon Prince's Ltd. had a chain of halls cast across England, large and shining halls in the centres of the towns and small and dirty ones in the suburbs. Dirty in more than one sense of the word. And the money from these innumerable pay boxes and bar counters came flooding into Vick's capacious reservoir. Albany would never admit that he was jealous of his brother's ever-enlarging wealth, but there was surely much in Vick's bouncing career over which a clergyman might shake a disapproving head. You couldn't deny that this money came from a trade that ministered to the worst appetites of men : from displays, for example, of high-kicking chorus girls whose main task was to give, from under a froth of petticoats, quick coy glimpses of their suspenders and the naked parts adjacent thereto ; from the suggestive songs and bawdy jokes of exceedingly low comedians ; from theatre bars where the beer and spirits splashed and flowed ; and, worst of all (one dropped one's voice as one mentioned this) from foyers and promenades where the feathered and bejewelled ladies offered their charms and their talents as at a hiring fair. Albany was surely entitled to say—but to himself only since this was no language for a clergyman—that it was better to be a poor parson than a wealthy pimp.

Still, like many of the jovial and easygoing sort Vick was generous with his money and his time, and after he had bought his large estate in Hampshire he gave himself to public service and public munificence. In due time he became a governor of the Mid-Hants County Hospital, a co-opted member of the Senate of Mid-Hampshire University, and chairman of the Conservative Party in his constituency. He gave a wing, the Victor Grahame Wing, to the hospital, a liberal endowment to the university, and twenty-thousand pounds to his party funds, so that, when his only son's death on the veldt was added to these benefactions, the Conservative Government could do little else than give him a baronetcy.

Of all this the brother, left to rest in a country rectory, despite abilities which he was confident were the equal of Vick's, could only say, when his wife spoke in wonder of Vick's talent for success, " I hope one doesn't measure success by the money amassed or the applause received. I trust one's values are less vulgar than that."

Once when Vick met him for the first time in ten years he called him ' an old puritan ', and Albany chose to be pleased with the appellation and regard it as a label of honour rather than of ridicule. For the more Vick succeeded and waxed fat in the world of the Flesh and the Devil, the more Albany chose to be (or to appear) a puritan in the world of the Spirit.

Until this moment. This moment of elation when Vick— poor old Vick—with a shot from his gun had blown open the Rector's prison doors and set him free. Free for a life of very different fashion. No one knew, not even wife or daughter, that for years past he had been sick of this life in Mosgrove. True enough that twenty-seven years ago he had wanted to come to the country to enjoy its peace and beauty and the long leisure of a country rector's life (though this last item he had never mentioned) but now he was sick of this solitary confinement behind the receding hills. He had hardly any educated person to talk with and little to do day after day but sit with his feet on a stool and kill the empty hours by reading, one after another, the sixpenny paper-backed novels of Charles Garvice, Guy Boothby or Rider Haggard. And always these tales of love of sport or other excitement pressed upon the ache of discontent in his heart. " I am getting old and missing life," he would think, dropping his book to his knees. " I am reading imaginary lives when I might be living myself. There's a lot of life owing to me, but if nothing happens soon, I shall never have it."

Sometimes he tried to read better stuff than these novels,

but even this austerer reading could, now and again, play the same trick upon his heart and press upon the pain. Once he was labouring through Walter Pater's *The Renaissance* and he came upon the passage, ' A counted number of pulses only is given to us of a variegated dramatic life. How shall we pass most swiftly from point to point and be present always at the focus where the greatest number of vital forces unite in their purest energy ? To burn always with this hard, gemlike flame is success in life.'

He dropped the volume to his knees, miserable with the thought that he had never burned with a gemlike flame.

Nor was this all. Only he knew, assuredly only he knew, that he had long wearied of his priestly labours and long ceased to believe in half the things he was obliged to preach to his few rustic people and teach to their snotty children. He would rejoice to be quit, not only of these tasks, but, even more, of the hypocrisy. And now he could be quit of both, and he did rejoice. He rejoiced with the ebony cane—but just then he observed a labourer, ruddy and grizzled, coming towards him with a midden fork on his shoulder, and instantly he stabilized the cane and arranged his face into a mask of grief.

" Ah'ternoon, Rector," said the man, touching his cap and halting before him. The rich smell of dung halted with him, radiating from fork and boots.

" Good afternoon, Stan."

" Things all well with ee, zur ? Ah 'ope so. All in good shape ? "

" Alas, no, Stan. Indeed no."

" But ye do be looking fine. Leastways, Ah thought zo. Looking vine."

" I'm not feeling fine. I've had some very, very bad news."

" Go on, zur ! " The man stared, and Albany was glad of an audience to hear the bad news.

" Yes, I've just heard that my brother has died. And tragically."

" What ? Did a' meet with some assident ? "

" No, Stan. It was—he died by his own hand."

" Oh, Lord, Lord ! Lord in Heaven ! But things do happen queer like that, zumtimes, zur. People can be took queer, zumtimes, when they're not zo young—meaning no disrespect. I'm very sorry for 'ee."

" Yes, and he was my only brother. We were boys together." There was pathos in these words and, since he was always moved

13

by pathos, and not least when he uttered it to himself, they raised a brief moisture to his eyes.

" Ah, yes, it must be a big blow for 'ee."

" It is."

" Nothing me and the missus can do for 'ee and the lady, I suppose ?."

" No, thank you, Stan. It is kind of you, but one must just bear these things. Well . . . good-bye, my dear fellow."

He gave to the labourer the stoical sweet smile of the afflicted, raised his right hand in a farewell that was almost episcopal with benediction, and walked on.

Free. Now he could do everything that he longed to do. He was not really old yet. Fifty-five was no great age, and in any case he was different from most men ; he was quite exceptionally youthful and vigorous. To be sure, there were times of gaiety and gusto, when he hardly felt thirty. Yes, he had plenty of time left to collect all that was owing to him.

He might even find love. But hush : this was a very private thought. He was still a parson, and his conscience told him that it was a shocking thought for a parson. He tried for a little to obey his conscience. He walked a little faster so as not to think it. But his heart was hungrier than his conscience was tender, and he went on thinking it. He considered it for a half-mile and more, because it was a thought that could enthrall as no other. He had never known real love or enjoyed beauty in his bed, as a man should. Delia had been a good and helpful wife but (not to mince his words) she had been something of a Plain Jane when he married her mainly because he saw Mosgrove Rectory behind her, and she was really (not to funk a truth) rather distressing to look at now. Was it too late, was he too old now, to find love and romance ? If he was no longer a parson—if he need pose no longer as a puritan—might he not . . . perhaps . . . Was he not an exceptionally handsome man (no need to be modest in a quiet lane) ? Six foot three, with wide shoulders, black hair silver at the ears, black eyes, a fine nose—a really splendid nose—and no one was to know that behind the pointed copper-and-silver moustaches and the neatly-pointed grey beard there was an upper lip too deep and a chin that receded a little—only a little, but enough to disappoint, and hence the shapely beard. Nor because of his fine height and broad shoulders was anyone to know that there was a little convex belly beneath his waistcoat and watch-chain.

He alone perceived the full truth about that belly when he lay in his bath and it rose before him like a rose-pink island above the waters.

Yes, a handsome man, thanks partly to the beard. Had not that gushing creature, Mrs. Peverel-Ames, described his appearance as ' princely ' and did she not tell everyone that her rector was one of the four handsomest men she had ever seen ? Of course she was a gusher—but there was something in it. Not one of the four handsomest men in the world, no, that was quite absurd ; but definitely above the average. Even high above the average. And all these good wares were wasting in the country. And time was passing. Take them to town, and what—what might they not win for him ?

His heart pulsed with anticipated pleasure. A quick, sweet thirst for it dried up his throat as he walked on.

There was a smile beneath the moustaches, a light in the black eyes, and a renewed swinging of the cane as he turned to walk homeward. Opening his door, he saw his wife in the passage and greeted her, " Well, Lady Grahame ! " before he perceived that this humour was untimely ; whereupon he coughed it away and made haste to add, " That's what you are now, I'm afraid, but one would hardly wish it at such a cost. It's a pitiful business."

Longing to discuss his plans for the future (but behind a mask of sadness), he said, " Come, Delia dear. Come into the study and let's talk. We must really talk. This is all very serious. It involves us in great changes."

" Changes ? Why ? " demanded Delia.

" Why ? Well, because . . . well, obviously . . . surely . . . but come and sit down." Was it going to be difficult to state a case to Delia ?

She sat down, but only at the brink of a chair, as if she could not think the changes would be many or require much talk ; and he, remembering his thoughts in the lane, looked at her. A long, withered, bone-showing woman with white hair. Incredible to think that she was now sixty-three and looking every year of her age, while he still felt like a man in his early prime and looked no more than, say, forty-five. Or perhaps forty-nine. Her features were long and thin, like her long, thin, and (yes, not to put too fine a point on it) scraggy body. Nearly always their expression was serious, and in repose, sometimes it was grim—so grim that her husband did not care to contemplate it, he being of neither a grim nor a melancholy cast, but sanguine and lively and at times even boisterous. She was thus grim, he thought, because her father, the admiral and churchwarden, had been a strict evangelical, and her husband had always posed as one, and she had never in sixty years questioned anything her father had taught her or anything her husband had preached in his pulpit while she sat below. Admirable the loyalty, and astonishing the passive credulity, of most women ; and especially clergymen's wives.

" You ask why there'll be—ah—changes. Well, I don't see, my dear, that we can stay here."

" Not stay here ? Why ever not ? "

" Well . . . don't you see : we shall be comparatively well-off. I hope that we—I mean, I've been given to understand that we shall have about two thousand a year."

" What does that matter ? We can do good with it."

" Yes, yes, of course. Certainly. Of course. I want to do good with it, but—— "

" You mean you want to leave Mosgrove ? "

" Yes. I feel that we . . . that I—— "

" Leave your lovely little Church ? Oh, no ! "

" Oh, *yes* ! " Not knowing how to describe his feelings, he began to get hot at her demand for them. " I've long thought I'd like to go. I've long been pretty miserable here. I—— "

" Miserable ? This is the first I've heard about your being miserable."

" Naturally. I'm not one to inflict my miseries on everyone around. But I *have* often suggested to you that I'm starved of intellectual companionship in this mossy spot. My interests are all intellectual, you'll allow, and you must surely see that there's not a single person here with whom I can enjoy a really intellectual talk. Except old Bait, and he's only here at odd times. Apart from old Bait there's not a creature here whose mind has changed since 1860, or thereabouts. Old Bait's the only oasis in this intellectual wilderness." Good phrasing ; almost a proof of what he was saying, that he was a man with a brain. " It's different for you. You have all the friends you want, because women, as I've often expounded to you, are never seriously troubled by intellectual starvation. As long as they can talk about persons and things they are happy, and one can talk about persons and things anywhere. They've no craving, like me, to discuss ideas—or perhaps it would be truer to say they don't mind what their topic is, so long as they're

16

talking. Isn't that so, ha, ha ? Oh, Mosgrove's all right for you, but it stifles me—Mosspot, the mossiest spot in England ! "

" But you wanted to come here ! When you first came and saw the loveliness of the country, you said it was a dream fulfilled."

" I know I did but I've—I've fulfilled my dream. I've been fulfilling it now for nearly thirty years, and I want some life for a change."

" Where do you propose to go ? "

" London, of course. Somewhere near old Bait. Yes, I'd like to live near old Bait. He's my best friend. My one friend." He spoke it with pathos and threw out his under-lip.

" You mean you'd resign your living ? "

" Yes, of course." Irritated, he began to walk about. " I can't take it with me."

" Well, I suppose you could give your services to some church."

" *What ?* "

She repeated the suggestion . . . " give your services to some church."

" Maybe, maybe." But he was pretty certain he was going to do nothing of the sort. He even doubted if he was going to attend church much more. He'd had so much of it, years and years of it, and so much of it had been hypocrisy. " I'm not at all sure that I'm not going to withdraw from active spiritual work for a while and think things out. I've long thought I'd like to give myself to some quiet thought about our various dogmas. And it may be that this is a God-sent opportunity, yes, literally a providential opportunity, to do so. I have never been able to give myself properly to thought here. I should have neglected my work if I had done so." As he said this, he saw himself in his closed study with his feet on the stool, finishing one paper-backed novel and starting another. " I want to consider very profoundly the more miraculous parts of our religion. They've troubled me for some time."

" But, Albany, this doesn't mean, surely, that you're losing your faith ? After all these years ? "

" Certainly not. Not at all. Of course not. It means—it means that, in a sense, I'm more religious than ever I was . . . more spiritual, shall we say . . . anxious to probe deeper . . . to get shut of anything that's even the tiniest bit hypocritical—"

But at that moment he heard a young voice singing in the sunlight of the garden and coming nearer to the french windows of his room. Softly, almost unconsciously, it was singing, and it came nearer.

> ' Ye banks and braes o' bonny Doon,
>   How can ye bloom sae fresh and fair. . . .'

Susannah. She had forgotten the disaster in the day, she who had not met her uncle five times in her life, and she was singing happily to herself as she came along the flower beds and glanced at crocus and daffodil, prunus and magnolia, and at the yellow forsythia bursting from the old wall like a rocket of stars.

> ' Oft hae I roved by bonny Doon
>   To see the rose and woodbine twine . . .'

Her low, sweet voice brought with it a sudden new idea, a new and excellent argument. " There's Susannah to be thought of. I've long thought that, if only for her sake, we ought to get out of this moss-grown spot. She's eighteen now and ought to have her chance of a full life. Yes, I've thought a lot about this, and if I do go, it'll be largely for her sake." And to himself he said, " Yes, I must try to feel this. And I do most sincerely feel it. It's true ; it's the truest thing I've said so far. And I can honestly say it to everyone." He opened the french windows and called, " Susannah darling, come here."

" Yes, Daddy dear." She stopped her song, abruptly, remembering that this was not a time for singing.

She came into the room, a slender girl, tall like him, with dark hair like his, and a wide brow above wide-spaced violet eyes ; and his heart swelled with a pride and a love that together were almost pain. Susannah, he liked to tell himself, was the one perfect thing in his life. From the day she was born he had indulged a sentimental dream that he would have a daughter whose beauty was matched by her affection, but she, for sixteen years, a noisy, rampant, ill-kempt girl, with her dark hair in her eyes, her skin less than perfect, and her flying limbs long and gawky—with an unstable temperament, now turbulent, now affectionate, now sullen—had blunted again and again this sharp eagerness to love ; and then, at sixteen, the miracle had happened : a competent, smug, bossy, quick-tempered little hoyden had bloomed into this graceful, gracious, seductive thing and at the same time fallen in love with her father, speaking of him as " a darling, a most beloved person." The whole of his dream had suddenly been granted him, and sometimes his heart could hardly bear the joy of it. He would look at her face, seeking this pleasure that was almost pain, even as, with a sigh at his heart, he avoided looking at Delia for fear of a disappointment that was certainly pain. Of course there were still occasions when the child's temper flared and she spat fire, but never with him, only with Delia or some other. And with Delia or some other it was quite pardonable, quite entertaining—even charming.

He looked at Susannah now as she came in with some daffodils in her hand, and he knew that this was the creature he loved best in all the world, after himself.

" Susannah, we have a lot to talk over. How would you like to leave Mosspot and go to London ? "

" Oh, Daddy *dear* ! " Her " Daddy dear " always went to his heart.

" Some nice interesting place such as old Bait lives in, where you could have heaps of young friends and go to all the theatres you want to. Shall we go, eh ? " He asked it brightly, and then remembered that his state was one of shock and sadness. " This has been a terrible business, of course, but I don't want it to upset you. It's no good pretending your Uncle Vick was anything to you. For me—well, he was my brother. We . . . we were boys together."

" Yes, I know, Daddy, I know." And she frowned, as if defeated in her longing to comfort him. This bending of her brows when her thought was defeated always seemed to him a strangely beautifying thing. How was it that a frown of perplexity could add its charm to a face ?

" I don't want you to give this tragic business another thought. Let's talk of pleasant things. This unhappy affair at least means that I can do great things for you. And that's the only thing that's of much interest to me now. *My* time is passed."

" Don't talk such rubbish ! Mummy, what awful nonsense that man does talk ! Daddy dear, you haven't begun to get old ; you don't look—well——" she put her hand on one side to consider him—" say, forty-nine." He could have wished she had said forty-five. " And you have never, in all the years I've known you, looked as handsome as you do now. I'm ever so proud of you."

" No, no," he protested in modesty, but hoping for more.

" Yes, you're beautiful, darling, and I shall love to show you off."

" Not beautiful, dearest. *Oh*, no."

" Yes, beautiful. I insist, beautiful."

" No, no ; beautiful I cannot allow. Distinguished, perhaps."

"Yes, appallingly distinguished. There's absolutely nobody who looks like you. I thank God for it daily. And, Daddy, I can't help feeling proud that you're now Sir Albany Grahame —is it very wrong of me ? It's such a lovely succession of sounds : Sir Albany Grahame. So like Strawberry Cre'am."

He was not sure that he cared for this joke. He too had been pleased with the sound of the name and it was perturbing to find it the stuff of a jest. But then it was only Susannah's mind which would arrive at a silly irreverence like that.

"I am glad you're pleased, young woman."

"And Mummy ' Lady Grahame ' ! Oh, I'm all excited. Is it very awful of me ? Yes, of course it is. I'm horrible."

"No, darling, just honest and not hypocritical. And I'm glad. Let's be done with hypocrisy. I've never had much use for it."

"I've tried to be miserable about it all, honestly I have, but it keeps stopping. But I quite understand it must be awful for you."

"Yes, yes . . . we were boys together. Still, there it is : I'm finding consolation in thinking of all that I can now do for Susannah."

"How sweet of you. Isn't that dear of him, Mummy ? "

"I've given much thought to the matter, and I've decided that I'm going to resign this living and take you to London."

"Oh, but, darling, you're not to sacrifice yourself for me. What would you do ? Get another church there ? "

"Maybe, maybe. I don't know yet."

"But what would you be ? Just a curate ? "

"Oh, dear me, no ! " This suggestion he found most unflattering. "I thought I might take a long rest. I have worked hard here."

"Does that mean we shan't have to go to church quite so much ? "

"Really, Susannah ! " her mother remonstrated. "What do you mean ? What a thing to say ! "

"Well, not being any longer the little souls at the Rectory, we could take it easy for a bit, couldn't we ? " Her father might be the tallest man in the parish and her mother taller than many women, and herself not small, but she always spoke of the family at the Rectory as ' the little souls '—except when she spoke of them as ' Susannah and the Elder.'

"No one need go to church who doesn't want to," said her father.

"Albany ! " Delia protested. "What are you saying to the child ? "

"I'll go once a Sunday if you want me to," Susannah promised. "That's surely enough for any child."

"Susannah!" Her mother sat shocked and staring.

Susannah turned towards her. "But I've told you for ages and ages, darling, that I only go to support the Family. I go because I'm fundamentally nice and don't want to let the Rectory down. If we aren't rectors any more——"

"You go because it's your duty to go. And as long as I'm your mother and have any say in the matter, you'll come to church with me."

"But, Mummy, I'm not at all sure that I believe half the things that you and Daddy believe. I try to, I try like anything, but I'm not sure that I succeed. It's sad, but——" and she shrugged her shoulders like one helpless.

Delia, seated on the brink of her chair, beat her toe impatiently. "I don't know what you're all coming to. Here's your father saying he wants to give everything up and 'think things out'——"

"Oh, can *I* think things out too?" A delightful prospect! "Oh, Daddy, shall we both take a long rest and think things out? What fun!"

This time Delia not only tapped impatiently with her toe but tossed an angry head. "I give it up. I don't know what you're all talking about. What is there to 'think out'? I personally don't change in my beliefs."

But Albany was watching Susannah's brightened eyes and lips and thinking, "Where does she get that charm and frankness? Not from her mother . . . who's a fool. And not from me . . . who am a horrible hypocrite." Aloud he said, with a teasing smile, "Woman, you get rather more beautiful as you get older."

"Oh!" she cried. "Oh, your very grateful servant!" And she swept into a little eighteenth-century curtsey, spreading her skirt. It was as beautiful a movement as he'd ever seen. Where did she get such grace? Not from Delia. Could it be from him?

"Yes, you're now a beautiful woman, strange to say."

"Oh, my angel!" she exclaimed in her gratitude. "What a lovely thing to say! And so like you to tell me. So immensely Albanian. But do go on talking about going to London. It'll be too truly lovely. We'll be the happiest of happy little souls."

Delia, conscious for the last two years of a relationship

21

between her daughter and her husband which left her uncomfortably on the ringside, a mere watcher, suddenly declared, " I don't think this is a moment to be talking in this flippant way. You seem to forget that your uncle is lying dead." And she went from the room, very emphatically.

Albany grimaced at Susannah. " Now you see ! You've offended your mother. You've said the wrong thing. So have I. We're both in disgrace. That was a stinger for both of us."

" But have I been very awful ? " she asked. " Have I said something awful ? I'm sure I have, but I don't know what it was."

" No, you were just being perfectly natural."

" Oh, but not too natural, I hope. That's the trouble with me, I say things, and I never know afterwards what I've said. I always come away from everyone wondering if I've said something utterly stupid or behaved in the silliest way. I do gush and go on so. What's so deplorable about me is that I'm so exactly like all other girls of my age. Full of silly feelings and gush. God, I hate the silliness of girls ! I don't wonder that, on the whole, the creatures are despised."

" Yes, they're rather insufferable. And now come and sit down and let's discuss our plans for London."

They sat together and spent a rich hour, painting pictures of great days in London and deploring in perfect harmony the intellectual stuffiness of old Mosspot.

And when she went from him, passing through the french windows into the garden again and singing to herself in her new happiness, he watched her and thought, " Yes, she's the greatest joy in my life. My one great comfort. I must hold fast to the idea of going to London largely for her sake, because that at least is a motive not wholly selfish."

CHAPTER TWO

THE WOOD

SIR ALBANY alighted from the blue Atlas bus at its halt by St. John's Wood Road Station. And the first thing he noticed, as he stood on the pavement, was the extraordinary width of the sky. The sky before him seemed wider and lighter than anywhere else in London. And standing there, leaning on his ebony stick, he saw why ; it was because its dome arched over wide green spaces, full of trees. He was standing at a noisy crossroads where five roads met. Immediately in front of him, on its island site was the white temple of St. John's Wood Chapel with the trees of its ancient burial-ground beside it, and the traffic of the five roads swirling before it ; on the left, within its grey wall, was the green area of Lord's Cricket Ground ; on the right the ample and timbered acres of Regents Park. The March day seemed lighter here because of this wide sky, and the air whiter and purer.

He turned into St. John's Wood Road and walked beneath the long curtain-wall of Lord's. He entered Grove End Road, and now he was really in the heart of the Wood, St. John's immemorial wood, and what a change of architectural mood was here from the tall terraced houses of Park Road along which he had come in his bus. At that junction where the five roads meet he seemed to have exchanged quite suddenly the eighteenth-century for the early nineteenth. There at that corner by Regents Park he had walked, very properly, into the Regency Period. No staid brick terraces here with their steps on the pavement and their kitchen windows peeping above it, but urbane little houses, square and white and hip-roofed, with little rectangular gardens around them and long grey garden walls to guard their privacy from pavement and carriageway. The first owners of these houses, it seemed, had wished to be each a little squire with a parcel of land for his own. Nearly all the garden gates were of wood and impermeable, except for the little monastic grilles which servants could slide open so as to learn who knocked at their masters' privacy. This Grove End Road wound on for a half-mile or more, and at every corner he glanced down the side-street and saw that it was much the same as every other street ; an avenue, that is to say, of detached and differentiated houses but given its unity by the long garden walls and the old trees that branched above them. Just such walls were on either side of him as he walked on : ripe old sooty walls, mellowed by a hundred years of London weather, overtopped by coarse-rooted ivy or sprawling creeper, mottled with green moss and yellow lichen. The low March sunlight, shining behind the branches flung blue openwork shadows on roadways whose colour was a pale fawn.

Here surely was the best of both worlds. Nowhere else in London were there so many trees to the acre and such quiet gardens so near its busy centre. Well was it named a wood.

23

It had been a pathless forest once, a haunt for the boar, the buck and the wild bull, with only the wattled huts of the swine-herds or the shy lairs of the outlaws among its greenwood shades ; then it became the woodland chase of some fat Prior of St. John of Jerusalem ; and now the little gentlemen of the nineteenth century had made it into a wood again, with their secluded gardens and their well-grown trees. Where else had the architects achieved such a balance between nature and building, between house and highway, between privacy and community ? Yes, he would live here.

81, Grove End Road. Here it was : the home of old Bait when he was not spending a week-end in his cottage at Mos-grove. And it was just the same as all the others, stucco-faced, cream-painted, with a walled garden around it and a shut garden gate, keeping the world in its place. It differed only in having a glass-covered way, festooned with a vine, from gate to front door.

Sir Albany rang at the door. An ancient parlourmaid opened to him. Her afternoon costume which was that of any plum-cheeked parlourmaid of eighteen—long black dress, long bibbed apron, and starched, frilled cap with long streamers—stressed unkindly that she was seventy and shrunken and old.

" Mr. Bait ? " inquired Sir Albany, as if there were some doubt about his still living here and still being her master. " He's expecting me, I think."

" Yes, sir," said the maid. " The Reverend Grahame, isn't it ? " And even as she said it, the round spectacles and long peeking nose of old Bait appeared round a door on the right. His eyes looked over the tops of the spectacles.

" Ah, Rector ! " he said. " Here we are. Come in."

" Good to see you, old man," said Albany, following Bait into the room on the right. " Good indeed." He said it with gusto, for he had a great affection for old Bait, an affection which he liked to think more remarkable than it was. Desperate for a friend in Mosgrove, he had elected Bait, the only candidate available, into the empty place, and then made of this place something like a throne in his heart. And never did he dare to doubt that Bait's affection was the equal of his own. " I have many things to discuss. I want your advice badly, old man."

" Yes, well, come in here. And let's shut the door before the wife knows you're here. One can't talk any continuous sense with a woman in the room. A woman's certain to divert you

24

up all sorts of unimportant and immaterial paths. They can't keep to one subject for ten seconds together. None can ; your woman, Delia, can't. Quick, quick. Come and sit down."

The room in which Bait quickly shut them was exactly the right frame for an old retired lawyer. Oblong and low-ceiled, it was filled with the fusty smell of a thousand untidy books ; of the stale smoke from cigarettes smoked one after another ; and of the old cracked leather on the armchairs before the fire-place : such a smell as assaults you when you step into an old bookshop that has not been aired for years. Before the most important of the deep easy chairs, Bait's own, stood a round leather hassock or *pouffe*, like a satellite in the orbit of its planet. Did you glance along the books you saw that many of them belonged to his active days as a lawyer : Chitty's *Statutes*, Mew's *Digest of Cases*, and the Law Reports of Chancery and King's Bench.

Old Bait seemed a tall man at first sight since he was thin and narrow but, standing before Sir Albany, who could give him five inches all round, he lost this semblance of height and retained only that of thinness. His hair, still black, and as thin as himself, allowed only a few strands to be forced back over his lofty bald cranium. All the bony base of his face protruded : frontal bone, nasal bone, and chin bone. His mouth seemed withdrawn beneath this prominent nose and chin, rather as if it would keep itself to itself. On either side of this narrow face the ears seemed unusually large. They extended like wings, and on cold days were red and on sunny days trans-parent.

In Mosgrove, when spending a week-end there, Bait always honoured the sweet countryside with a Norfolk jacket and knickerbockers, and above this country wear, since one expected the sun in the country, he perched a panama hat or a straw boater. Today, having come from some ceremony, he wore an old and loose frock coat, obviously retired and lazy like himself ; but there, on a side-table, lay the familiar panama, as yellow as a newspaper that had known twenty years of the sun. Whether in country wear or ceremonial wear Bait always walled up his loose-skinned neck in a high stand-up collar as white and upright as a strict lawyer's practice, and below this white wall a broad black tie above which his gold stud peeped like the rim of a yellow moon above a midnight horizon.

" So you want to live in the Wood," he began, throwing

himself into his own chair and settling his feet on the satellite hassock. " In the name of God, why ? "

" Because you've always told me that it was full of intelligent and interesting people. My coming here would be largely for Susannah's sake."

" Interesting ? What could I have meant by that ? Well, I suppose cranks and artists and actors are interesting fauna. And so are courtesans. These last especially."

" Courtesans, did you say ? " demanded Albany, leaning forward in his chair. Bait had spoken truly : these last were especially interesting.

" Yes, we've plenty of them, either still in practice or retired, like me."

" You mean—— "

" I mean the kept or cast-off mistresses of various wealthy rascals who've provided shady little villas for them in the Wood. From its earliest days, you know, our wood has always been a refuge for the outlaw and the castaway. Have a cigarette. Help yourself." Bait, looking over his spectacles, stubbed out one cigarette and took another from a box at his side with trembling nervous fingers. " But if you come to live here you must be careful to live in the very middle of the Wood. This St. John's Wood, you see, is an oasis in a horrible desert of Victorian vulgarity. Kilburn on the west, my God ! Baker Street on the south. Swiss Cottage on the north. If you come here, you must never venture across Maida Vale or you'll be in Kilburn. And, on the whole, you'd best not cross the Finchley Road more than you can help or you'll run into roads of outrageous Victorian palaces. You'll be among very terrible things. But the centre of the Wood—where we are now—has, I admit, some charm and character. Its houses sprang from a moment of good building iust before the Terror began. But, bless you, the moment lasted only a few years and was gone. Result— " Bait twitched up his very long nostrils and kept them on high ; and this sustained upward tweak, as of a man who sniffed, suggested that his view of the result was bleak indeed. " Result : Kilburn, Maida Vale, and Belsize Park. Belsize Park, my God ! And even here, even in these quite tolerable streets, two of our so-called artists have erected abominations that are an offence to all honest men. There's old Alma Tadema, in this road, who's built himself a pompous red palace which looks as if it had been spawned by the Albert Hall ; and old McWhirter, R.A., who, over there in the Abbey

26

Road, put up a house like a marzipan cake which I, for one can only pass with my eyes shut. We are famous for our artists, but I confess I recoil from most of them. Just go and look at the Art School in Elm Tree Road." Again that sharp distaste tweaked up his long nostrils, as he contemplated in imagination the Art School in Elm Tree Road. "You've only to pass it when the boys are coming and going, like bees at the door of a hive, to decide that it might well be the out-patients' department of a hospital for homosexuals and hermaphrodites. But I may be unfair to them. Perhaps I'm unfair."

"Those courtesans?" Sir Albany's interest, which Bait had awakened but not satisfied, could only come forth, from lips still clerical, in the shape of disapproval. "You don't mean, surely, that—er—this is an immoral quarter?"

"Well, in a sense, yes, but you must understand, my dear fellow, that such immorality as shelters here is of the most respectable. It's in its Sunday best. I am always delighted to see the way our little wood, our little Bois de St. Jean, preserves some of its ancient characteristics. It was always a bird sanctuary, and I think we may say it is one still.

"What on earth do you mean?"

Bait never smiled with lips or eyes when it was his humour to propound an extravagant thesis; either he kept his face impassive or he hooked up his nostrils as if in some dislike of what he was saying. "I mean that in the old days, the sportsmen of London would come fowling here where the game birds were to be found, and that is precisely what they still do. I'm no sportsman myself, and cannot say whether the noblemen and merchants of those days preserved their pheasants here, but they certainly do so now. And not only that; they seem to think it a nice shady little place where they can establish their ladies in comfortable nests after they themselves have decided to be good, or after their wives have discovered their sporting habits and enforced a similar issue. Yes, our retired Magdalens are quite a feature of the Wood. We all know them." And he gave the names of one or two of them, together with the names of their wealthy or noble protectors.

"Really?" exclaimed Sir Albany; and said little more, for he knew that if Bait were left uninterrupted he would continue to pour forth a jet of glistening absurdities from the vast reservoir within that bald head. "Is that so?"

"Certainly it is, and I'm not at all sure, Grahame, that some of these discarded ladies are not slowly turning, exactly as one might expect, into witches. And not they only, but one or two of our hitherto respectable spinsters too. Why not; it would be a natural development; and I'm not saying they know it's happening to them. The process is often unconscious. I offer no opinion on that. But you'll agree that there's every reason on earth why our Wood should breed its witches. Consider." He lit himself another cigarette with his trembling fingers, while the eyes behind the spectacles remained sober and unsmiling. He leaned back in his chair. " Consider, my dear fellow : this was once a swampy forest where many of these bedevilled old crones used to live and cackle. Very good ; but a place, I hold, gets impregnated with the emotions of its past habitués, and these emotions often retain a power that can affect all likely and susceptible subjects. Such, no doubt, is the explanation of all hauntings, in many of which I fully believe—don't you ? Now just think : our Wood is built by the side of a crossroads where five ways meet, and it's notorious that a crossroads was one of the many sinister places where these ladies would assemble to make their vows and practise their black arts and copulate with the Devil. But what's more, what's worse, on the immediate north of the crossroads is an old burial ground that was once a plague pit, and on the south that little green enclosure where they buried, not so long ago, the body of a murderer and suicide with a stake through his heart. Did you know that ? It's only seventy years since they put him there, so he should still be fairly fresh and able to work his unhappy spells upon us all."

Sir Albany nodded, grinning at this nonsense ; but Bait went on without a smile, and even with a hint in his nostrils of distaste for these undoubted facts, " Yes, I often wonder what unhallowed goings-on there are on that burial ground, say at Candlemas or on All Hallows Eve between midnight and cock-crow. All the world over, as you doubtless know, the witches have observed their Sabbaths in churchyards or in the neighbourhood of bones. Even the negroes practise their voodoo in cemeteries. If you come here, we'll go and prospect on a suitable night. Let's see : where are we ? " He leaned over to consult a diary on a table beside him. " March. Well, their next spring festival would be May Day Eve. No, better St. John's Eve, June 23rd, since that is St. John's Chapel and this is St. John's Wood."

" What would you hope to see ? "

" Oh, the old crones opening up the graves to get a few bones,

28

and the young virgins gathering their simples and herbs, and then, perhaps, the whole coven dancing among the tombs, with their skirts held up to their waists and holding each other's well-oiled fundaments. It should be worth seeing. If we were lucky, we might even see His Black Highness himself whipping 'em along. I can even conceive that he would lead them into the chapel for a Black Mass, and preach to them ; after which he'd put his fundament over the pulpit for them all to kiss."

" Good God ! "

" Yes, that is the *osculum infame*. I should like to see it, I *must* say."

" All very amusing ; and just how much of this do you expect me to believe ? "

" Do what you like, my boy. I'm not at all sure that I don't believe some of it. Not all, perhaps, but some. Who knows what elements of truth there may not be in these old super-stitions ? I'm very broad-minded in these matters. All said and done, it's no more difficult to believe in some of these strange enchantments and devil-possessions than in some of the things you parsons ask us to swallow ; it's easier, in fact, because we have proof that many extraordinary and inex-plicable phenomena do occur. It all depends whether you feel there are evil powers in the world—I do—and whether you suspect that certain persons can be possessed by forces alien to themselves—and I must say I do suspect this. You've only to look at some of our lonely woodland ladies to apprehend a slight aura of diablerie about them. A slight smell of sulphur, perhaps. You see them sitting alone in that old churchyard behind the chapel and the crossroads—and that's suspicious ; very suspicious. It may be a public garden now, but it was a burial ground once ; and there they sit with their reticules. *I* sit there sometimes too ; and, Lord help us, it may be that I'm becoming an incipient warlock myself ; I don't know ; I wouldn't say I didn't occasionally feel some of the symptoms. Sometimes when I'm looking into my shaving glass I don't feel at all happy about it. Horrible, hollow, hag-ridden features. What'll you do about your church work if you come here ? "

Having changed the subject, Bait swept the spectacles off his nose and began wiping them with a crimson handkerchief. Since he needed the spectacles only for reading or close work, and would keep them on his nose merely for their comfort and companionship—or because this was the most convenient place to hang them—his abrupt polishing of their lenses suggested that he would like to look into this new subject with some care. " Do you propose assisting at some church here ? In an honorary capacity, I imagine ? "

" Well . . . " This was difficult. In the past there had been warm, sometimes even choleric, arguments between Bait, who, though brought up as a Roman Catholic, had long been irritably contemptuous of, and inflammably hostile to, all orthodox creeds, and the Rector of Mosgrove, who didn't dare admit any loss of faith and accordingly argued in defence of the old dogmas just as irascibly. It was not yet time, it was much too soon, to say to Bait, " My dear chap, I have in the last few days become completely converted to your scepticism." But, since he did not propose to go to church much—if at all—once he was gone from Mosgrove, it would be as well to prepare old Bait for this curious phenomenon. So he said, " Well . . . I'm thinking of giving myself a long rest—I have worked hard—a kind of Sabbatical year, if you understand, in which I can just read and think. If there's any church here that suits me, I may give my services to it occasionally, but if not, I shall just devote myself to study. I have long wanted to do this. A parish priest has no time to *read*."

" A very fine idea ; and when do you think you'd come ? "

" In two or three months, perhaps. I have already written to the patron and the bishop."

" There's a house coming vacant in Circus Road next month."

" *Is* there ? " Sir Albany sprang alert. " Why didn't you tell me this before ? Is it a nice house ? "

" Not bad. It's bigger than this. Old Sir Vaysey Lowe, that fifteenth-rate composer, lived in it for thirty years, and he added a fine music room, which could be your study. It's sound-proof and you could read the holy Fathers there to your heart's content."

" Why, it sounds perfect ! Is it far from here ?"

" Not five minutes away. Circus Road runs parallel with this."

" Better and better. Let's go and look at it now."

" No, no ; wait till after tea and we'll go and look at it together."

" But I can't wait. What's the time ? Three o'clock. I'm going along now. I simply must." As impatient as a child who wants to unwrap a gift, he sprang from the chair.

" All right," agreed Bait, with a shrug. " But remember one thing. Remember what I said." He pushed the spectacles into their action stations, for reading, and picked up a book.

" If you take it, and bring your women there, sprinkle its threshold with holy water and say a brief prayer over it. That's a sovereign way, I believe, to insulate it from the evil spells of the witches. You are a holy man and should know how to do it. I may be wrong in my suspicions about some of our lady residents, but it's as well to take no risks. There's your Susannah. We don't want her corrupted. I wouldn't say but what there's something fey about her already."

" Never anyone less so," objected her father.

" Still," Bait submitted with an air of great reasonableness, " there's no sense in tempting the Devil." And he gave himself to his book.

With a laugh, and a wave of the hand to waft all such rubbish away, Sir Albany hurried from Bait's study into garden and street. After the close, junk-shop smell of that littered room the air of the leafy road seemed clean and cold. He hurried round the corner of Grove End Road, and his excitement increased as he swung into Circus Road and followed its serpentine curves between the garden walls. No. 62 was Sir Vaysey's house. Here was the wall of 58 . . . of 60 . . . and now— why this perhaps was his future garden wall. And this his gate. The gate had the usual monastic grille and above it a metal plate bearing the name ' Santa Monica '. The long wall was as tall as the average man and surmounted, for further privacy, by a trellis interlaced with the bines of rambler roses. But Sir Albany, so much taller than the average man, could look through the diamond openings of the trellis work. He did so : he stood, with the ebony cane held in both hands behind him, and one eye gazing through one clear diamond space. He saw an oblong house standing obliquely in its square of garden. It was cream-painted, except for the Regency veranda which ran along the whole front of the house and was painted green. Eight lime trees stood along the front garden and wall like soldiers in extended order. A very ancient and slanting tree, probably a mulberry, spread its branches over a quarter of the lawn. In a shell-hooded niche in the back wall stood a small stone reproduction, chipped and cracked and damply green, of the Medici Venus. The goddess's hand, which should have been screening, with a coy pudor, her lovely breasts from lickerish eyes, had long since fallen, leaving the virtuous arm truncated. Between the mulberry and this statuette white croquet hoops and coloured croquet pegs stood, or lolled, in their appointed places. Except one, which lay down.

Sir Albany gazed through the single diamond, stroking his long copper moustaches, fingering the neatly pointed grey beard, and dreaming dreams.

CHAPTER THREE

COMMANDER LUDLOW TAKES COMMAND

Less than three months later Sir Albany, Lady Grahame and Susannah were in that house called Santa Monica. It was mid-June ; all the trees of the Wood were full of leaf and either heavily drooping over the garden walls or thrusting forth their foliage till it almost canopied the camber as well as the pavement. In the garden of Santa Monica the scent of the eight limes was honey-sweet and seemed a tangible presence, touching one's cheek with a warm caress. The old slanted bole of the mulberry was hidden behind a curtain of broad leaves. The flower beds, well stocked by the departed Sir Vaysey, were abloom with sweet williams, campanulas, monk's hood, borrage, and thrift ; and, of course, with roses—roses everywhere.

Sir Albany had also bloomed into a blue bow-tie, a pale blue shirt, and a grey suit, and since these replaced the white clerical collar and dark garments they might be considered the flags and bunting of his new freedom. He was delighted with his new home and new neighbourhood ; not, perhaps, as completely delighted as he had hoped, but trying his hardest to be so. And frequently announcing that he was so. For Delia was manifestly entertaining doubts about this ' wild move,' and her implied criticisms greatly annoyed him. And the more annoyed he was with her, the more he resolved to be one-hundred-per-cent satisfied with the Wood. Sometimes he felt driven, even when no one was discussing either house or neighbourhood, to proclaim his complete satisfaction with both. This he did in the hope of provoking a hostile remark from Delia and so justifying a little pleasant heat, a release of some bottled-up expostulations, and a resentful withdrawal from the room.

One morning, when he'd been no more than four days in the house, he lit up a big post-breakfast cigar—he was proud of the big cigars which he could now afford—and strolled out into the roads to explore his new habitat. He had not gone far along his own Circus Road when he saw another solitary pedestrian coming towards him, a man of most striking figure and carriage. Sir Albany knew a trick or two for scanning an approaching figure without appearing to, and he now pretended to be studying the wall at his side, the sky above him, and the pavement across the road, while really considering every detail of the man before him. An elderly man ; tall as Sir Albany and as squarely made ; his nose a noble feature, as high-bridged and sharp as a hen-harrier's beak ; his face a square, shaven field for this central and capital feature ; his clothes at once old, outmoded and dandified—a black sack coat with braided edges, shepherd's plaid trousers, and a high winged collar in, the grip of a broad black cravat, which was the cushion for a black pearl pin. No hat, but a carnation in his button-hole, grey gloves on his hands, and a gold-headed cane swinging like a pendulum between two fingers.

Sir Albany might have tried not to stare, but this stranger was troubled by no such scruple. He stared at Sir Albany without stint or shame. Indeed he hoisted a gold-rimmed monocle, captive on a black ribbon, to his right eye that he might study an interesting object better. He did not even avert his eyes as he passed, and when he was six yards beyond Sir Albany, he turned about, stood still, swung the cane gently as a thurifer his thurible, and treated himself to a further scrutiny. Sir Albany had turned likewise to look at him, and, meeting that monocled eye, was abashed ; he coughed with his hand to his mouth, resumed forthwith his forward gaze, stroked his moustaches, and walked on, with never another turn of the head but with many a swing of the ebony stick.

Two mornings afterwards, since both, it seemed, were men of leisure who after breakfast took the morning air, they approached one another again. Sir Albany was careful this time to look at anything but the oncoming figure, but the stranger ran the ribboned monocle up to his eye like a flag to the masthead, stared with meeting brows, and stopped one pace before him.

" To hell ! " he said. " We're neighbours, aren't we ? Let's introduce ourselves. My name's Ludlow."

" Good morning, Mr. Ludlow."

" *Commander* Ludlow, to be accurate. And yours, sir ? "

" Grahame. Yes, Grahame."

" A bloody Scotchman. Well, delighted to make your acquaintance, Mr. Grahame."

33

Albany, a modest man—or, rather, one who liked to appear modest—did not correct the title, " Mr." But he did look forward with pleasure to the time when his new friend would become aware of his error. " Delighted to make yours, Commander."

" And what's your other name, sir ? "

" Albany."

" Good Christ, what a name ! And you've come to live at old Vaysey Lowe's house, San Jimmiano, or whatever it's called ? Well, that should be a change from the better : old Vaysey was a shocking man. He had to clear out because of his uric acid and his gout. Let's hope they've polished him off by now. I've seen you coming out of the house—I spend most of my time watching my neighbours—and I've seen your lady wife too. She's that long, rather skinny woman, isn't she ? And that's your lady daughter, I suppose, that very shapely craft with, if I may say so, a damnably pretty figure-head."

" Yes, that's my Susannah. Are *you* married, sir ? "

" Am I *not* ? Good heavens, yes. And the bloody woman's the bane of my life. I got rid of her some time ago, but I still think she'll kill me before she's done. The woman's a bitch."

Albany had never while in the collar of a parson heard such frankness, or such words, as these and at first he was shaken by them, but he arranged his face in a broad-minded expression and smiled. And suddenly, as he remembered his grey suit and bow tie, he perceived that the Commander would have no knowledge of his ecclesiastical background, and felt pleased that men now talked with him as they talked with one another, and not as they talked with clergymen.

" She lives at Blackheath now," the Commander was saying, " and I sincerely hope she dies soon. But, alas ! she's only sixty, so she'll probably kill me first."

" You have no family ? "

" They're all out in the world now, sir. Two married girls and a lad who's in the Argentine. Can't think how I ever managed to do the necessary and get them out of that woman. Come into my house and have a drink."

" What ? At this hour ? "

" Yes. Yes, rather ! Why not ? The sun's over the yard-arm, I think. That's my house there. We're very near neigh-bours, you see. Come along." He put a friendly hand on Albany's elbow. " Come aboard, sir, and very welcome."

34

Unlike Bait's house and Albany's, the house to which he led him showed itself to be a semi-detached, cement-rendered villa with a basement and many steps up to its front door. The garden around the twin houses was divided into two by an oak fence and a row of aspiring poplars whose peaks swayed gently in an unfelt breeze, high above the slate roof and chimneys. " It's a small house," said the Commander, turning the key in the door, " but it's big enough for me, and all I can afford, as long as I've got to keep that foul woman."

The room into which he ushered his visitor was very much smaller than Bait's study, and one's first impression was that one had walked into a tiny nautical museum. Chimney piece, bookshelves, cupboard tops, everything that offered a flat surface supported old ships' instruments such as sextants, quadrants and astrolabes ; models of old naval cannon with their bar shot, chain shot and grape ; and, most picturesque of all, a collection of model sailing ships which the Commander identified for Albany as an Elizabethan man-of-war, a Spanish caravel, a Flemish carrack, an eighteenth-century sloop and a brig of Nelson's time.

" Easy to see you're a sailor," said Albany.

" Oh, I don't know," the Commander demurred. " It's more often land-lubbers who collect this kind of junk. I happen to like it. Sit down and drink. Sink yourself there."

He pointed to one of two comfortable chairs before the chimney breast. Near the two chairs was a low round table and on it two spirit decanters in a mahogany case. The lid of the case was open and hanging back, so that round cut-glass stoppers looked out of the case, side by side, like twin babies looking over the side of their pram. The Commander flung a hand towards them. " You asked about my family. *That's* my family. And a much greater comfort they are to me than ever their predecessors were. Not but what I liked my kids when they were kids. But these two chaps are no trouble at all. Always quiet. Always smiling up at me. Always ready, at a moment's notice, to comfort the old man. Or— " and here he bent the whisky decanter over a tumbler—" To bow nicely before my friends." He filled the tumbler generously —even alarmingly. " Splash of soda ? Yes, but not too much, eh ? "

" Very nice little house this," ventured Albany, after sipping the powerful mixture.

" Not at all bad, but it has one fault."

" What is that ? "

" It's rather far on a wet night from the Lord's Tavern. The Tavern is my favourite pub. Is it yours ? On wet nights I usually make the Eyre Arms my port of call. I like public house life, don't you ? It reminds me of happy days in the ward room. We'll go out and visit a pub in a minute. How are you liking this neighbourhood ? "

" I'm loving it. And you ? You like it ? "

" Oh, yes, well enough. It amuses me. You've learned, I suppose, that it's largely a place for artists, journalists, and whores."

This last word Albany had never heard spoken aloud except at a church lectern, but he quickly re-set the broadmindedness on his face, and Commander Ludlow remained quite unaware that he'd administered a shock. On the contrary he continued in the same vein. " There's a whore living opposite," he said.

Albany, more interested than he would have admitted, swung his eyes to the window that he might see this house which sheltered sin. The Commander made no secret of his interest. He put up his monocle, leaned over the arm of his chair and gazed steadily at the small white villa. " Yes, that's her house, God bless her," he said, rising a few inches to scan it better. " But perhaps whore's too strong a word. She's merely the mistress of a wealthy old codger who's old enough to be her father. Bless the man, he comes three times a week, and he's older than I am. Nearly seventy, I should say. One can't help admiring him. I stand here and watch him drive up in his hansom and pay the cabby off, because the fellah won't be wanted for some time. Sometimes she opens the door to him herself, and fusses over him very prettily. It's sweet to watch. And sometimes they're unwise enough not to pull those holland blinds their full length, and then, if I bend down, I can see a good deal through the lace borders. It's interesting, very ; but it gives me a backache, stooping for half an hour and more. Don't think I blame 'em. Not at all. How can I ? I'm afraid I'm guilty myself of seeking in an irregular union the affection which my heart demands."

He spoke the words carelessly enough, sipping from his glass and wiping his lips with his finger, but they beat a bell in Albany's heart—a bell that bruised his heart. Nor did its notes cease to bruise his heart as the Commander, leaning back in his cushions so that his breast was upthrust, under the thick cravat and pearl pin, like the breast of a pouter pigeon, went on with rich satisfaction, " And, my boy, I don't mind telling you that I'm superbly catered for now. It's only in my latter days that I've known what sweetness and love can be. My God, it's wonderful. And she's a good woman, Grahame, if ever there was one, and—you may say what you like—basically pure. Her father was a county court judge. She's not so young, of course, but then I'm no chicken. A good and devoted woman, sir ; at Barnes, where she lives, she goes regularly to her church. No, I've no quarrel with these kind creatures who give a man a little happiness in this rather stinking world. Most of them in this neighbourhood are like that, I think, and I honour them for it. For two pins I'd dip my flag to them in the street. No, it's our artists I can't stand, and our long-haired actors, and, God's guts, our literary gents. Have you seen some of 'em ? They're ordure, my dear sir. Just ordure."

" Why, then, did you come to this neighbourhood ? "

" I should have thought that was obvious : to get as far away from my lady wife as possible. She had a fancy for Blackheath. Fine ! I put eight miles and the whole breadth of the Thames between us. Besides, old Budlier was here, my old friend, Colonel Budlier, one of the best. He's a bit too pi for me—a sidesman at the church and all that—and much too pally with the padres. I don't like padres, and that in spite of the fact that I'm really a religious man. Most of them are sanctimonious humbugs, you'll agree. Still, old Budlier's one of the best. He's an old widower, and I wish to God I was."

Albany, listening, was surprised to find how speedily his liking for this cold and clean-cutting frankness was growing in him. It was something he had never practised himself, and indeed never seen practised before. No hint of the usual humbug here. And it seemed as invigorating as a rude but fresh and untainted wind from the sea.

Meantime Commander Ludlow, having accepted and lit one of Albany's cigars, continued about Colonel Budlier. " He's only got his boy living with him. He's as poor as a church mouse, but he's managed somehow or other, by selling the clothes off his back, to send the lad to his old school, Clifton, and to Cambridge. And, my God, it's paid him. The boy's a splendid fellow. Wish he were my son. He's a cricketer of the very first flight. Why, sir, he got his blue last year, and it was his first year at Cambridge. What do you say to that ? He's one of the best fast bowlers in the country even if he is only nineteen. No great shakes at his books, of course—fast bowlers never are—but what does that matter? Last year he played twice for Middlesex, and he'll certainly play regularly for them when he comes down in a week or two. Plum Warner told me so in the pavilion at Lord's the other day. A good cigar this. Wish I could afford cigars. Come; you've finished that. Give me your glass."

Taking his visitor's glass, he poured out another half-tumbler of whisky and just touched it with soda-water. " There you are, sir. And then there was my lawyer, a dry, crusty old stick called Bait. He lives here and he found me this house. A good chap; his firm acted for me when I was getting rid of my Affliction—— "

" Bait! But good lord, man, I've known old Bait for twenty years. I count him my very best friend." Albany spoke with exaggerated fervour, in part because he was conscious of a little jealousy that the Commander should presume to speak as if his rights in old Bait were comparable with his own. In his excitement he drank somewhat deeply from the glass.

And in the same instant he learned that his head was confused. Delia was an adamant teetotaller, save only on Christmas day and very special occasions; the parish at Mosgrove had been a low-church parish; and for these two reasons, and because he was poor, he had never kept any alcoholic drink in the Rectory. For twenty-seven years he had been—and on the whole had been content to be—a teetotaller like his wife. Now, therefore, his head was quite unadapted to such fiery stuff as his host was mixing for him.

" It was because Bait, my dearest friend, lived here, that I came here," he said, negotiating the words with care, lest at any point he tripped.

" Well, upon my soul! So you know Bait? "

" I should say I do! Years longer than you've known him, I expect. Yeah . . . pretty sure o' that . . . years longer."

" But old Budlier? You don't know him? Well, let's go and see Budlier. He's a dear old man, one of the best." Suddenly, unexpectedly, somewhat bewilderingly, the Commander was on his feet, drinking down the last of his whisky and making ready to sally out. " You'll like the old man. He's only in Acacia Road, round the corner. Drink up."

Albany knew that it'd be better if he drank no more of that almost neat spirit, but he didn't like to show a weakness from which, apparently, his host didn't suffer, and he gulped it down. It immediately increased the haze in his head. The haze was now like a white and luminous fog in which his thoughts had indistinct edges and moved unsteadily and sometimes disappeared altogether.

Commandar Ludlow marched him out into the street, and as they pursued their course to Acacia Road, they came to the doors of the Eyre Arms. These doors inspired the Commander. They halted him on the pavement. " Better just come in and have a brief one. A good pub, this. You ought to get to know it."

" No, no," began Albany ; or perhaps ' begged ' would be the truer word.

" Yes, yes. Won't take a minute. And you'll see a very pretty barmaid. Come on."

And again Albany, not liking to appear less of a man than his companion, went into the saloon bar with him.

" What'll you have, Grahame ? "

" Oh, just a light beer—no more."

" Get along with you ! Hell and be damned, no ! You can't put beer on top of whisky. Two whiskies, please, Ethel darling."

When Albany had put this third whisky down, his head was like an upturned cup in which the luminous haze widened and narrowed and sometimes danced. It was only with some vagueness and imprecision of thought that he noticed, as they crossed into Acacia Road, that they had left the Regency period behind and entered upon the Gothic. But he did perceive this, even if foggily, and, to convince himself, and the Commander, that he had his thoughts in perfect control, he looked up at the steep gables, crenellated parapets and Gothic mouldings of these little stucco houses and said, " We've exchanged Regency for Gug-gothic " ; but the Commander made no comment, probably because he didn't know what his companion was talking about.

They had to mount ten steps to the Gothic doorway of the Colonel's house. Ludlow knocked, and the door was opened by a little round man with a clipped grey moustache that met cropped grey side-whiskers on his round cheeks. He had a fringe of white hair round his bald head, and this shining bald crown, framed in white, seemed to emphasize the little man's general roundness. His eyes were not very bright, but they were gentle and kindly. And just now they looked sad. Quite distressingly sad.

" Hallo, Ludlow. Come in, do."

" I've brought round a new neighbour to see you, Colonel. A Mr. Grahame, and one of the best, I'm sure."

" More than pleased," said the little man. " Come in."

" I've been telling him about your Tom."

The little colonel stopped abruptly and turned his head. " About Tom ? "

" Yes. About his cricket."

" Oh, then you haven't heard," he said. And he turned his face away and went on.

He took them into the front room. It had been the drawing-room once, and the product of a Victorian lady's taste, all draperies and ornaments, but now it was like a palimpsest, overwritten by a simple masculine hand. On the occasional tables with their fancy cloths were tobacco tins, pipes, cigarette boxes and piles of *Punch*. The white Indian carpet was stained with cigarette burns. A bureau, filled with Indian silver, had its writing shelf let down, and this shelf held a confusion of letters, books and bills. There was a grand piano covered with an Indian shawl, but this shawl was as a campus for family photographs in velvet or silver frames. Many of these were photographs of a boy with a charming round face—obviously the boy, Tom, at various ages. Tom at six or so, in a dark velvet suit with a pointed lace collar ; Tom in an Eton suit with a stiff white collar and shirt-front ; Tom in the flannel and blazer of the Clifton First XI and a boater hat. The worst intrusion into the dead lady's room was a roll-top office desk which stood in the window before plush curtains. On its top, however, in the place of honour, as a man conceives it, was a photograph of a woman in a costume of the nineties, with her hair brought to a knot on the top of her head and her slim body in a princess gown with bell skirt and vast leg-of-mutton sleeves. In the corner by the door a sheaf of bulrushes and pampas grass rose from an up-ended drain-pipe, enamelled green. Both rushes and grass looked more than usually dead, but probably the Colonel had never cared to remove them, since it was his dead lady who arranged them there.

" Do sit down, Ludlow," he said, clearing newspapers off an easy chair. " And you too, sir."

All sat down, and for a while there was silence. Albany observed a quick glance by Ludlow at a table and a cupboard and surmised that he was thinking, " No hope of a drink." For his part he was glad of this barrenness ; he didn't at all want to be offered a drink.

Perhaps Colonel Budlier detected the Commander's thought, for he said, " Would you like a cup of tea ? I can easily get some made for you."

But the Commander was certain he didn't want a cup of tea ; Albany insisted that he didn't want one either, and the silence fell again.

At last Ludlow said, " How's Tom ? He'll be home soon, won't he ? His term ends in a week or two, doesn't it ? "

Colonel Budlier looked straight into his visitor's eyes—but very sadly. " He's home already," he said.

" Home ? Why, how's that ? I thought these Cambridge boys never came down till the end of June."

" I've had bad news, Ludlow. Very bad news."

" I'm sorry, old man. What is it ? I thought you were looking a bit green. Is someone dead, and Tom home for the funeral ? "

" No, he's been sent down. In disgrace."

" Has he indeed ? Oh well, ha, ha, what does that matter ? It's not the end of the world."

" But he's been sent down finally. For good and all."

" What : expelled ? "

" Yes, that's another word for it."

" But they can't do that ! Don't be absurd. He's a blue. He's their best fast bowler. What's the rumpus about ? "

" He's not been behaving well."

" Well, hell and be damned, he's only nineteen ! You don't want him to be a prig and a milksop. What's he done ? "

" He's been carrying on with a shopkeeper's daughter."

" And good for him ! D'you hear that, Grahame ? Come, come, colonel, what's the harm in that ? Who doesn't at his age ? What did he do ? Get into bed with her ? "

" I'm afraid he seduced her."

" Well, why not ? She probably encouraged him to, while pretending not to. I know the sly little baggages. Of course she lured him on, a fine handsome lad like that. A blue. And a county cricketer. Good God, it's natural."

The Colonel shook his head, unable to absolve his son.

" Oh, cheer up," Ludlow comforted him. " If she practically asked him into bed, I don't see that it's done her much harm, or him either. I rather approve of a lad having a little practice before he gets married. He should learn his trade."

" No, he was wrong," said the Colonel who, as a lifelong churchman, and a sidesman withal, couldn't tolerate for a moment such libertine views. " Very wrong." He said it sadly. " Ruining an innocent girl."

" Ruining my arse ! " objected Ludlow. " Bet your life it was more than half her fault. She probably used every art she'd got, even if she didn't know she was doing it. They're like that, bless their little susceptible hearts ! I shudder to remember how many quite modest—well, *fairly* modest—little fillies got me into their beds before I was twenty-one. I was putty in their hands, and they seduced me far and wide. Tom's fair game for them too, a nice affectionate boy. She's not in calf, is she ? "

" What ? " The old Colonel was a little deaf, and as Ludlow had dropped his voice, he put a hollowed hand behind his ear, turned it towards the speaker. " What did you say ? "

" She's not going to calve, is she ? "

" Calve ? No, no. There's no talk of that."

" Well, then. . . ." Ludlow clearly wondered what all the worry was about.

" It's the immorality of it," submitted the Colonel.

And Albany, feeling he ought to contribute something to the talk, supported him. " Yes, it's the act one has to consider, not the consequences."

" I don't see that . . ." grumbled Ludlow. " No, I don't. . . Who split on him, if she's not going to calve ? "

" The father reported him to his college and the Senior Tutor, after consultation with the Master, sent him down at once."

" Did you ever hear such idiocy, when they need a fast bowler like him ? They must be mad."

" They gave him a Mock Funeral," said the Colonel with a sad little smile.

" What's that ? "

" A procession to the station with carriages and mourners and hymns. They sang, ' Now the labourer's task is o'er '." And even the Colonel had to allow his smile to widen a little.

" Ha, ha, ha ! " laughed Ludlow. " I'd like to have seen that. Poor Tom ! "

" They sang ' Day of Wrath ' too, and sang it splendidly, Tom says. It was a long way to the station."

If you know a poem perfectly, it is difficult not to show your knowledge by quoting part of it, and Albany promptly did so. " ' What shall I, frail man, be pleading, Who for me be interceding. . . . ' "

"Yes, and some of them even sang it in Latin," said the Colonel.

"*I'd* have interceded for him," declared Ludlow. "Dismissed the service for a little thing like that! A damnably steep punishment, don't you think, Grahame?"

Albany might be in a grey suit and bow tie, but the feel of his cassock was still about him, and he was hardly more ready than the Colonel to accept Ludlow's extreme libertinism. Besides, sooner or later, he'd have to tell these gentlemen that he was—or recently had been—a padre, and this was another reason for him to offer a proper comment now. So he said, "I suppose they thought it was what they *had* to do."

"They could have thought out something. With a bowler like Tom."

"But the morals of a university are more important than its cricket."

Ludlow at first looked as if he'd need some persuading of this, but when, after thought, he concluded that it wasn't really arguable, he replied reluctantly, "Yes . . . of course . . . but . . . it's not as if he'd forged a cheque or stolen the cricket club funds."

The Colonel looked sadly at the window. "He robbed a young girl of her all," he said.

"Not a bit! She only lent him her all for ten minutes or so. And if you ask me, she got back a damned good dividend on the loan. Of course she did, with a handsome lad like Tom. But I tell you what: Middlesex'll be glad of this. They won't ask any indiscreet questions as to why he's available so soon. Not they!"

But the Colonel was in no mood for levity. "It's a great blow to me. I had to sell my boots to send him to Cambridge, and now it's all wasted."

"It's not wasted. It's made him into a lad of perfect manners and every inch a gentleman. There's lot's he can still do."

"Yes, but *what*? He was reading Law——"

At that moment came the sound of the front door opening and shutting. And the Colonel said, "*Sssh* . . . here he is. Don't talk about it in front of him."

A tall youth burst into the room. "I say, Dad . . ." he began, and then saw the two visitors and apologized. "Oh, I'm sorry, Commander."

"Come in, and meet our new neighbour, Tom. Grahame, this is Tom Budlier, and one of the best."

Here certainly was the face in the photographs, and it was a charming face, Albany thought. The blue eyes were large and frank with nothing furtive in them ; all the features were straight and pleasing, except the chin, which might, perhaps, be considered a little weak. The only expression in the eyes just now was one of sadness, like his father's ; and this surely did him credit. As tall and slight as his father was short and rounded, he clearly inherited much from the lady on the roll-top desk. His light brown hair was plentiful and piebald ; that is to say it changed its colour so sharply in places that you hardly knew whether to call it brown or beige or barley-straw.

Ludlow was instantly inspired by his entrance and rose from his chair. " Tom, it's good to have you back. Come along, we'll celebrate your homecoming. You're lucky to have the Ordnance Arms just across the road. Wish I'd a pub opposite me. Come along, Colonel. Let's drink the boy's health and a hundred wickets for Middlesex."

" No, no." The Colonel shook his head, in no mood to be festive. " Not now. I can't drink at this time of the day."

" Well, Tom will, I'm sure ? " And Tom said, " Well . . ." as if he ought to demur ; but, in fact, he seemed quite ready.

" And Grahame, you've got to wet your new friendship with Tom Budlier of Middlesex. Come along, both of you."

And the Commander marched them out of the house and across the road towards that convenient hostel, the Ordnance Arms. " Come along, boys," he said, and laid his hand upon its door.

But here Tom hesitated. He stood still on the pavement. " No," he entreated. " No . . . wait . . . please " And Albany, surprised by a faint ring of sadness in the boy's voice, turned and looked at him. Yes, his eyes, looking at Ludlow, were still dulled, like his father's, with sadness.

" What the hell . . ." began Ludlow, but the boy interrupted him. " Commander," he said, " you've heard about me ? "

" Heard about you ? " Ludlow, also seeing the sadness, was prompt with comforting lies. " What are you talking about ? I've heard you were going to play for Middlesex as soon as you were home. Yes, your father was full of that."

" Why do you think I'm at home now ? "

" I don't know. What is it ? Leave on shore ? "

" No, I've been kicked out in disgrace. And kicked out for ever."

" No ? Go on ! You don't say so ! Kicked out ? You're

44

exaggerating, Tommy. Why in hell should they kick you out ? "

" Because . . ." and Tom, standing there on the pavement, told them the whole story which they'd just heard from his father. Ludlow expressed amazement. And indignation. You would have thought that the story was so new to him, so unforeseen, as to seem incredible. " Good God ! " he said again and again. " Good God ! " And the boy, words tumbling from his mouth, explained, " It's the old man I'm worrying about. I hate having hurt him. He gave up everything so that I could go to Cambridge and now I've ruined it all. Oh, God, I'm a cad ; a first-class cad ; an out-and-out stinking cad." Ludlow tried to interpose a " No, you're not, Tom," but the boy had to continue his outburst, drowning any suggestion of comfort. He insisted that he was a cad. He wouldn't hear that he wasn't a cad. Oh, it wasn't the girl he was thinking about ; she'd be all right ; there hadn't been anything like love between them ; it was the old man he was worrying about ; the poor old governor. The old boy had given up everything, every bloody thing, so as to give him an allowance at Cambridge ; he'd even given up his cigars, and he used to love his cigars. And he'd never be able to smoke them any more because he'd already spent so much. He, Tom, must get some sort of job so as to buy the old boy cigars. Christ, he was a beast ; he was a selfish beast ; all men, as far as he could see, were selfish beasts—all except the old man who was a good bloke. Completely good and, damn it all to hell, worthy of a better son.

A trace of tears ; and a turning away of his head. So the Commander, standing with his back to the tavern door, was able to get a word in. He denied that Tom was a beast ; argued that he was a thoroughly decent fellah ; and maintained, with genial oaths, that this penitence was excessive. But Tom insisted, almost angrily, that no punishment was too bad for him, since he ought to have thought of the consequences to the old man ; to which Ludlow retorted that he thought the punishment most damnably steep—cashiering a lad for his first little slip !—and so did Grahame here—but Tom, with mounting heat, declared that he fully agreed with it, that he reckoned he'd asked for it, that he was damned if he was going to whine about it, and that he was a bloody pig. And all this time Albany was no more than a spectator of this friendly content, swinging his interested gaze from one combatant to the other,

45

and back again, as does a spectator of a tennis tourney. He had an excellent close view of the bout from his place on the pavement.

The boy, his eyes most earnest and sad, was now vowing amendment, swearing he'd never do anything to disappoint the governor again, and calling down a vengeance on himself if he should fail in this resolution ; and Ludlow was enjoining him not to fret so much about it and assuring him, for his comfort, that he himself—and old Grahame here—had been in just such big scrapes when they were young.

" That's so, isn't it, Grahame ? You've often been in worse disgrace than this, haven't you, old son ? " Albany had certainly never been in such disgrace as this, but, to help the boy, and because he was still in imperfect control of his thought and words, he answered, " Assuredly. Most assuredly."

" Yes, of course," said the Commander nodding, " and look what fine fellahs we are now. Don't you worry. Come inside and have a stiff whisky."

" No, not whisky," said the boy, eyes still penitent. " I rcckon it was too much whisky that did it. I've done with whisky. The old man doesn't like me to be always drinking whisky. Just a beer. A half pint. And mild."

" Well, I don't care what you have, but cheer up. It's June, and the cricket season, and Lord's is just down the road. In we go."

" Oh, well," said the boy tossing his head so that the brown, pied hair went off his brow. " To hell . . . I suppose everything'll come all right."

" Not a doubt of it. Does he look the sort that's going to mess up his life, Grahame ? "

" He certainly doesn't."

And with that they all abandoned the pavement and went into the Ordnance Arms.

The Eyre Arms had been empty when Ludlow and Albany turned in there for a viaticum, because it had been early in the day, but this saloon was now crowded with dinner-hour customers ; and so many of these hailed Ludlow with lifted glasses, saluting hands, and shouted greetings that Albany guessed that the Commander was in the habit of steering his magnificent hull (with its fine beak at the prow) into public houses situated at every point of the compass from his berth in Circus Road.

He presented Albany to some of them. "My new friend, Grahame. Big chap, isn't he? Young Tom Budlier you all know. Seen him in action at Lord's. And now what's for everybody? Whisky?"

He bought drinks for eight or nine of them, and when, turning to Tom, he said, "Beer?" the boy answered, "No, dash it! I'll have whisky too. Why not?" Albany said, "Just a small beer, please;" but once again Ludlow protested, "Hell, no! Beer on whisky is just so much bilge-water;" and Albany, anxious to do the right thing in an unfamiliar place, agreed to another whisky.

The talk of these eight or nine friends was now loud and merry, and Albany was the only one out of it. Ludlow sat on a high stool, and the others stood around, save one who sat on the opposite stool; and Albany was on the outside of the circle, wistfully aware that he had not as yet any public house ease. Shut away all his life, by his clerical coat and his puritan pretensions, from tavern talk and ways, he was quite unable to blend with these loud, boisterous, and sometimes bawdy fellows. So much was this so, so conscious was he of his shyness, his illness-at-ease, and his 'not-belonging', that he felt at times a longing to escape from them, and into loneliness. But he wouldn't do this. He had not come to London to do this. So he tried his best to blend. He made efforts at bonhomie. Nobody laughed louder at their jokes than he, standing there on their fringe. His laugh was his request to be accepted as one of them. Once—twice—he learned forward to insert a comment into their talk—but their voices went on unheeding, and his comment was lost for ever. He even, while standing there unspoken to, put together a joke of his own and tried—several times—to intrude it into the chatter. "Look, Commander," he tried to say, "how long do you intend to stay tied up to this wharf and taking in supplies?" Did it succeed, he intended to follow it up with some witty variations on it, such as, "Your hold must be pretty full now," or "I should think your cargo'd soon be afloat." But time and again, as he leaned forward and began the joke, it was beaten back, like the horns of a sensitive snail, by someone's voice. At last, however, in an inexplicable lull, he got it spoken, and followed it with a loud uneasy guffaw. But apparently it had misfired, because his guffaw was the only one. And very loud it sounded in its loneliness. He felt a shame for it; a cold shame.

Now another of the company was standing his round.

47

" What's yours, Commander ?   And yours, Tom ?   And yours Mr. Grahame, sir ?   Same again ? "

" Oh, well . . ." It was not, apparently, the custom to refuse, so he said, " Thank you.   It's very kind of you."

" Fine.   Six whiskies.   One gin.   One Bass."

Six whiskies.   So far as he could remember, this was his sixth this morning.   And the remarkable thing was that this sixth whisky, as he sipped it, seemed to cure all the discomposure and doubt produced by its five predecessors.   It changed that luminous haze in his head into a great brightness.   His head seemed filled with a new, bright air that was charged with life-giving substances.   That doubt as to whether or not he felt sick had changed into a magnificent sense of well-being. Now at last he felt able—and more than able—to play the talking game with these good fellows.   He was at ease.   When Ludlow said, " Albany, my boy," he answered, " Ludlow, my son," and was delighted to hear himself doing so.   He heard his voice quite as much as any of the others ; he even caught himself uttering some of Ludlow's expletives.   When somebody said, " Don't you chaps ever go to work ? " he heard the late Rector of Mosgrove say, " Work ?   Whatever's that ?   Work my behind ! "   And if he was surprised to catch this remark, he was also pleased.   He was finding friends.   He was on terms of friendliness with good fellows in a pub.   He had made a joke at which they laughed.   Admirable fellows.   Most loveable fellows.

" My turn now," he said.   And was rather glad when most of them declined, because he was quite unused to spending money freely in a pub.

There was no sign of Ludlow going.   Or of Tom going. Tom was now as lively as any of them, his penitence put to sleep by his third and fourth whiskies, and his eyes bright again with youth and laughter.   But he himself must really go. Delia waited at home.   And Susannah.   " Well, I've got a home if you haven't, chaps.   And I've got a wife ; I'm a man under authority.   Shall I send an ambulance for you, Commander Ludlier ?   Budlow, I mean ?   No ?   Nor you too, Tom ? All right, good day, my dear lads."

And he came out alone, less than perfectly steady on his feet, but not much less, and thinking, " I am making friends.   This is what I wanted to do . . .   I am living my life . . .   At last . . .   I was dead and am alive . . .   It is not too late to live.   Good-hearted chaps, those ;   men of goodwill, and I rejoiced in their company. I love my kind. That is obvious. I may have many faults, but I clearly love my kind."

It was the next day, in the morning at about nine o'clock, that Albany, reading the *Standard* in his study chair over his post-breakfast cigar, heard a sharp knocking at the front door and the quick steps of the maid hurrying to answer this summons. No postman's or pedlar's knock this ; it was the ratta-tat-tat of a visitor—But whose—whose at nine in the morning ?

" It's a Commander Ludlow, sir," said the maid. " He says could he have a word with you. He says you know him. A tall old gentleman with an eyeglass."

" Commander Ludlow ! Why, of course. He's our neighbour. Show him in here."

Ludlow entered, very erect, with his ribboned monocle screwed home beside his honey-buzzard beak, a white flower in his lapel, and his gold-topped cane and grey gloves in his hand. He was very much the fine old gentleman in frayed, old-fashioned clothes, tut—what was this anxiety, this distress, this suggestion of shame in his eyes ?

" My dear chap," he began, as soon as he was three paces within the room and could come to a stand-still and drop the monocle to his vest. "I've come to apologize. Most humbly."

" But what in the world for ? Sit down. And have a cigar."

" No, I won't sit down, nor stay. I'll just beg your forgiveness and then seek some place of penitence and tears. Had it not been too late last night, I'd have come then, but it was ten o'clock before Bait told me."

" I don't know what you're talking about, Commander. You've done nothing to offend me."

" But how can that me ? " Ludlow was astonished. He replaced the monocle to consider Albany's unoffended face. " I took you into a public house."

" I know you did."

" To be accurate, I took you into two public houses."

" What of that ? "

" But you're a padre. Bait told me so. We'd just finished a game of chess and were discussing you. I was never so upset in my life. A parson ! Good Lord. And I talked about whores ! "

" You did."

" And I told you about my, er, my *chère amie* at Barnes."

Albany nodded.

"And I used bad language, I'm sure. I always do. How was I to know you were a padre when you were wandering about in plain-clothes and smoking a cigar as long as a sixteen-inch gun. It didn't give me a chance. Why, at one time I said I didn't like padres."

"My dear fellow, I was a padre till recently, but I'm now retired——"

"But you're still a padre. You're still a holy man. You're still entitled to our respect. Oh, yes. And Bait said that you and your wife were strict as hell—no strong liquor in the house, ever."

"My wife is rather strait-laced, certainly. I am not. Anything *but*," Albany assured him with a sudden anxious fervour. "And I like people to talk to me as they would to anyone else."

"But I don't understand that. You can't want us to talk in the presence of Holy Church as we would in the ward room. No, that can't be right. I apologize unreservedly. Why, I talked about young Tom Budlier learning his trade as a husband. And about the grocer's daughter enjoying it. Good God. And I suggested—I suggested, my dear chap, that you'd often been in far worse disgrace than poor young Tom. Fancy saying that to a padre! You really must forgive me."

"If you think forgiveness is necessary——"

"But that isn't all, Grahame. There's something else. Bait tells me you're a baronet, and I was calling you Mister all the time. Not that I should mind what I said to a baronet. I've known plenty of baronets, and most of 'em were as foul-mouthed as I am. My first skipper was a bart, and he had a tongue like a bilge-pump. But not before the padre. Never before the padre.

"Well, I do appreciate this apology, Commander, but it wasn't necessary. Now have a drink."

"No. Oh no!" The Commander raised a very decided hand. This morning at any rate he was going to behave properly before the Church. "No, I wouldn't dream of it. At this time of the day. You do accept my assurance, don't you, that I'd have said none of these things if only you hadn't been dressed up like an ordinary man? You do? Good. Then I don't say that in half an hour or so I shan't give myself a little stiffener. This has been a shattering experience."

50

CHAPTER FOUR

THE PARTY

ALWAYS, even within the puritan walls of Mosgrove Rectory, Albany had been subject to sudden eruptions of irrational and apparently unwarranted gaiety. Usually these lively attacks seized him in his study when he was weary of reading a novel or of wandering about the carpet with nothing to do. Boredom was best overcome by an outburst of jollity. He would issue from the study like a lion in search of meat, and, finding Delia or Susannah, or both, would play the fool before them, his high spirits even causing him, as he spoke ridiculous things, to thrust his hands into his pockets and dance a gentle tap-dance, heel and toe.

It was strange, he often thought, that shyness should inhibit him from heartiness with strangers while in the home his jocularity had surely an element of genius. Perhaps it was that the animal spirits which he could not vent among more easily sociable men had to spurt over Delia and Susannah.

Such a comicoleptic fit seized upon him a few mornings after this visit from Commander Ludlow. As usual, it swept into him like a possession of the devil, and he flung down his book and marched at a quick step into the dining-room, where both wife and daughter were seated at the table, the mother embroidering a cushion cover, the girl sewing an undergarment.

"Anybody jolly?" he demanded, and since neither replied, but both, after looking up, went on with their sewing, he answered his own question. "No. Clearly not. Nobody jolly. The atmosphere is wintry."

"I'm jolly," Susannah averred, holding up a lacy edge through which she had just threaded some pink ribbon, and frowning at it. "I'm overwhelmingly jolly."

"Good. That's fine. And is your father being thought of with affection?"

"Yes. Great affection. Pass the scissors, Mummy. Colossal affection."

"I'm glad of that. It's important. And your mother: is she feeling sufficiently romantic about her old man?"

Delia made a sound like 'Tut-tut.'

So Albany directed his talents towards Susannah, who was

usually a little more receptive. " Your mother is not amused. Alas ! no. Let me in no way disturb you, child, but what is it you are making ? Curtains for the kitchen ? "

" Don't be absurd. You can see perfectly well what I am making. And I am very busy at it. Could you go away ? "

" What was that ? What did you say ? "

" I said, Go away."

" You did ? Well, I am never one to crush the spirits of a young girl, but I must suggest that that is no way to speak to your father."

" Oh, Mummy, do something about it. Don't just sit there sewing. Send him away."

" Really, young woman ! I take great exception to that : encouraging your mother to be unpleasant."

" Now look, Daddy." Susannah laid down her sewing as one would appeal to his good sense, and he made her a little bow in acknowledgment of this courtesy. " Listen. Mummy and I are busy. Couldn't you go for a little walk ? Just once or twice round the houses."

" All right then. I shan't tell you of a wonderful idea that has just come to me. An idea that would have greatly appealed to you. But it's not necessary that you should hear it—— "

" Oh *yes*, Daddy, *please*."

" Am I to be allowed to finish ? Do I have audience ? I will go for a walk, and whether or not I shall come back I don't yet know. I have one great gift, and it's the ability to perceive where I'm not appreciated ; where, in short, I'm not wanted."

" But what was the idea ? In case we never see you again, you *must* tell us."

" *Oh*, no ! " he assured her. " Not now. Certainly not now. Umbrage has been taken."

" Gosh, isn't he maddening, Mummy ? And he imagines it's funny. But still, I'll say I'm sorry, if you like. What was the idea ? "

" I thought . . . yes, I thought that, now we're settled in this attractive little home, we should have a party. A house-warming."

" Oh *yes*, Daddy ! "

" A party ? " Delia looked up, and rested her needle. " But we hardly know anyone yet. Nobody except the Baits, and I can't imagine Mr. Bait caring much about a party."

Now since these words suggested that Delia was still nursing her dislike of this ' wild move ' to town, they were just the sort of words he liked to extract from her, so that he could be incensed by them. He was incensed now.

"On the contrary, I have already made heaps of friends. I love this place. And some of them are most interesting friends too."

"Who?"

"There's Commander Ludlow——"

"A most horrible man——"

"Oh, no, Mummy," interposed Susannah. "He's rather a pet. I love him."

"And there's dear old Colonel Budlier and his boy."

"That boy!" Delia lowered her eyes on her work. "But he's not a nice boy. He's a bad boy."

"I disagree with you entirely. He's an exceedingly nice boy."

"Nice, you think! Hasn't he just disgraced himself at Cambridge?"

Susannah's eyes widened with interest. She knew the boy only by sight, and this was the first time she'd heard he was in disgrace. It threw a fascination over his figure like that of a handcuffed convict on a station platform. "Why, what's he done?" she demanded. "What are you talking about?"

"Never you mind," said her mother. "It's nothing you should know."

"But why not? What rot. What absolute rot."

"He's been sent down from his college, my dear," said Albany, desiring, as far as possible, to take the opposite line from his wife's. "That's all."

"But whatever for?"

"Sent down for ever, poor boy," he added, to give the news its full drama.

"Why, was it something very terrible?"

Albany felt he had gone far enough. "It's not something I care to talk about to a young girl."

"Exactly," Delia agreed. "And that's the very reason I don't desire him here. I have some standards."

"And that's where you're entirely wrong. It's the very reason why we should have him here."

"Tush," muttered Delia, or something like it.

And Susannah, turning her eyes towards this sound, announced to the room in general. "There's clearly a detective job for me here. A girl can't be left in ignorance like this."

But Albany had no ears for her.

53

" I can pity the boy even if you can't," he informed Delia.

" I don't know what you're both talking about," sighed Susannah. " I haven't understood a word, but I quite agree with Daddy."

" You don't know anything about it," her mother snubbed her. " And I hope you never will."

" She knows everything about how to treat someone in trouble," Albany corrected. " She knows that you don't kick a man when he's down. Still less a boy." All his jollity was dispersed. He felt like an empty vessel sour and stained with ancient dregs. He no longer danced his little jig, but stood quite still like a man who'd been wounded in his *amour propre* and thus immobolized. " Hell and be damned," he said, having caught this oath from Ludlow, " I'm not going to push him further down. I'm going to do everything to help him. Either he comes to my party, or we don't have a party at all. Are we to be Pharisees ? "

" I have some standards."

" Yes, and dam-awful standards too." He saw Susannah gasp and stare. " The standards of the Pharisee. My idea of Christianity is very different from yours ; it is that when a lad's sinned, you don't turn your back on him, but stretch out a hand to help him." These words, having magnanimity and pathos, shot appreciative tears up into his eyes. " And let me tell you this : a party there's going to be. With all my new friends. *And* Tom Budlier. Largely for *his* sake. So now you know ! " Wherewith he went from the room and back to the study, his attack of gaiety completely cured.

The clock was about to strike midnight, and Albany much pleased with the success of his party, led the procession into the supper-room. He went first with Mrs. Bait, as the senior lady and oldest friend, on his arm. Next came old Colonel Budlier with a lady—Albany was not quite clear whom. Then came some other acquaintances of Delia's with their men ; then Ludlow and Susannah ; then young Tom Budlier with Delia's unmarried sister, Emily Freestone-Hay ; and lastly Delia herself on Bait's arm.

It was a well-dressed procession, and a host could be proud of it. The women looked well in their laces and flounces ; Delia, he could not but admit, was looking quite handsome in a gown of blue velvet with a " dog-collar " of six strings of pearls about her thin neck, like the collar so invariably worn by the Queen ; and as for Susannah, she looked lovelier than ever before, he thought, in a gown of coral velvet with a deep bertha of cream lace and a square band of black velvet ribbon to frame her fresh young breast and shoulders. She pressed upon his heart with her beauty. The men too—some of them looked most distinguished, he thought : himself, for instance, in a layman's full evening dress ; and Ludlow in the full evening dress of twenty years before ; and young Tom—he was a pleasing figure too in his black dinner-jacket suit.

It was a noisily vocal procession because there had been much to enliven the guests since nine o'clock. At first tea and coffee had waited in the dining-room, for the gentlemen to take the ladies to ; and in the study whisky and soda had waited for the gentlemen to take themselves to, if they preferred it. Ludlow had preferred it. He had visited the decanter many times, taking Bait there for a drink, and Coloniel Budlier, and Tom, and his host ; and himself, on occasions, quietly.

At first the party had moved stiffly, as if it were something just out of bed and still unsteady and inclined to yawn ; and Albany had been afraid for it, and secretly unhappy. The guests had just sat around the room, straining to make conversation with their neighbours, or striving with louder remarks, supposedly comic, to bring some laughter into the evening. Since it was not a young persons' party, Susannah had sat on a remote chair, silent and solitary and abstracted, so that he pitied her and went up to her and asked in a whisper, " Dull ? " to which she replied, lying a little, but brightly, " No, darling. Susannah's very happy. Susannah likes to be with the Elders." And young Tom, at first, had been plainly unhappy. Delia had received him with a wilful coolness, for which her husband was furious with her ; the other women had hardly spoken to him at all, as if they desired him to remember his disgrace ; and he had spent the first hour either leaning against the door-post or seated with that refuge of the drawing-room destitute—the family photograph album. And often, as Albany noticed, he was staring at Susannah with a goopish stare as if she were the first girl he's ever seen properly and this the first time he'd perceived what feminine beauty could be. Susannah had not seldom glanced covertly at him, but only because she was fascinated by the sight of a disgraced youth. It seemed extraordinary that anyone with such an open and pleasing countenance and such delightful piebald hair should have done something which had shocked a university.

In an effort to brighten his host Commander Ludlow, in a quiet corner, had offered, since he'd received a licence from Albany to talk always with him as with his shipmates, to tell him a dirty story. Albany, only recently out of his cassock, had declared that he never liked indecent stories, that they didn't even begin to amuse him ; but Ludlow had retorted ' Gammon and punk ' and related the history. It was about a man at a party, who had gone into the men's dressing-room in obedience to a natural call and found only a china receptacle there for his need, and, hearing women's voices approaching, as if under the impression that it was *their* withdrawing-room, had rushed through the nearest door with his shameful china burden in his hand, only to find himself in the dancing-room among the waltzers—and " Ha, ha, ha ! " laughed Albany ; " HA, HA, HA !'" louder and longer than for many a day.

It was Ludlow, encouraged by an eighth or ninth visit to the decanter, who at last set the party alight. He suggested round games, and Susannah leapt up saying, " Yes, yes ! " and Tom snapped the photograph album shut as if he too were ready to be gay. They played, Consequences, Person and Thing, and at the end, Musical Chairs. Ludlow might be the Master of the Ceremonies, and Susannah the Mistress, but the astonishing thing was that old Bait, after his visits with Ludlow to the decanters, was as frolicsome as any. He was almost the Life of the Party. In the Musical Chairs his laughter was as loud and his prancing as sprightly as that of the young persons, Susannah and Tom. His agility between the chairs far surpassed Albany's, though he, too, was getting younger every minute.

At one point Susannah and Tom, as the two young ones, were sent out together to be the ' Person ' and the ' Thing ', and they chose to be ' Commander Ludlow and his Monocle.' Tom was marvellously liberated by these uproarious games, and all barriers of shyness were down between him and Susannah. He was elated to be in such beautiful company, and he and she went back among the guests, hand-in-hand, Susannah as the Commander and Tom as the Monocle, and perhaps Susannah's arm as the monocle's ribbon. Delia looked not a little nettled to see these two children thus linked and excitedly happy together.

It was Ludlow who had demanded Musical Chairs, but Bait and Albany and Susannah and Tom had been as ready for the game as he, and immediately began arranging the chairs.

56

Others helped; and only Delia, annoyed with ' that Tom Bud-lier ' for being so riotous and forgetful of his disgrace, set her face in grim disapproval. Susannah won the game easily, being the youngest and most active of all, but Bait was an honourable second.

Thus Albany could be overjoyed with the success of his party as he led his guests to the supper-room. The supper-room was the dining-room converted into a buffet-bar by the caterer. A long table stretched before the windows. In its centre was a gold-plush mat with a row of leaves around it and a silver epergne rising from its midst, crowned with a dish of many-coloured fruits. Dresden fruit dishes stood around this field of the cloth of gold. Soup was being served from a tureen by the caterer's waiter and by Albany's parlourmaid and house-maid. Claret cup, rum punch and sherry went round on trays, and later champagne, to toast the new home. When the cham-pagne had lifted still higher the exuberance of the guests and the pitch of their voices, Albany, seized by one of his uplifts of gaiety, picked up a champagne bottle and a glass and slipped from the supper-room to the kitchen.

He was well aware by this time that he'd had all the drink that his inexpert head could stand, but just as a mountain walker will not allow to his happier companions that he's getting dizzy, so Albany was unwilling to admit that his head was less strong and manly than Bait's or Ludlow's or young Tom's. But he had to concentrate on controlling his dancing thoughts—and the behaviour of his breaths—as he walked towards the kitchen.

Here he found Mrs. Kenny, the cook, and Amy, the little kitchen maid.

Mrs. Kenny had been their cook for seventeen years. A tall, thin, grey woman, of similar build to Delia, but even thinner, she had been the wife—and was now the widow—of a cowman in Mosgrove. This cowman, James Kenny, a strict Methodist and lay preacher, had been well pleased that his wife should work at the Rectory, because it was a godly household where the mistress, a strict evangelical even if a churchwoman, ob-served the Sabbath properly and allowed, as a rule, no strong drink on her table. It was not that Mrs. Kenny was a sworn teetotaller. She would always accept a coy glass of wine on Christmas Day when Albany insisted that they must drink her health as " the maker of the feast " and she felt it her duty to respond by drinking to the health of the family.

It was with this in mind that he had now come into her kitchen with a champagne bottle and a glass. He was going to insist that she must drink to the new home.

Mrs. Kenny, as he entered, was sitting at the kitchen table with one half-closed fist resting on it, and a most odd contemplative, glassy look in her eyes. As he came in she gave him, after some silent contemplation of his face, a little bow as a dignified greeting. This bow achieved, she said, " Yesss . . ." but to whom, and why, was not clear, for she was now gazing again into the vacancy before her. Once, her eyes moving slowly to the right, she descried him again, and smiled in the friendliest way, and bowed. Amy, the little kitchen maid, cast a glance first at her, and then at her master, and giggled.

" Mrs. Kenny," he said, covering up any discomfort he might feel at her strange appearance, " we can't have you left out of all this. You've got to have a glass of champagne, just this once, as it's a very special occasion."

" Special occasion," repeated Mrs. Kenny, still staring in abstraction straight before her, even though after a few seconds she had to draw in her chin sharply to hold down a slight eructation.

" Mrs. Kenny," he asked, " are you feeling all right ? "

She looked up at him, apprehended with an effort his presence and with a further effort, his identity, and said " Pardon ? "

" Are you quite well ? "

" Yes, I expect so," she said. " Yesss . . ."

Little Amy stood at the side of the table, giggling behind her fingers. And Albany saw on the sideboard two of the rum bottles which had been used for the punch. Both were empty, and beside them was a tumbler. He guessed that Mrs. Kenny, tired by the exertions of the night, had, in a moment of weakness, her husband being dead, drunk of the unrequired rum and, finding it a wonderful reviver, had sought more and more of such reinstatement.

It would be as well if she didn't lay champagne on top of the rum, but he couldn't offend her self-esteem by an instantaneous withdrawal with the bottle (for he was a weak and soft-hearted man) so he said only, as he began to pour, " I'm sure you've had a very tiring time. This'll do you good."

Mrs. Kenny raised a bland hand of rejection. " No. No, thank you. I was *that* tired I did have a sip. I had a few sips to keep me going. Amy knows I had a few sips because I felt wore out. But purely as med'sin. I was not meself at all. As med'sin. Mr. Kenny always allowed that."

"He was perfectly right, so now have a sip of this."

"Perfectly what ? "

"Right."

"Yes, I daresay. Right. Fancy that now."

"Now then, here we are. Here's your medicine, Mrs. Kenny."

"Wawl . . ." When Mrs. Kenny was in doubt about something and needed to linger on the word ' Well . . . ' she always extended it into ' Wawl . . . ' so now she gazed in doubt at the glass and said, " Wawl . . . as you know, I never take alcol as a rawl. Not as a rawl, I don't."

" Not as a rule, perhaps, but to-day's different."

" I don't take it as a peverage, pardon, beverage," she corrected, accepting the glass and laying it on the table. " Only as a ped'sin. And only very occasionally. Christ, my feet ! " She bent down, ground the legs of her chair round, removed her shoes, came to the surface, and twinkled her toes up and down. " Christ, that's better."

" Oh, Mrs. Kenny ! " Amy breathed, shocked.

Albany pretended not to have heard. This was surely the first time Mrs. Kenny had taken a sacred name in vain, but did not this sudden release by the rum show how often in her fifty years she had ached to do so ?

The feet eased, she fingered her glass and twirled it.

" And you, Amy ? " Albany invited. " We must find a glass for you."

" Shouldn't give drink to children like her," said Mrs. Kenny, when she discerned, through her mists, what was toward.

" It won't do her any harm this once."

" Any harm this once," repeated Mrs. Kenny, and sipped. But you understand, Amy : more harm done by drink than by anything else in the world. Mush more. Mr. Kenny always said the doors to the pubbly, *hic*, pubbly-cows were the gateway to the Devil, which if what he said was right . . . as it was . . . you shouldn't ought to be . . . at your age . . ." But the rest sank into a slough of silence.

Albany, having poured an inch of champagne into a tumbler for Amy, lifted his glass. " May we all be happy in our new home."

" Pardon ? " asked Mrs. Kenny. " What you say ? "

" May we all be very happy here."

" Oh, yes, I see. Yes, I agree. I agree with that. May you be health and happiness, you and the Mistress and Miss Hosannah. I very much hope so. Pardon." Putting her fingers to her lips she covered an infant regurgitation. " It does come back on me, that stuff—rum, was it ? Comes back. Comes back on me again and again. I remember Misso—yes, excuse me—sannah when she was a little comic of three. Or four. I used to say to Mr. Kenny, she's a proper little caution she is ; I wonder what she'll grow up into. And now she's grown up. And she looks lovely to-night, I *must* say, though I don't approve of that there dress you've bought her. It shows too much. It's not nice when there's young men about. It's asking for trouble, Mr. Kenny always said. A woman shouldn't show her nakedness to the men. Her bosom and all. Not a young woman. It wouldn't matter with an old boiler like me."

Amy stared at her master to learn how he would take this rebuke.

" Don't you think, Mrs. Kenny," he said, " that after your tiring day you ought to get to bed ? "

" Here's your health," she answered ; and added after reflection, " A girl shouldn't show her bosoms."

" The master arst if you'd like to go to bed," Amy explained.

" Give over giggling now, Amy. Just because Master ah'st you t'drink's health. Giggling's silly."

" Come, Mrs. Kenny," Albany submitted. " I should go to bed.

" Bed ? " she echoed. " Bed ? " And frowned, trying to get a firm grip on what the word connoted. " Oh, yes . . . Bed . . ." She was now *au fait* with it.

" Yes, you've had a very exhausting time and should get some rest. There's nothing more to do."

" No, nothing more," she agreed sadly. They were sad words, and she spoke them rather as if a death, long expected, had come at last to the house. " Wawl . . ." She pressed her hands on the table to aid herself in rising. " If the ladies and gentlemen wouldn't mind, I'll—pardon, sir "—once more she had to smother a small eruption, caused, no doubt, by this leaning forward in an effort to rise—" I'll make my way upstairs. Has everything been all right, sir ? "

" Everything's been splendid, Mrs. Kenny."

" Yes, everything splendid," she agreed. " Is me lady satisfied ? I can't get used to calling her me lady, I can't really."

" She thinks you've done wonders."

"Done what?" Mrs. Kenny, tall as a clothes prop, stood by the table, partly stayed in position by the tips of her long knuckly fingers, while she awaited some light on this question.

"Wonders."

"Oh, yes. Wonders. Wonders never cease. That girl should be in her bed ages ago. Goo'night, sir. Amy . . . go to your bed . . ."

Albany hurried back to the supper-room, longing to tell Susannah of Mrs. Kenny's incredible lapse. And Susannah, hearing, cried. "No? Kenny tight? Oh, I must go and see her. Oh, Mummy, Mrs. Kenny's tight."

"Oh, what an evening!" Delia deplored, beating a foot. "I never thought we should come to this sort of thing. So is that horrible man, Commander Ludlow. I've never seen such an exhibition. And that dreadful boy has had far too much too. And what's happened to Mr. Bait I don't know. If you approve of this sort of thing, I never shall. What will Mr. and Mrs. Forrester think?"

"They're getting quite lively themselves," said Susannah.

The fun was indeed boisterous about the buffet table. The caterer's waiter, either in natural goodwill or in the interest of his master, had been refilling glasses at every opportunity; and now Ludlow and Tom were standing face to face, lifting their glasses to one another and singing, "Wi'a hundred piper's an'a', an'a'," finishing each verse with the proper little shriek; while Bait, one hand on high, one hand on hip, footed a little Highland fling to the lilting air, his shriek, at the end of it, being the shrillest in the room. And his smile the brightest. The most expansive.

Colonel Budlier, seated against the wall, watched his boy with a gentle smile, as if pleased to see him happy.

Ludlow, seeing that his host was back in the room, sploshed some wine into a glass and over the cloth and drew him towards it; then put an arm about his shoulder and hugged him against his side and inquired, "Where've you been? We've wanted you. We've got to have a speech. A toast to the house. Bait, you're an o'friend. No? Well, Tom, you're the youngest. You won't? Oh, well, if no one else will, I must . . . Gentlemen, the King. The King, God bless him." He shot his monocle from his eye that he might more freely address them on the qualities of the King. "The old boy had a job to follow the old queen, as we know. He'd been a bit of a sport while the old dear was alive, but since he ascended the throne he's discharged his duties like a man. He's done more for peace than all these blasted Liberal swine put together. Peace with honour." With eyes brightly bedewed, if a little blood-flecked, he smiled benevolently upon all the company, and broke into a little song, staring at Bait all the time, as if he expected him to join in. " ' There'll be no war . . . as long as we've a king . . . like good King Edward . . .' " Bait did not join in, but only grinned ; and the Commander was left to conduct his own performance with the champagne glass in his hand. " Peace and prosperity. Peace and prosperity to your new home, Albany and Lady Delia and the lovely Susannah. Not that there'll be much more prosperity for any of us now that these Liberal swine are in power. It looks like the end of everything to me. This Lloyd George rat—you remember what he was, don't you ?—a pro-Boer, only a few years ago, while you and I were dying for our country. And it's not only these Liberal swine ; it's these Labour swine. The House of Commons always used to be a house of gentlemen, but now, my God, these fellahs sit there in tweed caps and red ties. It's the end of everything. It seems to me, ladies and gentlemen, that unless at the next election we—what the devil do you want, sir ? Go away." This was to the waiter who had been going round with the bottle to refill the guests' glasses and was now at the Commander's glass, waiting for it to come to rest, for Ludlow was using it to emphasize his points. " Go away, I tell you. Who is this fellah, Albany ? What does he want ? " But suddenly he perceived what the waiter wanted, and his attitude to him changed. It changed like a burst of sunlight out of a storm-cloud. " Yes. Yes, I will. Come here. Fill it up. Thank you, steward. It's the end of everything." He sipped from the newly-filled glass. " England will be finished, and the Empire a thing of the past. What I say is, we must get rid of this Lloyd George fellah, or we shall have revolution. That's what he's after : nothing less than revolution."

" I disagree entirely," Bait interrupted ; not that he, as an old-fashioned Liberal, approved of Lloyd George, but that, as a lover of argument, he must always, if possible, take the opposite position from a speaker. " Lloyd George is a radical, but that doesn't mean he's a revolutionary."

" My dear sir." Ludlow addressed him pityingly, almost beseechingly. " My dear sir, do you deny that Socialists, by very definition, are revolutionaries ? "

" I do not."

" And these Radicals, aren't they, for all practical purposes, Socialists ? "

" Some are, perhaps."

" And isn't this Lloyd George a pig of a Radical ? "

" Undoubtedly."

" Then, for all practical purposes, he's a revolutionary."

" Oh dear, no ! Palpably you don't understand the first principles of Logic. That's an illicit process of the minor term."

" It's nothing of the sort. It's a *what* ? "

" An illicit process of the minor term. Your minor term was particular in your minor premise, and you made it universal in your conclusion."

" *Did* I ? Did I indeed ? "

" Yes. You broke the Fourth Rule of the Syllogism. Unless a term is distributed in your premises, you cannot distribute it in your conclusion."

" Distribute my—— " began Ludlow, but he saved himself in the presence of ladies, and suggested that Bait should distribute his aunt.

" A proposition, to be definite," Bait was meanwhile explaining " must make clear whether it is predicating something of the whole or the part. I recommend you to study Aristotle's *dicta de omni et nullo*."

Ludlow's blood-flecked eyes which had been so brightly bedewed and smiling were now filmed over with a temporary confusion. At last he said, " I take it, sir, that you are giving us some of your legal stuff, and as nine-tenths of legal stuff is so much abracadabra, I do not propose to argue with you."

" And that," laughed Bait, " is a perfect example of the Third Material Fallacy or *Ignoratio Elenchi*. It's perhaps the most famous example of the *Ignoratio Elenchi*, to wit, the *argumentum ad hominem*."

And Albany, standing by amused, said, " That's right." Having been put through a course of Logic at his Theological College, thirty years before, he recognized this handsome term, *Ignoratio Elenchi*, was pleased to meet it again, and eager to display his acquaintance with it. " *Ignoratio Elenchi*, or Ignorance of the Refutation, and resort to abuse instead."

" What the devil are you all talking about ? There's no need for you to butt in, Albany. Look here, Bait—— " but there could be no further argument with Bait, for Bait had left him and was now seated against the wall beside an elderly lady (of whose name, nature, and residence he had no idea at all) and was expounding to her, leaning forward to do so, the Three Parts of Logical Doctrine and the Three Primary Laws of Thought. And since she made a show of interest, he dealt very thoroughly with the fallacy of which Ludlow had been guilty, differentiating for her with examples—and gestures—the *argumentum ad hominem*, the *argumentum ad ignorantiam*, and the *argumentum ad verecundiam*. The only valid argument, he assured her, was the *argumentum ex concesso*.

So Ludlow, continuing his speech, had to address it to his host and to any others around who were listening. " My only comfort, ladies and gentlemen, is that these Liberal and Radical swine can't achieve all their purposes at once, and the present system will probably last my time. When the disaster comes, you and I, Albany, will not be there to see it. It's young Tom here, and your lovely lady daughter, that I'm anxious about. Good night, sir." This was to the waiter who had gone out to wash some spoons but whom the orator supposed to be retiring for the night. " Ah, well, even for Tom and Susannah, it will be all the same a hundred years hence. We must all die." He said this cheerfully at first, conceiving it to be a comforting thought, but, having brooded a few seconds on it, he repeated it sadly. " We must all die. Death will come to all. Steward ! Oh, he's gone, has he ? Well, girl, you there ! Thank you. I will. Just a little more."

In couples, or one by one, the people went. Bait and his wife went ; old Colonel Budlier and Tom went, the Colonel smiling a gentle thank-you. Strange ladies thanked Albany for " a really lovely party " and he smiled in acknowledgment, said " I'm *so* glad you enjoyed it," and resolved to ask Delia who they were. Only Ludlow remained, having no woman to make him go. In his present exhilaration he was in no mood to go. In the dining-room, amongst the litter and refuse of the party he sat against the wall and continued his prophecies of disaster. Albany yawned behind a hand, Susannah sat smiling at the exhibition, and Delia beat an impatient foot.

At length Albany, with a " Look, old boy ; hadn't we better all go to bed ? " got him to his feet and encouraged him out of the room and into the passage. Here the Commander turned to leave the house by the back door, but they brought him about and got him to the front door, where he tried to go down a step that didn't exist, and nearly fell forward on to the gravel. He turned and looked rebukingly at the place where the step ought to have been and was not. All the way, from the chair by the wall along the passage, and to the garden gate, he foretold the ultimate destruction of his country's greatness, and at the gatepost, solemnly shaking his host by the hand, he swore eternal friendship. " Well, home now. One must go home some time. Good-bye, my dear boy. Home. Nothing is perfect : go'bye, my son." He set his face steadfastly towards his part of the street, braced back his shoulders, and gave himself his orders. " Now then : full speed ahead for home."

Albany returned into the house to find Delia in the disordered dining-room, demonstrating her anger by hurrying this way and that, to pick up oddments of paper, gather up fallen crumbs, straighten chairs, or thrust them grudgingly aside, so as to get at some offensive litter dropped behind them.

" That dreadful man ! " she exclaimed, now that Albany was returned from launching Ludlow on his way. " Coming here and making a beast of himself. I've never seen such an exhibition. And not he only."

Albany had come into the room, pretty sure that his party was going to be abused and determined to be angry if this happened. " I wouldn't say that he made a beast of himself at all. He had drunk a little too much ; that was all. It was a very nice party. A grand party."

" I thought he was sweet," said Susannah. " He and Daddy, two enormous men playing Musical Chairs—and Commander Ludlow at his sweetest, making his little speech ! "

" How *can* you, Susannah ? Oh, heavens, what are we coming to ? They had all drunk too much. How you can bring such people to the house and let Susannah see such things, I don't know. If it had not been for the sake of the other guests I'd have walked straight out of the room."

" It was a very fine party. Very fine."

He said this so unhappily, with such disappointment and loneliness in his voice, that Susannah, her bowels of compassion troubled, rushed to him and threw arms about his neck to reassure him.

" Steady ! " he begged, for though he was comforted by her compassion, he was momentarily shaken by this affectionate assault which was too like a cavalry charge.

But she rose on her toes to reach his cheek and kiss him. " You mustn't look sad when you're so enormous," she said.

" It's too pathetic. It was a lovely party, darling. Susannah enjoyed every minute of it."

It was near the luncheon hour next day when the garden gate clicked, and Albany, looking out of his window, saw Ludlow coming up the path. Ludlow seemed in perfect order this morning, his suit well brushed, his monocle firm in his eye, his carnation well seated in his buttonhole, and a clean silk handkerchief within his frayed shirt-cuff. But lest Delia should first encounter him and be less than polite, Albany hurried to open the door himself. He opened it before Ludlow was ready for this event, and it was clear that this sudden and premature opening disturbed the Commander like a shot across his bows. " Hell ! " he protested. " I haven't rung yet."

" I saw you from the window."

" Yes, but give me time. Don't disorganize me. I've only just got myself in order for a very difficult job, and I don't want to be jarred in any way. May I come in a minute ? This has got to be got through. A bad business, but let us not funk it."

" Why, of course, come in." Albany led him past the eye of Delia, at the drawing-room door, into the study. " Sit down, old boy."

" No, I must get it over at once. It's damn difficult." He raised his eyebrows that the eyeglass might fall : it fell rather despairingly. " I've come to make my apologies to your lady wife and beautiful daughter. Could you summon them ? "

" Apologies ? What for ? "

" Because I gather that my behaviour last night was unworthy of a gentleman."

" Wherever did you get that idea from ? "

" From old Colonel Budlier. I had a slight headache this morning and went out for a little into the cold air, and I met old Budlier. We got talking about your excellent party, and he told me he thought your lady wife was shocked when I was making that speech. So I asked him if he thought I ought to come and apologize, and he said it never did any harm to say one was sorry. Well, old Budlier's a better man than I am, a sidesman at church and all that, so I decided I'd better do as he said. I hope I'm not a coward, but I confess I've been walking round summoning up my courage—and, well, here I am, to eat my humble pie."

" It's very nice of you, Commander."

" I made a speech. I remember that. What did I say ? Any words unfit for a lady's ears ? "

" Not one. It was politics mostly."

" Politics ? What had they to do with anything ? "

" Not a great deal, perhaps."

" Grahame, Grahame old boy, tell me truly : I didn't talk about—well, the ladies of the town ? Not before the lady wife and daughter ? "

" You did not."

" Thank God. Thank *God* ! Was there a how-d'ye-do after I'd gone ? "

" No, no ; nothing much ; we all went to bed. But if you like I'll tell Delia what you say."

" D'you think that'll be enough ? I'm not a coward. She's a formidable lady, certainly, but I'm not a coward. I can go through with it."

" It's not necessary, old chap. I'm sure she'll be touched by your visit."

" And your charming daughter ? She'll continue to think well of me ? "

" She says she loves you."

" She does ? In spite of all ? "

" Yes. She calls you a pet."

" And a pet ? I am greatly relieved. I couldn't bear to be thought ill of by anything so beautiful. The old hags don't matter : they can think what they like. Has anyone else apologized ? "

" No."

" Well, they ought to. Bait was as tight as I was . . . or wasn't he ? " he asked in an anxious afterthought.

" He was very talkative, certainly."

" He must have been tight. Why, he's rising seventy and he nearly won the Musical Chairs. What did he talk about ? "

" The Three Primary Laws of Thought, I think."

" Good Lord ! What are they ? "

" No idea. I used to know once, but I've forgotten."

" Some legal rigmarole, I imagine. Well, Albany, old boy, as Nelson said, ' Thank God I've done my duty,' but it's been a shaker, I don't mind telling you. I must go and have a drink. Come along too. *Yes*, come on ! "

" No, thank you. It's just on our lunch time."

" Oh, well, I'm in no condition for lunch myself. I must go into dock for repairs first." He put the monocle in his eye to be ready for the street, as another man puts on a hat. " You really will make my apologies to the good lady. That's very generous of you. Perhaps, after all, I *am* a bit of a coward. Well, good-bye, sir, good-bye."

Albany escorted him to the door, and he passed out of the garden, a very erect and well-brushed penitent. At the gate he turned, not eastwards towards his home, but westwards towards St. John's Wood Road, the Lord's Tavern and re-cuperation.

CHAPTER FIVE

DELIA

INDEED nothing is perfect, as the Commander said, and Albany's delight in his new habitation was falling short of his dream. He was happier than he had been in Mosgrove, but not happy enough. He was pleased that people were now talking to him as man to man, because he'd hidden for ever in a cupboard his dark clerical garments. This free, unfettered talk gave him a sense of having stepped out of a grey sleep into an awareness of the real world, as it lay under the sun. In himself he was conscious of an extraordinarily pleasing transfiguration. No longer need he make a show of principles and practices which he had long ceased to believe in and perform, and oh, the sense of health and well-being this freedom gave him ! Nor did he doubt that with freedom he had changed into something better as well as happier. Sometimes he was amazed how complete was the change from the Parson of Mosgrove into Sir Albany Grahame of St. John's Wood. It was as if the very substance of his brain had changed. In his covert thoughts he would liken himself to one of those Christmas cracker magic flowers which at first sight appeared no more than a tight little disc of paper, but on being put into a glass of water opened out and became a brilliant flower. Some of this new efflorescence was expressed in the layman's clothes which he now wore, but by no means all of it, because he thought it best to keep these un-clerical blossomings quiet and unobtrusive at present so as not to alarm Delia.

He was happy, then, in this new enlargement ; but there was a disappointment, a secret disappointment. It lay in this, that

he was not making friends more easily among the ' interesting '
people for whom the Wood was famous, its intellectuals and
artists and composers and theatrical folk. Ludlow was no
intellectual, nor dear old Colonel Budlier ; and certainly not
young Tom. Nor any of the hearty fellows to whom Ludlow
had introduced him in the public houses. . . .

Thus he was still more lonely than he liked, and too much
of his days he spent walking along the streets behind the big
expensive cigars of which he was now so proud, and thinking
his solitary and for ever silent thoughts behind their smoke.
When first he walked these streets he had been pleased with
the long garden walls, so old and ripe, so heavily embroidered
here and there with the plush of lichen and moss, so elegantly
shawled with the taut and blackening ivy or the bright loose-
hanging Virginia creeper. They seemed the very essence of
this leafy suburb ; and so they were ; but their meaning was
seclusion. Their wooden gates were always closed, and through
the monastic gratings of those gates no man might peer. Behind
them the little houses in their squares of garden had been built
for privacy and most of them guarded their secrecy still. He
would walk past the walls and hear the knocking of croquet balls
or the snapping of a lady's shears among her flower-beds or the
broken drone of a lawn-mower ; but he learned nothing of
these householders as the weeks and months went by. He
looked up at the window boxes on the sills of upper storeys and
wondered what went on behind their scarlet or pink geraniums,
their white marguerites and their blue lobelia. Or he would
stand behind his own window boxes and look out at his own
garden wall and feel (though not a word of this to Delia) a
little shut in—shut away from the full life which he so wanted
to find before it was too late. He would look across the sunlit
plush of his lawn to the eight limes that stood like sentinels along
the wall, and he would hear beyond their high curtain the
passing steps of invisible men or the zig-zag journey of the
lamplighter crossing from gas-lamp to gas-lamp ; and beyond
these nearer sounds the continuing rumour of London's traffic,
as if the dome of the sky were the trumpet-mouth of a great
sea-shell and this rumour the endless sigh within it.
Sometimes, because of this shut-in feeling he would go out
through the gate in his wall to walk the streets again ; and then
in the fallen dusk, or in the grape-blue darkness, he would
hear from some shadowy recess the murmuring of two muted

voices, one male, one female, and the whisper of kisses, and his heart would fill, most oddly, with a sweetness that was imagined and a regret that was real.

What was it old Pater had said ? He had said that success in life was to be always at the focus where vital forces were united and there to burn with a gem-like flame. Well, the weeks were passing and the months, and Sir Albany couldn't believe that he was yet burning with a gem-like flame.

Sometimes he walked around the houses or into the Park with Bait, and he would account this an item on the credit side. Granted, of course, that some of old Bait's ideas were extravagant and extraordinary, but he was always amusing when expounding theories in which he only half believed, and immensely provocative when he did believe in them (or maintained he did) and must defend them with heat. To be provoked by Bait into a hot disputation, as happened often, was to be enkindled into vigorous and pulsing life.

One of Bait's favourite topics was occult phenomena, and there lives no man whom the Occult cannot fascinate and even enthral. Walking at Albany's side, pishing and pshawing at all opposition, Bait would hold forth on telepathy, hypnosis, the sublimal consciousness, clairvoyance and precognition. He explained clairvoyance and precognition by simply denying the reality of Time. Man's reason, he said, was adapted for use only in a spatio-temporal world and nowhere else, but this ' world of experience ' was illusory and, to put it crudely but exactly, all-my-eye ; every mystic knew there was no such thing as progressive time, streaming from past to future, but only an Eternal Now, an Endless Present. Thus the future existed in the timeless present, and a clairvoyant's power of precognition was simply an ability to get glimpses of it. Everybody had this power in embryo ; did we not all have moments of premonition and occasionally experiences that could only be described as precognition ? In dreams, for example—and on dreams Bait was tremendous. Albany did not know if he was in Circus Road or in the Park, or indeed under the sky at all, when Bait descanted on dreams.

Dreams led him to the works of a certain Dr. Sigmund Freud, whose astonishing contents were just now seeping into the cognizance and chatter of intellectuals. So catholic were Bait's interests, so capacious and hospitable his mind, that he was as ready to expound and defend the deterministic views of this

Dr. Freud as the surely indeterministic views of the mystics with their Eternal Now. That Psychoanalysis and Occultism were quarrelsome housemates didn't disturb him at all. Albany, laughing, would liken him to a mediæval scholastic, so did he torture reason into the service of faith. And at this Bait would get quite hot, declaring with pish's and pshaw's that men had no right to say Incompatibles couldn't exist just because their poor human brains weren't organized to understand how. Where his vaunted Logic and his Primary Laws of Thought were at this point, who could say ?

Sometimes he interpreted Albany's dreams for him in the manner of Dr. Freud, and with considerable shocks for his listener. Hardly one of these interpretations but was extremely indecent—and extremely interesting. And possible—just possible. Albany poised and pouted his lips over them in wonder. Could these things be ? Argumentation shot between them like electric sparks all the way round the houses or along the glades of the Park. Soon Bait was interpreting not only his dreams but his little mannerisms, his set habits, and these interpretations were no less indecent and interesting.

That swinging of his ebony cane as he walked, did it not signify a suppressed desire to display the phallus, or, perhaps, a fear of impotence and therefore a desire to compensate for this inadequacy by an extension of his personality in the form of a walking stick ?

Good lord !

Or that frequent dangling of the stick behind his back, did it not denote homosexual proclivities and a hidden wish for anal intercourse ?

God, no !

That excessive distress when he left the stick on a seat in the park and knew no happiness till he'd recovered it. Manifestly a castration complex.

His pride in, and play with, his big cigar. Clearly an infantile phenomenon. It related to a stage of development earlier than the more overtly sexual or anal : to wit, the oral stage. The cigar held near his mouth, or twisted within his lips, were reminiscent of his mother's breast.

Never heard such nonsense.

That continual soothing of, and smoothing of, his long moustaches. This might be no more than a form of recreation for their owner, but Bait didn't think so ; he held that it was desire to draw the attention of all to these proofs of virility.

71

And when you considered the moustaches and the long cigar together—but here Bait's explication was such as is best left within the covers of a textbook.

Albany, though wondering how much of this was true, would argue that it was all jargon, fudge and moonshine ; that his moustaches signified nothing more than moustaches ; that his cigar implied nothing more than the comfort of a smoke ; and that his ebony cane merely represented his desire for a companion on his walks who didn't talk rubbish. But he came away from these talkative walks with Bait, happily stimulated, full of new ideas, and smoothing his moustaches.

Albany's body was less ready than his mind to shake off the habits of fifty years ; and this, on one occasion, produced a blunder that festered as a sore in his memory for years. It happened in a theatre. He was getting real happiness from taking Delia and Susannah to theatres—especially Susannah. Susannah, bred in a village, had not seen three plays in her life, and he, determined that she should be on his side in this matter of coming to town, took her to every play of whose fame she had heard and whose famous actor-managers she longed to see. Some of these famous men in their famous plays they had to seek out in suburban theatres : Mr. Martin Harvey in *The Breed of the Treshams*, Mr. and Mrs. Kendal in *The Elder Miss Blossom*, a most moving play, and August van Biene in *The Broken Melody*, a yet more devastating piece that dissolved Susannah in a cascade of tears, and did much the same to her father.

It was at the new King's Theatre, in Hammersmith, that Albany's evening was ruined—and his memory permanently wounded—by his body's blunder. The play was *The Belle of New York*, and their seats were near the middle of the front row. Very nearly late, they had but a minute to get to them before the house-lights went down. The orchestra was playing the overture and the Grahames clambered hurriedly past the people's knees before tier upon tier of watching eyes. Now, all clergymen, on reaching their seat in a church pew, put their hat on the floor and kneel down for a moment of private prayer ; and Albany, on this occasion, having attained his tip-up seat, laid his hat under it and his programme on the circle's parapet and knelt down to pray.

" *Gosh*, no ! " begged Susannah.

Fortunately, even as the crowd in the circle tittered and his blush distilled in sweat upon his temples, the house-lights went out, his shame was drowned in darkness, and *The Belle of New York* began.

Albany was often very unhappy that he did not love Delia more. He had to confess to himself that he was glad when he heard that she was out of the house, or that she was shortly going out. And this was not a happy admission. He would take the unhappiness into his study and, shutting the door upon the world, sink deep into his deep chair, and brood and brood upon it. His new study was a most comfortable place to brood in. He had converted the long music room of Sir Vaysey Lowe into the kind of study he had always desired : a long Turkey carpet on the floor, the largest and deepest of leather " club " chairs, a handsome writing table, handsome book-shelves all along one wall, and usually the smell of a lately-smoked Havana filling the room with its dignity and comfort. To this soft and compassionate room he would come for these lonely meditations on his lack of love for Delia. In the deep chair with his feet on the footstool he would either smoke a cigar, lifting it now and again from his mouth to brood with lips set tight, or, too unhappy even to light a cigar he would twist the long brown moustaches or finger the neat, pointed grey beard. The situation, he would feel, was pathetic, almost tragic, and not for himself only, but for poor Delia too. There was he, a lonely, hungry man ; and there was she, at this moment certainly not loved.

Sunday morning was always a time of such discomfort and strain. The discomfort endured from breakfast time to church bell. It sprang from the knowledge that Delia was quite de-termined to go to church and that he was equally determined not to. The bells of St. John's Wood Chapel, that little cathe-dral of the Wood on its leafy island-site, rang without rest from half-past ten to eleven, sounding their summons to the faithful like Delia, and their rebuke to the faithless like Albany. When the wind was in the east their notes were loud in Circus Road and beat uncomfortably on the conscience of Sir Albany in his study.

In his first weeks at Santa Monica he had made a point of slipping away from the breakfast table on these Sunday morn-ings that he might elude any controversy. He went either into the study and shut its door like a blank discouragement in the face of talk or he went quickly into the street for a walk, whistling nonchalantly. But he could not adopt these evasive manœuvres every Sunday morning, and now, all too often, the argument sprang up and filled the house from the middle of breakfast to the middle of church bell. " I can't understand," said Delia one morning, when she was already in the hall in toque and veil. " Not to go to church, and you a clergyman ! I can't understand this change. *I* do not change." And he, instead of retorting, as he would have liked to do, " No, that's the trouble. Your mind set like concrete fifty years ago, and you make the mistake of being proud of it," attempted to be humorous. " My dear Delia," he said, " I must have accumulated an enormous treasury of merit during thirty years of going to church four times every Sunday, and I reckon that's a capital on which I can draw for a long time yet." But Delia wouldn't allow that this was a subject to joke about. She only maintained her look of acid disapprobation and even, to be sure, increased the acidity. Then he got angry and demanded in a louder voice, " Haven't I told you that I want a little free time to think things out ? Haven't I made it clear that I've a strong desire to take my religion into the wilderness and think it all out ? I haven't thought it out yet."

" I do not understand. You a clergyman ! "

" Oh, my God ! " He tossed his head impatiently at this blunt-brained unwillingness even to listen to what he was saying. " Surely it is simple enough. I'm grateful for the opportunity afforded to me by my poor dear brother's death to think things out properly. It's not that I'm irreligious. If anything, it means that I'm more religious than ever I was."

But, still refusing to understand—were not the bells ringing ? —she picked up prayer book and gloves, drew on the gloves angrily and commanded, " Come on, Susannah."

" But, Mummy, Susannah would like to think things out too," submitted Susannah.

" Don't talk like that ! There ! See what you've done to the girl. She no longer wants to come to church."

" Sometimes she wants to," corrected Susannah, " but not always ; not absolutely every Sunday. Next Sunday I'm going to think things out."

" You're going to do nothing of the sort. Come on ! "

And away towards the door she went, with her lips pressed together and her fingers drawing on the gloves in a most un-Christian fashion.

Then he was sullen indeed. He didn't at all like this demonstration in front of him, and as further points in his favour leapt up for presentation he stated them loudly as she went through the door. " I'm fundamentally twice as religious as you are. As your beloved Tennyson says, ' There lives more faith in honest doubt, believe me, than . . .' "

But she conceded no answer. She shut the door on his quotation. She wasn't going to argue with anyone. Her churchgoing, in the old days, had been a duty ; it was now an angry passion. She walked to the gate and towards the bells, holding her head high, buttoning up the gloves, and drawing Susannah after her ; while he, in some rage, watched her from his window. " That's a demonstration in force," he told himself. " To humiliate me. And I don't like demonstrations in force. I'm not going to be demonstrated in force to. Pah ! The sainted woman ! "

He imagined her walking along Circus Road towards the church bells, supremely confident that she was right and he wrong. Maddening that cocksureness ! She with a brain that was incapable of independent thought, and incapable of criticizing herself ! " I do not change." That rigidity which she supposed to be a fine thing instead of a stupid ! Her quick, loud, easy dogmatisms, her arrogant, unshakable rulings. They were not open to question because she was the daughter of an admiral-churchwarden and the wife of a rector. They were all the same, these women like Delia ; he'd met many of them in the church ; they were as quick and loud and self-confident as their minds were limited and their views illiberal.

" I do not change. I have my standards. I keep my standards." And the other day : " It's no good : I've never liked indecent stories ; and I'm not going to begin now " ; whereupon he'd played Ludlow's trick upon her, narrating the merry tale of the man who'd carried that embarrassing and humiliating vessel by mistake into the ballroom—and *the trick didn't work ;* it failed as completely with her as it had succeeded with him ; she got up and went from the room.

And this new spiritual hero of hers, the Reverend Mark Armour, D.D., incumbent of the Chapel. She declared that he was ' wonderful ' ; and Albany didn't know, but couldn't help wondering whether the man wasn't probably as big a hypocrite as *he* had been. But, if he was, Delia would never perceive it, any more than she'd ever perceived it in her husband. Oh, the passive credulity of women ! Their readiness to be slavish disciples ! This thought suddenly introduced a very horrible question. Did she perhaps discuss him with the Reverend Dr. Armour ? Did she submit his frailties to the Doctor ? Did she think him inferior to this jewel in character and—worse still—in intelligence ?

So much did this horrible notion fester that next Sunday he resolved that if there were to be demonstrations in force they should come from both sides. He rose from the breakfast table and demonstrated in force before she could. " I," he said, " am going for a nice long walk. I may meet Ludlow in which case I shall probably have a drink with him at the Lord's Tavern. Or I may go into old Bait's and have a game of chess with him." And out of the room he went, and very soon out of the gate, a newspaper instead of a prayer book profanely under his arm, and his stick irreligiously swinging.

The strain between them was above the surface now in a way it had never been at Mosgrove. As long as he had been a practising clergyman, pretending to the same puritanism and the same dogmatisms as hers, the chain that bound them had been able to sag. But now it was taut. He could feel all the time her steady effort to get him into a respectable state again ; that is to say, to make him go to church again, to break his connection with men like Ludlow who took him into pubs, to fix him again in the mould (as she conceived it) of a religious gentleman, fit mate for a churchwarden's daughter. He found this covert but continuing campaign a most hampering business, because he was really more afraid of her watching eyes and her displeasure than he cared to own.

And all the time, as has been said, he would have liked to love her properly. Partly for her sake, but more largely for his own, that he might be free from a recurring pain. And this intermittent dislike of her was a very real pain. Albany would discern this latter motive and sigh at his self-centredness, but the situation remained : either for her sake or his own he must try to believe he loved her. One evening, thinking these thoughts, and made unhappy by them, he went from his home (which was hurting him) and went to sit with Bait. Their talk, as ever, visited a dozen fields, and it was Albany who, because his heart was still oppressed by the conviction that he didn't love Delia properly, diverted the talk to the subject of marriage. And when Bait threw himself most willingly into a diatribe against women and a jeremiad about marriage, Albany nodded occasionally, but sometimes shook his head ; and when

76

an opportunity came for him to speak, he declared, " Yes, some of that may be true, but I am lucky. I have a golden wife. . . . in many ways." And turning his eyes aside to stare into vacancy, he continued, " Yes, I should say that mine has been a perfect marriage . . . in some ways."

Bait nodded in his turn, but, preferring to deal with less happy affairs, diverged into cynical comments about old Sir Colin and Lady Maybrick, who lived across the road, and the state of the union there. " You've only got to look at old Maybrick and his woman, you've only got to see them walking along the road, or hear them sparring at a party, to realize that he's *fatigatus et aegrotus* with her."

" What did you say ? " Albany had not quite caught the Latin.

" *Fatigatus et aegrotus*," Bait repeated with no small relish. " Tired and sick of her."

It was a melancholy fact, but undisputable, that as Bait translated the two Latin words, a string in Albany's heart vibrated in sympathetic accord.

CHAPTER SIX

THE BRIGHT MORNING HAZE

WHEN, as so often happened, Albany went out after breakfast to enjoy the morning air, he might have seen, had his eyes not been misted by his thoughts, another wanderer on the pavements of Circus Road. It was remarkable that he never once observed him because this youthful figure was in the road and strolling past the wall of Santa Monica almost every morning after that house-warming party. True that at the first glimpse of Sir Albany he would turn about to hide his face, or swing out of sight into Elm Tree Road, but, even so, one would have supposed that on one morning or another these two strollers must have come face to face in the vicinity of Albany's gate. For Tom Budlier would walk past the house again and again, and very slowly that he might not quickly lose its nearness. He would walk to a corner and there turn to watch the house a little ; and sometimes he hurried round three sides of a square to come into Circus Road again. Then, after a halt, he would saunter past the Grahame's wall, gazing up like a love-rapt serenader at a first-floor window which he'd decided must be Susannah's bedroom ; imagining her there at midnight in her exquisite sleep ; and happily uninformed that it was the bedroom of Sir Albany.

Just now Tom had much time on his hands. He was supposed to be considering what he would do in the future, what plans he must make, now that his Cambridge career had ended at the guillotine, and sometimes, breakfast being over, he did in fact sit down with these difficult thoughts, or pace a room with them, but after a dutiful fifteen minutes, or even an effortful half-hour, his will died in his body, and he abandoned this dim future for the present bright enslavement of Circus Road. There was all time in front of him, he thought, and at this very moment Susannah might be making ready to come out of her gate.

It was not that he was less penitent now than he had been on the pavement outside the Ordnance Arms. Rather was he the more distressed by the disgrace that invested him, now that he'd seen the only girl worth calling a girl, and learned that she was a parson's daughter. Or an ex-parson's : he was not quite clear about Sir Albany's present status—any more than Sir Albany was. But it seemed certain that Susannah, brought-up in a parsonage, if she knew the nature of his disgrace, must think him bad indeed. What infernal luck to meet this overwhelming girl, the girl who made all other girls seem irrelevant, if not redundant, just when he was moving about the world in a cloud of disgrace.

And he was certain she knew something of the shameful story, first, because, when they sat together at the party, the only two young ones there, she had talked of their schools but avoided all mention of Cambridge, and secondly, because she had palpably striven to be nice to him after her mother, that damned hag, had so deliberately given him the cold douche. But if this delicately nurtured and high-minded girl had been told of his disgrace, she must in fairness be told also that he was not unashamed of what he had done and was resolving to make amends to his old father in the future. These points in his favour ought certainly to be exhibited to her.

His frequent visits to the pavements of Circus Road achieved their aim at last. He saw Susannah turn out of her gate and walk westwards towards Grove End Road. Now Elm Tree Road swings out of Circus Road to meet the long, winding Grove End Road at a lower corner, and Tom sprinted through this fortunate channel, dashed through a posse of loungers by the Art School, and emerged into Grove End Road—but his issue into this road was as slow and innocent as if it had no more interest for him than any other. This innocence he emphasized by a lift of his eyebrows, and a light of surprised recognition in his eyes, as he perceived Susannah Grahame only twenty steps away. Nor, in his considerateness, did he let her think that he was noticing the deep wine-colour which had rushed into her cheeks at this sudden sight of him. But with what pleasure, with what a spring of hope, he noticed it !

"Hallo," he stuttered ; and asked in as indifferent a manner as he could achieve, "Where are you off to ? "

"Me ?" she answered, almost as if he must mean someone else. "Oh, I'm going to the station."

"Which station ? "

"St. John's Wood Road Station. I'm going to town."

"Could I walk there with you ? I was just walking around for the sake of walking. I didn't come out with any particular purpose."

"Why, of course come too, if you'd like to."

"That was a wonderful party," he said, when they were walking side by side.

"I'm so glad you liked it." And she told him about Commander Ludlow's ' heart-breaking visit of apology ' and about ' Our Kenny's extraordinary lapse ', talking very fast, almost as if it were safer to be talking ; walking very fast, almost as if she half wished to escape from him ; and never once looking at him, as if his face could make her afraid.

"I do like your father," he said, for something to say.

"Yes, he's rather a poppet."

"He's so terrifically handsome, don't you think ? "

"Yes, I do. And I daily thank God for it."

"I say, need we hurry like this ? "

"Oh, I'm sorry. Was I hurrying ? "

The sun was high above the houses now in a burnished sky, and the shadows of the chimney stacks lay blue on roofs of violet slate ; the roadways were saffron-tinted between the flung blue shadows of the trees, and every street ran through the sunlight into a bright blue haze. The morning, brilliant with hope, was very like their minds. For their minds, at twenty, held more light than shadow ; and every long vista melted into a bright haze of morning.

They turned into St. John's Wood Road, and there before

them was the long, high curtain-wall of Lord's. To see that wall was to remind Tom that his cricket at least was something in his favour and, since she knew of things to his discredit, he was surely entitled to make some mention of this.

" Ever been to Lord's ? " he asked. " Ever seen any county cricket ? "

" No, but I should love to. You're awfully good at cricket, aren't you ? "

" Oh, I wouldn't say that. I bowl a bit."

" Commander Ludlow said you played for Middlesex at Lord's."

" Yes, I was given a trial in one or two matches last year."

" And you did awfully well, didn't you ? "

" Well, I was lucky. I took a few wickets, and on each occasion I was sent in to bat late, when the bowling was tired, so I was able to knock it around a bit. I made—well, to tell the truth, I made seventy once . . . seventy-three, to be exact. But the bowling was tired, of course."

" I'd love to see you play. You will be playing this season ? "

" Well . . . yes . . . I *have* been asked to . . ."

" Oh, *please, can* I come when you do ? "

" But of course ! You could come as my guest, and—— "

" Oh, that'd be too wonderful ! "

" But I shall be terribly nervous."

" Why ? "

" Oh I don't know. With you there. . . ."

" But I shall be praying for you. Praying like anything. Oh, I *know* you'd do wonders. When will it be ? Commander Ludlow said you'd been asked to play regularly."

" Yes . . . well, I have been . . . more or less. . . ."

And still she said nothing about Cambridge. He must learn how much she knew. " I did play for Cambridge."

" Oh, yes ? " And there she left this little fact where he had laid it down ; left it untouched.

" You know I was sent down from Cambridge ? "

" Sent down ? " She was pretending she didn't know what the phrase meant.

" Yes, expelled. Kicked out. Did you know that ? "

" Yes, I did, as a matter of fact."

" And do you know what for ? "

" No, I don't think I do. All I know is that Commander Ludlow said it was a shame."

" Oh, no, it wasn't. I deserved every bit of it."

80

"I'm sure you didn't. I'm sure it was a shame."

"But I *did*." He was quite angry with her for questioning the extent of his guilt. "I've no sympathy with myself. I don't want you to think that. I let the old man down badly. It was a bad show."

"I think your father's such a dear." So did she change the subject.

"He is. He's the best old thing ever. You know he's a sidesman at All Saints? I do think there's something wonderful about some of these simple old colonels who paddle off to their Holy Communion every Sunday at eight o'clock. I'm afraid I don't go. He's a much better person than I am."

"I don't see why you should say that."

"I say it because I know it." He was almost angry again. "I'm a ghastly disappointment to him."

"I don't believe it."

"Yes, yes, I am," he insisted. "But I've made up my mind to make it up to him somehow. I fully intend——"

But, oh, the callous indifference of Life, its insensitiveness to one's desire to tell a story well and finish it off properly, its lack of all feeling for a fine climax, its beastly *shapelessness* Just as he was about to expose his surely creditable vows of reparation, they reached the doors of the Metropolitan station, and she had halted and was saying hesitatingly. "I must go now. I'm in rather a hurry . . . really."

"Yes, of course," he agreed accepting the imperfections of Life, its torn and jagged ends. "Good-bye, then. Good-bye for the present."

Standing in the sunlight and watching her in the dusk of the booking office, he saw her take her ticket, turn once again to smile at him, and then hurry down the stairs to the platform below, like a rabbit scurrying into the shelter of its burrow.

She was gone now, and he turned away to traverse the busy, throbbing cross-roads and stroll homeward by Wellington Road, between the east wall of Lord's and the old burial ground, now a timbered and shady garden. He walked alone now, but he was happy in his loneliness because he was exalted. His head was lit with a glow that surpassed the sunlight without. And if yesterday he'd had plans for fine achievement—or, rather, hopes, because the plans were still as amorphous as the bright, vapoury haze at the end of the road—these hopes were all-important now. He must give them shape ; convert them into plans. Soon. At once. "There's no one like her. Oh, my

God ! No one at all. Hell, I'll do anything. *Be* anything.
What can I do ? What can I start doing to-morrow ? To-
morrow, as ever was. . . ."

And while he considered this, Susannah was being carried
along under London in a hurrying, beating train. The engine's
smoke and steam, imprisoned in the deep tunnel, went clouding
past her window. Her compartment was empty, because it
was long past the London rush hour. And in that empty
compartment her heart was speeding, and beating, like the
train. Her lips were parted, despite the smoky air, because
she was drawing in sharp breaths of happiness. Her breast
was in a strange condition, inflated, as it seemed with air that
was more like light. She might be deep down in a subterran-
ean darkness, but her head, down there, was like a little moving
focus of light.

She knew that he had come into her streets to find her. Her
father might not have noticed him there, but she had seen him
many times. The first time had been from her window, as she
sat brushing her hair. Through the curtains she had seen him
loitering along and looking up at her house. A mere chance
that she had seen him then, but since that interesting moment,
she had come often to the same window, after breakfast, to see
if he came again. And on many an ensuing morning she saw
him pass slowly and glance up furtively. She called him ' The
Great Duke Ferdinand.'

This needs explaining. Tom was a tall and good-looking
boy but with his light brown, two-shaded hair and his fair
English skin, he was not in the least like a Grand Duke of the
Medici. But it so happened that in her last year at school
Susannah's English mistress, who was given to gush about
poetry, had insisted that she must read for her moral improvement Browning's *Rabbi Ben Ezra :* ' Let age approve of youth,
and death complete the same ; ' and for this purpose she had
presented her with a small limp-leather book containing a
selection of Browning's poems. But Susannah had been far
more interested in the poem that neighboured *Rabbi Ben Ezra*,
and this was *The Statue and the Bust.* This poem, she told
herself, was ' terrific.' She read it over and over again till
many of its stanzas were haunting refrains in her mind.

The excellent instruction of this poem—which amounts in
simple words to this, that if a chance of love is around, you
should not just dream happily about it day after day, but should

secure it before it is too late—in short, and to put it very crudely, that you should get out and get on with it—this instruction made a deep impression on her. And surely now there was a faint resemblance between Susannah looking from her window at Tom Budlier loitering in the road and the Riccardi's bride gazing out from her palace at the Great Duke Ferdinand riding by. *De te fabula.* And Susannah had no intention of being like the woman in the poem who did nothing, nothing at all but postpone and dream, ' till the glory dropped from their youth and love.'

> ' So we resolve on a thing and sleep :
> So did the lady ages ago. . . .
>
> But next day passed, and next day yet,
> With still fresh cause to wait one day more
> Ere each leaped over the parapet.'

This morning Susannah had seen Tom there, had exclaimed, " Ah, the Great Duke Ferdinand," and, mindful of the poet's counsel, had promptly leaped over the parapet. She ran from the house to encounter him somewhere, though the encounter of course must appear an accident. At her gate, however, seeing him in the distance, she had yielded to panic and turned the opposite way to escape him. Quickly she had got herself into the safety of Grove End Road and been truly surprised by his sudden egress from Elm Tree Road. In her state of over-throw, caused by this materialization, she had said the first thing that entered her head, namely, that she was going to the station and to town. And now, as a result of this complete but surely venial lie she was obliged to travel in this stupid steamy train to the next station which was Baker Street. Who on earth wanted to go to Baker Street ? All she could do at Baker Street was to turn round and travel home again. " Heavens, I'm a liar ! " But what else could she have said ? Not even God, if He was a God of mercy, could have expected her to say, " I came out in the hope of meeting you."

Was she in love ? She didn't know, but she hoped so with an excited hope. Her first feeling had been one of extreme interest, because of his disgrace, and of swelling pity, because her mother had been so cold to him. He had looked so sad at the party and had brightened up so wonderfully when she had taken him in hand. And when she had taken him by the hand to drag him into the drawing-room as ' Commander Ludlow's monocle ' the effect on her had been strange. There had been a vibrating of her nerves all the way from her finger tips to her heart.

She knew every detail of his disgrace. Her parents ' poor darlings', might suppose that she knew nothing of such matters, but she knew all. The nuns at her convent school had accepted, with the same simple faith that they gave to their religion, that their delicate charges, reared in religious homes, knew as little about sex at sixteen years of age as at six. Whereas it was at school, and at sixteen, that she had learned, with an engrossed interest, the ultimate truths about licit and illicit love. Mabelle Prinny had brought to school, enthusiastically, and passed around among her classmates, a book entitled *Wedded Joy*. And Mabelle was an earl's daughter. Mabelle's real name was Mabel Bursford-Prynne, but she was sixteen, an age when ' Mabel ' seemed unromantic, and even to savour of the pantry. So she wrote herself ' Mabelle.' Susannah had read Mabelle's enthralling volume, lying prone upon the school grass under the farthest trees, her elbows screening it from the surrounding fields and hills. She had read it all one golden afternoon with an avid appetite, no small agitation of her whole being, and a pulsating guilt. Sometimes, as new knowledge burst upon her, she exclaimed, " Crikey ! " And as the knowledge increased, she told the grass beneath her, " The Elders would have forty fits if they knew Susannah was reading this."

So she was able to understand Tom Budlier's sin. Its nature had been disclosed to her, most unexpectedly, and rather coyly, by Mrs. Kenny in her kitchen. And Susannah, questioning and listening with an ardent interest, had been clear-eyed enough to perceive that Mrs. Kenny was enjoying this ostensibly moral discourse on matters usually hidden. Mrs. Kenny might imply in her talk that the facts of sex were both sacred and indecent—a view that knit Susannah's brows in some confusion—but there was no doubt, thought Susannah, that Mrs. Kenny was indulging her hidden desires with a new freedom, now that Mr. Kenny was no more. As the child of Delia and Albany, Susannah naturally considered Tom's offence a very serious one, but she wanted to love him in spite of it, and now, in the train, she was digging into memory to find some good in him. There was his love for his dear old father . . . and . . . and . . . his liking for *her* father . . . and . . . and . . . Was that all she could find for the present ? Well, even if he *was* very weak, Christianity said one must forgive, and for once in a way she determined to honour this precept. And somehow she

84

found it easier to forgive him because her mother found it impossible.

Baker Street. Who on earth wanted to be at Baker Street ? Nothing to do but go home again. But since it was always a weariness, duller than a twice-told tale, to go home the way one had come, she left the station and walked homeward along Park Road through the sparkling, sun-flushed morning. It was only a mile or so, and she had long, slim, striding legs like those of an Andolan antelope. Park Road brought her to the entrance of St. John's Wood Road station where, fifty minutes before, she had parted from Tom. She saw the threshold on which they had said their good-byes and was astonished that it had now taken to itself a certain sacredness. Strange that the dusty entrance to a booking office could be thus anointed ! That it could be endued with power to drive at the heart ! " I must be," she thought with a leap of conviction, " quite a lot in love." She recalled a haunting couplet from that poem. It told how love came suddenly to the Grand Duke as he rode by the lady's window. " And lo, a blade for a knight's surprise Filled the fine empty sheath of a man." Could it not be applied to her ? Had she not been, until this exciting hour, an empty sheath ?

The next morning Tom was at their door, asking for her father. He was being shown into the study. And she in the dining-room was waiting, transfixed, with a thumb at her teeth.

Tom was telling Albany that he would be playing for Middlesex against Gloucester next Thursday and asking if he'd care to come as his guest and sit in the Members' exclosure. " And I think your daughter said once that she'd like to see a match too." Tom had decided that, in view of his present clouded reputation, he had better invite ' the old boy ' rather than his daughter, leaving the daughter's invitation to appear as an afterthought. In any case it was improbable, was it not, that an old parson would allow his daughter to venture without a chaperon into a predominantly masculine assemblage like the crowd at Lord's. Of course he had hoped that the old boy would say, " No, you two young people go," but this did not happen. Sir Albany was as delighted as a schoolboy. " Why, my dear Tom, there's nothing I should enjoy more. I'm the world's best watcher of first-class cricket. But usually I've had to go in the sixpenny seats. This'll be marvellous. And I think Susannah might enjoy it. Anyhow, it's part of her education to see some first-class cricket." He seemed to think that he was the principal guest and Susannah no more than an appendage—and a doubtful appendage at that.

" And Lady Grahame ? " asked Tom, discharging a duty but hoping passionately the hag wouldn't come. " I think . . . I think perhaps I could get three places . . . but I'm not sure."

" No, no ; Delia won't want to come." Albany, no more than Tom, wished Delia to be there. " But I think Susannah might like to. Susannah, here ! Here, quickly ! Great news. Tom Budlier's asking us—you remember Tom, don't you— he's very kindly asking us to come to Lord's next Thursday when he'll be playing. *Now* you'll see something. The real thing ! Not the village cricket you saw at Mosgrove."

" Oh, how superb ! " Susannah's hands gripped each other with excitement. " Oh, I'm thrilled to bits. Shall we see you bowl ? "

" Not unless we lose the toss. And perhaps not then. You may see me bat. But I'm the rottenest bat."

" Don't you believe him, child. He's quite famous as a hitter."

" Yes, sir, but that's not batting."

" It's one kind of batting, and great stuff to watch."

" Oh, I'm longing for Thursday ! " cried Susannah. " I shall be so proud. Will you come and walk with us in the interval so that everybody will know we belong to you ? "

" Not if I go and make a duck. I shan't put you to a public shame then."

" Oh, but you won't make a duck. I'll *will* that you don't. And you'll take heaps of wickets."

" Yes," said the equally enthusiastic father. " Bowl 'em all out, Tom. Bump 'em, boy ! Knocks their caps off for them. Who cares for Gloucester ? This is tremendous, Susannah."

Now it was Wednesday, but the rain was falling, falling, upon the gardens of the Wood and upon the great field of Lord's within its high walls. It was falling, not violently, but stead- fastly, so that the grass of the croquet lawns looked sodden and sad, and the geraniums drooped in their window-boxes, the hollyhocks stooped over the garden beds, and the limes hung their leaves heavily, drippingly, above the garden walls.

Two people watched from their windows that tireless rain of a Wednesday long ago. Susannah went often to her window and looked out at the wet grass, the stable cloud-blanket, and the grey spines of rain slanting across the darkness in the trees. She looked and looked, and found no place of comfort anywhere. " Oh, but it mustn't rain to-morrow," she said, with a hand at the curtains and a foot beating anxiously. " Oh, God, make it stop. It can't go on like this for ever. But perhaps it's a good thing that it should rain to-day, because it'll rain itself out and be gloriously fine to-morrow."

Tom stood likewise at a window and stared at the rain. It was the window of his study. The little white Gothic house in Acacia Road, with its steep gable and battlements, held only Tom, his father, and their housekeeper, so Tom was able to have a sitting-room of his own on the top floor and call it his study. Here were his books and his pictures ; and the pictures were more revealing than the books, which were not many. One was of Andromeda chained to her rock, and it hung there less because he was interested in the legend of Perseus and Andromeda, or because he took an æsthetic delight in the artist's draughtsmanship, than because the lovely figure of Andromeda wore nothing at all but her chains. Other pictures were of school and college groups in which Tom figured ; the First Eleven at Clifton, the Freshmen's Team at Cambridge, and the Oxford and Cambridge Elevens of last year seated together before the pavilion at Lord's. On his writing desk stood a picture of his father in uniform and, opposite it, one of his dead mother in a wide picture-hat and bell-bottomed skirt. Along his mantelpiece stood a row of picture postcards, glossy portraits at twopence apiece of actresses who had delighted his eyes. Here were Marie Studholme, Mabel Love, Gabrielle Ray, Phyllis Dare, and Gertie Miller—of Gertie Miller three ; as well there might be, of so delicious a trifle. Till yesterday all of these, with their smiling loveliness, had given him moments of pleasure when he wearied of reading and glanced their way, but now Susannah had bereft them of power. They smiled at him as he stood by the window, all showing regular and radiant teeth, and some with their heads archly inclined, but he didn't turn once to look at them. The big new meershaum pipe, which he was striving by unremitted smoking to colour a deep chestnut brown, meant more to him than they.

He, like Susannah, stared at the changeless sky. " Oh, if only it would break up and change to bright sunlight. Then we should have a drying wicket ; a beautiful treacherous wicket ; a sticky dog wicket ; the perfect wicket for spin bowlers

like Hearne and Tarrant and for fast bowlers like Tom Budlier."
He dreamed of a triumph on that bowler's wicket to-morrow,
and of the tributes that would be paid him in the next day's
papers. " Mr. T. J. Budlier and Hearne were almost unplay-
able, especially the former." " Mr. Budlier took five wickets
for twenty-one runs . . ." " took seven wickets for thirty-
three . . ." " took all ten wickets. Tarrant also bowled
well." " Mr. T. J. Budlier is certainly a great acquisition to
Middlesex." " On returning to the pavilion he received an
ovation."

Towards evening the clouds above the rain began to whiten
and brighten ; they cracked and drew apart, and the travelling
sun appeared in the rifts. In the morning London awoke to
a sky empty of all but a jovial sun that was plainly out to make
a day of it ; and Tom, staring in his pyjamas at the universal
brightness, exclaimed, " My God ! God is on my side. Oh,
God, send them in first. Of Thy goodness and mercy send
the Gloucester lads in to bat first and let me bowl them
out."

Not that his pleasure was undiluted. Nay, diluted is the
word for it. His nervousness, as the clock ticked round from
nine to ten, debilitated the pleasure by diluting and melting it.
His heart seemed to vary its beating with a bubbling, and his
stomach to desire nothing but emptiness, so that it drove him
more than once to the privy. His speech tripped over his
words as he talked with his father, and his breathing stood
still at certain thoughts. He didn't know, as he wandered to
a window, whether he envied the people who were walking
towards unpublic occupations, or pitied them ; he wasn't sure
that he didn't want the rain to return in power and cancel the
match. A crowd of twenty thousand seated round the cricket
field, with Susannah among them !

He weighed the possibility of feigning sickness.

But he set his lips and closed a fist. And the fist trembled
with resolve. " I'm *not* going to fail. I'm going to bowl as
never before. With everything I've got. Oh God, send them in
first. This is the test of my life. I must come through it."
It seemed to him that he would be bowling not only at the
Gloucester wickets but at the high barrier of disgrace between
him and Susannah. Every wicket he shattered would help to
smash that barrier down. And after this triumph to-day he
would set about improving his prospects—and his character—
so as to be more worthy of Susannah. He was not sure how

88

he was going to begin this general improvement, but that misty question could wait : the immediate business, between now and sunset, was to bowl as never before in his life.

Now it was near the hour, and Albany and Susannah were in Grove End Road, approaching the gates of Lord's. They were walking fast, not because they were late, but because Albany was charged, like a super-heated locomotive, with enthusiasm and information. Susannah was dressed for the warm day in a frock of white muslin and a large flowered hat and carried her lace-fringed parasol. Her father had honoured the sun, and their purpose beneath the sun, with his lightest grey suit and a panama hat. In his enthusiasm he was saying, " You'll see Plum Warner, and B. J. Bosanquet who really invented the googly ball and Warman, who's probably the fastest bowler alive—unless our Tom's as fast. You'll see some of the greatest cricketers of the day." Of himself he was saying, with modesty, that he was never a very good batsman, only a hitter, but he gave her to understand that he'd been an uncommonly big hitter in his day. " Had the height and reach, you see. *And* the strength." He told her of some of his biggest hits. At one point there was a halt on the pavement while he showed her with his walking stick what was meant by an off-drive, a cut, and a hit to leg. And after that demonstration, walking on, he made some doughty off-drives with the stick while he expatiated on the art, the poetry, the skills of the game. No one, he said, could really appreciate it who was not its scholar, whose eyes were not trained—just as a musical ear was trained—to detect every nuance and variation and grace-note in a supremely difficult art-form. It needed trained discrimination, he said. It was beyond the understanding of Americans, he said. Susannah, though giving some response to this pæan, for he was speaking with power, was thinking rather of a single performer than of these subtle nuances. Would they see Tom bowl ? she asked ; and her father, the expert, answered, " I think we may probably see him both bowl and bat, since it'll be a bowler's wicket to-day, and one side'll be bundled out and the other side have to go in and bat before the day's over."

Now they were at the Main Gate, with the crowds streaming in beside them, and here was Tom waiting for them—Tom in his white flannels and a blazer of blue and yellow stripes.

" Ah, I see you wear a Quidnunc's blazer," said the expert.

"That's because he's a Cambridge blue, Susannah. They don't award that to everybody."

"No, no . . . Yes . . . c-come along," Tom stuttered. "I'm going to put you with my f-father."

"Aren't you frightfully nervous ? " asked Susannah. "With this shocking crowd ? "

"Oh, n-no. I've done this before. Before bigger crowds." But then he recalled his vows of improvement and determined to be done with this lying. "Yes, though—perhaps, I am—a bit. Yes, a bib-bit."

And Susannah, seeing that his hands were trembling, said to herself. "Oh, the poor darling," and to God, "Oh God, help him;" and then to him, for his comfort, "I should be nearly dead. As it is, I'm nervous for you. It's rather awful when you've got someone of your own playing."

"Of your *own* ! " laughed her father. " She's adopted you quickly, Tom."

"Oh, you know what I mean," objected Susannah, a blush flooding up under her large hat.

He took them to the seats of the privileged in the Members' enclosure beyond the pavilion, and sat them next to his father and Commander Ludlow ; then with a nervous smile left them. Susannah was now between her father and the little old Colonel Budlier, who sat there with his plump hands clasped over the crook of his old ash cane, and his kind gentle smile on his round face. From the seat beyond him Commander Ludlow jerked a thumb at the smile, scanned it through his monocle, and said, " The Colonel's trying to pretend he's not sick with pride about his boy. He's pretending it's all in the day's work to have a boy playing for his county. I'm busy assuring him there can't be anything wrong with a boy who plays cricket like Tom, because cricket develops all that's best in them. Isn't that so, Grahame ? "

" I quite agree," said Albany, who'd played cricket in his day.

The Colonel only smiled. Colonel Budlier accepted all such banter with a smile and little more, because he had no opinion of his own wit and was convinced that most men were cleverer than he. And because of this simplicity in the Colonel Albany always felt at ease with him. Here was a man, better no doubt than he, but naïver, simpler, one whose intellectual superior he undoubtedly was.

Bait was not of the company. Albany had asked him if he

was coming, but he has pish'd and pshaw'd about " that shocking cult down the road and its enervating influence on its
thousands of idle addicts ; " he had expressed his astonishment
that Albany could sit impounded in one of those pens throughout a whole day, and had reminded him that the ground at
Lord's had once been a dairy farm with pig-styes all round and
that, in his view, it was not much better now ; and finally he
had quoted with approval a statute of Edward IV which en-
acted that anyone allowing this unseemly game, this *ludus
inhonestus*, to be played on his premises would be liable to three
years' imprisonment, and anyone actually playing it to two
years' imprisonment, a ten-pounds fine, and the destruction
of his implements.

Susannah, her bosom a vessel compact of eager anticipation
and windy anxiety, gazed at the huge arena before them, a
brilliant green under the blazing eye of the sun. It was like
a huge green salver bounded by a white rail. Behind the
white rail the people were crowding on to the benches or on
to the tiers of the tall white stands. Pigeons waddled and
sparrows hopped about the borders of the trim turf, indifferent
to the incoming multitudes and the forthcoming game, and
interested only in the seeds to be found among the grass. On
a soft breeze from the south-east came the scent of mown wet
grass and the sounds of bats-upon-balls in the Nursery nets.
From farther still, from beyond the high curtain walls came
the voices of newsboys at the gates, shouting their mid-day
sporting editions and the low murmur and purling of London's
traffic on the highways and at the crossroads.

At her side Albany, inspired by the scene, was pointing out
to her what he called " the immemorial features of an English
cricket ground in summer : " the fathers with their small schoolboy sons ; the unfathered urchins with pink, outstanding ears
and their lunches in satchels prepared by devoted but un-
cricketing mothers ; the parsons, old and young, sprinkled all
over the stands because they alone could snatch a whole day off
from their week-day labours ; and the old grey men of all
classes who'd done for ever with week-day labour and could
sit smoking the hours away or dozing in a quiet spell or telling
strangers at their sides of feats they had witnessed in the past.

Albany himself was doing exactly this. A cigar in his mouth,
he was speaking with the Colonel of the immortals he'd seen
in his youth : of Alfred Shaw and the Honourable Ivo Bligh
and Alfred Lyttleton and A. G. Steel ; of Spofforth, the demon

bowler, and Blackham, the stumper who took the demon's deliveries as if they were tennis balls ; of Tom Richardson, 'the greatest fast bowler England ever produced,' and of a team of giants he had watched here at Lord's just twenty years ago, at the Lord's Centenary Match.

" Some of these are only men of legend now," he said to Susannah, who was listening ; for he was in lyrical mood. " Shaw died the other day. The hungry generations tread them down. Yes, they were giants, but who knows, we may be looking at giants to-day who will be legendary heroes in fifty years time."

Oh, yes, he was in lyrical mood. He directed Susannah's eyes to the cropped and shining turf and said it was the most sacred grass in the world and had been so for a hundred years ; he turned her eyes towards the crimson and ochre pavilion and assured her that, as the headquarters of cricket all over the world, it was to this most noble religion as the Vatican to the Universal Church ; he spoke of the ' Noblemen and Gentlemen of the Marylebone Cricket Club,' long dead now, who'd sat in that pavilion ; and as a fitting coda to these dithyrambs, he concluded cheerfully, " One day we too shall be ghosts."

The pavilion bell. Three double chimes at noon day, as if it were a monks' bell ringing for Sext. It brought all wanderers back to their seats ; it speeded the drinkers at the Tavern or Pavilion bars ; it hurried the feet of those who had only just threaded the turnstiles. Five minutes, and the game would begin. Susannah's heart raced.

Here came the umpires, loitering out of the players' pavilion, one of them tossing the little red ball, the sacred focus of it all, the little red apple of discord, from right hand to left and back again. And now which captain will lead his men on to the field, MacGregor of Middlesex or Newell of Gloucester ? Ah, it is MacGregor who is leading out his gentlemen amateurs, Warner, Bosanquet, Douglas and Littlejohn—and, last of them all, Tom Budlier. Tom comes shyly, for he is the youngest, the ' new boy ' in this procession of celebrities. Warner and Bosanquet halt, wait, and say a few words to him ; maybe for his encouragement ; and Susannah can feel, across a hundred yards of grass, that Tom is flattered that the great men deign to speak with him. He is pale and palpably nervous ; and she is at prayer. Now come the professionals from their humbler pavilion ; Tarrant and Hearne and Trott and Hendren. A brief minute, and Gloucester's two opening batsmen appear.

One goes to the popping crease at the Pavilion end and takes his guard. MacGregor tosses the ball to Trott.

" We shan't see our Tom yet," says Albany, the expert, to Susannah. " They'll put on their spin bowlers first. You'll see. Hearne'll follow Trott, and if these two don't come off, they'll try out their new fast bowler, Mr. Tom Budlier."

Susannah is almost glad they are not going to ask Tom to bowl.

The first ball. And the first over. And the second over. Slow scoring because each batsman is poking cautiously at the spinning ball or leaving it to dance alone. Over after over with only singles hit, or stolen, here and there. Then a ' maiden over,' and another to follow it.

" Why is it called a ' maiden ' if no one scores ? " asked Susannah of her father.

" A maiden ? " He is embarrassed, not liking to speak to a young daughter of a *virgo intacta*, a virgin unscored off. So he laughs and says, " Perhaps it's a corruption of ' made none.' Eh, Ludlow ? "

But look : a pause while MacGregor changes the bowling. He is tossing the ball from palm to palm. What now ? Will he try out his fast bowler ? Will he throw the ball to Tom ? He does, and Susannah's heart is a trembling ball of solicitude, panic and hope.

" What did I tell you ? " boasts Albany.

The generous crowd applauds this choice of Tom. He is young, new, full of promise, and popular with them because of some ferocious, profitable, and amusing bowling-spells last year. Tom and his captain set a new field : three slips and a gully and the stumper well back from the wicket.

" Three slips and a gully ! Whoosh ! " exclaims the expert. " He's going to bowl fast."

" And a silly mid-off and a silly mid-on," adds Ludlow, another expert. " He's going to bump 'em."

Now Tom takes many, very many, strides from the bowling crease ; he strides, it seems, fully a quarter of the way to the boundary ; and the crowd laughs because the length of Tom's run up to the wicket promises an attack packed with venom and a ball like a bullet. He scratches the grass with his boot to mark his starting place and swings his arm round and round to loosen it up. He is ready, and a silence awaits his performance—a silence in which Susannah accelerates her prayer, in some hope that God is watching the game from His pavilion in the sky. Tom begins his run, and it is indeed an extraordinary and villainous affair. He pounds towards the wicket in a menacing, head-first crouch as low as his strides are long, as if his final aim were to butt the batsman in the stomach instead of bowling a ball at him. His strides quicken as he nears the crease ; a yard this side of it he leaps from off the face of the world and hurls himself and his arm forward : the ball shoots from his hand as if yonder batsman were an offence to all honest men and it would be a public service to assassinate him.

"Wide," signals the umpire. And there is a roar of laughter. Tom's first ball is a disaster, and Susannah's heart dies.

"He's nervous," says Albany.

Colonel Budlier's hands still rest upon his stick, but his gentle, happy smile has diminished ; so Susannah prays for him too.

"Never mind," Ludlow encourages him. "He's not in form yet. Give the boy time. Give him time."

Tom, a little shamed, has gone back to his starting place. He swings again his guilty arm to teach it to behave better. And now his low crouching, menacing run seems yet more vicious than before as if he must justify himself after that first failure. Never before, surely, such a leap from the spurned earth ; such a fling of his arm ; would he send the arm as well as the ball at the batsman ?

A full toss. The batsman slams it to the boundary. A roar of scornful laughter for the bowler ; a roll of applause for the batsman. It is the first boundary of the match. And it was hit off our Tom.

"Oh, my God ! " says Ludlow. And he makes a joke which pleases him all the more because it surprises him with its felicity. "Poor Tom Bowling ! Now he's gone aloft."

"Never mind, Colonel," says Albany. "He hasn't really begun yet."

"Why not let the umpire bowl instead ? " calls a wag in the crowd.

But Tom is back at his base. An object of public laughter just now, he flings back his tumbled hair, palms the remainder of it away with his sweating hand, wipes his brow with his bare forearm, and rubs the ball dry on his shirt. Then he braces back his shoulders and begins a yet more malicious run.

A good ball this. The batsman lifts his bat, but decides to leave it alone.

"Ah, better ! " says Ludlow. And the Colonel smiles gently again.

All the next three balls are good—untouchable—and Susannah, who has been in a deplorable state, breathes rather more easily——but not much more.

Now it is Hearne who bowls, and three runs are taken off him this over ; three singles.

Tom again. And Susannah at prayer again. Perhaps the prayer is answered ; perhaps power from on high descends upon Tom, for the power he now puts into each ball is surely analagous with the energy which the Almighty put into the great ball of the world when He sent it spinning. Or when he sent Lucifer spinning. The ball strikes the earth and leaps off it, spurning it.

" Jesus Christ ! " says Ludlow, forgetting Susannah's presence and the Colonel's a sidesman. " He's getting it up to an awkward height. Something'll happen soon."

" An ugly rise that," says the voice of an unknown behind Susannah. " Face-high bouncers these. Something'll happen soon."

What happened, however, was not caused by the ball's rising but by its shooting. It shot and hit the batsman above the knee, so that he danced in pain. And skipped and hopped and doubtless blasphemed. He walked round and round, and round and round, lifting up his knee and sinking it, and stooping and rubbing it. And Susannah, while pitying the dancer, was guilty of a base hope that he would now be completely demoralized and very willingly yield his wicket to Tom's next ball. This wish was certainly not ' cricket,' but if Tom could get a wicket it would encourage him.

The man did not, however, do this. He played Tom's last two as if they were incandescent cannon balls and, his ordeal over, began to dance again.

No wickets had fallen as yet, nor did one fall in Hearne's next over.

And Tom has the ball again. His first delivery whips past batsman and stumper both, and spins to the boundary for four byes. " No fault of the bowler's, that," say the wiseacres. " There was a devil in that ball. No one knew anything about it. An inch straighter and it'd have spreadeagled his wicket."

The crowd waits in silence. Budlier is bowling well. The batsman plays the next ball respectfully. The third ball is a little short ; the batsman plays forward to it, and *snick* ! it's in the wicket-keeper's hands. " *How-zat ?* " The shout can be heard in Baker Street. A mile away. How's that, umpire ?

95

The umpire's index finger points heavenward like the finger of the Baptist in Leonardo's picture. Small boys yell " Got him ! *Got* him !" The batsman walks homeways, using his bat like a walking-stick. And here comes his successor, with his bat under his arm, while he draws on his batting gloves.

He takes his guard. Tom takes the ball ; he takes his long, striding, pounding run ; the ball shoots on to the new-comer's pads—one hears the impact—and from field and ringside, from old men's voices and shrill boy's voices, comes the bellowed inquiry, "*HOWZAT?*" I say it was a shout that could be heard in Gloucestershire. "*HOW WER ZAT?*"

The umpire's finger points once more to the Throne of Forgiveness. The batsman returns the way he came. Small boys dance.

Two wickets in two balls. Will he get his third wicket with his next ball ? Will he do the hat-trick ? Twenty thousand people are loving Tom Budlier like their son. Their silent desire for his success is every whit as great as that of the Colonel, his father, behind that gentle smile. Even the ranks of Gloucestershire aren't quite sure that they don't hope he'll do it.

But he does not ; the batsman plays his next ball, and a sigh of disappointment rings the field. Nor does his sixth and last ball trouble the batsman. Still, two wickets and no runs in six balls makes a fine over, and twenty thousand people, including the supporters of Gloucesterhsire, applaud it. So far Budlier has taken two wickets for fourteen runs.

Now Bosanquet, from the far end, is bowling his celebrated googlies, and they divert the crowd, breaking this way and that way and both ways, while the batsman stares at them, bewildered, and wondering if he is awake or sober. " The wicket's certainly taking spin," says the expert. " But there's always lift and fire in a Lord's pitch." Bosanquet, however, gets no wicket and tosses the ball back to Tom.

Some of the spectators (especially the small boys), remembering Tom's last fine over, and much liking his vehement charge and attack, give him a mutter of applause.

To their delight he looses the same cannonade, hurling his whole body after the ball so that you would think that each delivery must shoot his arm out of its socket and tear asunder the muscles of his back. But apparently it leaves him unwrecked, for he follows up each delivery in hope of a catch, and, when within reach, stops the hardest ball. " He's a wonderful fielder to his own bowling," says the expert. Five such balls he sends down ; no run is taken off them ; the sixth smashes the batsman's wicket into its constituent parts. Over ; and Tom, brushing his forelock off his brow with his wet forearm, resumes his cap from the umpire's hand as if he is not hearing the cheers and prolonged applause.

The wicket-keeper, before crossing to the other end, hands his cap to the umpire, as if Tom's bowling has made him sweat, and his head is seen to be bald. " Don't wonder," says Ludlow, " with Tom bowling like this. He'll be white before the end of the day."

Tom's analysis is now three wickets for fourteen.

And no one else has yet taken a wicket.

Good enough ; but in the course of Bosanquet's next over there comes that grey disappointment which treads always on the heels of success and is doubtless designed by the gods to teach a man that perfection unsullied is not to be had in this world.

Tom is fielding at extra-cover, and perhaps he is dreaming of those three sweet wickets, remembering that last ball which burst the wicket like a bomb, thinking that Susannah saw that ball and heard the cheers, but—a catch is slashed towards him off an impish Bosanquet ball ; it comes into his hands before he is out of his dreams ; he fumbles and drops it. The groans all round the field, twenty thousand groans, make a sound as bitter as the cheers were sweet. He hears his name from every point of the compass : " That was Budlier . . . Budlier . . . Tom Budlier, and it was a dolly catch." His sickness in this moment is not worse than Susannah's on her seat far away.

All right ! Passionately he locks his lips together and vows to make amends in the next over—much as (though he has forgotten this) he resolved upon amendment after his disgrace at Cambridge.

But lest his dreams should soar too high on the wings of pride, the gods continue their chastening ; they grant sight at last to the Gloucestershire batsmen so that they see his fastest balls as large as lazily drifting balloons and slam them with the best of their bats, driving, cutting and pulling them. They score boundaries. His rich and glowing analysis begins to look like watered wine.

" They're hitting him about now," said Ludlow. " He's tiring."

" Yes, he'll come off," agrees the Colonel, since it is right to speak modestly of one's son.

" Oh, *no* ! " pleads Susannah.

And even as she begs of the distant captain to let Tom go on for a little longer, the cry goes up from Tom's very voice, a young excited voice, "*Got him !*" with a run forward and a low lunge of his right arm he has caught the driven ball five inches from the ground. Caught and bowled Budlier. *And* what a catch ! Amends. Budlier four for thirty-two.

And no one else has taken a wicket yet.

" He'll last till lunch time now," said Ludlow. " Don't you worry, Susannah. No one's going to take him off while he's getting wickets like this."

Bosanquet gets his first wicket before lunch, and the gods, deciding that they have chastened Tom sufficiently, suffer him to creep a little nearer the forbidden perfection. With the last ball of the last over before lunch (a pretty moment to do it in) he shatters a wicket and turns to take his cap from the umpire, as if he is now free to rest and take food.

The team comes towards the pavilion, and all the applause is for Tom. The Noblemen and Gentlemen in the pavilion stand up to clap him. At first he pretends not to realize that it's all for him, but since this deceit cannot be maintained, for they are saying, " Bravo, Budlier," and " Good show, Tom," he touches his cap and runs up the step into the shelter of the dressing-room.

Soon in his blue and yellow blazer he has come to talk with his father and guests. " I hope you're not bored," he says to Susannah.

" Bored ! " she answers. " *Bored !* "

" Well done, my boy," says the gentle old Colonel. " You did well."

" Did well ! " scoffs the Commander. " Why, he's done wonders."

" Oh, but the wicket's a gift to anybody," says Tom deprecatingly. " And one of my wickets was just a fluke."

" Still, five for forty-four," says the Commander, patting him on the back.

" Oh, but I was splendidly backed up by the fielders. And I dropped one awful catch."

The people are looking at him and Susannah. They are asking each other, Is Susannah his fiancée ? And Susannah, knowing this well, is pleased to be thought so. Tom has to return to the pavilion and lunch with his fellow-players, so his guests have a meal together in the Members' Luncheon

Room. After this they join the gentlemen and ladies promenading over the green grass and pausing to look at the pitch. The sun is in midday mood, so Susannah, like the other summer-dressed ladies, puts up her cream parasol, lace-edged, and feels fashionable and ' in the manner '—the grand manner of Lord's.

Ding, *dong*, ding *dong* went the monastery bell ; and quickly the promenade dispersed and the green plain was empty of all except the two white-coated umpires dawdling towards the wickets.

Of course, when the players came out, Tom was immediately put on to bowl again. His captain lobbed the ball into his hand, and Tom strolled towards his base, to the applause of the affectionate crowd. Susannah loved them all for loving Tom.

" He'll bowl unchanged throughout the innings now," said his father. " And he should get some of these last wickets. He's got the rabbits in front of him now."

" Oh, I hope he gets them *all*," she said, leaning forward in her seat to watch.

But Jack Hearne began the rot among the rabbits. Of the four wickets still to fall he took two, and Susannah, anxious to see Tom take them and to hear the roared appreciation of the crowd, was impatient with the man. More interested in Tom's success than in Middlesex's, she prayed in her seat, every time Hearne assumed the ball, that he would bowl very nicely and creditably, but get no wicket. He did not get a third wicket, and now Tom had his chance again. Before him was Mills of Gloucester, No. 9 in the batting order, a fine bowler but no great shakes with the bat. God give Tom his wicket.

Mills of Gloucester played the first ball of this so dangerous young bowler with an apprehensive carefulness that made the crowd laugh. He played the second ball likewise. The third, which Tom had artfully pitched a little short and much slower, he played straight into the bowler's hand. *Caught !* C. and b. Budlier. A wild, intemperate cheer, for seemingly the crowd like Susannah, wants Tom to multiply his total. Budlier now six for fifty-two. Away went Mills, taking his duck's egg back to his mates, and out came the last batsman, Dennett, like a sacrifice. A good man, Dennett, a pillar of his side, their steadiest bowler, and not the worst of batsmen. Oh, God, let Tom get him, and not that man Hearne. Dennett was drawing on his batting gloves as he came to the altar, and a loud jolly

99

voice shouted, " Never mind them, George. You won't need 'em." Much laughter. Dennett took his guard and was ready, but not, perhaps, happy, for his bat was patting and patting his block-hole. Tom had three balls left of his over : could he get him and finish off the enemy ? He began his long, pounding, crouching run—for a second Susannah thought it was hardly fair to bowl as brutally at these last poor tail-enders as at the great opening batsmen, but the thought had no time to develop. Tom was at the wicket, he had leapt from off the circumference of the Earth, he had flung his arm over till head, torso and hinder leg were almost parallel with the ground, his ball, it would appear, was the fastest of the match, for no one seemed to see it, certainly the batsman didn't see it, the only thing anyone saw was the off-stump leaping in-dignantly into the air and the middle stump throwing itself on to its back for the final count. The perfect finish to Tom's career to-day. Seven wickets for nine runs apiece. Glouces-ter's total only a hundred and ten, and Budlier the cause of the rout. And he the people's hero, as he walked shyly behind the older and more celebrated amateurs back to the pavilion.

It was still only three on a bright afternoon, and Albany said to Susannah. " There's more than three hours to go. We may yet see him bat before the day's out. He goes in No. 7, and wickets are cheap to-day."

" Oh, I hope we do ; and I hope he does well," exclaimed Susannah.

" He's done well enough for one day, whatever happens," said the Commander.

They did see him bat. The Middlesex men found it as hard to make runs on this perplexing and repulsive wicket as their opponents, and as hard to protect their stumps. There was no keeping the bat above the buck-jumping ball. One by one they went sadly home to the pavilion. Save for the humour of watching these ' returned empties ' going back to the cellar, the game was providing little entertainment for the crowd. Their only interest now was whether Middlesex, their home team, could reach and pass the enemy's score of a hundred and ten. It didn't look as if they could, as the afternoon wore away, and they only poked unhappily at the worrying balls for over after over, gathering no flowers by the way. If one of them did pluck a run from somewhere the crowd greeted this triumph with a prolonged sardonic cheer. But for the most part they yawned and were silent. The somnolent stillness of late afternoon came silently in and possessed the whole walled field of Lord's and all within its compass, except the white players loitering to and fro. The very flags on the two pavilion masts fell asleep. So did the trees around the ground ; they slept. So did some of the old parsons in the stands, and some of the Noblemen and Gentlemen in the pavilion ; they slumped in their seats and with opened mouths slept, dreaming perhaps that they were twenty again and slogging balls to a boundary. The pigeons and sparrows returned to the outfield and waddled and pecked there, confident that no more hard-driven balls would come bouncing amongst them to vex their leisure. In the stillness one heard all sounds, near or far, with an extraordinary clarity : the padding of the players' feet, the smack of bat upon ball, the gust of laughter as a batsman ducked to dodge a head-high bumper, and the clicking of turnstiles as a few late-comers hurried in to see the end of the day.

All day the sky had been clean and lustred, like the skin of a child's blue balloon, and the sun, unvisited by cloud, had laid a golden sheen on the well-trimmed grass, but now a white flocculence was piling up in the west and occasionally a grey mass passed across the sun, changing the luminous grass to a dull green and then allowing it to light up again. The clock on the Tower pointed to five, and the shadows of the pavilion began to stretch across the drowsy plain.

Five wickets down, and now a high pressure of nervousness inflated Susannah's heart, for Tom must come from the pavilion to the crease and perform in public again. He appeared, running down the steps, and the crowd, having made him their favourite for the day, applauded his long figure directly they recognized it. Susannah could hardly watch him, as he walked with a long hurrying stride to the wicket. She suspected, from his too-quick walk, that nervousness was throbbing like an engine in *his* breast too. Unable to watch longer, she looked down upon her lap. And prayed.

But Tom, out there, was less nervous than she imagined. His success with the ball was a fount of happiness in his memory, and he was thinking that, even if he failed now with the bat, he'd done what he'd determined to do ; he'd bowled down some of the barrier between him and Susannah. Inspired by this memory, he was telling himself that on this brute of a wicket he was going to hit out at everything and gather a boundary or two, even a six with luck, before the brute beat him. To judge from the lives of his predecessors, it was as likely to beat him if he played carefully. So away with prudence. Let's see what audacity will do.

But the wicket was even more incomprehensible than he had supposed; the ball danced about in the most illogical way, its every break, whether to off or to leg, a complete non-sequitur, and Tom's start was exceedingly shaky. It must be appearing deplorable, childish, to Susannah. He could do nothing but dab the ball down cautiously or leave it to fly past him. And after two or three overs of this helpless and inglorious play the crowd began to laugh at him. This galled him, and he slammed at a ball and missed it; whereupon a group in the crowd gave him a satirical clap. He turned and looked at them, and his look said, "So easy to play this bowling from your place in the stand, you fools." But people, observing the look, only laughed. Off his next hit he snatched his first run, and the satirists applauded; and he loathed them for mocking him before Susannah. Still, he had now broken his duck, and his relief balanced (though only in part) the pain of ridicule. The consciousness of Susannah in her seat kept his nervousness throbbing, so that he could not stand still while his partner was batting, but must walk round and round, and up and down, by his crease. And when he took his place to bat again he must tap and tap at his block before each ball came to him. And when it came he could only make dabs at it, either putting it away or missing it altogether. The bowler, perceiving this unease, tried to finish him off with a ball so fast and merciless that Susannah flung her hand to her mouth and murmured, "Oh, the wickedness of it!" The ball, just touched by Tom, leapt over a slip-fieldsman only an inch out of his reach.

Now the fieldsmen paid him the poor compliment—him, a hitter!—of closing in around his bat in the hope of a catch. This genial insult made the crowd laugh. Laugh in pity for him. Then something happened in Tom. Never before had the field closed in on him. Nor a crowd laughed at him for impotent play. They would treat him as a rabbit, would they? All right; he hitched up his trousers, tested his bat, and looked all round the field for a safe place to put the ball when he'd slammed it over the heads of these insolent fieldsmen. He swept his eyes over the whole of the outfield, where the pigeons were enjoying a promenade, uninterested in the game, and inexpectant of any balls in their quiet country, now that the day, with its many noises, was dwindling into the stillness of evening. A comedian, observing this sweep of Tom's eyes, shouted, " Have a look at the wicket, too, Tom—— " and drew a laugh from every seat in the ground.

" All right, fool ! " thought Tom ; and he locked his lips, gripped his bat hard, and faced the bowler. The ball was a good length, but he stretched a long leg half-way down the pitch (or so it seemed) and drove it with a furious resounding smack high above these fielders who'd dared to close in on him. It flew like a howitzer shell and touched earth only a few feet from the boundary rail, scattering the pigeons like sea-spray. It banged against the white rail. A four ; almost a six.

A roar of delighted laughter from the crowd, whose ridicule was now directed at the discomfited fieldsmen. And long applause, affectionate this time, not ironic.

That glorious laugh set Tom free. Set him on fire. After that, as the papers said next morning, he "could do nothing wrong "; he played, they said, "like one inspired". To hell with nerves and idiotic wickets and cocksure fieldsmen ! Out he went to the next ball and sent it to the leg boundary, stampeding again those loudly dissenting pigeons. Two fours in succession. Two storms of applause. Such a double is an intoxicating draught for any man, and now Tom's play flew in the face of sense and theory and succeeded everywhere. By using his long stride he converted good-length balls into bad-length balls, stepping back to make them long hops, stepping forward to make them half volleys, or running right out of his crease to hit them full-toss. One of these full-tosses he slogged into the Mound Stand for six, lifting the people there to their feet in alarm and all the small boys on the ground to their feet in joy. Now it was the Gloucester bowlers and fielders who were demoralized. They bowled less well, fielded less well, and he took every advantage of this decline. Four . . . two . . . three. . . four again. Ecstasy among the small boys.

Sir Albany did not rise with the small boys and dance on feet, but in his enthusiasm he leaned forward with his hands on his knees and jerked up and down as if he had springs in his big buttocks. " That's right, Tom. Smite him to the four winds of heaven." His comments were perfervid, and sometimes they were witty, because he too was inspired. When Tom leaned back on his right foot and hit a perfect-length ball right over the head of mid-on, he exclaimed, " But that is blasphemy, my boy ; blasphemy ! People don't *do* such things, ha, ha, ha ! " When the boy scored a three immediately after a four, " But this is gluttony," he protested, " gluttony." And when Tom hit out at Dennett, Gloucester's finest bowler, and drove him along the ground for four, he shook his head in mock disapproval and declared, " That's no way to talk to your father." Susannah had no such wit available ; overcome by this too sudden and too exciting display, she could only bewail, " Oh, my stomach ! " and, " Oh, I can't stand this " and " Oh, please. . . ."

Commander Ludlow, monocle up, hands on knees, was as exalted as Sir Albany and occasionally slapped the Colonel, his smiling and happy neighbour, on back or thigh, to congratulate him on such a son. " Indiscreet, sir, indiscreet," he said to the far-away Tom, as the boy ran out to a ball, " but that's the idea. Bash the stuffing out of them." And " Very sweet, sir ; very sweet ! " as Tom cut a ball cleanly through the slips. And " Hell, Colonel ! The lad isn't stopping in his garden," as Tom went chasse-ing out to a shortish ball.

" Fate generally chooses to crown one man a day," said a voice behind Susannah. This certainly seemed true to-day. Fate crowned Tom its favourite, as he played on and on through an evening of sunlight and shadow. It allowed him to hit the four that lifted the Middlesex total above that of their opponents ; and it allowed this hit to be a boundary. It allowed him to hit a ball so hard that it hit the pavilion railing and rolled back to the players, saving a fieldsman the trouble of running to fetch it. It allowed him, when he was in with the last man and snatching every possible run, to run runs that couldn't surely be run, but were. His young, excited voice rang over the field, " *Yes !* " One MORE ! "

But these too-bright displays cannot last for long. The higher the flames, the sooner the ash. Of course Tom, attempting while there was yet time a tremendous swipe for six, sent a ball like a rocket into the deep field, wild applause following it—but lo ! a man running ! Would he catch it ? Would he ? Oh, no, no, no ! But he did ; and a great groan assaulted the sky above Lord's. Then applause, generous applause, for a magnificent catch.

All out, and cricket over for the day, since it was now after six. Tom returning with the Gloucester fieldsman, was given the ovation he had dreamed of yesterday, as he watched the

rain. He touched his cap to the cheering crowd and ran out
of their sight into the pavilion. The people streamed away to
the gates, the Commander, the Colonel, Albany and Susannah
among them. As they moved slowly because of the press,
Susannah heard a woman in front of her say, " What a most
attractive young man ! So modest and shy ! " and she knew
that she was plunged into the bottom of love. " I'm sunk,"
she said to herself. " Sunk beyond hope." Tom's first battle
was indeed won. He made a way to them, to say good-bye
before they were out of the ground, and Albany said to him,
" You'll remember this day, my boy, when you're an old grey
man like me, and sitting by the fire."

He returned to the pavilion ; and they passed out ; and all
the others with them. Lord's lay deserted. A great airy
structure of excitement, like the invisible and evanescent palace
it was, had collapsed into silence, and there was nothing left
but the green veldt and the white railings and the empty white
stands.

CHAPTER SEVEN

MISS PRUDENCE MADDOW

BAIT and Ludlow had spoken of the discarded mistresses in the
Wood, the late Magdalens in their small establishments behind
their garden walls. ' Birds in the sanctuary,' Bait had called
them. Albany, listening, had been more interested in them
than he cared to show to either of his informers, and in apparently casual chats with these willing talkers he had contrived
to ascertain which these ladies were (there had been no difficulty whatever in inducing the Commander to talk of them) and
where they lived. And now sometimes, on his idle and lonely
walks, he would take his cigar in the direction of their quiet
houses and consider their windows and doors as he passed.
It might be that at the end of the road, or at a curve in the
road, he would halt and, half-sitting on his ebony stick, glance
back at one of these houses and indulge a cigar dream, perhaps
twisting his long moustache-ends as he did so. Usually he
moved on at last, leaving the dream behind him with some
such thought as " Too late now. . . . Too old. . . . It is something that has passed me by."

His interest was not by any means merely prurient or personal.

It could fill with deep pity (of which he was proud) or with deep thoughts (of which he was also proud) about Life's harshness to women, its unfairness to men, and the general human dilemma. Indeed these impersonal thoughts were usually uppermost when he saw one of these fading ladies go by.

There was Miss Kate Eldrington of the little house called Villa Rica. His pity, when he saw her, was certainly akin to love : a distant, disinterested, compassionate love. She was a tall, fair slender woman in early middle age, with flashes of grey in her hair and a sweet sad expression on her still youthful and rounded face. What beauty she must have had twenty years since, when she was the lavishly decorated mistress of that little financier, Sir Adriel Zimmermann !

Then there was Jane Graybrooke whom the world knew to have been the mistress, long years ago, of a once-famous young poet, and the inspiration of his only lyrics that lived still and were likely, some said, to live always. She had given him this little immortality, and now she was a shabby, thin-lipped, dreary-eyed woman, getting fat.

Most pitiful of all was a little round-backed woman with untidy grey hairs and hastily mended garments, who swayed homeward from the public houses in Maida Vale, bemused with gin and muttering to herself or to people whom she passed. She stood still upon the pavement to mutter to these. And she was Gertie Hazeldine, the daintiest of comediennes and dancers and the treasured plaything of the late Percy Brabbant, impresario and lessee of the old Princess Opera House, that gay home of Comic Opera and Musical Comedy whose dust lay somewhere beneath the mountain of Bush House, at the foot of Drury Lane.

But there was one of these ' birds in the sanctuary ' whose plumage hadn't moulted at all and whose song was still lively. This was Miss Maddow in her large square house in Waterloo Close. All the Wood, if not all the world, knew that Prudence Maddow had been the mistress of the Earl of Clanbethry who had kept her in this big pale mansion during the years in which he was separated from his countess. They knew too (for did she not say to her confidantes, and they repeat the saying, " I am now put out to grass, my dears " ?) that directly that bitter and intransigent lady, the Earl's first countess, died and enabled him to marry again and be respectable, he left her in the large house, settled a comfortable income upon her, and visited her no more.

Waterloo Close was, and still is, a little secretive avenue on the north side of Lord's Ground. It was so private in those days that it had gates across its wide roadway, and it was only through these gates that you could enter or leave it, because it ended in a blind garden wall. For the whole of its length, which was not a hundred yards, it was shadowed by over-spreading trees. Within this leafy seclusion it held only five large houses, each in its square tree-shadowed garden, and each large enough, in a neighbourhood of small villas, to be called a mansion. Miss Maddow's house, No. 3, was just like its sisters on either side. Three stories high and encased in cream stucco, with painted shutters flanking the windows, its pale rectangular faces were partly visible and partly veiled from view by the trees in its garden ; ilex, chestnut, maple and ash. The shadows of these trees played upon the stucco, and often their green branches, gently swaying, were reflected in the windows. A brick wall protected the garden, but much of its brickwork was hidden by hanging creepers which reached almost to the sidewalk, like a harlot's tresses wantonly let down.

The lady of this mansion was a figure to draw the public eye, and perhaps the women's eyes more than the men's when she swept from her portico and garden in a gown of taffeta silk whose lace-trimmed bodice had stoles reaching to the very flounce of her skirt, or in a dress of foulard silk, all velvet and lace trimmings, with a skirt like a bell. Her waist was small and riveted in corsets so tight that her bosom billowed above them. Her hair was reddish rather than auburn, and the women maintained that it was dyed. Often a carriage waited for her near her house, an open victoria hired from Gregson's Livery and Bait Stables, and on some days it had to wait so long, while she prepared for the Park, that the coachman walked his horse up and down, and round and round, to keep it amused, or warm, or awake. But she swept out to it at last in a long black coat and long suede gloves and a spotted veil to hold her Paris hat in place and protect her complexion from the wind. On a sunny day she would sit in the carriage, holding a silk parasol edged with a frill and adorned with a black bow on its long handle.

And one day Sir Albany came wandering into the Close to study the houses, and he saw that her gate was open. He stopped to look in at the many-shadowed garden. Its grass, so far as the spreading trees would allow it to grow, was as well groomed, and the flower beds as well ordered, as the costumes of the lady herself. And while he stood there gazing, behind his cigar and its blue-grey smoke, she came round from behind the house with a pair of garden scissors in one hand and a cluster of roses in the other. She smiled as she approached him, almost as if she had guessed he was there.

" Oh, you must forgive me," he hastily apologized, removing his cigar. " I was admiring your lovely garden."

" Would you like to see it ? Do come in. You are Sir Albany Grahame, aren't you ? "

" Now how do you know that ? " he asked with an archness to which he was always subject in the presence of strange women. But he was pleased to be recognized and named.

" Well, you are not an inconspicuous figure, are you ? " she answered, her head a little to one side, her manner not less arch than his. " So very big ! And, may I say, so—*distingué* ? I made haste to learn your name. I'm disgracefully inquisitive, you see. I *have* to know who everyone is."

" May I inquire your name ? " he asked with a little bow, just as if he didn't know it already.

" I'm Prudence Maddow. But I'm a quite unimportant person. Come in."

She walked him round her flower beds, and he pretended to much interest and admiration. He looked up at her house. " You have a large house here."

" Yes, much too large for one simple woman. Would you like to see it ? And perhaps have a little drink ? "

" I most certainly should. I feel sure you've decorated it beautifully."

" I don't know why you should think that. But come along in." And she led him up three steps and through open french windows into a large drawing-room. As he followed behind he grew aware of a stronger fragrance than that of the roses. It came from her slight body and reminded him of an arcade of stalls at Earl's Court Exhibition, where exotic scents were sold. Once they were within the walls of the room it seemed to strengthen and enfold him.

" Do sit down while I run and put these flowers in water. Then I'll get you a nice little drink."

She went from the room, and he sat alone in it. He glanced around it. The large room was as bare of pictures, ornaments, knick-knacks and draperies as his own drawing-room was full of them. There was something self-conscious and assertive about its contrast with all the other drawing-rooms he knew. The wall-paper, pastel grey, was plain as a sheet, except in one corner where a pattern of lean and twisting green stalks rose from the yellow skirting to the yellow picture-rail. No picture broke the bareness of the walls except two oblong Japanese prints, and they hung, not on either side of the mantelpiece, but on either side of the corner with the stalks. All the furniture was tenuous and tall and appeared to be unstained elm or oak, so pale it was. Never before had he seen sitting-room furniture that was not a good dark brown. The piano, a baby grand, was of some bleached wood and almost white. There was a chaise-lounge of French Directoire style that immediately recalled pictures of Madame Récamier reclining, and seemed admirably suited to the daytime rest of its present lady. The only patches of colour on the furnishings were the many cushions on a settee wide enough to sit three or four persons in comfort, side by side. Here was a sophistication he did not understand, and he shifted uneasily in his chair and felt inferior. He had not yet heard the words *art nouveau*, but the phenomenon was all around him.

Miss Maddow returned, and all her fragrance came with her. " Oh, no ! " she cried. " Don't sit on that ridiculous little chair. You're much too big for it. You extinguish it. So tall—and so broad too ! Sit on the sofa and be comfortable, and what will you have ? Sherry . . . or a whisky ? Dear me, how I love the smell of a cigar. Every room should have traces of it. Would you be shocked if I smoked too ? " She took a cigarette from a white wood box, put it in a holder as long as a pencil, and lit it with a match from a tasselled case.

" Shocked ! Why should I be shocked ? " he exclaimed, though, in fact, he was—a little.

" I'm afraid I smoke far too much. It's living alone, you see. You did say sherry, didn't you ? " From a low cabinet she fetched a decanter and two cut glasses, filled the glasses on a little low table, and sank gracefully on to the chaise-lounge leaning back on its cushions. " Now sit there and tell me how you like St. John's Wood. Have you made many friends ? "

" Oh, yes. I've some very good friends. I came from the desert of the country to find friends, and I think I may say I'm doing so."

" Oh, do tell me all ! Other people's aspirations are my meat and drink."

He began his tale, and she leaned forward to listen, holding the long cigarette-holder as it might be a straight line of sympathy between her chaise-lounge and his sofa. He began with a trickle of information but, before he knew what was happening, the trickle, attracted by the broad, deep pool of her sympathy, broke through all dams and poured forth in a voluminous, enlarging and (he feared) reprehensible cataract. He listened to the torrent coming from his mouth in an ever-swelling volume, and carrying intimate confidences on its stream, and was far from certain that he ought to be telling such things, but nevertheless, continuing to tell them. And she continued to make soft sounds of agreement and sympathy, sometimes fanning her cigarette smoke from between them, as if it were the ordinary constraint between less sophisticated people, so unnecessary and, where there was sense, so absurd.

He spoke of the ' intellectual difficulties ' which had put an end to his service in the Church. It had been a very difficult thing to do, to break with all his Past, he said ; making of this late crisis in his affairs an interesting, moving, even a dramatic tale. The figure in the tale had distinction : he moved through the events as a man of deep thought and high purpose, the hero of a spiritual conflict who'd been loyal in the end to his highest instincts. " On the whole, it was perhaps one of the saddest and yet one of the best things I ever did." And she said, " Oh, I understand, I understand, so perfectly." It was not, he explained, that he had no religion left ; not at all ; he liked to think that, fundamentally, he was now more religious than he ever was, but more rational, more intellectual—if she understood. She understood. Yes, he believed that he was a sincerer person, a, well, a finer person in every way now that he was done with the effort to maintain an impossible loyalty. She more than understood. And would he ever go back to the Church, she asked. No, he thought not : he felt now towards the old Church as a grown man towards his old mother, loving her with his heart but gone far from her in his head. " That's a perfect description," she declared. " And your wife ? " He was not clear how this transition had come about, so she elucidated, " Does your wife feel the same way as you do ? " And straightway he was borne on the flood towards the most unrestrained confidences about himself and Delia. After all, these were interesting and human matters. No, Delia was very different in some ways, he said. Very different. " She was perfectly content with our narrow existence in Mosgrove, but

I wanted to escape—into some Life. And I did escape. But only just in time. I'm not growing any younger, you see, ha, ha, ha."

"Nonsense!" she protested. "Why you're in your prime. A man is at his best at your age. What are you? Fifty?"

"Fifty-five, I'm afraid."

"And what is that? No age at all, in a man."

So he continued about his wife. Delia was a golden wife . . . in many ways. She was a much nobler person than he was. . . in many ways. Of that he was sure. She would be in Heaven while he was waiting outside, but there was this difference between them, that she was simple while he was complicated. She was a satisfied person while he was, and would be for ever, a seeker—a restless seeker. These last phrases pleased him, and he decided he was doing well. So well that perhaps this would be a good final chord on which to close this opening movement, which had already been, perhaps, too full and varied, and rendered rather too *presto* and *con brio*. So he leaned forward and said, "I must be going now."

"Oh, no," she begged. "It's *so* interesting. Tell me about your beautiful daughter. I have seen her. She's so lovely."

"You think so?"

"Why, of course! And isn't there every reason why she should be beautiful?"

A compliment to him? It couldn't apply to Delia. Ah, his daughter, he said, was the joy of his life—with the implication, unperceived by him, but certainly perceived by Miss Maddow, that his wife did not occupy that position. He painted an idealized picture of his relations with Susannah. Never the least friction between them. She could spit fire at others sometimes, but to him she gave nothing but love and agreement. She took all her beliefs from him. It was charming, really, because so many of the modern young girls were in revolt from their parents.

"Oh, yes, but this is different. I can see everything. She must be so proud of you."

"Proud? Why?" He desired to hear more of this.

"Now you're fishing! Of course she's proud of you. Look, my dear"—that 'my dear,' like Susannah's 'Daddy dear,' went straight to his hungry heart—"I used to adore my father, but he was never a handsome man. He was distinguished, but not in appearance. He was short and fat, never huge and strong like you, and as I should have liked my father to be. Indeed he was seldom free from illness whereas you look as though you'd never had a day's illness in your life."

This set wide the gate to a discussion about his heart which didn't tire after a thirty-mile walk, and about his wind which had shown itself, on a Swiss mountain, to be as good as that of young men in their twenties, and about his stomach which could digest most things. At this point his sense of fairness touched him on the elbow and whispered that it was time he allowed her to talk about herself. Not that he felt he'd been boring her. Women were so different from men and seemed to like hearing other people talk about themselves.

How make way for her ? He looked round the dove-grey walls of the room. " This is a charming room," he said. " Unlike any other I know. You have great taste, I think."

She rushed into the place he had opened for her. " That is probably my French blood," she said.

" French ! "

" Yes, my mother was French, but my father was as English as they make them. He was ' D.G.M.' of the *Westminster Gazette*."

" Oh, yes ? " agreed Albany, trying to cover the fact that he'd never heard of ' D.G.M.' and not succeeding.

" You haven't heard of him, have you ? He was the paper's dramatic critic and signed his articles " D.G.M." His real name was Donald Augustus Maddow, but he couldn't very well sign ' D.A.M.' " She loosed a silver trill of laughter. " Not as a critic. So he signed " D.G.M."—G for Gus, which all his friends called him. He died five years ago. And the pity of it was, we were estranged before he died. It was very, very sad. He didn't approve of what I was doing but, just like you, I was determined to lead my own life." Albany perceived that she'd said this lest he knew all about the Earl of Clanbethry. " That he couldn't understand was one of the tragedies of my life—but let's forget that. I owe him much. He taught me all the literature I know, and because I'm bilingual I've been able to earn nice little sums, translating from the French."

" You have translated books ? "

" Yes, several."

" And they have been published ? "

" Of course. What do you suppose ? I review French books too."

"That *is* interesting." He had a simple, almost rustic admiration for anyone whose writings had appeared in volume form. Or, for that matter, in print.

"It was my greatest grief when the link between me and Papa broke. I loved him so. I sometimes think that it is because of my childish love for him that I've always liked men older than myself. Twenty years older at least." (Twenty. And she, say, forty. He, fifty-five . . . well. . . .) "It may be," she suggested, gazing through the open french windows at her shadowed garden, "that I am always looking for a father."

Sir Albany nodded.

"Or it may be," she amended, bringing her eyes back to him, "that no man is tolerable till he is past forty. And some men are quite abominably attractive in their fifties."

The Sèvres clock on the mantelshelf, with its tiny bell, struck midday. He rose. "I must go. I really must."

She rose too. "But you will come again. Often, I hope. Let this be the beginning of a friendship."

"I certainly will, if I may. It has been a most pleasant encounter." And over her hand he gave her the small gallant bow to which he was always driven when complimenting a strange woman. The more beautiful the woman, the more completely this gallantry came down upon him and drove him. "Thank you for it."

"It's been delightful for me too. Very sweet. This way, my dear."

She led him to the french windows, watched him down the steps, and fluttered a hand at him as he went through her gate.

When he was out of that shady Close and in the bright, open street, he began to feel ashamed of his garrulous outburst; repenting at leisure. Those intemperate confidences had escaped from him and leapt about with a life of their own, exactly as if his brain had been set afire, and the strings of his tongue loosed, by a draught of unaccustomed wine.

In the loneliness of his study sometimes, behind its closed door, Albany would stand before the fireplace, with his coat-tails over his arms, and count up the friends he'd made since he came to town. Old Bait. "I have a good and permanent friend now in Bait. He gives me the intellectual companionship I so badly need." And Ludlow. "The Commander's no intellectual, but he's a Man. He's real masculine company

such as I have been shut away from too long." And the good
fellows in the pubs—for Albany went often now into the Eyre
Arms or Lord's Tavern. "They're real good fellows. Excel-
lent fellows, all of them. Then there's dear old Colonel
Budlier, very simple, but one of the best. And young Tom.
I love young Tom. I love all Youth."

And the members of his club. Yes, he had a club now.
Bait, for years a member of the Savage, had got him elected
at once: was not Sir Albany the brother of Sir Vick who'd
been one of the most jovial savages of them all? Albany was
very proud of having a London club. To whomsoever possible
he mentioned that he was a member of the Savage, and if
they didn't know much about this famous club, he explained,
with pride, that its interests were Literature, the Stage, and
Art. And, when possible, he slipped in the information that
whereas most men had to wait years to be elected a 'savage',
he had been elected directly his name was proposed.

But in his heart he knew that he was but a poor savage,
a quiet, restrained and, as you might say, tamed savage. As
in the pub, so in the club, it was always an effort to break
through his self-consciousness, his social inexpertness, and mix
easily with these noisy, buoyant debonair souls. He seemed
incapable of their spontaneous fellowship. Too often he was
but a lonely wanderer in the club rooms or a silent diner at a
table of merry talkers. But he did not tell Delia of this faliure.
He gave her to understand that at his club he was finding at
last the Life he longed for.

Life? How much life had he really found? There before
the empty fireplace he would assess his gains. Lord's . . .
Ludlow's pubs . . . the Savage . . . Miss Maddow. The greatest of these, considered as Life, was certainly Miss Maddow.

He was visiting Prudence Maddow frequently now, and in
her pale feminine room, enjoying her flatteries, he was far more
at ease than in any of the leathery and masculine rooms at
the Savage. "Come whenever you like," she had said, "and
have a nice little drink and talk. It's kindness to come and
talk with a lonely woman. The only thing is, you must let
me know beforehand if you're coming. You mustn't take me
by surprise. You must ask me if it's convenient. You see, I
might have friends coming—*women* friends—and you don't want
to run into a hen-party. Or I might be going to my club."

Her *club*? She, a woman, had a club?

"Oh, yes, dear: it's the Ladies' Lyceum in Piccadilly. I'm

one of its foundation members. Our interests are The Arts and Literature."

Just the same as *his* club, he said proudly.

" Yes, and why shouldn't we poor women have such clubs too ? The Lyceum is a god-send to a poor lonely creature like me. I go there some three times a week, so you must give me a ring if ever you feel like coming round for a nice chat."

" A ring ? " He did not understand.

" Yes. Telephone me."

" You have a telephone ? " She was the first person he'd met who had a telephone in their home. He himself had not used a telephone six times in his life. He tried to hide his surprise from her, and did not succeed.

One advantage that his club gave him was that it provided a pretext for leaving Circus Road when he intended to go to Waterloo Close. He could say to Delia, " I delight in my club. It's a source of great happiness to me. I had nothing like this in Mosspot, and after years in the wilderness I've earned the right to a little society of men of my own kind," and then go off to Miss Maddow. There was no sense in hurting Delia with unnecessary information about Miss Maddow. Sometimes, to ease his conscience, he did actually go to the club for a little, and read the papers there in silence and solitude, before coming back to St. John's Wood and Waterloo Close.

And so at last came an evening when he really did sip from a wine-cup of Life that had never been offered him before. An evening with a tremendous close. An evening of triumph.

She sat on her chaise-longue, looking beautiful in a silk tea-gown, all pendent with pointed lace. Its neckline was dropped just enough to show the opening valley between her breasts. Its three-quarter length sleeves, as fringed with pointed lace as the ends of an expensive Christmas cracker, unveiled her slim arms to the elbow whenever in a graceful gesture, she swung one hand or the other through the air. He also had taken pains with his dress, and he felt that they were a smart, even a high-society couple, sitting there with the whisky decanter on the coffee table between them and her long cigarette-holder in her fingers and his long cigar between his lips.

After some animated talk, silence and blue smoke-clouds drifted between them. Then suddenly, talking the holder from her lips and blowing a last cloud away as if it were a last reticence, she said, " I suppose you know all about me ? "

" No," he answered, his smile a lie.

" Well . . ."   She gazed at the rings on her fingers.   " You've told me so much about yourself.   I feel I ought to tell you a few things about me.   Besides, I hate all deceptions.   I cannot bear anything false."

He said that he too hated all lying.

" You have heard of Lord Clanbethry ? " she asked, not lifting her eyes from her diamonds.

He knew the name, he said.

" He and I were lovers."

" You mean . . . ? " He didn't like to utter the word " mistress."

" Yes, I was his mistress for many years.   He ruined my life for me.   He took me as a girl and made me love him.   I loved him very much and believed I was right in giving him all he asked.   That was what Papa couldn't understand.   I really did lose everything by it, because I had the chance of a wonderful position as the editor of a woman's paper, but he wouldn't hear of my taking it.   And then, of course, if I hadn't given my best years to him, I might have married some good man. . . ."

" You couldn't marry him ? "

" My dear, he was married already.   Oh, heavily married, but separated.   She died only a few years ago, and then he married again."

" But why not you—why didn't he marry you ? "

" Because one doesn't.   One doesn't marry a mistress one has besmirched.   Besides, he likes them young.   He was twenty years older than me when we first met, and he's nearly forty years older than his present choice.   And I dare say he didn't think a mere writer's daughter was good enough for him. This present child is the niece of his friend, Lord Fortesgarde."

" And he doesn't see you any more ? "

" Oh no . . . no. . . .   He's sixty now, and a model of virtue."

" But *you*—you could marry someone else now ? "

She smiled sadly, as though at his ignorance of life.   " One doesn't marry easily after a liaison like that.   I could never hide it.   Too many sweet and uncharitable people know all about it.   Besides, I could not lie to a man.   I do not lie easily."

" Some men would understand, I think."

This she seemed not to have heard.   She was looking through the smoke of her cigarette and saying with some acidity, " Child after child he's had by this young thing of his.   Three in four years !   Still, I doubt not they are beautiful.   He was very good-looking, as big and tall as you—I've always liked big

116

men—and as handsome, my dear. But no, perhaps not *quite* as handsome, not quite so *distingue*."

His pleasure in this praise was so acute as to be a discomfort, and he thrust it aside by talking of something else. " I do appreciate your telling me all this. It is an honour, I feel."

" I wouldn't tell many people, certainly, but we are friends, I think I may say very good friends now, and I want you to understand all about me."

" Friends ? Of course we are friends. Since we are telling the truth, let me say that the best evenings I've ever spent have been these with you."

" I'm so glad." She smiled very brightly and stretched out a hand to ask for his.

Their hands met and joined ; she kept silence and continued to stare at him ; he gathered all his courage—it took time because this was a new and untried country for him—and asked at last, " May I . . . might I kiss you ? "

She did not remove her eyes and answered only, " I should love you to kiss me."

He drew her to his sofa, and they sank into its genial and abetting embrace. His first kiss was a gentle thing, but it was as a match to his long-imprisoned passion ; the second and third kiss cast open the prison doors, and the captive rushed to its joy. She kissed with passion too, murmuring between one visit of his lips and the next, " Who could help loving you ? " Delia had never given him anything like this. Never in her life had she seemed to realize that he longed for it ; that his body and his heart and, yes, his soul, needed it.

He gazed down at Prue's face, pinioned within the crook of his arm ; at the pearls in her ears, and the serried pearls about her slim neck—and stood upon a peak of pleasure that he'd never supposed he would scale.

And when at last, he said, " I must go . . . I must go," and she said, " Darling, must you really ? But you will come again, often, often ? I will do anything for you. You must be happy," he wondered, his heart troubled by an exquisite fear, what she meant by " I will do anything for you."

He went out into the dark street, taking with him a heart shaken by his conquest. A light in his head bemused all his thinking. It was the excitement, much magnified, of a school-boy who has kissed a girl for the first time. And, passing through the gate of Waterloo Close, he thought, " I am living at last. A club . . . and Lord's . . . and love. . . ."

CHAPTER EIGHT

THE WAY TO THE TOMBS

A TRIUMPH so rare must be told to someone. But to whom? No confidant in sight but old Bait. Such a pity that he could not tell Delia and awake her to his attractions. Bait, that avowed misogynist, was not perhaps the ideal audience for such a story, but he would be interested—beyond question, interested ; and he was his best friend, the one with whom he could always discuss his problems. And this matter of Prue Maddow he could certainly present to Bait as a problem ; he need not appear to be parading it as a triumph. So all next day he was impatient for the evening when he could wander round to Bait's and say, " Old man, I've something to discuss with you. I always bring my little problems to you."

And now it was evening, and dinner was done, and he was in Grove End Road, approaching the gate in Bait's long garden wall. They were good moments as he passed through the gate and stood on Bait's threshold and rang his bell. Bait himself opened the door, and Albany said in a dropped voice, " You free for an hour, old man ? I need your advice rather badly, old chap. I've something to discuss with a vengeance now."

" Well, come in," said Bait, examining him over the top of his spectacles, after hearing this mysterious inquiry. Bait's velvet smoking-jacket with its frogged buttonholes hung loosely from his lean shoulders, and he looked very ready for the comfort of a chair and a chat.

They went into Bait's fusty room and sat themselves in the old cracked leather chairs before the fireplace. The stub of a cigarette which Bait had just discarded was still smoking in an ash-tray, and he took another from the box and lit it with his nervous, shaking fingers. It was not necessary to offer one to his visitor, for Albany was smoking his after-dinner cigar. He flung himself into his chair and his feet on to the hassock. " Well, what is it ? What is the problem ? "

And Albany began. " Well, old boy, it's like this. Delia is a wonderful wife to me in many ways, but—I wouldn't tell this to anyone but you—we've long ceased to live together as husband and wife. Now this absence of the ordinary marital relations means nothing to her, but you will agree, I think, that it's—well, unsatisfactory for a man. For a man who is still, if I may so put it, in his full vigour. You don't mind my discussing these things with you, do you ? "

Bait shook his head. No, he did not mind.

" No . . . well . . . I am perhaps unique, old man, in that I have never in all my fifty-five years sought a woman except in wedlock. I remember you once called me a puritan, ha, ha, ha. I suppose I have been."

Bait took off his spectacles, dangled them between finger and thumb, and waited for more.

And Albany, charged with the interest that envelopes a talk about sex, continued, " Still, I must confess, puritan or no, that I've often been tempted to seek in an illicit union the comfort which my heart desires." A phrase of Ludlow's that had rooted in his mind. " Yes, I'm afraid I have."

Bait nodded and swung the spectacles, while his lips tightened into a small grim smile.

" Now I know," said Albany, looking away from that smile, " that you're cynical about Prudence Maddow and my affection, my very real affection, for her, but——" And, fixing his eyes on Bait's again he told the story of last night. He came with pride to the climax which he had so longed to tell. " She just came straight to my arms, old man."

" She did ? "

" Yes, and she said—she said, ' Who could help loving you ? ' I was terribly touched."

" And then ? "

" What do you mean : ' And then ? ' "

" Did you stop there ? Was that all ? "

" Of course it was all. Naturally it was all. . . . It was all for the time being," he added, almost as an apology.

" And what now ? Do you make her your mistress ? "

" That's where I need your advice, old son. I have no doubt I could do so," he stated proudly. " No doubt whatever. I have no doubt she would give herself to me to-morrow."

" Nor have I."

Had old Bait laughed in his nose as he said this ? Albany preferred not to think so. He didn't want his triumph dimmed by any breath of cynicism. " She almost said so. She said, ' I will do anything for you.' "

" Well, that's comprehensive enough."

" Yes, and my point is, would you condemn me if I took what I really believe would be given me ? My affection is deep——"

"My dear fellow, who am I to give you advice? In my youth when I was still a good Catholic, I could have answered you straight out of the book. But now that I am the thorough-going sceptic I know no answer. You should know it. You are a clergyman."

At this Albany glanced away, quickly, at the bookshelves, "I ought to have told you before," he stated after a pause "that I have been for some time "—he didn't know how to put it—"for quite a long time approaching your position. I am largely converted to a position like yours. Not perhaps to complete scepticism, but to doubt. It's only after much thought that I've arrived at this position, but there it is. I'm almost as much a renegade from my church as you from yours."

Bait parted the grimly closed lips. "Strange," he said, "how often clergymen come into money and doubt at the same time."

"Yes, I feared you'd say that, ha, ha, ha. Yes, that's the obvious thing to say, ha, ha, ha. But really, Bait old boy, I've been intellectually ill-at-ease for a very long time. And now, in this matter, I do really find it difficult to believe that two people are not to be allowed to give each other a little happiness. It's not as if I advocated promiscuity. No, no. I don't believe in that. And, whether you believe me or not, it's her affection and understanding that I desire far more than——"

"Than her bed." While Albany was trying to think of a euphemism, Bait supplied, thus brutally, the sense of the matter.

"Well, yes." Albany admitted this interpretation, but hastened back to more spiritual needs. "I'm sure you understand this hunger for the spiritual healing a woman can give you."

"Do I now? I'm not at all sure that I do. Do you really think that women are fit company for adult men? I don't. One in ten thousand may be, but that is all." He was so emphatic about this that he leapt from his chair and walked up and down while he argued the case against women, a distaste for the creatures sitting high in his nostrils. "My dear chap, you have only to look at the creatures—look at their cheeks and their features and their hands and their voices to see that they are cases of arrested development. They've infantilism written all over them. It stares you in the face that they're not adult. And they're not only physically arrested at some adolescent stage—say fifteen or sixteen—but morally and spiritually too. Of moral or spiritual vision they have none. They just have a moral tight-lacing when it's in fashion, but usually the first man that comes along can undo the laces for them. Spiritually they're at the level of the fourth form : always instantaneous in judgment and condemnation. And that's spiritual infantilism. I say they are the greatest lie in Nature, the wickedest deception that Nature practices upon us poor men : to the eye and the touch they are all softness and smoothness, while inside they are as hard as the oldest rocks of the earth."

" Oh, no ! I won't have that. I disagree with you entirely. They are capable of unselfishness far beyond us men."

" Pshaw ! Pah ! " Bait whipped off his glasses and used them to sweep all such feeble thinking aside. " Except for a saint here and there, their unselfishness extends only to their own people, and therefore its no more than an extended selfishness. Beyond the limits of their own little circle they are more selfish and grasping and unforgiving than any man. And intellectually they're negligible, save for an odd freak here and there. Which of them is capable of a really objective judgment ? And another thing : only stand above them and watch them lighting a fire. You'll see they don't understand the first principles of combustion. Why the fire ever comes alight I don't know : it may be something to do with witch-craft. And another most convincing point, Grahame : look at their letters : they've no grasp of the need for, or the prin-ciples of, punctuation. None whatever ; and that's proof of uncontrolled and imprecise minds. Wit they may have sometimes, but a clear, unbiased intelligence never. Yes, they're retarded physically, spiritually and mentally. A half-finished and wholly unsatisfactory effort. And when they cease to be retarded they grow beards and deep voices and are neither male nor female. From beginning to end I can make nothing of 'em. As an idea, I disapprove of them."

" So ? " laughed Albany.

" Undoubtedly so. I agree with St. Clement of Alexandria, who wrote, ' Every woman ought to be filled with shame at the thought that she is a woman.' I've a fancy that St. Paul had something of the same idea."

" I see. Then you wouldn't agree that, in spite of all this, they have grace and charm and can give a man something that no one else can give ? "

" I will admit that they have some chemical power of making a fool of a man. And all I can say is, if you find it a pleasant folly, why, there's a case for playing the fool."

" Do you suggest then that I should do this ? "

" Do what ? "

Albany didn't like to put it into words. " Do what we were talking about."

" Yes, what were we talking about ? " Bait paused in his pacing and strove to remember. He remembered. " Oh, yes . . . If you accept no longer the writ of your church, by all means do it . . . if you can keep your self-respect."

" Oh, I can do that . . . I think," Albany averred.

Bait began to walk again. " I must say I'm glad to hear that you've thrown over the bonds of your Church. I've always wondered how an adult man could give any loyalty to a Church that doesn't know its mind about anything. It's good enough for women, who've no powers of criticism, but what appeal it can have for a grown man, unless he's extraordinarily simple-minded——"

" *What?* " Albany was hurt, wounded to a quick, by the sudden fear that Bait all these years had been regarding him as simple-minded. And Bait made the wound worse by adding, " The men in your Church, it has always seemed to me, must be either more naïve and *ingenu* than any man ought to be or hypocrites. Probably the majority of them are hypocrites, especially the parsons. A Church that doesn't know what it believes about the Bible or the Creeds or the Mass or Matrimony——"

" Nonsense ! Absolute nonsense ! "

" The Church I had the honour to desert was at least clear about everything——"

" Yes, clear about the Earth being flat, and Galileo a liar, and Hell under the Earth, and everlasting torment for all those who dared to reject its despotism or question its puerile dogmas. The opposite is true : the Church, the modern-minded and inquiring Church, which I had the honour to desert, is the only one to which a man of intelligence——"

" What you don't see, sir—— " began Bait.

" I see anything that you see."

" Oh, no, you don't. *Oh*, no ! "

" Oh, yes, I do. Oh, yes I do. If you knew anything about my Church's history——"

" There's been no Church history since the Reformation,"

announced Bait. " There's only been religious controversy."

This was a remark that would bear thinking on, but Albany was not disposed to think on anything just now. " What I can't see," he said, " is how any intelligent man can believe in a Church built on a bog of exploded lies."

" Rubbish ! Tosh, sir, tosh ! Once grant the premise of a supernaturally revealed religion, and the Church of Rome is a palace built of majestic logic, as beautiful as any proposition in Higher Mathematics."

" Higher Fiddlesticks."

" I, personally, do not accept the premise, but that doesn't matter. Logic isn't interested in whether a main proposition is true, but only in the validity of the argument. The argument is valid. If you understand the first thing about Catholic theology——"

" I beg to remind you that I've passed examinations in Theology. And with distinction." This was not true : he had not passed ' with distinction" ; but in the heat of battle he was loading his gun with any shot that came to hand.

Bait waved this interposition aside, as something which bore not at all on his argument and therefore impeded unnecessarily its flow. " We believe that our Church—I mean, my late Church—is the depository of the one ancient and unchangeable faith, while yours is the depository of ten thousand heterogeneous opinions, and no more. A Church without a clear creed and clear rules isn't a church at all, but a mob."

" And *I* say your Church is the depository for every unworthy compromise with the primitive instincts of half-educated men : images, relics, pardons——"

" All right. It's built on a bog. But a bog is a slightly better foundation than empty air. *Your* church is based on empty air. You say it's based on the inspiration of the Bible. But you must accept that the Holy Spirit is in the Church, guiding it, before you can accept the Bible. To do anything else is like some silly old woman who tries to prove her every belief by quoting some text in Scripture. The old simpleton can't see that you've got to prove the Scripture first. And that's only done by accepting the Church as divinely guided. The Church wrote the Book, the Church pronounces it divine, the Church keeps it, interprets it, and "—here he stopped his angry pacing and stood before Albany, to let him have this one full in his face—" imposes its conclusions on her children under pain of damnation. Quite simple."

"Yes, simple for the simple-minded." Albany was glad to get this sharp-edged flint, 'simple-minded,' thrown back.

But Bait took no cognizance of the flint. He began a new walk around the room. "We very properly divide the Church into the *Ecclesia Docens*, that's to say the pastors who do the teaching, and the *Ecclesia Credens*, that's the people who believe it . . . under pain of damnation. Or, if you like, you can call them the *Ordo Clericalis* and the *Ordo Laicalis*."

"There's no need to throw your Latin at me. I know Latin, too."

Bait gave no heed to this, but went on with his walk and his Latin. "Unlike your *omnium gatherum* of heresies, our creed is that which has been believed everywhere, always, and by all, *quod ubique, semper, et ab omnibus.*"

"Exactly. And it has not been believed *semper.*"

"My dear fool, the *ubique* and the *ab omnibus* prove the *semper*. What has once been believed everywhere and by all must be believed always. The Holy Spirit doesn't make mistakes. Concede that the Holy Spirit is in the Church and *ergo*, it's infallible. That seems elementary."

Invariably Bait's philosophy, when heated by argument, became little more than a furnace for roasting his opponent. And Albany's did no less. Each was now far more interested in reducing the other to silence than in convincing him. So Albany left Infallibility on one side, and turned on a different heat. "Mariolatry! Who ever heard such nonsense? Worshipping a middle-aged village woman."

"And there, my dear ignoramus, you don't know what you're talking about. There is no Mariolatry in my Church—er—my late Church. Perhaps you don't know the difference between *Latria* and *Dulia*."

"I not know!" exclaimed Albany (who didn't). "I was trained in Theology. You wasn't—weren't, I mean."

"Well, what is it? Let's hear you define it."

"No, thank you. *I* didn't introduce the words."

Bait, who'd halted for the definition, resumed his walk. "*Latria* is the worship due to God alone, and *Dulia* is a lower form of worship that can be given to persons and things not divine. Mere veneration, if you like. For example, the whole of your Church gives *dulia* to the Bible. I once invented a word for this. Bibliodulia."

"Very clever," said Albany, his nostrils dilating even as Bait's were wont to do.

" Yes." Bait agreed with him. " And, personally, I think it more sensible to give *dulia* to a warm, living woman than to paper, leather, and printer's ink."

" I know all about *dulia*," said Albany (who now did). " Let me tell you : if I were a Catholic, I'd bow my head in shame at my Church's record of bloody persecutions."

But Bait was not going to bow his head. He was going to explain and justify. " The Church claims power over the bodies of heretics for the sake of the souls of the faithful. Perfectly logical. The State does no less in the matter of foot-and-mouth disease and fowl pest. Further, the Church claims the right of inflicting physical punishment upon the bodies of the faithful as well as some punishment upon their souls. But whether "—he stopped the walk and applied an arm of his spectacles to the interstices of his teeth, while he gave the question thought—" whether this right is *jure divino* or by the *lex non scripta* of the Church, I am not prepared to say. It is disputed among doctors."

Now Albany leapt up from his chair. The cigar at his lips was now out, and he alone was alight. " I'm not going to stay here and listen to such rubbish. You don't believe a word of it yourself ; you're just an argumentative cuss ; that's all."

" I believe most completely in the logic of the position. I accept with admiration the logic of Pope Leo XII's encyclical on Human Liberty, wherein he affirms categorically that it is contrary to reason that error and truth should have equal rights. There's no arguing with that—always provided a man is so fortunate as to know what the Truth is."

" Oh, shut your gob, if you can." Albany walked towards the door.

" Of course if you're going to lose your temper and run away."

" I'm not losing my temper."

" Oh, yes, you are. You're losing your temper because I'm keeping mine. It's a most common phenomenon."

" My temper is in an excellent state. And I'm certainly not running away. I just don't choose to waste my time in un-profitable logomachy." Thank Heaven he'd found a good sounding word to balance Bait's Latinity. He reached the door. " If saintly men like Laud and Andrews and Jeremy Taylor——"

" And that," interrupted Bait, accompanying him into the

passage, " is the *argumentum ad verecundiam* and one of the most ancient fallacies."

" Oh, *is* it ? " sneered Albany. " *Ad verecundiam*," he repeated, to show that he knew the Latin.

" Yes, it is ; and it's more worthy of a silly woman than of a man, because it proves just nothing."

" I'll say no more," said Albany with dignity, opening the front door for himself.

" There's no more to say," suggested Bait. " You and your bibliodulia ! There's nothing to be got out of bibliodulia."

" Oh, yes, there is," Albany began, but the door shut behind him, like the crisp closing of Bait's lips, and he found himself under the sky again, with his body shaking.

He walked homeward, very hot in the head, and pleased with the heat. And at the same time sad. Utterly sad. But as long as the heat remained the sadness was in the background behind the flames. As long as he could keep the coals alight he was satisfied and even exultant. Bait might be a good lawyer, but he was an old fool too. Now that he'd retired from busying himself with the laws of this world, he was plunging into the laws of a moonshine world. Witches, ghosts, evil spirits, psycho-analysis, time an illusion, all that nonsense about women . . . And Bait imagined himself his superior in intelligence !

He was able to keep the coals alight all the way home and as far as his study. But in the study they dimmed and became ashes, and then his heart was a lump of sadness and Life seemed as empty as the room in which he stood. Bait was his greatest friend, his one really satisfying friend ; and, desperate for friends, he didn't dare lose his affection for Bait, or his faith in Bait's affection for him. " He was my greatest friend. Who else is there that I care for as I cared for him ?

" But I'm damned if I'll apologize.

" Or will I, perhaps ?

" But he's impossible. Quite impossible. I no longer love him as I did." But this thought was too great a pain to hold. " No, I still love him, but he's impossible."

His sadness went up with him to his bedroom ; it got into bed with him and lay beside him ; and, in the morning, it rose with him and walked at his side to his dressing-table. And now, in the bright morning, its name was less Sorrow than Remorse. As he brushed his beard, looking at his unhappy face in the mirror, he had no doubt that it was Remorse. His distress was only intermitted by moments of satisfaction with the beard and moustaches. He punctuated remorse with twists of the moustaches. These achieved, he asked of the sad face. " How did it happen ? It happened because he implied I was simple-minded, and I am vain and self-centred and cannot stand a breath of criticism. I thought I loved old Bait, but I love no one but myself. That is me. Of course he was very rude at the end ; " You and your bibliodulia." I must look up *dulia*. But I started it. He merely implied that I'd been simple-minded or a hypocrite for fifty years, and dammit, he was only too right. I've been both. If I was anything but a mass of quivering self-love "—he felt a small pride in this phrase—" I should have met his words with humour. I ought to have done. I *am* humorous, I'm a very humorous man, but not if my disgusting self-love is so much as pricked. Self-love like that shuts you up from loving anyone properly. Yes, I see that more and more clearly every day. And there's no happiness in this world unless you love someone at least as much as yourself. I see that."

He went slowly down to breakfast full of remorse and vision ; and of pride in the vision, because he was sure that it was something to which Delia, with all her churchgoing, would never attain. At breakfast he spoke hardly three words to Susannah, and none at all to Delia. Breakfast over, he went from the house without a word to anyone. As the front door closed on him, Susannah, who'd been watching him over her plate and her fork, said to her mother, " He's not a happy little soul this morning, He's ever so unjolly." And Delia answered, " Yes, what's the matter now ? What's offended him ? Have *I* said something ? "

" Probably," said Susannah.

" Oh, dear ! Dear heaven, where do you suppose he's gone ? "

" To walk round the churchyard."

" Round the churchyard ? "

" Yes, he always walks round the churchyard when he's not as happy as he'd like to be. It's so sweet."

" Why ? What pleasure does he get out of that ? "

" He chooses his grave, I think," said Susannah.

And in saying this Susannah was nearer the truth than she knew. A favourite walk of his, when melancholy, was in the public garden behind the Chapel, under its fine old trees and among its derelict tombs. There he could think sad thoughts, deep thoughts, about Life and Death, sauntering along between the gambolling children, the young nurses watching them, the old men musing behind their pipes, and the old dead tombs. He was soon among the tombs this morning and gathering food for his melancholy from their neglected and perishing inscriptions.

"Mr. Stephen Pettigrew. Died April 4th, 1815." Then *his* conflicts and griefs had been over for nearly a hundred years. And for sixty or seventy of those years he had been forgotten. He had lain there as if he had never been. A little while and his name on the tomb would be indecipherable. "To the enduring memory of Mr. Simon Lord." Enduring! And already his name and the worn stone were almost one. 'Simon Lord'—was he a brother of Thomas Lord whose cricket ground lay yonder across the highway? 'Died 3rd July.' Right in the cricket season. 'Aged 71 years.' He himself was fifty five, and that would mean sixteen more years to live. 'Sir Albany Grahame. Died 9th May.' Died in the beauty of the spring, when all the trees were bursting with green and the flowers into bloom, under the life-giving sun. 'Sir Albany Grahame. Aged 71 years. At Rest.' For ten years, or even twenty, his gravestone would be visited, and then it would be given over to the moss and the lichen and the slow, raking fingers of wind and rain. In 1950, perhaps, some wanderer in the garden might glance at his listing head-stone and half wish to be himself at rest.

He wandered on, not wholly unhappy to think of his tall broad figure, passing from tomb to tomb, as a symbol of the long passion of mankind; a poetic symbol, and a pathetic.

"In memory of my darling father." He saw this inscription and wondered if Susannah would perhaps put something like that over him. He looked at other inscriptions and chose those which he would like to imagine marking the place where he lay. 'His children rise up and call him blessed.' 'A devoted husband and father.' 'After long suffering, bravely born. . . .' 'With a cheery smile and a wave of the hand, He has wandered into an unknown land.'

Since no one was watching him as he strolled on, with his stick held in two hands behind him, he let his head shake despondently as he thought, " I'd like to be remembered with love. But there it is: one only gets out of this world what one puts into it; and I don't really put love into it. Fifty-five, and I'm still wrapped up in myself, still bound tight in the swaddling clothes of self." It was infantile—as old Bait said the minds of women were. " I have no real human sympathy—not really." What was love but loss in others, and he could never lose himself now. Too old, too fixed. Filled with this fear that he would never love anyone now, he endured a very real pain among the tombs. Oh, if only, even at this late hour, he could step out of himself. " I would like to do some good before I die, and be remembered with love. Whom do I love properly ? For whom am I capable of sacrificing myself ? No one, no one on earth, unless it's Susannah. Yes, Susannah is my only hope." He drew on his cigar and inhaled a little hope with the smoke, and a small breath of comfort. He must try to sacrifice himself more and more for Susannah. Susannah's happiness, henceforward, must be his primary motive ; his own happiness secondary. Then perhaps, with this daily training in self-sacrifice, he would find himself, after a time, better able to be self-forgetful with others. This led his thoughts to Bait. Yes, he must put his resolutions into practice and, whether Bait was rude to him, or he to Bait, he must do ' the big thing ' and go and apologize. He and Bait must shake hands and say God bless you and swear brothers. This was an affecting picture and, in his troubled condition, it slightly moistened his eyes.

Turning around to leave the garden and apologize to Bait and swear brothers, he was so impressed with the happiness that was now filling him, the sweet serenity that was settling down in the place of dejection, that he had thoughts of going back into the Church and preaching love, and self-sacrifice, to everyone. Of preaching it all, for the first time in his life, with the power of a passionate discovery. And after a most moving reconciliation with Bait on his doorstep, in which each declared, "The fault was mine" and "No, I was to blame" and almost quarrelled again as they competed in self-condemnation, Albany walking homeward and swinging on high a rejuvenated stick, could almost wonder if he was going to do this.

But the trouble was that, now that his grief was removed, and his pain healed, he felt no longer an immediate need of religion ; and this modification of his thoughts was uncommonly like relief. This general sense of relief and recovered well-being made him feel almost as gay as, two hours ago, he had been sad. He went into the house, singing gently to himself. And Susannah, hearing the shutting of the front door, and his voice at song in the hall, and then the shutting of his study door, dashed down the stairs to the dining-room where her mother was, and said, " It's all right. Don't worry any more. He's back from the tombs."

CHAPTER NINE

THE FIRST EVER

IF Albany liked to believe he was finding Life at last, Susannah was quite sure she was doing so. Ever since that morning walk under the long wall of Lord's to the Underground Station, and that midsummer day when she watched Tom's triumph within the wall, she had been saying to herself, " I have only just come alive." St. John's Wood Road was now an enchanted track because the wall of Lord's accompanied it most of the way and ended opposite the Underground Station. She had heard of the Wailing Wall in Jerusalem, so she called this wall (but to herself only) the Rejoicing Wall. She never went into the streets without a hope of meeting Tom, unless she learned from the sports page of *The Times*, which she now studied daily, that he was playing for Middlesex in some distant county. She showed an unusual willingness to go on ' errands ' for her mother, because the shops were in St. John's Wood Terrace and the High Street and so very near his home in Acacia Road. One morning, when she read that he was to play at Lord's, she made an excuse for shopping in St. John's Wood Terrace and walked homeward by Acacia Road, which was not a very successful stratagem since she did not once dare to look up at his white Gothic house but passed it quickly by, staring straight ahead of her. She did, however, two minutes later, meet Tom at the corner of her own Circus Road, and while happy to suspect that he'd been adopting the same expedient as herself, thanked God for His timing of this encounter because, had it happened a minute before, Tom must have seen her coming out of his Acacia Road. She flung out a smile of surprise as though she'd hardly realized he was in London, and even, before she could stop the wickedness, told a lie. " I thought you were away at Old Trafford or somewhere."

" No," he said. " I'm playing at Lord's to-day."

" Oh, *are* you ? " she asked, eyebrows lifted in surprise.

" Are they playing at Lord's ? Oh, I wish I could come.
I've fallen in love with cricket. It's a disease with me, now."

" Oh, *do* come. *Please* come. You must. The season is
dying. There are only two more matches at Lord's."

" Oh, I must then. I simply must. I love it so. Look,
I'll rush home and ask if I can come."

She ran home to her father. " Daddy, I accidentally met
Tom Budlier. He says Middlesex are playing at Lord's and
it's their last match but one. Can I go and see it ? I'm like
you now ; I can watch cricket for ever."

Her father was up from his chair before she'd finished her
word. As enthusiastic as she, he said he was coming too,
and thanked her for the information. This was not what
she had intended, but she must accept it. She hadn't the
heart to show a trace of disappointment. " Poor sweet, he's
so enthusiastic ! " And they set off together, Albany expounding, in words that glowed, what a joy it was to him that she, a
girl, wanted to come and watch cricket with him. " I've always
wanted an enthusiastic companion to come with me, and my
only sorrow about your being a girl was that we'd never go off
to watch cricket together. And here we are, going off together,"
whereupon he put his arm into hers as a symbol of this happy
marriage of two minds. His happiness, she thought, was touching, and she decided that she was pleased to be sacrificed in so
good a cause.

They took seats before the Tavern, where, said Albany,
you met everybody sooner or later. He gazed out at the green
oval field, and at the crowds climbing into the stands, and at
the Noblemen and Gentlemen sitting in the Pavilion with their
top hats tipped forward to shade their eyes ; and he exclaimed,
" This is Life, Susannah ; I love this."

And so it was for all three days of that match. All the time
he sat with her in the mellow August sun and discoursed learnedly
on the finesses of the game and the great men of the past ; and
Tom, though he came once or twice to visit them, was shy of
Sir Albany and for the most part kept away. He contented
himself with fighting out there for Susannah's admiration and
for the good opinion of her father.

And then it was the last match : Middlesex *v.* Kent. And
still her father came, effervescent with high spirits : he came
on the first day and the second and the third. And the third
day was the Last Day. It was the end of a summer song. The
red rash of autumn chequered the trees ; a few tired leaves

filtered down ; and the sadness of a Last Time lay upon the roofs of the stands and the white railings and the great grass level, which was now a dull green under its English cloud.

On this third day, just as the players went in to lunch the rain came. It came out of the cloud in splashing torrents and drenched the grass and the trees and the drooping flags of the pavilion. Albany, ever the expert, announced, " No more play to-day ; you can be sure of that. This is the End. This is the Curtain. Very sad. I could weep. Come, my dear, we may as well go."

But she pleaded, " Oh, let me stay. It's the Last Match, and it may clear up. They may play a little more."

" Stay a little if you like, but it'll be no use. I know when a pitch is soaked. There's no hope."

" All the same I'll stay."

So he left her, and she stood with a few other invincibles, under the shelter of the Tavern awning.

When the heavy shower stopped, she, like others, dawdled across the grass to inspect the pitch. Or, rather, she, the only woman among them, went to be espied by Tom in the pavilion.

The ruse succeeded, for she was scarcely back on the Tavern ground before Tom in his blue and yellow blazer came hastening towards her. The rain came again, and they went and sat together under cover. There was hardly anyone else near them now. Even the most hopeful had given up hope. And at three the news came travelling round the ground that the captains had decided " No further play."

" All over," said Tom. " All over till next year. Look, you must come to tea somewhere. Not here. We must go and do something jolly. We must celebrate the End. Will you come ?"

She was frightened by the invitation, having always understood that it was wrong to go out alone with a man, but she said, Yes, staring at him with fearful eyes and conceding this much to her conscience that she said it so as hardly to be heard.

" Your father wouldn't mind, would he ? I shouldn't like to—you know—upset him. He's so decent."

" No . . . no . . . I don't think he would."

So Tom hurried back to the dressing-room and changed and came to her again; and they ran through the rain, out of the gates and along the Rejoicing Wall to the Underground Station. In the Underground train they were scuttled along, with a rattling and a ringing, over the iron veins of London, far beneath its foundations and its highways and its parks, to

Baker Street, and Piccadilly. They sat side by side in silence, because each was embarrassed by the nearness of the other and each was wondering to what issue they were going. Near the Circus they took tea in a café, talking across the table uneasily. After tea Tom asked, " What can we do now ? You don't want to go home at once." But she said, " Oh, I ought to. They'll know that the match was over long ago," and, so saying, became a party to their deceit.

" They may not know. It's stopped raining. And if the match had gone on, you'd have been there till after six."

" Yes, but . . ." She didn't want to join him in this deceit —or, rather, she didn't want to appear to be doing so.

" Come along," he encouraged her. " Let's do something jolly. Ever seen any moving pictures ? "

" No. Not proper ones."

" Well, they're quite fun. There's the New Century Biograph Theatre in Lyme Street by Leicester Square. Let's go there."

" Do you think we ought to ? "

" Yes, I think so. Yes, of course. Come on."

" Well . . . for a little, perhaps. But I mustn't stay long."

The New Century Biograph Theatre was no more than a long hall with a stage at one end and red-plush tip-up seats on its unraked floor. A taut white sheet was hung high above the stage so that all could see it above the heads in front of them. Below the stage, and screened by a red curtain, a pianist with a shock of grey hair sat at an upright piano in such a position that his eyes—and his hands—could follow the events on the sheet. The long room was lit by gas chandeliers, but Susannah and Tom had hardly taken their seats behind some sixty other people when the gas jets dimmed slowly down through a twilight into darkness.

" Oh, dear ! " murmured Susannah as the visible world departed from her and darkness buried all.

But now a striped white beam, in which the dust of London danced, shot from a little square window behind them, and the first picture, an ' actuality ', began its motions on the sheet. It was a boxing match, or a few minutes of one, between Joe Hagen, the Stockwell Terror, and Big Barney Rose, the Kilburn Storm. Its events flickered at great speed and in a succession of jerks, behind a continuing rain-storm of scratches.

" Big Barney's our boy," whispered Tom. " Kilburn's in Middlesex."

" It appears to be raining in Kilburn," said Susannah.

The 'actuality' lasted only fourteen minutes, and was followed by a 'comedy feature' about ghosts in a haunted house; and of this Tom said in his best Cambridge manner, "How quite extraordinarily unfunny."

Next came a romantic piece about two lovers in a punt on the river. There was much passionate, if jerky kissing in this romantic reel, and Susannah said, "Oh dear! I'm sure I oughtn't to be seeing this."

Then came a 'drama', called 'The Gallows Road', which included a murder, a chase of the murderer over the roof-tops and a final execution-morning scene, complete with a surpliced chaplain holding open a pray-book, and prison warders jerking the trussed victim out of his cell to the gallows.

"Oh, my heavens!" sighed Susannah; and Tom felt justified in laying a hand upon her to calm her.

All the time the pianist, whose shock of grey hair and enormous black cravat showed that he still dreamed of himself as a famous artist, adapted his music to the situations on the sheet, providing sweetness for love, and thunder for disaster. He played trills for the comedians as they cascaded down a collapsing staircase in the House of Mystery, and the Dead March in 'Saul' for the last moments of the murderer. When love or death did not demand softness he played loud so as to drown the whirring noise of the projector behind the white striped beam.

Directly the murderer had gone to his punishment and been succeeded by a white blank he brought the Dead March to an untimely end (like the murderer) and started the National Anthem in time for a coloured portrait of the King.

The gas lights went up, and the people streamed out into Lyme Street and Leicester Square.

It was now evening, ten past six by a clock in the square, and raining.

"Oh, it's raining, raining," Susannah bewailed, as Tom with a hand at her elbow guided her through the press of people outside Daly's and the Empire, "oh, this rain! They'll know I couldn't have been at Lord's all this time."

"I'll get you back as quickly as possible," said Tom. "We'll take a cab. Hi!" and he raised a hand to a hansom jingling by.

"Oh, no," she protested, for she had gathered from her mother that while a hansom was the proper conveyance for a man coming home and reasonably proper for a man and his wife, it was a dubious vehicle for a woman alone, and next door to an immoral place for a man and woman unmarried.

But Tom apparently (and only apparently) had no knowledge of these assessments, and the hansom which he had hailed was now at the kerb to receive them.

" But no ! " Susannah persisted. " It's—it'll be so expensive. It's miles to St. John's Wood."

" Pop in," ordered Tom ; and to the bowler-hatted driver, perched high up in the weather, he said, " Lord's, please," and got in beside her.

Lord's ! Obviously he had said this because she must alight from the cab out of sight of her home. Again she must appear as his fellow in a conspiracy.

They were in the cab together now, and Tom closed the aprons, and let down the glass shields against the rain. They were boxed in, and the cab bowled off with them.

" I said Lord's," he explained, " because I couldn't very well drive you to your door."

" Of course not," she agreed. " They'd never understand us coming home in a cab like this. Silly, isn't it ? "

" Absolutely stupid. As though there were anything in it ! "

" No . . . of course not. . . ."

But they were silent and fidgety as the horse went clopping along Regent Street, Portland Place, and the Marylebone Road, and the rain struck on the glass shields and ran down in rivulets and rills.

It was warm in the cab with aprons closed and window down ; they were shut in with a smell of leather and dust and stale cigar smoke ; but, none the less, Delia and her puritans were right : the hansoms of London, before they fled from our midst, were an invitation to love, and their worn, dusty seats were thrones of danger for young persons like Tom and Susannah. Did you like, you might think of this hansom on the Marylebone Road half a century ago as a big pram with two babies tucked in it and its bowler-hatted driver as a veiled nursemaid whose thoughts were astray from his charges ; or, better, as a little enclosed world spinning through the traffic with the driver above the roof, like God out of sight above the world, at once immanent and transcendent. The chemistry of love, which makes the world go round, was at its work within. Tom fidgeted in his seat ; he leaned an inch nearer her ; he looked out anxiously at the haunches of the pony lolloping into Park Road, all too fast. Soon they would see the white Doric portico of St. John's Wood Chapel and the wide arch of sky above the open places.

135

He adventured an arm behind her waist. She leaned forward so as to avoid knowledge of this advance.

"Susannah," he began.

"Yes?" she answered as if she couldn't imagine what was coming.

His arm closed round her. "You're quite the loveliest thing I've ever known."

"Don't be ridiculous," she said, looking out of her window at the wall of Regents Park.

He placed a kiss on her averted cheek, and she begged, "No, no, *please*," as if in pain, though, in fact, it was joy, a high joy, to be within the arm of that young gladiator whom the multitude at Lord's had acclaimed.

"Kiss me properly," he entreated; and she said, "No, no," —as the situation required.

But he, unconvinced by this refusal, turned her face towards him, while she strove to thrust him away—as the situation certainly required.

He kissed her on the mouth, and that kiss was too much for his strength and his scruples; it inflamed his desire, and he drew her roughly against him and forced more kisses on her lips and with a hand felt for, and pressed upon, her breast.

Now—believing what she imagined she ought to believe— she persuaded herself that she was angry; and because the anger quickly became a pleasurable fire within her, she deliberately raised it higher by thinking of that girl at Cambridge and asked herself if he supposed . . . ?

"Leave me alone," she cried, dragging her body from him and pushing him away. "What do you think I am?"

But he presumed to laugh at her so rightful and proper anger, and to attempt her face again. Then, as she drew away, she shot at him with a poisoned word, "I'm not *your* type of girl. Don't you think so."

"*My* type?" His hands had fallen to his side, and his body sunk back. "What do you mean? Not *my* type?"

"You know what I mean."

"I do not know at all."

"Why did you have to leave Cambridge?"

Ah, yes, she had ended his adventure now. She had struck upon an old wound and left him sick. "No, my dear, you are not my type if you can throw that in my face. I did wrong, I know, but I thought I'd paid my penalty. I thought you were different from the others. I thought you were lovely and

136

kind to me in spite of that, and perhaps because of it. God, how one gets things wrong!" The pillared portico of the Chapel was in sight now, and the great sky above and about it; and heedlessly, heartlessly, the pony trotted onward, clip-clop, his harness jingling.

"I, too, thought you were different. I never thought you'd —you'd do what you tried to do." Her words brought back the anger. "I don't like that sort of thing. I don't know why you should think I should. It's an insult to suppose I should put up with it."

"I see," he said to the Chapel, and the wide sky ahead. "You're like all girls—like all the rest. You make us think you like us; you do all you can to make us love you——"

"I did *not*!"

"Oh, yes, you did—in a hundred little ways—you all do—"

"I'll never speak to you again."

"You're all the same; when you've made us want you, and we try to take a little, you slap us in the face and say we're beasts. Perhaps I went too far. If I did, I'm sorry. Does that make any difference?"

"None whatever. I never want to see you again."

"Fine! Well, now we know where we are. O.K., love. I'm not going to worry. I can find someone else."

Did his words start in her more of anger or of pain? She did not know. But better to give the anger pride of place. Let the anger do the speaking; muzzle the pain; he must not perceive the pain. Let the anger speak, and speak loud. "You certainly can. As far as I am concerned."

"All right. So let it be. Here we are, my child. Lord's. Lord's where we've often been rather happy. But that's over. Everything's over. Such fun!" He knocked on the roof, and the driver above opened his trap. "We'll stop here," Tom said through the trap.

"Aye, aye, sir," said the driver, who was apparently an old sailor.

And the cab went up to the kerb, and they alighted at the very doors of the Underground station, whose threshold, when they crossed it but a few hours ago, had been a sacred place, enshrining a memory and effusing happiness. Tom stepped down first and saying, "Come, beloved, trip down. Trip down, sweetie," stretched up a hand to help her, but she refused to notice that guilty and discredited thing.

He pointed up Wellington Road on the left of the Chapel.

"That's your best way home. I'll go this way. Then I shan't inconvenience you with my presence. Good-bye."

"Good-bye."

Without a turn of the head he crossed the five-ways cross-roads towards the High Street on the other side of the Chapel's garden of trees and tombs.

And so they walked to their homes with a green island of dead tombs between them. Susannah did not once look through the railings of the Burial Ground to see his figure walking parallel with hers on the farther side. So long as she could be seen of him she walked at a decent pace and with her head high ; but directly she had turned into Circus Road, she ran. She ran because she was wretched and it was late.

At her knock Delia came to the door. Fortunately Delia knew nothing about cricket and was unapprised that rain, even if only intermittent, could put a stop to all play as early as three o'clock. So all she said was, " Good gracious ! Have you been at Lord's all this time ? I don't think it's quite nice, a girl hanging about there, among all those men."

With only a muttered answer Susannah hurried up the stairs to her bedroom, glad to have passed that barrier so easily. In her bedroom she closed the door so as to be alone with her thoughts. What *were* they ? She hardly knew, because they were in conflict with one another. She wanted to think that anger, a most proper and meritorious anger, was the chief of them, but—what about this other thought that leapt up and thrust itself into view whenever the anger rested ? It was a thought that had exultation and excitement in it ; it was a joyous thought, no denying this ; it told her again and again that she had been kissed for the first time—and *properly* kissed —with passion. . . .

But with indecent passion, she reminded herself, that she might stir up the anger again, and bid it fight this inappropriate exhilaration. He had done this and that. He had treated her as if she were easy fruit to gather, and cheap. He had laid his hand upon her breast—but as she remembered this, the joy, which was being so savagely pummelled, began to reveal its reserves of strength and get on top in the fight . . .

A knock at the door. She started and walked quickly to her dressing table and pretended to be combing her hair.

" Susannah darling ? " It was her father.

" Yes, Daddy ? " Never a more innocent expression on her

face. She looked straight into his eyes because she knew it was what people did who had nothing to conceal.

"I've something to show you; something interesting." He closed the door. "No, I haven't really; I only said that for your mother to hear. Now, Susannah darling, where have you been?"

Albany's emotions, for the last two hours, had been more imbued with pleasure than he would have liked to admit. His satisfaction that he knew all about cricket whereas Delia knew nothing about it; his pity for Delia in her ignorance about wet wickets and prematurely drawn stumps; his admiration for his shrewdness which guessed that Susannah and Tom had been on some escapade together (Lord knew where); the prospect of exhibiting this sagacity to Susannah and 'catching her out' (which, unhappily, can have its relish, even though the victim is our daughter); his picture of himself as one who would be much gentler and more understanding than Delia; his pride in being the natural protector of his daughter—all these emotions were pleasurable, though doubtless they should not have been.

"Where have I been?" Susannah echoed the words as though surprised at them. "At Lord's," she said, maintaining that straight, honest stare.

"What? Ever since lunch? Surely they didn't play any more?"

"No, as a matter of fact, they didn't."

"Then they must have announced 'no further play' ages ago."

"Oh, yes, they did. So . . . so we went and had some tea." What more natural?

"Who's 'we'?"

"Why, Tom and me, of course."

"A long tea. It's nearly seven o'clock."

"Is it? Is it really?"

"Darling, I am not a fool. You haven't been drinking tea all this time at Lord's. Where was it?"

She confessed to the tea-shop in Piccadilly. And he, in pursuit of his vision of himself as the exceptionally understanding and tolerant, but wisely admonitory, parent, began, "Well, my dear, I don't want to be the old-fashioned father, I never want to come between two young people, but——"

"But you needn't worry," she interrupted. "We're never going to see each other again."

Startled by this abrupt statement, and by a sadness in her face, he asked, " What do you mean ? Have you quarrelled ? "

" Yes. And it's a final quarrel. I can promise you that."

" But why ? What has happened ? "

She told him of the brief struggle in the cab, putting forth the proper show of anger. Tom had forced his kisses upon her. He had crushed her against him, and pressed his hands upon her. He had supposed that she was there for him to do what he liked with.

And Albany, listening, remembered his embrace of Prudence Maddow, and the way his passion had mounted, and the things which he had done. And the words of disapproval and condemnation which a year ago he must have spoken died behind his lips. He kept silence from good words and, instead, took a turn about the room.

Surprised that he did not speak, Susannah asked, " It was awful of him, wasn't it ? "

He stopped in front of her. " I can forgive him," he said.

" Forgive him ! I can't. And I won't. Daddy, do you mean that ? "

" Yes, dear. Men are very weak when they've got a beautiful woman in front of them. And you're a beautiful young woman now, I'm sorry to say."

" But, Daddy, don't you think it's awful to kiss a girl in a cab ? What on earth would Mother say ? "

" She'd be horrified. Good heavens, yes ! "

" And he went on after I'd told him to stop. That was awful, wasn't it ? " She wanted to keep her disdain, her grievance, and her right to punish him.

" It was wrong, yes. He's a weak young man, I'm afraid. But, then, so are we all. And he's young. Tell me, Susannah, was that the first time you've been kissed ? "

" Of *course* it was ! "

" And didn't you enjoy it ? "

" No ! " she affirmed indignantly. " Certainly not ! "

" Come, tell me the truth, darling." And he smiled at her, tolerantly. " Don't just say what you think it right to say. Isn't the truth that you enjoyed it ? "

" Well . . . of course . . . yes . . . in a way, yes."

" Rather exciting, was it ? "

" Well, it did rather reduce me to curds and whey. Yes, it did . . . I'm afraid."

Albany nodded, smiling still.

" But he went *on* doing it," she reminded him. " And he said I'd encouraged him."

" Well, hadn't you ? "

" Of course not ! "

" My dear, do you mean to say you've never let him feel you liked him quite a lot ? "

" Perhaps I have sometimes . . . a little . . . now and then."

" Yes, well then I think we can forgive him for that first kiss. These are the 1900's, you know, and the times have been changing while we've been buried in Mosspot. I sometimes think we're rather like rustics come to town, you and I and your mother."

" Oh, I'm not a rustic, am I ? " Horror stood in her eyes. " Oh, heavens, I don't want to be a rustic."

" No, you were right to show him he couldn't take liberties with you. Quite right, and now—— "

" Oh, but he won't think I was rustic, will he ? Oh, how confusing it all is ! I thought I was being clever, but was I only being rustic ? "

" No, you were right. But now that he's had a sharp lesson, what do you say to punishing him no more ? I think it's a pity, if you're growing fond of each other, to let this keep you apart. Susannah, how fond of him are you ? "

" Daddy, I think I love him."

" I think you do too. It may be only a passing fancy for each other, but that's what you and he have got to find out. I think I want you to go on being happy with him. Would it make you happy again if I went and saw him, and told him he was wrong, of course, but managed to bring about a reconciliation ? "

" Oh, Daddy, darling, *will* you ? Yes, do, please. That *would* be so completely Albanian of you."

With those words in his ears Albany went from her room, a vessel charged with happiness and content. He was proud of the wisdom he had shown, the understanding he had preached, the admiration he had won, and the work of rescue (always a flattering occupation) to which he was going. He went first to the white Gothic villa in Acacia Road, but here old Colonel Budlier told him that Tom was gone out : Tom had come home about an hour ago, looking very unhappy, and gone out again without a word to anyone.

Albany went down the steps, wondering. Then, abruptly, he crossed the road to the Ordnance Arms. And there, in the bar, as he had surmised, he saw Tom sitting against the wall before a little table. The boy's chin was dropped in the deepest dejection and his eyes gazed into the emptiness of a whisky glass on the table. Doubtless the emptied glass was symbolizing the emptiness of his life, now that Susannah was lost to him ; he twisted its stem between his fingers, but otherwise did not move at all. Seated there, he was the picture of a youth who, in despair or remorse, was giving himself to whisky and forgetfulness.

Albany bought himself a tot of whisky and carried it towards the boy. Tom, hearing his approach, looked up. The despairing eyes took on a frightened look as if he were wondering whether an indignant father had come with talk of a horse-whip. So Albany immediately put out a smile.

" Well, Tom," he said, and sat down beside him. " I've heard all about the great quarrel."

" Has Susannah told you ? Is she very angry with me ? "

" She was."

" I'm a beast. I'm a loathsome beast. I kissed her once, and it was so lovely that I lost my head. I'll never do anything again to hurt her. I swear and vow it. I've been sitting here telling myself that if only we could get back to where we were this morning, I'd never do anything like that again. I've been calling down all sorts of vengeance on my head if I ever do anything to hurt her again. I hope God'll strike me dead if I do."

Never, thought Albany, was there a boy with such a talent for penitence, such a turn for the austerest (even if only temporary) purposes of amendment. He covered his smile by smoothing with forefinger and hand the length of both moustaches. Then he disclosed the smile. " You have, have you ? Well, that's fine."

" Yes, I have, truly, sir. I suppose you couldn't tell her this. No, of course not. She's done with me for ever. And I don't wonder."

" I will certainly tell her. Look here, Tom : she's fond of you, I think, and happy with you, and I want her to go on being happy. She's everything to me, and her happiness means more to me than anything else in the world." Ah, if only he could make this true. He was going to try to. " I know you'll never do anything like that again. Now have a cigar. You are fond of her ? "

" I love her better than anything else in the world."

" Well, what shall we do then ? I want you two young people to be happy together, though you're too young to talk of love yet. You've got to get to know each other better, and, Tom, you must get settled before we think of anything serious."

" I know, sir. And you won't tell Lady Grahame anything about this, will you ? She doesn't like me—doesn't like me in the least—and I don't wonder."

" No, this shall stay between you and me and Susannah. Let's see : it seems dreadful to ask a cricketer to come and play croquet, but your season's over ; would you care to come on Monday for tea and a game, and I promise Susannah will welcome you."

" Oh, sir—you're wonderful. I love croquet."

" Yes, it's not too bad a game in the failing sunlight after tea. Come along then, Tom, and we'll all be happy again."

Albany was certainly happy when he came away from the public house. He swung his stick as he walked homeward with the story of what he'd done, a story in which he would figure handsomely as father and peacemaker. " I love that boy. I love all young people. He's weak, of course, but so are we all." The stick continued to accompany him home with triumphant circles and arcs, and the plumes of smoke from his cigar were a celebration in the evening air.

CHAPTER TEN

MRS. CLAPTON, JEAN, AND EDDIE

THE letter was brought to Albany in his study at nine in the morning. It was unstamped and had been pushed through the door. He looked at the handwriting, which was strange, and at the front and back of the envelope, which was not very clean. Tearing it open, he considered the address. " 16 Elber Square." A near neighbour then. He looked for the signature. This was difficult to find because the writing was closely packed, and crossed, and the last words had been inserted in the top left-hand corner of the front page. " C. A. Clapton ? " Who on earth was C. A. Clapton ? Date there was none, and of punctuation very little. The last words of every line turned down like a drooping tail, so as to remain attached to the main body and save space. Evidently a person who was poor or parsimonious, and not very well educated.

" Dear Sir Albany I have only just heard that you have come to live close to us Amy Denton Bullock told me and Jean and Eddie coming out of church last evening"—who the devil was Amy Denton Bullock?—" I *was* surprised. Only fancy I said to Jean and Eddie your father's brother has come to live—— "

What ? Their father's brother ? Some children of Vick's ? Now he read on avidly.

" Life is strange Who would have thought it I wonder if Vick ever spoke of me to you I feel he must have done—— "

Never, my dear woman, never.

" It is of course twenty years and more since we had to part Life is full of tragedy he was the only person I ever loved even though he didn't treat me too well in the end and I believe though perhaps it is wrong to say it that he loved me better than well you know what I mean. In those distant days he often used to speak of you and your noble work—— "

Sounds like Vick !

" It was a terrible shock to me when I read of his death I opened the paper and there it was I had to break it to the children who know the truth now though they used to think they were Mr. Clapton's children I know I can trust you a clergyman not to speak of these things. Vick bought this house for me and the children years ago when we decided to part and he settled a sum of money on us Vick always did what was right for his children I'll say that for him but of course things have been much more difficult than ever he knew especially since my operation."

So then, Vick like others, like Lord Clanbethry, had retired his mistress at a suitable age and settled the discarded lady in the quiet of St. John's Wood.

" I have to work and slave for the children It was better when Eddie was earning money at the undertakers but now he is at the theological college it is all putting out and none coming in but I always wanted him to be a clergyman hes cut out for it You will be interested in my Eddie since hes going to be a clergyman too It was no good his going to the college till he was 21 so he worked at Johnson and Buss the furnishers and undertakers doing most of the clerical work in the undertaking department and he worked at his Latin in the evenings. He used to say that he arranged for the people's Last Buss home hes full of fun and will have his joke. He says now hes going to polish off their souls instead of their bodies Sometimes his jokes are rather naughty Jean is a good girl too she is 25 now and works at an antiques shop in Park Road I didn't quite like her being in a shop, but antiques are different and it is run by a lady Molly Prendergast and Jean has a feeling for beautiful old things she is very artistic. I hear you have a lovely daughter Mrs. Cooper Bradley says she saw what must have been her——"

And who the hell was Mrs. Cooper Bradley?

"It would be nice if she and Jean could be friends. I do hope you will come and see us in our little home one day I feel you could advise my Eddie so much since he is going to be a clergyman Both Jean and Eddie send their love to their Uncle Albany though they have never met you——"

Uncle Albany! Well, here was news! He hurried towards the door to carry this wholly unexpected and high-seasoned dish to Delia, but before touching the handle of the door he stopped. He prided himself on his ability to keep a confidence, largely because Delia had no such ability. And soon, as he waited by the door handle, this pride in his trustworthiness mastered his longing to divulge the story.

He went back to the fireplace. Reading the letter again, he suspected, with some fear, that this woman had lively notions of extracting money from him, and he deliberated, for an unworthy minute, whether to leave the letter unanswered and so discourage the lady for good. But curiosity transcended the fear, a desire to be kind, and even noble, joined the curiosity, and so did a sudden tenderness for the girl Jean. After all, she was his niece, a new niece, and he allowed a sentimental dream to form in the smoke of his cigar, a dream about a beautiful girl to whom he was the kindest and most loving of uncles, and by whom he was greatly loved. 'I love my uncle Albany better than anyone else in the world. He is perfectly *sweet*. And he's been like a father to me.'

Curiosity and conscience and aspiration, and this pleasing dream, drove him forth. Almost as excitely as a child going to a theatre where an enthralling story will be told he went to 16 Elber Square.

Elber Square was remarkable for not being a square but a curving road of narrow Victorian houses vested from basement to cornice in cream or grey stucco. Terraced houses with deep basements and steep steps to their front doors, they had none of the charm of the little detached or semi-detached villas behind their garden walls. All had a look of distressed gentility, and one imagined them inhabited by indigent gentle-women who eased their distress by taking in paying guests or letting off furnished rooms. A few years more and they would have lost the last of their gentility and become hives of the poor.

He walked up the steps and pulled a bell handle. And, standing there on the threshold, he became conscious of a pair of eyes peering at him through the lace curtains of the bay window at his side.

The curiosity behind those eyes brought their owner, with a shuffling sound, to the door. She opened it, and Albany saw a woman of about fifty, with a fat, heaving body and face made hard by a fallen mouth and those peering, loveless eyes. The grey hair where it did not drop in strings and wisps was bundled and pinned on the top of her head, as if she had not long been out of bed. Her feet, bare, stood in old felt bedroom slippers of which one toe was worn away so that a big and untrimmed toenail peeped out. This fat slattern—was she once the be-loved of Vick ? Twenty-five years ago was she slim and graceful and pretty enough for Vick to buy ?

" Miss Clapton ? " Remembering that other discarded mis-tress, Miss Maddow, he made the mistake of saying ' Miss.'

" *Mrs*. Clapton," she corrected, still staring at him inquisi-tively.

" My name is Sir Albany Grahame."

" Oh ! But I thought you were a clergyman." Her eyes swept his bow tie, blue collar, and blue shirt.

" So I was till recently."

" Oh, but you really must excuse me looking like this. I have all the housework to do. I have no domestic staff nowadays."

" I shouldn't have come so early. But I was *so* interested in your letter."

" Yes, well do come in, but I *am* ashamed for you to see me like this. You're just in time to see Eddie. Lucky you came when he was at home. He goes back to college next week. *Eddie !* " She yelled this up the staircase. " *Ed-dee !* Here's your Uncle Albany. He's in his bath. He couldn't get the stove going before. Come into the drawing-room."

As they went along the passage, the door of a back room opened an inch, and a pair of old eyes scanned him. The door shut quietly. A lodger ?

The drawing room was the front room behind the lace cur-tains and the bay window. It was as slatternly as its lady. Garments lay piled on piano and chairs. A tea-cup half full of cold tea stood on a table by a basket of undarned socks. Newspapers and ragged magazines sat in the easy chairs or on the worn carpet at their sides. The silver frames of the photographs on the mantelshelf were black as lead.

Albany's eyes sought these photographs : one of Vick in his thirties, and yonder one of a young and pretty Mrs. Clapton with her two children at her knees, self-consciously posed and smiling. Above the mantel hung an enlargement of her in a low-necked velvet dress with a diamond brooch at her bosom and diamond-drops in her ears. His eyes fell from this richly soft and jewelled lady to the woman now seated before him. She had sat herself on the brink of an upholstered chair, forgetting her *déshabillé* in the interest his coming had aroused. Once, starting to cross her legs, she uncovered a bare and swollen ankle, but she quickly remembered this danger and withdrew the slippered feet into the shelter of her skirt.

Albany was only anxious now to escape from this disordered home, but his courtesy forbade an immediate flight, and his compassion too.

He sank himself into the chair opposite her.

Something fell with a thump on the ceiling above ; footsteps creaked across it ; and through the floorboards came the hum of a deep voice singing.

" That's my Eddie," she explained. " That's the bathroom just above. He must have just finished his bath."

As an ex-parson Albany recognized the tune coming through the floor. It was a jovial hymn, ' Hark, hark, my soul ! Angelic songs are swelling,' but this deep voice was droning it like a dirge—between the creakings and the thumps.

" Your letter was a complete surprise to me," he began. " Vick never said a word to me about you and the children."

" He didn't ? No, I daresay not. No, I can imagine that. I never want to say a word against him, but in some ways . . ." Tears formed in her eyes and she felt about her person for a handkerchief, finally drawing a crumpled one from the fold down the side of her chair. She blew her nose. Her nose was well-shaped but long at the point, and she turned this point to one side as she blew. It sprang back into its position when she released it. The handkerchief went back into its cache down the side of the chair.

To comfort her Albany said, " I saw very little of him in the last twenty years."

" It's twenty-seven years since we—since he and I first came together. Jean is twenty-five now. It's very sad for them. They've never had their rightful position in the world." The tears formed again, and her mouth twisted and worked as she controlled, or pretended to be controlling, them. " I don't care for myself any more but only for them."

Something tumbled with a bang overhead, while the deep voice droned, ' Far, far away, like bells at evening pealing . . ." To this accompaniment Albany was doing a mental sum. Vick had married Lena, his wife, more than thirty years ago.

" Then I suppose," he faltered, " I suppose you—yes, naturally—you and he came together after he'd married Lena."

" Oh, yes. It was all very sad. He had all my love, and that's why my life has been nothing but tragedy. But we were happy for some time. We had a dear little house in Winder-mere Road, West Kensington, and there my darling Jean and Eddie were born. I often go and look at it." This was too much for her : the tears leapt, and she blew her nose again so vigorously that she turned its point through several degrees. It sprang back indignantly. " But things couldn't go on. He came one dreadful day and said that Lena had got to hear of me, and everything must come to an end. He promised he would do all he could for me."

Albany, knowing his brother, wondered whether Vick hadn't tired of a fading mistress and invented this tale of Lena's discovery.

Mrs. Clapton replaced the handkerchief down the side of the chair. " He bought this house for us and settled a little money on me. It was not very much, considering that I gave my life to him. Things have been very difficult for us—very difficult indeed—especially since my operation."

Albany perceived that it would be indelicate to ask for details of the operation, and was glad that this should be so, because, while he knew no more about her operation than he did about her Mrs. Cooper Bradley, he was not anxious to have his dark-ness enlightened. He nodded sympathetically. " Tell me, Mrs.—no, I can't call you Mrs. Clapton—what is your name ? "

" Cornelia is my name. Yes. Cornelia Alice."

" Well, Cornelia, tell me : the children know the truth ? "

" Yes, but they've always gone as Percy's children."

" Percy ? "

" Yes. Mr. Clapton. We were married about three years after Vick went out of my life. But there again : things were all right at first, Percy was easy-going and good-natured, I never want to say a word against him, but he was not a moral man. Not at all moral. He didn't know what morality meant."

" Was that so ? " But who did, in this story ? " May I ask, what was his profession ? "

" He had no profession. He called himself a gentleman of independent means. He was the grandson of a Q.C. who made a great favourite of him and left him money—not much but just enough to live on. And he was a born gambler. I don't want to say anything against him, but he married me for the little money and the nice house and furniture I'd got from Vick. This gave him a nice home and what with his money and mine, and his winnings at cards—he was a marvellous whist player—he didn't have to work. Things were not too bad. He was really fond of the children at first, but sometimes he'd throw them in my face. Which wasn't nice."

" And did he die ? "

" No, he disappeared."

A thump above, and Albany's heart jumped from its seat. " Oh, Eddie ! " his mother protested. The voice came louder, as the singer stooped to the floor to pick up the article which had fallen : ' Angels, sing on . . . Sing us sweet fragments of the songs above. . . .'

" Disappeared, you said ? "

" Yes, he went off with Jimmy Greystone, a friend who was no good at all—just such another as himself. He said he and Jimmy were going off to Canada to make a lot of money and he'd send me huge sums and perhaps have me and the children out there, but it was all talk. That was the last I heard of him from that day to this. He just went out of my life."

" Have you never tried to find him and make him support you ? "

" How could I ? He knew too much. And he could be nasty and throw the children in my face. I couldn't tell the lawyers everything, could I ? Life's been very difficult for me."

" And Vick ? Didn't you ever go to him for help ? "

" Yes, and he did send me a sum to help with the children's education. Eddie went to Dalton House School in Abbey Road ; it's not a public school of course, but Mr. Williams is a B.A. London." She was clearly covering up some guiltiness about having sent Eddie to a cheap little school. " But I had to take them both away from school when they were about sixteen. I wrote to Vick telling him I couldn't manage, and he answered very sharply. It hurt me very much. He said he'd done all he could. Such nonsense, when he had all the money in the world! He said he didn't want to be bothered any more. So I decided that my task was to keep a little home over the children's heads—I regarded this as a sacred trust—and they must contribute a little to the housekeeping. I was ready to work and slave for them in the house, even taking in lodgers. I've one now. Through there." She pointed to the wall. "So Eddie went to Johnson and Buss's and Jean to 'Dorothy Dean's' the antique shop. I didn't like them going into shops, but an undertaker's is hardly a shop, is it? He didn't have to serve behind the counter. And there are lots of ladies in antique shops. Molly Prendergast who runs 'Dorothy Dean's' is a lady. I did my best for them."

Albany, listening, had little doubt what had happened. He had discerned, behind all these window-curtains woven of soft maternal words, the hard peering eyes of a self-centred and grasping woman, and he guessed that, directly she was sure that Vick was no longer watching, she had put the children out to work that they might bring money into her home and purse. Perhaps in her Eddie's case the selfishness had yielded an inch or two because she must have forced herself to contribute to his expenses at a Theological College, knowing that if she did this the Church would supply the rest, and so she would get something for nothing. But for Jean there would be no more. His heart went out again to this Jean, and his mind's eye went seeking her in her antique shop.

But just then they heard a heavy step on the stairs.

"Here's Eddie," said his mother, and Albany waited with no small interest to see his nephew. Would he be tall and handsome like Vick? Like Vick's brother?

Eddie entered, and Albany exclaimed within himself "Good God!" Eddie was small and fat with a protuberant belly like a bladder-frog's. His nose, too small for a man, and his moustache, of thin pale fluff, seemed but rudimentary. His eyes were small too, and appeared the smaller for the huge round spectacles that framed them. With these too-small features, and his oddly shaped body, he looked like a job not properly completed. His clothes seemed to stress this incompleteness: the suit of pepper-and-salt serge hung loosely about him; his stiff white collar was much too high; his stiff white shirt-front bulged, and was obviously a 'dickey'; and his stiff white cuffs, falling far below the sleeves, revealed that they were both detachable and reversible.

Vick's son! My nephew! Susannah's cousin! Good God!

But his manner was supremely self-satisfied. " Ah, Uncle,"
he began, and the deep rich voice came oddly from that un-
completed figure ; it seemed made for someone twice his size.
" Aha ! This is an occasion. Glad we meet at last." And he
came forward with a hand held as high as his shoulder, ready
to slap down heartily on his uncle's. It did slap down on it ;
it gripped it painfully and shook it many times—say three times
too often. " Aha ! This is indeed a pleasure. I trust my dear
mother has been entertaining you adequately. I am so sorry
not to have been presentable when you came, but I was per-
forming my ablutions. It was a somewhat late hour in the day
for such cleansing processes, but I was helping Mr. Mellor
at St. Stephen's till nine of the clock, and then needed a little
refreshment for the inner man, haw, haw, haw ; haw, haw."

This laugh of his could be described only as a loud but
diminishing neigh ; it was a succession of haws, and the last
in the succession was a belated, lagging, lazy haw, an also-ran
of a haw, well behind all the others. On paper the cachinna-
tion can be set down, if justice is to be done to it, only as :

    ' Haw, haw, haw . . .
      haw . . . .
                    haw'

He sat on the rim of a chair with his hands on his knees and
the long cuffs dropping over his wrists. " My dear mother
had been very naughty and suffered the fire to go out, so that it
was an hour before we could get the water at the required
temperature. But all's well that ends well, and I am clean
now, and clothed, and in my right mind, haw, haw, haw . . .
                     haw . . . .
                       haw."

" Eddie will have his little joke," said his mother proudly.
" And now I'll nip away and make myself presentable too."

" I shouldn't have come so early," Albany apologised, as the
lady went.

" Not at all, Uncle. I don't think we need stand on ceremony
with each other. I'm only sorry we have so little entertainment to offer you. The Exchequer won't run to much in this
abode. And how is my aunt, Lady Grahame ? And my charming cousin, Susannah ? I consider her a great addition to the
amenities of the neighbourhood. I hope we shall see much of
each other, though I am not given much to the Fair Sex as a
rule. I've had more serious matters to consider. My studies
have always precluded me from taking a real part in the social

life of our little suburb. I've had to keep my Nose to the Grinding Stone."

Albany listened and stared, fascinated. Here was foolishness enveloped in self-satisfaction. Obviously he had no consciousness that his appearance was foolish—on the contrary, he was well pleased with it—and no consciousness that his pompous polysyllables and ponderous humour were not good, but bad, and his ceaseless chatter not entertaining but an affliction.

And his mother was equally blind.

" Is Susannah meeting some nice young people ? " the voice went on. " Perhaps my sister and I could introduce her to some. There are many earnest young people in St. Stephen's congregation. Perhaps we could all forgather together one day and see what can be done in this important respect."

" Thank you. She has many friends," said Albany, thinking, The impudence of the puppy ! " She has become an habitué of Lord's."

" The Marylebone Cricket Club ? " Eddie gave it the more pompous name, fingering some threads of his moustache. " I'm afraid my inclinations have never leaned that way at all. Athletics have never been my Strong Forte. My tastes lie in the direction of Books. And how are you liking your new domicile in our leafy little suburb ? There are many more unsalubrious places, I think, than our Wood of the Baptist."

He was liking it very well, Albany said ; and inquired, " Could I smoke ? "

" Why, most assuredly you could. I fear I have no cigarettes or other specimens of the Weed—ah, you have a cigar ! Good. It's not a vice I have acquired yet, but I cannot say that I feel any condemnation of those who indulge—if they do it in moderation, of course. What church is the church of your attendance? I was mentioning you to Mr. Mellor this morning, because I hoped you might come and help us sometimes at St. Stephen's. There's a great opportunity for spiritual work here, so many of the Literary and Artistic Fraternity seem to have no sense of religion at all. I sometimes think that when in the fullness of time I am ordained, I should like to get my title here."

" You expect to be ordained soon ? "

" I hope to be admitted to the Diaconate next year as ever was. And then my idea is to have my mother and sister to live with me—until such time, of course, as I take unto myself a wife."

" You propose to marry, do you ? "

"Oh, yes." Not a doubt in his smug little mind that someone would delight to marry him ! And the extraordinary thing was, that someone would. "Oh, yes, indeed. A wife, if she's a properly earnest woman can be of great help to a parish priest. Every priest should take unto himself a wife."

"But could you afford to marry ? Your stipend would be only a hundred and thirty pounds or so."

"Yes, but my tastes are modest. I've never been addicted to the Creature Comforts and the Pleasures of the Table. Besides, it's possible that my spouse might be endowed with some of this world's goods. A little filthy lucre would be quite welcome, and I see no reason why one shouldn't make friends to that extent with the Mammon of Unrighteousness, haw, haw, haw . . . haw . . . . . . haw."

Lord, lord, how could he get away from this appalling fool ? He felt like a fly, caught on a fly-paper that was sticky with fool's talk. He took out his watch. "Heavens ! Nearly eleven. It's all been so interesting that I haven't noticed how time has flown. I must run. Run."

"Oh, must you ? "

"Yes, yes. My wife is waiting for me." He walked to the door and out into the passage, and all the way his nephew followed him with apologies for inadequate entertainment. That voluble voice interrupted these flowing apologies only to call up the stairs, "Ma ! *Ma* ! My good uncle's going," and then resumed them, beginning at the beginning again.

Cornelia Clapton came hurrying down the stairs, just as Eddie was telling Albany that he "wanted to get some tutoring in the vacations so as to help the family finances," and producing a professional card in the hope that his uncle might hear of some tutorable child. Albany looked at the card and with amazement read :

Mr. Eddi Bakewell-Clapton
Classical Tutor

"' Eddi ' ? Is that a misprint ? "

"Oh, no," Cornelia explained. "He likes it spelt like that. It looks more Saxon, he thinks."

"I see. And Bakewell ? *Bakewell*-Clapton ? "

"Yes, he likes to call himself that because my mother was a Bakewell, and Bakewell is the family name of the Earls of Prestatyn."

"Really ? How very interesting ! " But lord, lord, the

conceit, the pomposity, the eagerness for self-decoration, in a would-be priest whose citizenship was not of this world.

He managed to get from the house at last, though Mr. Bakewell-Clapton followed him down the steps and along the pavement with apologies and information and good wishes for his happiness in St. John's Wood and kind regards to his aunt and cousin and hopes that they would all forgather together soon. When it was finally clear to Mr. Bakewell-Clapton that the coupling between him and his uncle would hold no longer, he raised a fat palm shoulder-high for the last hearty farewell and smacked it down on the hand of the retreating guest, which he pressed and shook with vigour and vehemence. Manifestly he had a satisfying view of himself as a fine type of muscular Christian.

Albany sat at the luncheon table that day, bearing a burden of secrecy, and proud of his power to bear it. Luncheon and this praiseworthy silence over, he set off for Park Road to get a glimpse of the girl Jean. After the shock of Cornelia and Eddie he had not much hope that he would find in Jean the beautiful and lovable niece of his dream, and he walked the long road sadly, because prepared for disappointment. Here was the string of antique shops he had often noticed, suitably old-fashioned shops cut into the ground-floors of an old eighteenth-century terrace ; and there among them was ' Dorothy Dean's.' Silly affected name ! ' Dorothy Dean. Antiques ' : a little dusty shop whose wide window was crossed by the black glazing bars of an older day, and whose tall narrow door you had to approach up three narrow steps. And it was served by a daughter of Vick's ! He went up the steps, peered through a glass pane of the door, saw that the shop, though crammed with old furniture and ornaments and curios, was empty of any human figure, and accordingly with a gentle and nervous hand, pushed open the door. But as he stepped upon the mat within, a bell jangled loudly, startling him ; and he had barely time to notice the clutter of bric-à-brac amid which he stood—the old china, glass, plate and pewter, the horse brasses, warming pans, copper scuttles, ship's lanterns, coaching horns—barely time to smell the dust from a London roadway that was cupped in this multitude of vessels, when footsteps creaked in the back parts, and a tall girl emerged.

Albany took a step back, so shaken was he. Her resemblance

to Vick was like a flash in his eyes. This tall girl was as surely the child of Vick as her brother, that rudimentary creation, might be anyone's child—since God had never completed him.

"Can I show you something, sir?"

They were Vick's eyes looking at him. But everything which she had drawn from Vick was wrong in a girl. Vick's height had been matched by broad and powerful shoulders; her height was too great for a girl, and her figure too thin. Vick's nose had been a fine feature in a man; but in this girl it was too long, and it would seem that she scorned the blessings of powder. Her hands were large and heavy, like Vick's, and her feet too long. And those eyes might be Vick's eyes, but they were as sad—yes, and as distant and reserved and even hard—as Vick's were merry and friendly and twinkling. The auburn hair might have been beautiful, because it was clearly abundant, but she had strained much of the beauty from it by drawing it as austerely as possible from a parting in the centre to a large chignon at the neck.

"Could I show you something?" she repeated, for in this first moment of poignant encounter he had not spoken.

Well, there was one thing quite beautiful about her, and it was her voice: a low contralto, with beautiful modulations.

"You are Jean Clapton?"

"Yes."

"That is easy to see. My dear, you are so like your father."

A blush of shame rushed up to the strained hair, and he realized that he had blundered. He explained hastily, "I am your father's brother. Albany Grahame."

"Oh. . . ." She gazed at his features with interest, but little friendliness. "Oh, I see. Mother has been writing to you. I told her to let you alone. It was no wish of mine that she should pester you, Sir Albany."

Her head was high as she spoke, and he thought, A haughty young woman, this. So he smiled and said, "Don't call me Sir Albany. I am your uncle and you should address me as such—and affectionately, if you can."

"That would give a lot away, wouldn't it? You are not, I think, brother to the amiable and so amenable Mr. Percy Clapton. You know all about him, I suppose?"

"Yes."

"I guessed so. You have seen Mother, and she has spilled out everything to you. Usually it's the one thing under the sun that she's been able to hold her tongue about, because it suited her to do so, and it must have been Heaven's own relief to pour it out to you."

" The secret is safe with me. I pride myself on being able to keep a confidence."

" On the whole, I should prefer that you did."

" I'm only sorry I frightened you just now by mentioning your father, but I was overthrown by your likeness to him."

" I have no desire to be like him. I see no reason to remember him with anything but pain."

" You are bitter against him ? "

" And why not ? Aren't we his cast-outs ? Isn't Mother his cast-off clothing, and doesn't she look like it ? She received you in the drawing-room, I take it ? "

" Yes."

" Well, that must have been a sweet experience for you. Was the place a pig-sty, as usual ? "

" I didn't notice it," he lied.

" It must have been ; it's never anything else. Ah well, I suppose if you make a mess of your life with men, you make a mess of your drawing-room afterwards. And did you see Eddi Bakewell-Clapton ? E, double-d, i ? What do you think of him ? Don't you think he'll be an ornament to the Church ? "

" I daresay he'll do well enough."

" How he ever got into that Theological College beats me. They'll take anything these days. He talks as if he knew all about Latin and Greek now—he calls himself, if you'll only believe it, a Classical Tutor—and the truth is he only scraped through the entrance exam at the third try. I hope you were impressed by his complete self-satisfaction. Did you get a word in edgeways with either Mother or Mr. Bakewell-Clapton ? "

" A few."

" You surprise me. Usually our Eddie is so pleased with his own talk that he hates to stop it, and he goes on after everyone's retired from listening to him. He's quite capable of going on for a little when there's no one left in the room. But, more usually, he follows them out and continues to address them from three paces in the rear."

" Never mind Eddie. He seems to be settling himself in life fairly well. What are *you* going to do ? "

" Ask me another. I only wish I knew. What is there for me in this world ? "

" Plenty. You may get married."

" I can't see anyone marrying me, and I don't think I want

anyone to. I'm not impressed with marriage. Look at my real father with unacknowledged brats all over London and my reputed father, whose name I bear, a common runaway. Though I must say that sometimes, after listening to Mother for an hour or two, I don't blame him for going."

" Not all men are like that, Jean."

" I am not interested in men. I don't know why it is, but I hate them to be near me. I recoil from them if they touch me."

Albany did not say, ' The grapes are sour,' but he saw that this was the substance of her recoil. With her long body and large features she believed that the love of a man was out of her reach, out of her hope, and this belief disguised itself, for her comfort, as fastidiousness. Encouraged, the fastidiousness had become tough and prickly, like a cactus in the desert. He saw all of this in the haughty, unpowdered face and the severely disciplined hair. What he said was, " You have very good brains, my dear. That is obvious to me. And it is brains that determine your life, not parents."

" But I've no education. I'm not trained for anything. Mother took us away from school directly she was sure our father wouldn't hear of it. She meant us to pay for our keep, so that she could have all his money for herself, and she calls this ' keeping a little home over our heads.' That sickly slop may deceive Eddie but it doesn't deceive me."

" Is there anything in what you're doing here ? "

" Precisely nothing. Molly Prendergast, who runs the place, makes a good thing out of it by the simple process of taking a hundred-per-cent profit on everything. She prefers three-hundred-per-cent, of course, if she can get it. She's making a very pretty income, but what she's got she holds. I get a pound a week. God, the rapacity of women ! "

" She's married, is she ? "

" She's a widow."

" I suspected so. Widows have to fight for themselves, my dear."

" Maybe ; but it doesn't add to their attractiveness."

" I'm afraid you're not very happy."

" Happy ? Oh, I manage all right. But I do look sometimes at girls with fathers and unshadowed homes. You have a daughter, haven't you ? And she's beautiful."

" I'd like to think so."

" She is. I have seen her. It was silly of me, but, directly I heard about her, I went out of my way to walk past your house in the hope of seeing her. And I saw her at your gate, saying good-bye to a young man—someone she was calling Tom. Oh, yes, she's beautiful." As she spoke of this incident, gazing into his eyes, his pity swelled, because the words revealed so much. And her next words completed the revelation. " He's in love with her, I suppose. Ah well . . . good luck to them."

" Jean dear, is there anything I can do for you ? "

" I can't see that we are any responsibility of yours."

" Perhaps not ; but it may be that I just like you for yourself."

She dropped her eyes and unconsciously shook her head, as if perceiving no reason why he should like her.

" You must come and meet Susannah. And—and her mother," he added in a doubtful afterthought.

" They won't want to meet us."

" Oh, yes, they will. I'll go and arrange it at once. You and Susannah must be friends. You won't mind my telling them the truth, will you ? Come, you are my niece." And there among the antique bric-à-brac, some genuine, some false, he drew her to him, she resisting a little, and kissed her.

He hurried home. So hurries a child who has an exciting story to tell. He was looking forward to shocking Delia with these strange facts, to exhibiting his high-minded attitude towards them, and to quarrelling with her, should she decline to be as high-minded as he. Immediately he was in the house he called, ' Delia ! ' and ' Susannah ! ' and went into his study to wait for them. He took up his usual position before the fireplace, hands behind his back, impatient for the entry of his audience. Delia came from the dining-room and Susannah from her bedroom, scampering down the stairs.

It was a pleasure to walk to the window and back before beginning, " I have something of no small importance to tell you. Susannah, shut the door."

Delia looked scared. " Is it something serious ? "

" I confess it has come as a shock to me. I should have liked to keep it to myself, but—— "

" Albany, what on earth is it ? "

" Sit down. It is something we must discuss very seriously."

Delia sat herself on his desk chair, incompletely and uncomfortably. Susannah plunged into the comfort of the easy-chair at his side, drawing her legs up under her. He stood on the hearthrug, and the rug was his rostrum.

" It may interest you to know that we have a sister-in-law a few streets away."

" A sister-in-law ! "

" Even so ; and a nephew and a niece."

" A sister-in-law ! "   Susannah echoed her mother.

" Well, that perhaps is a courtesy title. But about the nephew and the niece there can be no question." And he told them the story of the house in Elber Square. He saw Delia's face darkening and her lips tightening. From this displeasing sight he turned to look at Susannah. *Her* face was brightening with amusement. Indeed, when he had finished the story, she said, " Oh, what fun ! "

And at once her mother rebuked her. " Fun ? It's not fun at all. How can you say such a thing ? It's a shocking business."

" Shocking or not," said Albany, " there it is. Safely there in Elber Square. The woman's a sloven and a wearisome chatter-box, the boy's an idiot, but there's something to the girl. For her sake we must be nice to them and welcome them."

" What ? Are you suggesting that I should receive this woman into my house ? "

" I certainly am."   He perceived with satisfaction, that the quarrel was about to start.   " For the girl's sake we will accept the mother and, God giving us strength and fortitude, Mr. Bakewell-Clapton too."

" But I'm not at all sure that I'm prepared to do any such thing."

" And why, pray ? "   This was as he desired : the quarrel was flaming up.

" Why ? Because she must be a completely immoral woman. I'm not accustomed to associating with such people. Do you forget that I am a churchwarden's daughter ? "

" All the more reason that you should act like a Christian."

" Rubbish. She must be a completely abandoned woman."

" Well, she's not going to be completely abandoned by me." A rejoinder which pleased him.   " There are the children. And one is my nephew, God help me, and the other my niece."

" They must accept the consequences of their parents' sin."

Here Susannah burst in.   " Oh, I don't see that, Mother."

" You know nothing about these things. The children are the fruit of sin."

" Yes, but not *their* sin, Mother."

" Exactly."   Albany in his enthusiasm for this support,

159

walked again to the window and back. " Susannah is perfectly right."

" I don't see why she should be made to associate with them. I can't see why your father has brought you into this at all ; I can't, really."

Albany disliked criticism of himself at any time, but never so hotly as when he was confident of his rightness and of his superiority to his critic. Now, stung like a bull by a dart, he raised his voice. " I did perfectly right in bringing her into it. I couldn't have been more right. I decided that she must show kindness to a girl less fortunate than herself, and I thank God that she has the sense to see that it's no fault of Jean's, or of that supreme idiot, Mr. Clapton, that their father sinned a quarter of a century ago. And they're not going to think that we think so. I bring my daughter up as a Christian. Good God in heaven, I'm more religious than any of you."

" Doesn't the Bible say the sins of the fathers shall be visited on the children ? The Bible is good enough for me."

" And it's not good enough for me when it says things like that."

" Oh ! " Delia submitted that this was blasphemy, and Albany was exasperated by the way she pronounced it blah's-phemy. " You set yourself up above God, do you ? "

" Certainly, if He's no better than that."

" Well, I never heard ! It's blah'sphemy. And you a parson. I don't know what's happened to you. You seem to have lost all your religion."

" Not at all. By no means. I'm more religious than ever I was."

" Well, I can't see that."

" More's the pity ; but, see it or not, you will call upon this woman."

" I will *not* call."

" Then you will invite her to this house, and her daughter, and—this is the extreme of Christianity—her idiot of a son."

" I shall do nothing of the sort."

" Then I shall. And, Susannah, you will go out of your way to be nice to this girl."

" I will do what I can, Daddy."

" Thank you, darling." His anger with Delia produced such a gratitude towards Susannah for her understanding and support that the tears came into his eyes. " I want you to be a friend to her."

" I will try to be, Daddy dear."

" If you like," said Delia, softening a little. " I will invite the children, but not the woman."

" No." He did not wish a quarrel which he was enjoying to lose one degree of its heat. Rather let him raise its temperature. " I'm not going to have her insulted like that. Bore and humbug and money-grabber she may be, but I'm not having her left at home like an untouchable. I'm not a good man, but I'm better than that. A little better than that, I hope." These, being pathetic words, even beautiful words, slightly increased the volume of tears in his eyes, and he dashed from the room lest the tears should be seen. His anger and his tears were infectious, so that Delia broke down too and dashed from the room. Susannah, discomfited by the sight of this double weeping, came third, and with a shrug of her shoulders and a spreading of her hands returned up stairs to her room.

CHAPTER ELEVEN

THE VISION *v.* THE HUNGER

DELIA and Susannah having gone from the study, Albany slipped back into it. He shut its door soundlessly and began to tread its carpet, eyes before his feet like a sheep browsing. Up and down, up and down, he was driven by a furnace within. " Incompatibility," he said. " Complete incompatibility." While he was a practising parson and living in a prison of pretences he had been obliged to hide this incompatibility even from himself, but now that he'd allowed his mind to walk out of its prison yards and into the open fields, he had to look straight at it and accept it, and be miserable. " There is no real understanding between us at all, and never can be. We are different minds. But thank God for Susannah. She is obviously my daughter and not Delia's. She is not hard and censorious ; she is gentle and kind, like me."

Always, sooner or later, a private misery urged him to get out of his house and under the sky, and now he felt a more than usually urgent desire to escape from it because it housed this incompatibility. To get out of it as one gets out of a hairshirt. The hall was empty : he slipped softly along it and out of the front door. Softly he shut the front door. Where to ?

To the Old Burial Ground where he could be melancholy among the children and the tombs ? " Yes," he said at first ; but then " No ", and turned towards the dead and ruined house in Willow Road. No better stage for melancholy than this haunted place of broken walls and breast-high weeds. And perhaps the fact that it had once been a proud and happy home drew his heavy heart towards it.

He came slowly into Willow Road and saw its broken roof above its jungle of trees. A pompous mansion with tall piers to its carriage gates, it had been the home of the most famous actor-manager of his day, and the most celebrated resident in the Wood ; and many a splendid soirée had he mounted here. But since his death, ten years ago, the estate owners had left it to decay and die too, in the hope of building, one day, a great block of flats there ; and now its carriage-way was a curving sweep of moss and thistles, nettles and docks ; and its avenue of sycamores had seeded among the stones, so that their saplings sprang from this brushwood of weeds. Ground ivy crept up the stone steps and over their balustrades ; fungi sprouted from the brickwork, where its stucco had fallen, and swelled like cysts from the trunks of the trees. The privets, once a trim hedge before the basement windows, were grown into tall trees, curtaining the ground-floor windows and brushing the sills of the first-floor. Litter, tossed over the garden walls, rotted in the green wilderness.

He stepped over the dwarf-walls and, parting entangled branches, brushed through the weeds and walked up the steps into the hall. Here, high above the staircase well, he saw the sky. He looked into the spacious reception room with its lofty windows. Most of its ceiling lay in chunks on the floor. Part of the floor had collapsed so that there was a crater of darkness in its midst. He stood in the doorway and imagined the great receptions in this once fine room, when lovely actresses stood talking to famous men, and voices and laughter and music beat against the walls and broke out into the night. So far as the sinking floors would allow it, he wandered about the house and was happy in his melancholy. Through an un-hinged and lolling back-door he went down some steps into the back garden. This, like the garden in front, had gone back to the wild. All lawns and beds lay drowned beneath a lake of weeds. In a far corner, beleaguered by the weeds, an old gipsy caravan stood under an ash-tree, its iron chimney lost among the pendent leaves. He had heard how this wandering gipsy home had come to rest in the actor's garden. The actor, charmed by it, had acquired it for his romantic drama, 'Romany Love', and when that spectacle took its last curtain, had brought it to his garden for his children's play. Those children had long grown up, and the caravan stayed beneath the ash-tree, discarded like some old omnibus worth nobody's effort to move.

And yet, not so long since, it had been the proud home, like this mansion itself, of the gipsy family whose name, 'Boswell', was still decipherable, in tarnished gold, on the door. All its panels were adorned with carvings of vine leaves and dragons and prancing horses, and all these carvings the departed gipsy hands had painted red and green and yellow and gold.

He brushed through the grasses and walked up its wooden steps. He looked in. Old broken toys still lay on its floor; torn children's books on its shelves; and bursting mattresses on its bunks, where once the actor's children had bedded down for the night in joy and terror.

Descending from the caravan, he stood in the garden. And looking up at the derelict house, he saw again the truth which he had seen among the tombs, that all things pass, and a man should do some good before he died, and love was the only thing to strive for between the first darkness and the last. He would like to do some good before he died. To do good and be remembered with love. Susannah had seemed his only hope among the tombs, but now there was Jean. He would like to be loved by Jean as well as Susannah. Or, rather, since he was in the mood to put unselfishness first, to be the benefactor, the one good thing, in that sad girl's life.

Such was his dream at first, but unfortunately the thought of Jean stirred the thought of Vick, and how Vick had lived to the full with his mistresses while there was time. And this reminded him of Delia's inability to satisfy his great hunger, and of Miss Maddow. And straightaway he was in the grip of a desire to go and visit Prudence Maddow and discuss with her the transitoriness of all things and his sadness—and, perhaps his hunger. And to kiss her. Let him, like Vick, live to the full while there was a chance of Life.

In a word, the fine vision of his spirit was defeated by the hunger in his body, and he walked out of the abandoned garden towards the secret by-way of Waterloo Close and Miss Haddow's sequestered home.

It was early evening as he walked up the steps of Miss

Maddow's house. The starched maid, opening to him, said, " Oh . . . yes, sir . . . I'm afraid the mistress is engaged," and stood hesitating, as if expecting him to retreat. But he said, " Could I wait ? " and she hesitated again and then asked him into the hall and, leaving him by the hat-stand, went into the drawing-room. From this room, as she opened the door, came the sound of a man's voice, and Prue's voice, laughing. The laughs stopped that the maid might speak. Then Prue's voice : " Show him into the dining-room. I won't be a minute."

Albany waited in the long brown dining-room. Through its walls he could hear those two voices, a murmuring which lasted for more than a minute and only closed with a high-pitched laugh from Prue and a low-pitched laugh from the man.

Now Prue came in to him, swishing and radiant in a pink silk tea-gown or peignoir (he didn't know what to call it) trimmed with an abundance of falling and swinging lace. It was an extremely *décolleté* gown, so that he saw the head of the avenue between her breasts, and his breath shortened with the desire to see more. The garment appeared to open down the front from neck to flounce : indeed, as she sank for a second to a chair, it opened and uncovered a black-stockinged knee. It was like a volume partly opened, and he longed to spread wide the covers and read.

" Oh, darling," she said, while quickly and most properly closing the volume, " you *are* a naughty boy. You must always let me know when you are coming. It's quite an accident that I am at home. If this man hadn't suddenly appeared, I should be on the way to my club. *Tsh !* " She dropped her voice and pointed mysteriously at the wall. " Do you know who it is ? My solicitor. My sweet lawyer-man. He's such a dear. He's trying to get back some money for me. He won't be long. Don't you worry. I'll get rid of him."

Since he must say something, he said the first thing that came to his lips. " Who are your lawyers ? "

So unlikely, so stupid, was the question that for a second she was unhandy with her answer.

" Who ? . . . Oh, they're Stephens and Clay, of Bedford Row. Yes. A very old firm. This is Mr. Stephens. He came quite unexpectedly—why, look, I'm still in my semi-negligée—but I just *had* to see him. It was important. Awful, isn't it ? Wouldn't matter if it'd been only you, but to receive one's lawyer like this ! Now you wait there like a good boy, and I'll—— "

" Oh, but if you're off to your club. I'll make myself scarce."

" No. Don't *you*. I'd much rather talk to you than go to that silly old club. I was only lonely. Stay here, and I'll quickly get rid of this incubus."

She raised a confidential and mischievous finger and with a swishing and rustling of silk sailed back into the drawing-room. Was there more laughter in that room ? Yes, but natural and friendly laughter, the put-him-at-his-ease laughter of a good hostess ; and soon the two of them came into the hall. Their voices were now quite loud. " Good-bye, Mr. Stephens. So kind of you to come in person." " Good-bye, Miss Maddow. Yes, I thought it safer to come in person."

Since the dining-room was a front room, he was able to stand at the window and see the solicitor depart. A slight man with sharp features and keen eyes, this Mr. Stephens looked like a lawyer, but hardly like a lawyer on business bent. No formal office attire his, but a sack suit of a cinnamon hue, a broad white stock, and bright brown shoes. As he went down the path he looked back and, without touching his brown derby hat, waved to his client with a blithe and most unlawyer-like gyrating of his hand.

He might look more like a jocund neighbour than a man of business, but Albany did not doubt Prue's word. He didn't doubt it because he didn't want to.

" Now, my dear," she said, coming into him and taking him by the hand. " Come out of this mortuary and into the drawing room. Come where it's warm and cosy." And she led him by the fingers into that delicate room of pastel greys and unstained woods. A rose-shaded oil lamp stood on a low table between settee and chaise-longue, and he saw within its thrown golden aureole a decanter of golden whisky, a silver-skirted siphon, and two empty tumblers of gleaming cut-glass. The lace-fringed holland blinds of the french windows were lowered, and the grey curtains partly drawn across them, but not enough to hide the twilight in the garden or mute the last singing of the birds.

" It's autumn now, and evening. Good. I never care for this room unless its autumn and evening. It's apt to be gloomy in the day time when the trees all round are full of leaves. I only really like it when I can light my lamps in it, here and there. Lovely amber light. Not gas ; oh, dear me, no ! In-candescent gas is a harsh, wicked light for us poor women who are no longer as young as we were. Let me give you a whisky. I gave the lawyer-man one. But first, aren't you going to give me a kiss ? "

He kissed her warmly, desire having been stirred by that glimpse within the gown ; but it was a small shock of disappointment that her breath should be tainted with whisky. However, as he put her away, he told himself that nothing was perfect in this world.

She swished around, finding a new glass from a cabinet and charging it for him ; then flung herself on to the chaise-longue, swinging her legs on to it and arranging the gown over them.

" You look sad," she said. " Anything happened to make you sad ? "

" Yes," he admitted. " Things have. I'm melancholy. I think I came to you for comfort."

" Now, how sweet of you ! But you must always let me know first. You might have missed me to-night. Now tell me all about it."

He spoke of his determination never to say a word against his wife, and so far from doing so, declared that she was a golden wife . . . in many ways. " Naturally we irritate each other sometimes but I don't go about abusing her to everyone I meet."

" And you're so right. I love you for your high principles. Men are so much more scrupulous than women. I hardly know a woman who ever stops complaining about her husband. You're so different. Now tell me all about it."

He was resolved, of course, not to reveal, or even to hint at, the truth about the Claptons, and he felt that this laudable restraint outweighed and paid for his dubious intention to talk about Delia. " I wanted Delia to help a little family in trouble—— "

" So like you ! "

" I can't tell you anything about them. That would be to reveal a confidence."

" Of course not. I wouldn't ask you to do any such thing. Do they live here ? "

" I'm not even going to tell you that. The mother is not, I'm afraid, technically a good woman. She's a woman who once—you know—— "

" Lived in sin," Prue supplied, taking the fence as surely as he shied back from it.

" Yes. And Delia declined to have anything to do with

her." Had he been looking at Prue, he might have observed a very hearty dislike of Delia in her face ; but she said only, " I think that's a pity, don't you ? "

" I most assuredly do. Of course I don't approve of these irregular unions, unless— " suddenly he remembered in whose room he sat and, furthermore, what he had in mind to do— " unless the circumstances are quite exceptional. There are times, of course, when something of the sort is justified."

" Exactly. Oh, you're so right. I believe so entirely with you that the only ideal is one man and one woman, each absolutely faithful to the other. My whole instinct lies that way. I'd never have consented to—— "

He waited for her words.

" —to my arrangement with Lord Clanbethry, if circumstances hadn't made anything else impossible. But . . . I loved him . . . I loved him." She opened helpless hands.

Albany nodded in sympathy, and wanted to get back to talk about himself. " When she refused to have this woman in her house, I got angry. I was rude. I can be rude sometimes," he added proudly.

" But I so understand ! "

" I raised my voice, I'm afraid. I don't like doing that, but I did—I was so angry. I really let go. I really let her hear from me. And I may say the whole family are coming to dinner. I was absolutely firm. I insisted upon it."

" Strong Man ! "

" No, it is not that ; it is just that I cannot stand intolerance and uncharitableness. With all my heart I believe in magnanimity and understanding. And Susannah, I'm glad to say agrees with me. She and I are as alike as two pins."

" And what did you do then ? "

" I walked out of the house, I was so miserable. I went and walked about the old ruined house in Willow Road."

Instantly she left her chaise-longue and put herself at his side on the sofa. " Oh, you poor dear ! " she said, laying a hand on his knee. " How unutterably sweet ! And then you came to me. I *am* touched."

He picked up her hand, still available on his knee. There was a silence while each gazed into the other's eyes, plumbing their depths for the possibilities lying there. " May I ? " he asked, drawing her towards him. Her silence was her answer, and she was in his arms, and his hand was gently pressing upon her breast. Passion mounting, he advanced his hand within the gown. "My dear, may I ?" he said most courteously. Her answer was so low, it was hardly a breath : " I want you to be happy." He began to be happy. He sought a deeper happiness. But now, for a second, she interrupted the happiness. " Wait," she said. " Just one second ; " and rose. The night was now dark outside, her lamps were bright, and the curtains were not fully drawn. She drew them all, so that the room became a privacy of dusk and gold ; she halted for a further second to shake their folds into place, and then came back to his arms.

This entracte, unforeseen and undesired, had somewhat chilled the passion, but she clearly expected him to resume, and he resumed. He adventured again, and, when he met any hindrance, she made straight his paths for him.

It is regrettable, but his chief emotion, as he went from that house, was pride. He had achieved a mistress. By his freedom from the old puritan fears, by his skills as a wooer, by his masculine quality and, presumably, his charm, he had won himself a woman—a woman of distinction and beauty. This had been Life. Life as nothing else was. Success in Life, Walter Pater had said, was to be present always at the focus, and there to burn with a gem-like flame . . . . A pity he could not hurry home and tell Delia of this success. Always before, because she was his wife, he had hurried home to her to report a triumph. Almost he could wish that she would hear of this success from other lips than his. It would teach her that if she did not approve of him, or desire him any more, there were others who did.

But if an exultation was his companion all the way home, a small shame also came limping beside and behind it, for the late professor of puritanism was still active within him, and did not easily rest.

CHAPTER TWELVE

THE DINNER PARTY

THEY stood in the dining room awaiting the entrance of the Claptons. The door-bell had just rung, and the feet of the Claptons were in the hall. Delia's expression, as they waited, was one of cold politeness, since she had been forced to receive them ; Albany's was one of vigilant anger, since he was contemplating a rare big quarrel at midnight, should this coldness offend his guests ; Susannah's was one of bright-eyed and impatient anticipation.

The maid announced them. Delia received Cornelia and Jean with sufficient affability ; as for Susannah, she was almost effusive. Albany's welcome was the more cordial because he perceived that the two women were dressed in their best for this occasion, and his pity was stirred. Cornelia was indeed overdressed : her bodice had a low neck-line behind which her bosom rose like an ocean swell ; her face was overpowdered so that her nose was white as summer dust and the crinkles of her skin held the chalky powder in cakes and threads. Jean, her tall body in a neat but obviously cheap party gown, had scorned, as usual, the embellishment of powder, but her hair was carefully, if severely, dressed, and her eyes were at once remote and haughty and sad. She tried, however, to smile graciously at her hostess and Susannah ; and her smile for Albany was like that of an old friend.

But the entry of the two women was quite overshadowed by the approach of Eddie at their tail. Having a high opinion of his social gifts he came forward with the right hand uplifted high, ready to swing down on each hand in turn and wring it genially, while pressing it painfully. " Ah, Auntie Delia," he said, " I am most happy to make your acquaintance. Aha, my dear cousin Susannah, this is indeed a pleasure. Well met. Ah, Uncle, we meet again. This is splendid." And he even put the genial hand on his uncle's back.

Delia and Susannah watched him with amazement ; Susannah with amusement also, and a trembling mouth.

They all sat down, Eddie on a square stool, with his hands spread over his knees and the detachable cuff's drooping over his hands. He leaned forward, ready to display his gift for social conversation. And soon the room was but a theatre for his long dissertations, while Delia and Susannah listened with fascinated astonishment. Jean turned her eyes away in palpable distaste, and Cornelia watched with a mother's pride.

" You like living in the Great Metropolis ? " he asked Delia, and, since her answer was no more than " In some ways, yes," he expatiated at length upon the comparative advantages of Life in the Capital and the Rural Scene, before turning towards Susannah, since he knew he must share out the advantage of his talk among all the ladies. " I hear one of your favourite pastimes, Susannah, is watching our National Game. I'm afraid I have but little opportunity for such recreation myself because I have to devote myself to my theological studies or to practising the exacting art of a tutor—— "

" A tutor ? " exclaimed Delia, for Albany had forgotten to mention that Mr. Bakewell-Clapton was a Classical Tutor.

" Yes," explained Cornelia, in the way women have of explaining their children, or their husbands, in their presence. " He teaches Latin to Mrs. Parkhurst's little boy who's taking his Common Entrance next term, but I'm afraid he only earns a very little money that way." And instantly Albany wondered, with apprehension, if she was making haste to minimize the family income with a view to seeking a subsidy later.

But even while she spoke, and while others turned to her voice, Eddie was continuing his disquisition on cricket and on subjects suggested thereby. " No," he was saying, " I cannot pretend to any great skill in the Field of Athletics. Circumstances compelled me to leave my school at a comparatively early age and, in any case, the manly and invigorating game of cricket played no great part in the curriculum of that little academy—— "

" It was quite a good school," put in Cornelia.

" *Your* education, my dear Susannah," pursued Eddie, not having heard his mother, " has long been completed, I suppose. The Higher Education is hardly a prerequisite for Fair Ladies like you, haw, haw . . . haw ; haw, haw . . . haw."

Susannah's head jerked back, so unprepared was she for this laugh like a broken-winded horse-cough.

Not noticing this spasm of withdrawal, incapable of suspecting any criticism of his entertaining talk, he treated the company to an ample consideration of the requisites of the Fair Sex, while Susannah, who was sitting next to her father, whispered, " This creature is a joy, Daddy."

He had now turned to Delia. " And what, Auntie," he inquired, " are your impressions of our Wood of the Baptist ? "

" Of what ? " demanded the hostess, perplexed.

" Eddie *will* have his joke," explained his mother. " He always calls it that."

" We must be of all the assistance we can to you in our little Wood. We are antique residents now," he said, and so justified his reputation as a cultured jester. There followed a lecture on the Knights of St. John of Jerusalem, their priory at

Kilburn, their ownership of the ancient greenwood, the St. John Ambulance Brigade, and subjects adjacent to these—while Albany went round with the sherry to sustain the listeners.

The recital was still in progress when the maid announced dinner, so Eddie continued it as they all walked out of the drawing-room and across the passage to the dining-room. He rattled on with the recital in their rear, like a kettle-drum thrumming behind a march. Abnormally short-sighted, he trod on the cat in the passage and exclaimed, " Oh, whatever's that ? " as the creature screamed and fled.

Delia still expected Grace to be said before meals, and Albany, never wanting to disappoint her unnecessarily, always said it, the family standing. This evening Cornelia and Jean perceived what was toward and remained standing ; but not Eddie, who sat down and unfolded his napkin while his host mumbled, ' *Benedictus benedicat, per* . . ", and then, observing that he ought to be standing, rose and stood erect, just as all the others sat down. He stood thus for a second, with the napkin dependant, till he saw through his thick lenses that he alone was up on high, whereupon he emitted the horse-laugh and lowered himself to a level with the rest.

Wines and food that night were good, for Albany had insisted on a fine entertainment, partly because he sincerely wanted to give these unfortunates a good time, partly because he wanted to exasperate Delia, and partly because, new to luxury, he liked to display it. The oval table shone with a damask cloth, cut glass, and silver ; and the soup was followed by a halibut paysanne, cutlets with pink frills and green peas, and an omelette soufflé with vanilla sauce. The wine was a Sauterne, Albany deciding that these uneducated palates would prefer a sweet wine.

All through the courses Eddie talked, sometimes leaving the food to get cold on his plate, while he rambled over a topic. He paid tribute to This Festive Board ; he discussed the chances of himself and Jean getting screwed on this excellent wine, since the Clapton Family was more accustomed to the Cup that Cheered but not Inebriated ; he ranged wide over his prospects after his ordination next year and dilated upon his hopes of having his revered mother to live with him at the scene of his labours, " till such time as he took unto himself a wife and kicked her out, haw, haw, haw ; haw, haw."

He had an accident with the main dish. After helping himself to a cutlet, peas and potatoes, he rose to pick up his table napkin, but unluckily, on sitting down again, his protruding and slightly batrachian belly caught the rim of his plate and tilted it upward so that some of its contents slid on to his waistcoat and some on to the floor. He exclaimed, " Oh dear ! *There* now ! " Cornelia said, " Oh dear, Eddie, oh dear ! " Jean went white with her private disgust ; and Susannah smothered with her fingers a laugh which had emerged as a scream. Albany said, " It's nothing, it's nothing " ; Delia assumed command of the cleansing and scavenging operations, and Eddie, standing above the disaster, apologized *in extenso*. He called it a distressing contretemps. The apologies continued, in serial contributions, for the next nine minutes. One instalment he flavoured with a joke which he felt to be worthy of his reputation. " *Re* that little contretemps of mine," he said, " it was a pity, wasn't it, that such excellent comestibles, which had been designed for the Inner Man, should have been applied to the Outer Man, haw, haw, haw . . . haw . . . haw."

When the meal was finished and all had risen, the ladies walked to the door, and he hurried behind them, conveying his weighty thanks to Delia and to Susannah for this Superb Repast, but Albany beckoned him back to the port decanter, that the ladies might retire unpursued ; whereupon Eddie turned about, said " Oh, yes, of course," and apologized twice and thrice for his mistake.

Albany, realizing that he must now endure his nephew alone for ten minutes or more, filled up his glass for him, lit a cigar for himself, and prepared to drown in a flood of boredom.

But the boredom was even more asphyxiating than he had feared. He craved to escape from it, and after only five minutes of it, he resolved to unload it on to Delia—though perceiving that this was unfair, since it was against her will that the Claptons were there. He rose from his chair, steered the young man still talking into the drawing-room, and there, to his surprise, found Delia and Cornelia gossiping together as fluently, and apparently with as much enjoyment, as two women sharing a wash-tub. They were engrossed in each other, sisters under the skin : Jean and Susannah, their hands asleep on their laps were left to sit in silence on the rims of their chairs and on the edges of the chatter. Albany, as he entered, had no doubt that the two women had been gabbling thus happily on a variety of subjects ever since they left the dining-room, but just now they were discussing Cornelia's operation and her doctors, the bad ones and the good, and the miracle which her surgeon, that delightful man and wonder-worker, had undoubtedly achieved.

"Oh lord, lord, lord," he thought, realizing what he must endure for a while longer. He took a chair, listened behind his cigar smoke, and tried to be charming when one or other of the ladies turned a remark towards him. But suddenly all possibility of further charm went from him. Eddie was now in competition with the two women, and since neither Delia nor Cornelia could compete with him in sustained verbosity, and his mother in any case always stopped to listen to him with pride, he soon had possession of the floor and was dilating on his plans for the evangelization of a London parish as soon as he was ordained. Albany withdrew from listening, contenting himself with a covert wink at Susannah and a sidelong grin for Jean. But his attention sprang alert when Cornelia took advantage of a momentary pause in Eddie's recital to comment, with her head laid to one side in appreciation, and her voice given its most sentimental tone, "To think that Eddie will be a clergyman in a few months' time! And isn't it rather wonderful to think that he, my poor old Eddie, will be taking up the burden which Albany laid down?"

"The idiot woman!" Albany exclaimed within himself. "The intolerable syrupy, sentimental fool!" That imbecile, that figure of fun, to be compared with *him*! To be regarded as capable of taking up a burden which *he* had laid down!

From that moment his silence was tight-lipped and complete. He played no further part in the conversazione except to undo the lips and give a hypocritical smile to Cornelia when, every now and then, she addressed a remark to his face. He burned within; the burning gradually sank into a smouldering; he saw his study in his mind's eye; and some ten minutes later, when no one was heeding him, he slipped away to the study and gave himself to his chair, his footstool, and his novel, leaving the Claptons to Delia.

And there most comfortably he remained, absorbed in a novel of Rider Haggard's, till Susannah, having grasped at length the nature of his desertion, rushed in upon him, saw him sitting there, and stammered, "Oh, the foul wickedness of it! Come back at once." But he only replied with a grin, and waved her back to her hospitable duties. "But this is gross!" she complained; and went. It was fully an hour before she returned, saying, "They're going, Daddy, praise be to Heaven. For God's sake, come. They're to be found in the hall." Since this was good news, he went out to them and said, charmingly, "Oh, must you go? Must you really?"

Eddie answered for them all. Yes, they really must, he said, and lifted high his palm to slap it down on each hand, while proffering to them all his continuous thanks for a most delightful experience and his renewed apologies for that little contretemps. " Reverting to my little contretemps, Uncle," he began ; and reverted to it at length, while Albany eased him towards the door. Out in the garden he spoke of their Beauty Sleep and the Tasks of To-morrow and went through the gate, thanking Albany first, and then Susannah, for a delightful experience. On the pavement, in the light of a gas lamp, there was some danger of his pressing their hands again—his palm had risen—but they evaded its incidence by quickly offering him their most friendly smiles and turning back to the house.

CHAPTER THIRTEEN

AN AUTUMN AND A WINTER

THAT Susannah and Tom were much in love with each other was now accepted by Delia and Albany : by Delia as a most displeasing fact which, it was to be hoped, would pass, and by Albany as a pretty affair which might or might not ripen into something more serious. Delia wouldn't hear of any engagement between them, and Albany, without telling Tom of Delia's hostility, explained to the boy, one day in his study, that he couldn't think of sanctioning an engagement unless Tom got himself a profession and adequate means. " Oh, yes, sir ; I quite see that," said Tom. " Naturally." Albany enjoyed this interview in the closed room because he felt a pride in being the protective father and a pleasure in the careful and kindly way he was dealing with the lad. Nothing heavy or pompous about his handling of the situation ! Rather a sympathetic and smiling attitude, as of one who could remember what it was like to be young. His words had surely been as well chosen as they were fluent, and it was plain that this boy respected and admired him. Indeed Tom's liking for him was as manifest as his dislike of Delia ; and this was pleasing.

Tom had assured him that he really would set about preparing himself for some profession. And he did ascend forthwith into a high tower of resolve. He was going to work really hard, he told Susannah, and not only for her sake, but for the old man, his father's, sake, whom he didn't want to disappoint again. It was a sincere resolution, made with all the gravity and fervour of twenty-one.

But what was he going to work *at* ?

Yes, what ? What was the profession to be ? This he could not specify at once. The tower was there ; his desk and his chair were there ; the paper and the pen were there ; but not yet the books, because he did not know what they should be. Should he read for the Civil Service Examination ? No, this awoke no answering enthusiasm in him. Should he study to be a Chartered Accountant. Good God, no ! The Church ? No, he was not good enough ; not a good man like Susannah's father.

Well, what, then ?

At Cambridge he had been reading Law before he was requested by the authorities to depart from their kingdom and escorted, so to say, by his fellows to the frontier ; and in those years he had ploughed a little way into books on Roman Law, Constitutional Law, and Jurisprudence at intervals between playing cricket or playing football or picnicking on the river ; and so it seemed plain that his best course now was to pursue this track and qualify as a barrister. Not a solicitor ; that was a stuffy job ; both Susannah and Tom were of opinion that a solicitor's was a stuffy job. A barrister, then. Yes, a barrister every time. Susannah was enthusiastic about Tom's being a barrister ; so much so that Tom couldn't help feeling her enthusiasm was a little facile : *she* wouldn't have to toil, with aching back and bursting brow, through massive works on Torts, Criminal Law, Equity, Contract, Legal History, and Conveyancing.

But he kissed her for the enthusiasm, even though it was facile, and went up into his high tower. He went up there to read, as he had gone to the wicket to bowl—in order to win Susannah for his wife and her father for his sponsor.

He furnished his tower (by which we understand his top-floor sitting-room) with all the best authors on the tedious subjects listed above ; he drew up a schedule of Working Hours—' 9.0 to 1.0, 5.0 to 7.0, 8.30 to 10 ' ; he bought two new meerschaum pipes to sustain him through laborious days ; he swept from his mantelshelf the picture-postcards of lovely actresses ; and this was a symbolical action—he was not clear of what ; he left Susannah's picture alone on the mantelshelf ; which though obvious in its symbolism was not perhaps very sensible, since her face might distract him at times from Clerk and Lindsell on Torts or Phipson on Evidence and Procedure ; and he sat down at his desk, thinking, " I'm really going to do this for her sake. And for the old boy's sake." Two of the first books he read, and the only two he read with any interest were two he had seen advertised in *T.P.'s Weekly:* ' The Brain and How to Use it ' and ' How to Pass Exams.'

All this he did with the great earnestness of youth.

But he found it difficult indeed to hold himself down on this important chair ; difficult to keep his eyes on the outspread volume and the notebook. A mounting dislike of the book acted as a brake on the wheels of his brain, and with a sigh he would glance at his watch in the hope that it was one o'clock, and learn that it was only eleven. He would force his eyes back on to the heavy-laden page, but after a little more study, any excuse—an interesting sound in the street, the need to buy some more tobacco, the desire for a red pencil with which to underline a serious passage—would raise him from the chair and give him a rest from it for a while.

He was quite resolved to behave properly and do this thing but—he was only twenty-one, and the endless avenue of Time seemed to extend before him.

Autumn marched through the Wood, turning the house-creepers crimson, snatching the rust-brown leaves from the trees, drawing the blue bonfire smoke over the garden walls, chilling the cheek as a man came forth to meet the day, and strewing the pavements with the shadows of emptied branches and the dapple of weak filtered sunlight. Winter came marching behind it, out of the grey mists, past the paraded trees which were blackened skeletons now and the wet gardens where only the ivy and the privets, the hollies and the conifers, were still green. Along roads hard with frost, or pavements greased by yesterday's fog, Winter marched by, its breath a cold blade and its only gift to the gardens the silver rime upon the grass. And in these pale winter days, perhaps because of the emptiness of the trees and the silence of the gardens and the stillness of the vast area of Lord's, the sound of London breathing and brooding was heard more clearly by people standing at their windows—say by Albany pensive in his study or Tom relaxing in his upper room. Wellington Road and Abbey Road, those wide highways, murmured all day with the hiss of wheels and the crepitation of hooves, and the Underground Railway rang and sighed and belched from the chasms where its tracks were open to the sky.

Albany had some happy times that winter, acting the kind and generous uncle to Jean Clapton. He took her to ' little dinners', sometimes quite costly meals, at Romany's and the Café Royal and the Cavour, where the stars of music hall and theatre might often be seen. He took her to theatres where he delighted to place her in the stalls and see her pleasure in sitting, for once, in a fashionable and expensive part of the house. He also gave her little presents now and again, saying when she told him he shouldn't, " Nonsense, Jeanie my dear; it's the privilege of an old uncle." In this business of being kind to Jean he was the happier because it seemed to partake of self-conquest rather than of self-seeking. It would have been more pleasantly exciting, doubtless, to have at his side the niece of his dreams, a girl of beauty and great charm, but since this factor was not present, then surely his generosity had a quality of unselfishness and he could believe that he was more religious now than he ever was.

Not but what he had a very real affection for Jean, and this, not only because a man will always feel a liking for someone to whom he has done a kindness, but because his affection was deepened by pity. It was clear to him that her mother, despite all that talk about the children being her ' sacred trust', had never released a penny to help Jean, but only to help her precious Eddie—and not too many pennies for him. Cornelia, just as he had foreseen, was now pestering him with long, closely-written, illegible letters, describing her Eddie's progress and hinting at his pecuniary needs. All of these he tossed into the waste-paper basket—but not unread, both because he found them interesting, and because he was fascinated by his detestation of her begging. He would have been disappointed if he had not discovered, somewhere in a letter, the hint that he should forward a remittance to a straitened home. It was a relief to come upon the hint, and then a sensuous pleasure to throw the letter into the waste-paper basket. She never seemed to notice that her last letter was unanswered, for she would write equally fully a few days later, and equally affably.

His companionship with Jean waxed the brighter for this hatred of Cornelia, because Jean herself had a most discerning contempt for the woman. Sometimes it plunged him into meditation, and set him smoothing his long moustaches, to think that he was so much more at ease talking with this girl (because she admired him) than with any man in club or pub.

Jean had consented to his telling the truth of their relationship to old Bait, ' my dearest friend, and one from whom I like to have no secrets,' and Bait had surprised him, when he unfolded the tale in Bait's dusty room, by proclaiming that, good God, he knew Jeanie Clapton well by sight and that his wife was on cackling terms with Cornelia Clapton because both women, being incapable of an intelligent scepticism, were persistent and tireless attendants at St. John's Wood Chapel, that preaching-box round the corner. And now this poor girl, afflicted with a mother like that, turned out to be Albany's niece ! Good Lord ! Albany had arrived only just in time, Bait suggested, because, unless he was much mistaken, the girl was in some danger of turning into a witch. There was every reason why she should do this.

" What ? At twenty-five ? Oh, no, Bait. That's impossible."

" Pshaw ! Stuff and nonsense. Don't you believe it. There've been plenty of girl witches. The transmogrification can begin at any age. Mind you, I'm not saying she's aware of what's going on inside her. The process, as I've told you, is often unconscious. Nor am I saying that she will ultimately make a compact with the Devil. There is, as it were, a novitiate. But that's not to say, mark you, that, whether she wants it or not, she won't have the evil eye. In truth, I'm not sure that she hasn't the beginnings of that interesting gift already. She's thrown me a most extraordinary look sometimes as she's passed me on the pavement. She hasn't *meant* any harm, of course, but a young woman with the evil eye can work her mischief without knowing it."

" My poor dear Jean ! No, Bait, I won't have it. I won't allow it."

" But she has all the early symptoms, my dear chap : remote eyes, a possessed look, increasingly masculine features, and that ruddy, unpowdered skin, slightly weatherbeaten, as if she'd been out all night. And she has pets, hasn't she ? "

" She has a cat, and a rabbit in a pen."

" Ah, that's bad. Undoubtedly, unless something's done, they'll turn into her familiars. You've only to look at cats to see their diablerie. And all rodents are suspicious. Then there's all that antique bric-à-brac in which she spends her time. I know the shop well, all horse bells and horse brasses and bits and bridles, and an old Welsh harp—mark that !—and mouldering collections of butterflies and bettles. It's all very symptomatic."

" But she doesn't want to be there. It's against her will that she's there."

' Exactly. Against her will. The matter is not within her consciousness or control. But if there's a hidden conflict the likely issue is that she'll turn into a white witch."

" And what, pray, is a white witch ? "

" A kindly and well-disposed witch who seeks to heal rather than to hurt, whereas black witches are eager only for mischief. They seek their own power, not your good. In a word, they take the Left Hand Path."

" I see."

" Yes, and then they begin making their evil brews from a most shocking pharmacopœia. You should study it. It makes excellent reading. No, on the whole, I think your Jeanie will be a white witch. If ever she becomes the real substantial thing you should have opportunities of learning it."

" How ? And when, if you please ? "

" Oh, by some mark on her left shoulder, when she wears a low dress ; say the imprint of a claw or the footprint of a hare. Or by some hint under her bodice of the supernumerary breasts wherewith she gives suck to her familiars. And if you want to be quite sure, take her to the seaside and throw her into the water. If she floats without any effort, that's a certain proof. All the fathers are agreed on this."

Albany nodded, as one who understood this instruction ; and Bait, rising to walk up and down with his spectacles dangling from his fingers, turned to another consideration.

" There's another point to consider, old man : her name, Jean. With a name like that she should have a predisposition towards diabolism. No woman called Jean or Joan or Janet should ever be trusted. They may secede to the Devil at any time—— "

" But confound it, Bait, old boy," Albany interrupted, " Jean was our mother's name, and it's my Susannah's name too—her second name."

" It is ? Oh dear. That's bad. That's worrying. The seeds must be in Susannah too. Get her married as quickly as possible. Jean in union with Grahame is a conjunction fraught with danger. Grahame is Scotch, you see. Hazardous ; very."

" But Jean Clapton's real name is Scotch too."

" How so ? How do you mean ? Clapton ? There's nothing wrong with Clapton."

"But that isn't really her name at all. Her legal name, I take it, is McVye. Cornelia was a McVye."

"McVye ! McVye ? But this is terrible. Jeanie McVye Oh, worse and worse. My dear chap, anything may happen. Witchcraft and the evil eye are as native to Scotland as the heather and the grouse. You knew that, didn't you ? It's probably something to do with the peat in the soil and the mist in the glens. Whether or not there are any witches left in England, everyone knows there are large covens of them in the highlands." Bait paused with never a smile in his eyes. He swung the spectacles between his fingers ; then tapped them on his teeth like a man in deep rumination. " I'm wondering," he said, " whether we should be altogether happy about the way she goes about doing good works. It's all rather strange. She's for ever, so my dear wife tells me, taking calf's foot jelly to the sick, and flowers to the bereaved, and church magazines to the parishioners ; she shops for the bedridden and reads with the blind and, when there are no other objects for her ministrations, takes foods to the birds in the Park. She goes quite often to church ; she is a frequent attendant at Holy Communion ; and yet she entirely refuses to take the Sacrament. What do you make of that ? I must say that, what with one thing and another, I can't help feeling that in good King James's days she'd have been apprehended and tried. And, I fear, *convicta et combusta*."

" I can make everything of it. She has talked it all over with me. Like me, she can't accept the orthodox dogmas, but she has a feeling for religion, and a longing for it, and she gets something—something mystical—out of the church services."

" Mystical, ha ! " Bait found this supicious.

" She just goes to church blindly and worships her unknown God, but she resolutely refuses to be a humbug. I honour her attitude. She's extraordinarily like me, in some ways."

" Yes, but I should take care . . . take care. All these suppressed, frustrated, semi-masculine virgins will turn, sooner or later, to someone who wants them, either to Christ or the Devil. You say she doesn't believe in the Church's dogmas— Well, you perceive the danger. Get her married before she leases herself to the Devil. The usual lease," he added, as a good lawyer should, swinging his glasses, " is seven years, with the option of renewal."

CHAPTER FOURTEEN

THE COMFORTERS

THAT winter, on a day late in February, Delia died. They found her, at nine in the morning, slumped and unconscious in a fireside chair ; they got her to her bed where she lay unconscious for three hours, and then died. The doctor spoke of cerebral embolism and chronic myocarditis.

Albany was shaken at first and wept as he looked down upon her. But even as he wept the little dungeoned seer within him came up and told him that he was pleased with the tears because they were genuine, and—what was worse—pleased that Susannah should be noting them. She comforted him with a kiss (which increased the tears) and he patted her back gratefully, as a man does who is in no condition to speak.

He retired into his study. And here he was not lightly shocked, he was greatly shocked, that the emotion within him which was bidding fair to become the strongest was pleasure. No one must ever know of this most improper condition, but he couldn't deny, however he might discommend, a feeling of exultation in a new freedom. It was an exultation similar to—and in this case even more deplorable than—that which he had felt on learning of Vick's death. Now, suddenly, he was liberated from the hard eyes of a puritan wife. And liberated from those puritan remnants in his own conscience. The comfort which he had been receiving from Prudence Maddow would now be immoral no more. Or, at any rate, much less immoral. That situation was greatly improved. And what possibilities of marriage with beauty, and perhaps with more youthful beauty than Prue's, did not now——

But let him not consider these possibilities as yet. It was not right. Not becoming. He would *not* think of them.

But if he succeeded in suppressing these thoughts, he could not overcome a certain relish for the drama of this event and for the pathos and importance with which it invested him. He tried to overcome it ; he strove to feel some more grief ; but it was no good. In less than twenty-four hours, by nine the next morning, he was a thoroughly happy man because he was interested and excited, and that is to be happy. He went out into the streets in the hope of meeting people whom he might inform of the sudden and grievous event. He felt that they ought to know, and he went forth into Circus Road and Grove End Road to put himself before them and receive their sympathy. February it might be, but the sway of winter was failing: the streets were full of sunlight and the breeze was warm with the first visiting breath of spring. Some of the birds were trying out their voices, like a few in an orchestra trying a stave or two on their flutes and piccolos.

Albany, hardly less, had the beginnings of a spring-song in his heart. He met several acquaintances and entertained them with his sad news; and their copious and moving sympathy (which more than once moistened his eyes) showed him the proper and picturesque part he must play in the next few days. He must withdraw into his study and stay there in solitude, like a man who has grief for a companion. So he strolled home and went into the dining-room to make a selection from the novels in the book-case. He cast an eye over his shoulder as he spread wide its glass doors. He felt guilty all the while they stood open. Quickly: which books should he take? Mrs. Humphry Ward, Hall Caine, Stanley Weyman, Marion Crawford—no, all these were too heavy, too serious; he didn't feel in the mood for these. He wanted something light. Or something exciting. He took in the end Nat Gould's 'The Pace that Kills,' Guy Boothby's 'Dr. Nikola,' and two school stories which he had always liked and felt he could read again, Dean Farrar's 'St. Winifred's' and Vachel's 'The Hill' (a most moving tale). Four books were quite a pile, and he waited till his route was clear before conveying them to his study. There he shut the door, built up the fire, and made himself very comfortable in his easy chair with the cushion well plumped behind his head and his long legs extended on to the footstool. He began on the adventures of Dr. Nikola, and when once the maid came into the room he lowered the book to his lap, with its spine and title to the wall.

At about eleven o'clock the maid announced, in a subdued voice to match her master's sorrow, "Commander Ludlow, sir. Will you see him?"

"Yes . . . yes . . ." he consented, as with sadness, though in fact he was well pleased to have a visitor with whom he could talk of the dramatic event. "I must see anyone who comes, Collins. It's kind of them to come, and we mustn't hurt their feelings. So show them in."

Ludlow came in, a very different Ludlow from the customary

182

jovial product of the late Queen's quarter-decks : his manner was adapted to a friend's desolation, not jovial but solemn, not noisy, but quiet. His eyes were moist and he came forward quietly, with a hand outstretched.

" I've just heard, old chap. I just came to offer my sympathy, my very great sympathy." The breath on which this sympathy travelled was flushed with whisky, and Albany guessed that he had strengthened himself, at home, or in a saloon, for this exacting work of condolence. To judge from the humidity of his eyes, he was perhaps a little drunk. " I feel for you, old son. I do, I do."

" It's very kind of you," said Albany in the proper voice of the bereaved.

" For a long time I couldn't decide whether to butt in upon your grief or not. I spent an hour debating the question with myself. But I decided that you could always turn me from your door, or kick me out of your room as soon as you'd had enough of me. We're good enough friends for that. We're good friends and kick me out, kick me out, if you want to."

" I'm very glad to see you. In times like these we need all the sympathy we can get."

" I know. It must be a terrific shock, old man."

" It is . . . it is . . . Naturally."

" You look pretty awful. Don't let it get you down. Don't let it sink you. If Life's taught me anything, it is that it's amazing what one can suffer and still keep afloat, with one's engines running." The Commander sat down uncomfortably, holding his hat between his knees. " I can imagine what you feel. You know, by the way, that my wife died a few months ago ? "

" No ? Is that so ? " Albany felt, and was properly ashamed to feel, a faint disappointment at having a rival in this field.

" Yes, but don't be upset about it. I gave praise to Heaven. It's very different with you. You were fortunate in your lady."

" I was indeed. In many ways."

" She loved you as a man longs to be loved. She used to say to me sometimes, ' Nobody could have a better husband than Albany. He's so gentle and kind. I think myself a very lucky woman.' Yes, she would say things like that. I'm not lying. I assure you I'm not."

Albany wondered. These didn't sound like Delia's words, and he knew that the Commander was always ready with comforting lies if he felt that a sufferer would be helped by them.

"Yes, I thought you'd like to know she said things like that. Well, now, is there anything I can do to help? Anything, say, on the business side? You can't be in any mood to attend to that. I'd cheerfully—— "

"No, it's kind of you, but the undertaker's seeing to all that. They're wonderful these undertakers; they just take everything off our hands and leave us to . . . to our grief."

"Well, I don't know what I can say except, Don't lose heart. One gets used to it."

"I suppose one does. Time heals all. Can I get you a drink?"

"No . . . no, no . . . don't you trouble about me . . . well, yes, perhaps."

Albany had long kept a decanter of whisky in the cupboard beneath his book-shelves. He prepared a drink for his visitor and carried one for himself to the mantelpiece.

The Commander sipped. "Soon things will interest you again," he promised. "Have no doubt about it. And you can be sure you'll meet your lady again. I'm not a saintly type, as you know, but I'm religious in my way. All sailors are. I've often taken Divine Service on board, and I've always taught my men, in every ship I've been in, to say their prayers, damn them. I go sometimes to old Colonel Budlier's church— at least, I've put in there once or twice. And I tell you, old fellow: I firmly believe in the Hereafter. I look forward to meeting my dear old mother again. And—between ourselves —a certain little lady who was all the world to me for a while, a few years ago. She gave me all, bless her—everything— though I could do nothing for her, tied up to that infernal woman. In the end she died. Died when she was under forty. I have suffered too, old boy, but I take comfort in the thought that we shall find again those we loved." He was now in tears.

He swallowed the rest of his drink in one draught, and rose. "I will go now. You don't want me hanging around at a time like this. You want to be alone. I know, I know." He stretched out both hands, and the gesture so touched Albany that he, in his turn, had to gulp back some tears. They shook hands vigorously with wet eyes.

Albany walked with him as far as the gate and saw him turn, not towards his home, but in the opposite direction.

Probably he was going towards the nearest public house, where he could undergo repairs after an agitating encounter.

His comforter having departed, in tears, Albany was able to feel again that exultation in his freedom. It was an exultation of which he so little approved that he sought to escape from it in the adventures of Dr. Nikola. But after a few pages his eyes wearied and his interest waned. The sun was shining into the room, inviting him to come out and enjoy the sweet freshness of this premature spring day. But, having begun this picture of himself as a man shut in with his sorrow, he did not wish to mar it. He had an artist's sense of perfection. So he picked up the novel again.

Soon after one the maid came in and asked if she could bring him in a little luncheon. Here in his study. On a tray.

" Eh ? What ? " he said, as if luncheon was the last thing he had in mind, though he'd been quite ready for it for some time. " Well, yes, Collins. Just a little."

" I see, sir. Just a little something nice." And she withdrew softly, sympathetically, while he was left hoping that she wouldn't interpret the word ' little ' too seriously, too pityingly.

When she brought in the tray, he looked at it with some anxiety and some disappointment. The portions on the plates were small—as for an invalid.

He ate everything with a good appetite, reading his novel the while, and, on emptying the plates, could have eaten much more, but he didn't like to ring and disappoint the maid.

When she had taken the tray away he considered the possibility of relieving this tedious incarceration by a game of Patience, but while he was wondering whether this would be practicable without a locking of the door, the maid returned and said, " Mr. Bait, sir."

It was a relief more welcome than any game of Patience. " Oh, come in, Bait, old boy," he said. " There's no one I'd rather see. Sit down, sit down." And he felt sentimental about old Bait, his dearest friend, who would be with him—faithfully at his side—in any sorrow. He even looked forward to the day when he could be at Bait's side in the loss of his wife. Bait in his best chair, he placed himself before the fire, with his hands in his pockets, his coat-tails over his arm, and his large buttocks towards the comfortable blaze.

Bait began by saying much that Ludlow had said : that Albany must send him away if he'd rather be alone ; that he

185

realized what Albany must be feeling ; and that no words of comfort from him could be of much use.

" Oh, but they are," Albany assured him. " They are, and we need them at a time like this."

" There *is* something I feel I should like to say."

" Please say it."

Bait looked away, drawing up his thin nostrils as if sniffing up the strength to say it. He took a cigarette from the box which Albany handed him, and lit it with nervous, quivering fingers. " As you know," he began, " I'm sceptical about many things, but I do believe—yes, quite firmly, I think—in survival after death. I would go so far as to say I've had proof of it."

" Proof ? " Albany stared.

" It seems like proof. Of late I've been doing considerable research into Spiritualism and—to put it mildly—I've been staggered by some of the phenomena. I have been attending the séances of Mrs. Grant, the trance medium. I've even had some private sittings with her."

" But, Bait, old boy, you never told me any of this."

" No. No, no. Why should I ? To tell the truth, I doubted if you, as a clergyman, would approve. I haven't even told my wife. And, on the whole, I'd as soon you didn't mention it to her."

" Of course not, old man." Albany saw that Bait, nearly seventy though he might be, and a lean old cynic, could still feel about these visits to the séance room as a schoolboy about his sly and reticent visits to a larder.

" Mrs. Repton-Wills invited me to come and sit with Mrs. Grant, and I consented to go. I was utterly sceptical at first —merely curious—and it was quite plain to me that Mrs. Repton-Wills was a completely uncritical *dévote* like most women—in fact, a very absurd woman. But I went along and, good Lord, the results were extraordinary. They were. They were eerie."

Albany went to the chair opposite Bait and sat in it, leaning forward. He was deeply interested ; as interested as he had been in the adventures of Dr. Nikola. " Tell me what happened."

" No, no. Not now. Some other day, perhaps, when you're less unhappy."

" No, tell me now. It'll take my mind off things."

Bait shook his head. He sniffed. He pulled at his cigarette. " No. I only wanted to say that I, for one—an old sceptic like me—am now pretty well convinced that we shall meet our loved ones in the Beyond. I'll say no more now."

"But you *must* Bait. You must tell me all now. You just can't get me all exci—I mean, you said it would be of comfort to me."

"Very well then. This first sitting was in Mrs. Repton-Wills's drawing-room. I was there and Mrs. Repton-Wills and another foolish woman and—who do you think?—old Colonel Budlier. He's never got over the loss of Tom's mother, they say, and he's always trying to get in touch with her. This Grant woman sat in an armchair pushed against the wall. She's a great fat woman of forty and obviously as stupid as an ox. That's one remarkable thing : when she's in a trance she seems to change her nature. Instead of being about as commonplace and inarticulate as a cow she suddenly draws on enormous funds of language. She becomes as fluent as a parson in his pulpit."

"Go on. What happened ? " Albany was still leaning forward in his chair.

"She said, ' My control is an Egyptian called Hierax who was famous in Egypt two thousand years ago. I hope you'll have a successful sitting.' Then, she sat quite still, her hands gripping the arms of her chair—" inspired by the story, Bait gripped the arms of *his* chair, and Albany, captivated by the story, did likewise. "She took deep breaths, and slowly her head began to droop forward again and again." Bait let his head fall forward two or three times in illustration, and the fascinated Albany unconsciously reproduced the movement, so that both were leaning forward and bowing to each other. Between them the fire fidgeted and flamed in an excitement of its own. " Then one of her arms fell down by the side of her chair, and her head went after it as if she'd been shot. But she pulled herself together, sat upright, and said in a deep voice quite unlike her own, ' Good evening, all.' Mrs. Repton-Wills, who's a fool, promptly answered, ' Good evening, dear Hierax. Have you any spirit friends to come through ? '"

"Yes ? And then ? " asked the staring Albany.

"Then Mrs. Grant, or Hierax, or whoever it was, said, ' Yes, I've a woman here, and I'm getting the name of the friend she wants to speak to. It's not clear yet. It's Pat . . . or Pete . . . or Pet. . . .' " Possessed by his subject, Bait imitated Mrs. Grant, or Hierax, or whoever it was, remarkably well. " Pat . . . Pete . . . Pet. . . . Now there was no one in the room named

Peter—old Budlier's a George—but I immediately wondered if the name could be Petlet."

" Petlet ? "

" Yes, you see, Grahame, I had a dear friend once, who passed over about twenty years ago, and she used to call me—it may seem absurd—Petlet. I must explain, old chap, something I've never told anyone before, but we're old friends, and I think all this may be of comfort to you. Great comfort. I shall have to speak of things you'll not approve of, I'm afraid. This was a woman who was all the world to me, and I to her—the one great love of my life—but it came too late. I had been married to Ada a dozen years. We had a few years of hidden happiness, and then agreed to part."

Albany was gazing at Bait who was gazing at the floor with tweaked-up nostrils. So old Bait—Bait who girded at women as half-finished creatures of poor sense and little use—Bait when he was a dry and sniffing old lawyer of nearly fifty—had adored and delighted in his woman—a woman with whom he exchanged, like Swift, the charms of a ' Little Language.'

" Well, believe it or not, Grahame, I had no sooner thought of her than the Grant woman, or Hierax, said, ' I think the word is Petlet.' And Mrs. Repton-Wills asked, ' Does anyone here think this is for them ? '—she's no sense of grammar ; no women have. And she went on, ' If so, ask dear Hierax the name of the spirit friend.' *I* wasn't going to say ' Is it so-and-so ' and give Mrs. Grant her clue, so I kept mum. But even as I was thinking of the right name, the deep voice said, ' I get the syllables Mar . . . Mary . . . or perhaps Marion.' " Bait paused here and looked at Albany. " Marion," he said, when satisfied that Albany was ready for the revelation, " was my dear one's name."

Albany only continued to stare.

" I whispered to Mrs. Repton-Wills that I had known a Marion, and she said, ' Ask if there's any message.' I was prepared to go that far, so I said ' Is there any message ? ' and the voice answered, ' She asks me to convey her love to you. She says it is greater than it ever was. She says she is always near you, helping you.' That was all."

" And not very much," suggested Albany.

" No, I came away far from convinced but interested enough to want to probe further, and I arranged a private sitting with the Grant woman at the London Psychic Association in St. Martin's Lane. But first I did some research into this fellow

Hierax, and I found that there'd been a Hierax who'd lived at Leontopolis in Egypt in the third century. He founded a society of ascetics who held that only celibates could enter the Kingdom of Heaven ; and I thought that this would be an interesting point to take up with him, if he and I got really friendly. He also denied the resurrection of the body—another interesting point, since he'd now taken up with Spiritualism. I went along to St. Martin's Lane and sat alone in a darkened room with the Grant, who went off into her usual trance, after a few palpitations and groans. Nothing happened at first, and then the deep voice said, ' Good afternoon, my son '—son to *me*, who am twice as old as the Grant ! Since I was his son I asked him a lot of questions about the daft views he'd held two thousand years ago. He was quite unabashed. Indeed, he was extremely reasonable. He allowed that he'd been wrong on the subject of virginity but contended that he'd not been so wrong on the question of the resurrection because the astral body, as he called it, was etheric. An interesting thought, and, discussing it with him, I quite forgot all about poor Mrs. Grant in her chair. But I wanted to ask other questions about Marion, and was wondering how to do it without offering any clues, when the voice said, ' I have a woman here who was striving to make contact with you before. Marion I think the name is. Does that convey anything to you ? ' I said, ' It might,' and asked if the woman could identify herself better. And the voice said, ' She seems to be a woman of about forty who passed on at that age. She is saying that she had a very great love for you, and I gather—I think I gather— that circumstances prevented you marrying and you agreed to part. She is saying, ' I have been with you, near you, ever since I passed on, but I could never get through to you.' She's saying she is glad you kept all her letters in that box and—I see the glint of gold—some gold trinket, I think, which she gave you.' Well, Grahame, she died in her forties ; I've always kept her letters hidden in an old iron box ; and when we parted she gave me a gold cigarette case to remember her by. Here it is." He produced it from a breast pocket. " It's never been away from me from that day to this," he said, and was so moved by the words that, greatly to Albany's surprise, and somewhat to his discomfort, he could not, for a while, go on.

" Extraordinary ! " said Albany, to help him. " And was that all ? "

" No . . ." Bait gulped. " The voice said, ' I am seeing

water, sparkling water. It is a river or the sea, and I get the impression of great happiness on the water.' Well, you see, Grahame, we—we sometimes, Marion and I, rowed together on the Thames at Maidenhead. We crossed the Channel too —to Paris. The voice went on, ' I see a little room—in a house or cottage among trees, I think, and the same happiness there.' And well, Grahame, there *was* a—she had a cottage among the Surrey pines where I would visit her."

" Extraordinary."

" I am not an easy man to convince, as you know, but these and other experiences have, I think, satisfied me that anyone who was very close to us in life—as my Marion was—is even closer to us after death ; and I thought it would comfort you to feel that Delia was still near you, and watching over you."

Albany's heart sank in alarm at the words. He felt as if a choice gift had suddenly been taken back again, a reprieve suddenly cancelled. But he managed to say, " Thank you, old chap. It was nice of you to have told me. It *is* comforting."

So little comforting was this idea that Delia henceforth would be ever near him and watching over him—accompanying him to Waterloo Close—that, after Bait was gone, he had to sit in his chair, bring the tips of his fingers together, and dispose of it. Old Bait was as crazy as a coot. Not one of his ' proofs ' but could be attributed to guesswork and perhaps, here and there, to thought reading. How safe to begin with a name like Mary, and to mention letters and sparkling water (all lovers went on the river) and golden trinkets and a secret place, in cottage or country hotel, for the guilty assignations.

No, he didn't believe any of it ; he wouldn't believe any of it.

But—his thoughts ran on in the chair—what revelations had come to him directly he had sloughed off his clerical habit and, in so doing, dropped the wool from his eyes ! Ludlow with his woman ; Prue Maddow and the ease with which she was won ; Cornelia and Vick ; and now Bait—Bait of all people with his Marion !

He sat in his chair for an hour or more, dwelling upon these revelations and his blindness in the old days. It approached tea-time and he was now feeling exceedingly hungry. Having wearied of Dr. Nikola, he picked up the newspaper again ; but in this, most unfortunately, he read of an official banquet last night. And as he read of the guests sitting down to Severn salmon, a baron of beef and Aylesbury ducklings, his appetite flourished within him, so that at last he resolved to go from the house, ostensibly on a sad man's walk, but really to obtain food. He rose to go, but at that instant the maid announced, ' Mr. Bakewell-Clapton, sir.'

" Oh, hell, no ! " He said it quite loudly and hoped that either it hadn't reached the maid's ears or that, if it had, it would only stimulate her compassion. This intolerable fool ! This consummate coxcomb and bore ! And, heaven help us, was *he* coming too with proofs of the survival in the Beyond of a late mistress ? Anything seemed possible now.

Eddie came forward with his hand uplifted, ready to slam down, not this time in hearty good-fellowship, but in an embryo minister's professional sympathy. " Ah, my dear, dear Uncle," the big deep voice began, and the hand came down—there was no evading it. It descended mightily, and pressed and pressed Albany's hand, and would not let it go. Albany extracted it at last, but Eddie hardly observed its departure because he was explaining in a plethora of words that there was so little he could say. " What can I say, my dear Uncle ? What am I to say ? "

Having now both hands free, Albany spread apart their empty palms. " Nothing, Eddie. One must just bear these things."

Eddie, however, having come upon this ministering mission, was not disposed to say nothing. He sat down, placed his large hands on his knees, pushed back the stiff white cuffs as they fell, replaced the hands, and discussed at length the condition of the faithful dead. He touched upon the Church's distinction between the Souls Expectant and the Saints Triumphant. Where was the good of his theological studies if they couldn't be unstabled and given a canter on an occasion like this ? Albany sat down, half-way through the course and lit himself a cigar. He tut-tutted behind its smoke, unheard. Plain that the fool had been preparing this discourse all the way from Elber Square to Circus Road and that he was much enjoying it.

" You have our prayers, Uncle, my dear mother's and Jean's and mine. We are praying that you may be strengthened and upheld. And I do think, Uncle, that a bereavement like this is more easily borne by people like you and us because we have our faith. I'm sure it's of great comfort to you to think that my dear auntie is now in a place of peace and happiness where she will be amply repaid for all her misery here—— "

" Misery ! " interrupted Albany. " *What* misery ? "

" Ah, you know, Uncle, what I mean. This is a Vale of Tears, after all."

" I consider," said Albany, " that she was a fortunate woman."

" In some ways, yes."

" In *many* ways."

" Yes, of course, of course, but *re* her exact state of beatitude now. I don't know what you hold about the condition of the faithful dead but I personally hold, after my studies of the Fathers, that there's an intermediate state for all disembodied souls—except, of course, the saints who go straight to Heaven and glory. Mind you, the saints, in my view, don't attain to their perfect consummation and bliss until after the Universal Resurrection and the General Judgment, but that they are in Heaven and in possession of felicity, I must believe in common with all the Fathers, not one of whom denies it—unless it be Irenæus. That is what I hold *re* the Glorified Souls, and *re* the Church Expectant. Now *re* Auntie. She would not have claimed, and not even you would have claimed, that she was the perfect saint and fit to go straight to glory. I hold then that she is in some happy place where her venial sins are being cleansed, and that we may justly pray for her. I am no Ritualist Heaven knows, but I do go with the late Dean Farrar— " Albany cast an eye at Dean Farrar's ' St. Winifred's ' to make sure that its spine and title were turned from the lecturer— " who was anything but a High Churchman, but he does say in his ' Mercy and Judgment ' that our Reformers recognized this intermediate state. He says they implied it quite clearly in their strong denunciation of the doctrine of psychopan-nychia—— "

Albany, who had retired from serious attention for some time and, since he couldn't openly sigh, had canalized his impatience down his long right leg to his foot where it extruded itself in tap after tap on the carpet, now glanced up in a moment of interest. " What did you say ? " he asked. Better to pretend he hadn't heard than to admit an unfamiliarity with this remarkable word.

" Psychopannychia, Uncle : the long night of sleep which, as some heretics have maintained, extends between death and the Judgment."

" Oh, yes : psychopannychia." Albany nodded brightly, as in recognition of an old friend. " Yes ; quite." And there he shut his lips and preserved silence, not wishing, as an ex-theologian, to reveal that this was his first view of the handsome word and his first meeting with the doctrine it connoted.

And Eddie went on. He went on and on. " I must hold that this middle state is a realm of continued development where souls are purified and ripened for the Last Judgment, and so, reverting to Auntie, she is now in a place where she can be, and should be, helped by our prayers. Yes, that is what I hold, and shall preach fearlessly, *re* Prayers for the Dead. If that is to be a heretic, then I am a heretic."

Never seemed a man more pleased with an ambiguous position.

" I do agree with all you say, Eddie. Most heartily. It was kind of you to come and help me like this, but now I have to go out. I—— " He rose from his chair.

" Let me go along with you, Uncle. I'd love to. We could talk further. There might be more I could say."

" No, no, no. No. Don't think me rude if I say that, on the whole, I'd rather be alone. You will understand, won't you ? "

" Oh, yes, I quite understand. Perfectly. Of course, of course." Eddie was enthusiastic about this line. " I'll go instead and comfort my fair cousin, shall I ? "

" Yes. You'd like to talk to Susannah, I'm sure," said Albany. " She's there in the dining-room."

" But first, Uncle, when are the Obsequies ? "

" The—er ? "

" The Last Sad Rites."

" Oh, I see. The Funeral. Yes, it's on Friday."

" I only wish she could have lived a few months longer so that I could have taken a part as an ordained minister. I should have loved to."

I'm sure he would, thought Albany ; and he sidled quickly from the study, mumbling a last good-bye. But the unceasing, unquenchable sympathy followed him out of the room, along the passage, and through the front door into the garden. Here was the final handshake. Eddie's hand soared aloft and came down like a steam-hammer on to his uncle's, pressing it even more vigorously than before, since this was its last chance to minister the full Christian sympathy. As quickly as was decent Albany hurried out of danger into the street, and Eddie, almost as hastily, turned round to enter the house and be of Christian service to Susannah.

Delia had been an active member of the congregation at

St. John's Wood Chapel, and the people assembled in large numbers for her funeral service there. It was a fine service, with clergy and choir in their stalls and the people filling all the pews except those in the galleries, and Albany had to admit to himself, without approval, even with censure, that there were aspects of it which he enjoyed. He had bought himself recently the frock coat of a layman, and he was pleased to wear it now, with gloves and a silk hat newly ironed and shining. Tall as he was, and broad, with his grey beard and moustaches well trimmed and his hair silvering, he could not but know that he made a distinguished figure when embellished by this formal attire : had not Prudence Maddow often said, " No one looks like you when you're arrayed in your state garments ? " As he walked up the nave before this large congregation he knew that all eyes must be following him, and he was glad to be a sight worthy of them. He had invited only a few as guests at the funeral—old Bait because he was his dearest friend, and the Claptons because he wanted Jean there, and such of Delia's relatives as were available—so the *cortège* was but small that at the end of the service he led down the nave to the carriages ; but he was touched and flattered to see all his friends and acquaintances there in their darkest clothes : Commander Ludlow with his eyeglass in his eye surveying the procession ; old Colonel Budlier in an ancient frock coat, with young Tom at his side ; all his servants ; and not a few of his tradespeople, with whom he was on the most amiable terms because he was always ready to exchange a jest with them over their counters. In the back seat of all he saw Prudence Maddow, dressed in black satin with a sable cape and muff, long black gloves and large black hat, to honour the occasion. It was nice, he thought, of Prudence to be there.

CHAPTER FIFTEEN

SUMMER AND LORD'S AGAIN

A FEW weeks, and the first warmth of summer came in like a tide. It soaked into the earth of the St. John's Wood gardens, starring their lawns with daisies and dressing the flower-beds with wall-flowers and tulips of all colours, and small, smiling violet pansies. It ran up the boles of the St. John's Wood

, seven-y...
...ciana D'Oroz...
...of a poor Italia...
...er in the village of...
...na, sits down and...
...riously writes a letter.

Every Sunday these letters

...we
...our
...the
...o preach
...I hope to
...d by living
simplicity."

..cake"
...e may be
...n Hollywood
...hat is smutty
..."
...at if she were
...ts that meant
...evealing clothes
...hem.
...atic. and if those

SKIDS,
TURNS
TIMES

...le were slightly
...t night when their
...ed on the icy sur-
... grass verge and
...hree times on the
...   near

...kno...
tions
good

The...
Oakley...
give pa...
every...
Children...
Said 19...
mond yest...
ship is a...
Parish Chu...
adopted the...

"It all hap...
some films...
children. W...
like to help,...
the "Save...
in London....

"We wer...
some unf...
we picked...
£2 10s ev...
Fund.

"In...
Lucia...
parc...
swe...

Legg...
...about th...
...eed for a c...
...naw is not at a...

oy," he tells me, "I'll subject ...
...st come through it without ...
...ter
...and
...has
...en it
...for all
...kept on
...to make
...n.

...t Easter
...s Parker,
...e decided
...Alan had
He was
...s proposi-
...is chance
...re often

...tion about
...ty for, at
...e really

...ll-round
scoring
...later

...able a player to take chances."
...the

**dribbling his way in to lay on
Wishart's second.**

Centre-half A l e c Young,
brought back to take over from
the injured Clunie, had his
weak moments against Celtic,
but in his latest outing he was
something like his old confident dominating self.

Oh those points!

This most recent success has
put Aberdeen once more in the
running for the championship.
They must be regretting more
than ever the non-under-
standable shedding of points
to less talented teams.

Hearts are at the top and I
cannot recall when they were
last there at this critical stage
of the League championship.
They have got there without
the usual ballyhoo.

...ARPEN UP

Within 12 minutes of the
start, Alan Boyd provided a
...irst class emulation of
...aham Leggat's opportunism
...giving his side the lead. Six
...utes from the interv...
...ser headed hom...

T...
M...
of Div...
no wonde...
me your...
centre-half
football and
too. Just li...
seems to be
up in knots—
THIRD LA...
ACHE AT M...
Last time
against Stone...
November 4. ...
Rangers' Watt ...
wasn't dropped ...
from the coalfie...
a grin "I got quit...
Third tried to p...
switching Wark a...
bamboozle Alex, ...
didn't come off.
Alex is a big bo...
Johnstone team a...
only one ambition
for the boys."
That, of course
Pattillo's one big
On Saturday, ...

M...

trees till the chestnuts and elms were in half-leaf, the sycamores nearly full, and the limes and beeches tinted all over with pink buds and brown. It ran up the branches and filled the chaffinch with his defiant and repeated song. A little more, and all the limes and beeches had slipped their gloves of pink and brown, powdering the lawns with pink under the limes and brown under the beeches. Soon all the lilacs and laburnums, heavy with flower, were drooping over the long garden walls and scattering over the pavements their shadows and their blossom.

And of course this high quickening tide was hardly less in the veins of Susannah in Circus Road and Tom in Acacia Road. The wintry mourning for her mother could not survive this warm incitement of May. Even in the first of the spring, only a month or so after her mother's death, it had been difficult to be as sad as she felt she ought to be, and now it was very difficult not to be thinking of Tom all day and of her love for him. This love, only at its beginning, proved more powerful than her love for her mother which had never been as complete as she would have liked it to be, and never comparable with her adoration of her father, which she now found so delightful.

Besides, she had never enjoyed such freedom as now. Like Albany, though with less need and therefore less relief, she was free at last from the watching and puritan eyes of her mother. In fact, there was now no one to forbid her anything. Fathers were different from mothers, and her father, watching her not at all, was usually shut in his study with a book or absent at his club three miles away. He seemed to be going often to his club these days, and she could only imagine that he was lonely and sad and hoped to be ' taken out of himself ' by a little comradeship with his men friends.

Delia had always insisted that at places where she would meet Tom, or other dubious and probably untrustworthy young men, she must be chaperoned by herself, her father, or some married woman ; but now she was able to pronounce this old-fashioned and to steal, ever and again, an unchaperoned hour with Tom. Happy, bewilderingly happy, were these secret meetings because each gave the other all that was possible, all that was legitimate, this side of marriage ; or, to put it more simply, they spent most of the time frantically kissing. Happy hours they might be, but whether hallowed too Susannah could never determine, because she could never shake off the idea that this seethe of love within her, this surge that dried the throat and swelled and beat in the body, must partake of the nature of sin.

With the summer came garden parties, but Susannah, still in mourning, could not go to these unless they were charitable affairs. There was one great house in Hall Road, with a walled garden of some acres, well timbered with oaks and limes and noted for its long poplar avenue ; and here among the trees the wealthy hostess arranged fêtes and bazaars in aid of this charity or that. Susannah attended these galas at the earnest request of the hostess, and Tom made a point of supporting the charity too. And then sometimes they would wander together down the poplar avenue to a secluded bower against the coachmen's cottages and sit there hand in hand and often lip to lip. It was only later in the summer that Susannah felt free to go to croquet and tennis parties, but occasionally she and her father invited a few friends for a little quiet croquet on their own lawn, and Albany saw no reason why Tom should not be one of the company. Often he arranged these games for Jean's sake, whom he was now persuaded he loved next best to Susannah and then perhaps the players would be Jean and Tom and Susannah and himself. " I am always happy with young people," he said.

Of course, if Eddie was home from his college, he had to come too, and his mother with him. Then the sides might be The Grahames v. The Claptons, while Cornelia sat watching. Albany did not object to this, because he so delighted in cannoning Mr. Bakewell-Clapton's ball when it was beautifully placed before its hoop—as it might be Mr. Clapton himself before the gate of Holy Orders—and driving it to the remotest corner of the garden, somewhere among the rhododendrons or the rose-bushes. If among the prickly roses, so much the better. He would rest on his own mallet and watch Mr. Bakewell-Clapton looking for it. With Jeanie's ball he was always gentle. He enjoyed also being indignant with Mr. Clapton, and directing towards Susannah a grimace of despair and resignation when that heavy-handed young man hit the lawn instead of the ball, and, apologizing profusely, endeavoured to repair the damage with a large flat foot. He enjoyed registering this impatience and stoical fortitude when Eddie, who placed his mother above all others, left the game to minister in some way to her comfort ; to get a cushion for her back or to move her chair into the shade. Albany would wait, leaning on his mallet, while he cast despairing glances at Susannah, or shrugged long-suffering shoulders at Jean, or consulted his watch for the diversion of both. To Eddie he said, " Ah, you've returned," when the filial duties were discharged.

All the same he did think that these attentions to his mother were rather less revolting aspects of Mr. Bakewell-Clapton than most, and he did understand why Cornelia, if no one else, loved him. When the game was done he enjoyed above all his regular practice of transferring Eddie, who'd be following him around with some long-winded analysis of the game just done, to his hostess, who was certainly Susannah. And when, the guests having gone, she rushed into his study, crying, " Oh, the foul wickedness of it ! " and calling it " a dastardly trick," he enjoyed grinning at her and propounding, " But, child, I thought you'd like to see more of your cousin. And hear more from him." If then she called his behaviour ' piggish ' and his present grin ' idiotic ', because the trick wasn't funny at all, he liked to maintain the grin and say, " Nonsense, dear child. You are the hostess, and it is the first duty of a hostess to keep her guests happy by listening to their talk. Don't worry ; you're coming along very nicely as a hostess. Besides the Reverend Mr. Clapton is obviously much attached to you. He prefers you to me, I'm afraid. But it's natural, and I won't stand in the way of either of you. Youth to youth."

Yes, Susannah was Albany's hostess and housekeeper now, and he loved to see her in the hostess's place at his table or to have her sitting in the big chair opposite him of an evening, the lady of the house. And Susannah too was pleased with this position of responsibility and authority. Among other things it enabled her to go shopping in St. John's Wood Terrace and the High Street, which busy bazaars were but a few yards from Acacia Road, so that there was always a chance that she might meet Tom on the pavement. She did meet him, oddly often. Again and again it seemed that he had been forced to desert his desk by some need of tobacco or pipe-cleaners or a box of matches. And then they would stand and gossip for quite a long spell. On Sundays they met sometimes at church. Susannah went to St. John's Wood Chapel alone because her father was no churchgoer now, and Tom went there alone too, because *his* father was a sidesman at All Saints and one who never failed to parade for duty. Tom preferred the singing in the Chapel, he told the good old man, and he went as a rule to a pew in the front row of the gallery from which he could look down upon Susannah in the nave. After the service, if the Sunday was fine, these two would sit in the public garden among the mossed tombs, and some of the women of the congregation, strolling under the trees, would stare at them as they passed, with eyes and lorgnettes and probably lips that reprobated the licence of the modern girl.

Sometimes, on week days, they ran away to places that Susannah had long wanted to see. They went to Soho and in a French restaurant enjoyed a five-course dinner for one and sixpence. They went to Limehouse and Chinatown, though not to this grimy Orient till Susannah had besought of Tom, " They won't cut us up, will they, and make us into chop suey ? " They went to Oxford (by cheap excursion) and strolled the academic streets, staring at the pinnacles and battlements and domes, Susannah with gasps of admiration, but Tom with assertions that Oxford was no more beautiful than Cambridge.

But the visit that was happiest and guiltiest of all was to a place not many hundred yards from home. It was to the caravan among the high weeds in the ruinous and melancholy garden of the old actor-manager. They stood among the weeds looking at the gilded carvings, so tarnished now, on the wagon's side, and at the name of the gipsy family, ' Boswell ' on its doors ; and they spoke with a real poetic appreciation of the days when this gay nomadic home went touring the roads of England and halted at sundown on some grass verge by the wayside. Tom said, " God, I'd like to wander away in a caravan and do a little horse-dealing—and maybe a little horse-stealing too—and never put foot on a pavement again. *You* could do a little fortune-telling and petty pilfering, and we could be really happy at last." This was the first time she heard a new note in Tom, a longing to escape from cities and pavements and books (books on Law, that is) into the stretching counties and their green empty fields.

Like her father, many months before, they parted the tall grasses and the high entangled weeds and walked up the wooden steps into the cold caravan. They saw, as he saw, the broken toys on shelf and floor, the little cracked kettle on the rusty range and the torn and stained mattresses on the bunks. And again Tom said, " I wish we could harness a horse to this old bus and go off for ever along country roads, never minding where we halted next. I could be a travelling tinker and you could make baskets and brooms and mend the farmer's chairs. Gosh, I'd be happy, dawdling on to the next county and the next. But you'd have to be there, lady, to share my enthusiasm with me. You understand that, I hope."

" Yes," she said, with bright assenting eyes, and he took her into his arms for a kiss. But it was much more than a kiss. It was the usual hard, hungry, unbreakable hold, the usual impetuous, incalescent, almost brutal kissing, and at last he sank with her to one of the bunks and there, hidden away in a jungle of weeds they lay together in an endless embrace, the appetite of each for the other only heightened as it was thus roughly fed.

This emancipation of Susannah was disastrous for Tom's reading. How could he read from nine to one when Susannah might be in the High Street, shopping ? How read on an afternoon when her father was away and she might be snatched and taken to some place that was lonely and quiet and, if possible, green and lovely ? How plod through Law books when the grass was dry again at Lord's, and that great round plain, with its bowling crease in the middle was waiting for him, and the great white stands were waiting for Susannah ? What chance had dry books against the dry grass of Lord's ? Why, if you walked along Wellington Road, you could hear the horse-mower drowsing over the outfield and humming its monotonous, sweet overture to the next day's play. Nor was Lord's the only cricket field in England. Sitting with his head bowed over a book, he saw the pleasant ground at Hove stretched among the seaside houses, and the beautiful Saffrons ground at Eastbourne framed by its fringe of majestic trees. And other grounds in harsher scenes : the Oval amid the Surrey tenements and Old Trafford beneath the heavy Manchester sky.

He had been invited to play regularly for Middlesex but his father had intimated very gently—so gently that it was impossible to disappoint him—that it would be wrong, at this stage, to intermit his studies for weeks at a time. It was Commander Ludlow who in the end, demolished this argument. " Blah, sir ! Waffle ! " he said. " The boy can only be young once. And think of this, Colonel : he may play for England one day, and then some big firm will probably give him a well-paid job and set him free in the summer months to play first class cricket. They often do this because it's a first class advertisement for them. Stop him playing now and you may prevent his getting a much better job than devilling for some old barrister." Tom, hearing this, knew in his heart that he wasn't good enough to play for England, but with some pricks of conscience because he loved his father, he let the argument stand. The Colonel, a simple-minded man, accepted it because he loved his son, and so Tom was able to close his books and descend, six steps at a time, from his High Tower.

Susannah was very proud when, after his performance in the field, he came and sat beside her in his blue-and-yellow blazer, and she heard the people whispering, " That's Budlier. There : the tall fair chap with the piebald hair." Sometimes they said, " That's his girl," and her heart dissolved into exquisite air.

But where at such times was her father who so loved to watch cricket ? At first he had declared, for her pleasure, that he and she would go together to every match that season ; and to the first two matches they had gone together, Albany happy to think that she could be so happy with him. But when Tom had come and sat with them once or twice, this happy mist dispersed of a sudden before his eyes, and he saw clearly that he'd been a fool ; that he was ' one too many ' on this particular bench ; that these two young people wanted to be alone, and Susannah hadn't the heart to tell him so. So next time he made excuses for not accompanying her, though he longed to see the game. It was one of his better deeds—and he thought so too. And, thinking so, he continued in this generous path for the rest of the season. Let the young people be happy. But sometimes, unable to keep away from an interesting match, he slipped into the ground by the north-east gate and sat in the cheap seats, safely hidden among a multitude of people who had no friends in the pavilion. From his seat among the unprivileged he would look across the field to the Members' stand till he descried Susannah. And if she was seated by a patch of blue and yellow, which was Tom, he was made happy by her happiness, and his loneliness was eased. A few minutes before play ended he would slip from the ground and be in his study with a book when she arrived home.

June, July, August : always the cricket season swept too fast towards its close like all beauty ; and it was at one of the late August matches, when Susannah and Tom were sitting together, he awaiting his turn to bat, that he said, " Susannah, listen. I've something to tell you. Something tremendous. I've had a Revelation. I think I've had a Call."

"But how thrilling!" she said. "I'm so glad, though I don't know what you're talking about."

"I'm sure it's a Call. It's a Call like your old man must have had when he decided to be a parson."

"You're not going to be a parson!"

"No. But it was the same sort of a Call. I suddenly knew exactly what I wanted to do with my life—what I'm *going* to do—for certain—somehow—one day."

"But you're going to be a barrister, aren't you?"

"No. That went up in smoke in my moment of revelation. I tell you, it was like Conversion; I'm sure it was. I found a sort of religion I could really love; and if you can call it a religion, then I can be as devout in it as my old man is in his. I can be a perfect saint."

"Oh, do tell me. Tell me," she begged, laying a hand on his knee for a second—which she always loved to do when there was plain justification for it. "And perhaps I can be saintly too."

"It happened yesterday in front of a wheat-stack. With Bill Judd." Bill Judd was one of Tom's Cambridge friends (he'd attended Tom's funeral in a cassock and surplice) and his father, a wealthy landowner in Hampshire, had arranged a house-party for the Middlesex *v.* Hampshire match. Tom and another Middlesex amateur had been among the guests. "You remember it was the Judds whose house-party I went to."

"Yes. Was it nice?"

"Nice enough. Just six girls and the same number of men."

"What sort of girls?" The girls, for Susannah, had momentarily obscured the Revelation.

"Oh, just girls. Nothing to write home about."

"Pretty?"

"Some of them, but not as pretty as Susannah."

"I think I'm glad of that."

"But I fell in love, all the same. That's the whole point." Her heart fell like a dropped catch. "In love?"

"Yes. With an idea."

The heart eased—but not quite; it had been too shaken. "Oh . . . I see . . . what idea?"

"The Judds have a large farm, and Bill Judd works it with his old man. What a wonderful life! I spent the day with him yesterday because our match finished on Tuesday. Fancy, if Hampshire hadn't beaten us by an innings and given us a free day, my whole life might never have been changed. On Tuesday I was a drifter; to-day I'm a Man with a Purpose."

" The purpose being ? "

" I will tell you. Don't interrupt. Their farm is on the Wiltshire border and it rises up from a little river to the ridge of the downs; and, Susannah, if you look at it from the ridge, it looks like a patchwork bedspread flung over the downs. The house and the steading—what a lovely word !—were on the slope, but oh, they were so mossy and weathered that they seemed to have grown out of the earth along with the elms at their side—— "

" Gosh, Tom. But this is poetry ! "

" Yes. Probably it is. I was most terribly moved. But don't interrupt. And don't laugh. On the lovely soft turf the sheep were feeding, and half way down the hill you could see the shepherd's cottage. Oh, well hit, Pinkie. It's a four, by Jove ! A four." This was the first time he'd really noticed the game. He'd been seeing a downland farm, not the field of Lord's. " Bill and I were up and out at six o'clock, and, Susannah, my sweet, you simply don't know how lovely the sun is when it's only been up an hour. We met the carters and the day-labourers and arranged the day's work with them. Then we went up to the sheepfolds on the slope and then down again to the horses in the stackyard and had a talk with the head carter; then we went to the dairy to see the head dairyman, and then home to breakfast. And what a breakfast ! You can't imagine what breakfast can be like if one's been out on the hills for hours. After breakfast we went to a field and saw the pitchers loading the wheat on to wagons, and when the boys led the horses away to the rick—and what horses ! what lovely, gentle, patient beasts !—we followed them and watched the men emptying the wagons and building up the ricks. And it was then that I saw the Light. I was inspired. Yes, I think perhaps you're right. I ought to have been a poet. Anyhow, I saw in that moment that I wanted to be a farmer and that I *would* be a farmer, somehow or other, one day." He gazed out at the cricket field, but the eyes of his mind were seeing his English farm as those of a boy who wants to go to sea will descry the Indies or the Spice Islands.

" A *gentleman* farmer, I suppose," Susannah put in, anxiously.

" Of course, of course. Like Bill Judd and his old man. And, Susannah, when I suddenly knew all this it was like——

well, it was a kind of breathless excitement like when I first kissed a girl. I'm sure, as I say, it was like Conversion—like what your old man must have felt when he really got religion. I'd found mine! And a host of smells confirmed it for me all day long. They kind-of-shouted that I was right, and patted me on the back—— "

" Smells? What smells? "

" Oh, the smell of the straw in the yard and the thatch on the ricks and the earth on my hands and the dung in the midden —and, above all, the smell of the cows coming in to be milked. Golly, I knew then that I wanted to be done for ever with London and its everlasting grey streets. I'm off, I'm going."

" But, Tom—— " she began in dismay.

But he ran on, unheeding. " It's amazing the truths I saw yesterday. I knew that I wasn't a desk-type at all and that I was only fully alive when I was digging in the garden or wielding a cricket bat or controlling a galloping horse—or, yes, if I may mention it, when I was making love to you."

" I'm glad I came in somewhere, even if it was after the horse."

" Yes, at these times one just *is ;* at a desk one only half *is*. And I think I would add another time : when you and I are having a real old row. I certainly come alive then. Got him! Pinkie's out. What a ball! What a snooter! Young woman, I must go. I bat soon. But look : it won't be only heavy back-breaking work, fighting the earth at all weathers—though I shall love that. Bill Judd says I could make opportunities for an occasional game of first-class cricket and certainly play every Saturday afternoon with the village team. And any day of the week there'd be a tennis party somewhere."

" Have you told your father all this? "

" No. Only you. Hell, it only happened yesterday. But the old guv'nor won't like it. His notion is that you can't be a gentleman unless you're in one of the services or sit at a table in a black coat. But that's the trap. That's the trap he's got me into, with the best will in the world. And I intend to break out of it. I saw that I'd *got* to break out of it. But, Susannah, tell me, how would you like it? How would you like to be a farmer's wife? A *gentleman* farmer's. There'd be tennis parties," he repeated anxiously, " and . . . and hunting . . . I could keep a hunter for you."

" But, Tom, are you sure that this isn't just a sudden romantic notion? I come from the country, and I know something about farming. It can be heart-breaking, endless, messy work."

"I know all that; I know every bit of it; I know that farming's largely slogging through mud and pitching muck; and the fact remains that the smell of manure stirs something in the depths of me. Something that I'm going to obey. See?"

"But how? How are you going to do all this? You've no money."

"Yes, how? I don't know. I suppose I'd have to go first to an Agricultural College and then rent or buy a farm."

"And that'd cost an awful lot."

"Quite a spot yes."

"Well then, how can you do it?"

"Don't know, my sweet. But one knows when one's going to do something. I shall get there somehow. And make a success of it. Get some exemplary bloke to finance me, perhaps, and pay him back one day. Bill says farming's been getting more and more prosperous ever since the Boer War and that, if this war with Germany comes, every farmer will be sitting on velvet."

Susannah, not yet accustomed to this strange and sudden idea, and a little frightened by it, remained silent for a little, and then, not to disappoint him said, "I'm sure you'll do it."

"I'm sure I shall too. But you—what about you? Blast! Trott's out. I must rush and put on my pads. Susannah, what do you think of it? Could you be as enthusiastic as me? You would come with me, wouldn't you?"

He had risen to go to the dressing-room, and she smiled up at him above her and rested her fingers on his hand. (This also she loved to do.) "My dear," she said, "I want to be with you always . . . always . . . and to do everything for you."

This was true, but she was disturbed, none the less, by this new and surprising ambition of Tom's. She was not at all sure that she wanted to bury herself again in the country. Tom, town-bred, longed for life in the country; she, country-bred, loved her new life in town. Tom's craving was the reverse of her father's longing, and her own, to escape from the empty fields of Mosgrove and find a fuller life in London. But she told herself, as she walked about her room with the problem, that if Tom wanted to be a farmer, she must go with him like a loyal wife; and she was helped in this resolve by the poems, and the ethics, of Miss Adelaide Procter. Almost her favourite book, just at this time, was *Legends and Lyrics*, by

Adelaide Procter. This assembly of sad little rhymes about love and loss and mortality had made such an appeal to her that it was now honoured by horizontal lines pencilled beneath whole stanzas or by vertical lines dashed enthusiastically against their sides. If a stanza, or a whole poem, had seemed exceptionally beautiful, it had been doubly honoured : underscored heavily and given as many as three fervid lines in the margin. One such poem (with a three-line whip) was *Friend Sorrow* :

> ' Do not cheat thy heart and tell her
>   " Grief will pass away,
> Hope for fairer things in future
>   And forget to-day "—
> Tell her, if you will, that sorrow
>   Need not come in vain ;
> Tell her that the lesson taught her
>   Far outweighs the pain.'

For Susannah might be only a little more inclined to church-going than her father, but Delia's upbringing had left her with a love of all pious, high-minded and self-sacrificing sentiments.

And now, as she instructed herself that she must help Tom in his career and follow him, if necessary to a farm, it was these words from Miss Procter that stood in her mind :

> ' I do not ask, O Lord, that Life may be
>   A pleasant road ;
> I do not ask that Thou wouldst take from me
>   Aught of its load.'

No. Love was worth nothing, she told herself, if it was not ready to go anywhere and do anything. If Tom had been in the Diplomatic Service and sent as a colonial governor to Weihaiwei or somewhere, would she not have had to go with him ? Or if he had decided to become a missionary (so likely !) would she not have gone with him to the Fiji Islands (where were they ?) and laboured at his side ? And now he was not asking her to go to Weihaiwei but only to a farm in Wiltshire. And he'd promised her that there'd be tennis parties and very likely a horse of her own and hunting. " I am ready to go," she decided, assuring herself that she was being loyal to the best in her, even as Tom was being loyal to the call in the smell of manure. " Yes, I am more than ready."

She felt a self-respect akin to that which supported her father in the cheaper seats at Lord's.

Tom continued at every meeting to pour out his hopes for his future as a farmer. " Two years' training at, say, the Carter-Weyman's Agricultural College—say, a hundred a year, all told. Rent a farm of about five hundred acres, with a nice farmhouse, a few cottages and suitable buildings, at, say fifteen shillings an acre. Buy it one day, at, say fifteen pounds an acre. On twenty years' purchase value—— "

" But," interrupted Susannah, " unless my arithmetic's all wrong, that makes seven thousand five hundred pounds."

" It does, my sweet, and, what's more, Bill Judd says that an owner-occupier would need as many pounds an acre if he's going to work his land as it ought to be worked."

" Well, then ; where is all this shocking amount of money coming from ? "

Tom didn't know. He talked vaguely of banks advancing some of it and of himself raising the rest ; of working like twenty niggers till he'd paid off every debt ; of wars coming to his help ; and of his certainty that, if only he could get started, he'd make a success of it.

One day he came with an exciting new idea that had been given him by an exciting new friend. This ' absolutely top-hole chap ' was Charlie Dyson who lived in one of those huge mansions in St. John's Wood Park—that road of Victorian palaces which led out of his own Acacia Road. He had met Charlie in the Prince of Wales pub which was almost exactly half-way between their two homes. Charlie's old man was Arthur Dyson, of Dyson and Miers, the Theatrical Managers—" you've heard of them, haven't you ? Your old uncle was something in that line, wasn't he ? Well, as you'll guess, old man Dyson is just about as rich as your old uncle ; he keeps several carriages and a couple of coachmen. But Charlie's refused to go into the business with him : he says he can get all the fun out of it, the free tickets and everything, without sitting all day in a smelly office. *His* great interest is motor-cars. He's got a motor-car of his own and he knows all there is to be known about them. And this is the point, Susannah darling, my heart, he's certain that if one gets into the motor trade as quickly as possible, one can make bags of money."

Susannah smiled and looked eager, to please him, but she didn't really believe. " But how wonderful ! " she said.

" Yes, and Charlie says he has no use now for his old man's carriages and coachmen. He says that horses are finished. Soon there won't be a horse left in London, unless there are one or two on show at the Zoo. He says that the boom in motoring is going to be enormous, and I think he's right. You've only got to stand by the Underground Station—d'you remember the entrance, my heart's delight ?—stand there and watch the traffic swishing about the crossroads to see that he's right. There are almost as many motor-cars as there are carriages and carts. Why, they're so common now that no one turns a head to look at them."

" Yes, but what can you do about all this ? You can't be in the motor-car business and a farmer as well."

" True enough, my sweet, but I *can* be a motor salesman for a time till I've made a decent blob of money on commissions and such. Charlie says he's thinking of being a motor salesman himself, but of course he only wants the money to spend on his own pleasures, whereas *I* want it to put into the good earth ! To sow it down for pasture, child, and see my herds grazing on it ! Gee, by all that's holy, I may not be much good at seeing beauty in poems as you do, but I *can* see poetry in good farming. Like hell I can ! "

A little while and Susannah became jealous of this unseen Charlie. Tom spent much less of his time with her now, and nearly always Charlie Dyson figured in his excuses : he had been motoring to the sea with Charlie, or he had been to Brooklands with Charlie, or he'd been lunching with Charlie at the Royal Automobile Club. After a time, though she hated to admit this, she was not sure that she trusted his excuses.

And she began to be very unhappy. " I am now no more than a pleasant habit for him, a comfortable piece of furniture in his life. We're not married yet, and won't be for years, and yet he already treats me like a wife." And the gross unfairness of it all was that, as his love dwindled down into a quiet glow, hers was only heightened. It was heightened by this fall in the temperature and by the frequent absences it appeared to involve. His neglect, like a cold air, was blowing her love into flame.

Autumn slow-marched again into the Wood, an autumn cloudy and wet, and as Susannah strolled along the pavements with her hands thrust deep into the pockets of her raincoat, the state of the roads, moist and beautiful and untidy, matched well with her melancholy mood. The creepers, red as ripe apples, drooped lax and listless tresses over the garden walls ; the yellow leaves speckled the damp pavements and settled like a silt in the gutters, where they lisped and shuddered as the fretful wind touched them. From behind the garden walls came the scent of summer grass cut for the last time and perhaps the sound of a gardener raking the dead leaves into a pile with a swish as of lazy sea-breakers. Blue mists filled the farthest distances, making ghosts of the buildings behind them and merging their blue, like a cauldron's low smoke, into the milk-grey skies. And Susannah, strolling down these autumnal vistas, saw their beauty but drew more dejection from it than joy. Her sadness tuned in only with the sighing in the tree-tops, the helpless stutter of the dead leaves as the wind went fidgeting among them, and the impatient hiss of carriage wheels on the wet and leaf-strewn roads.

The sadness had one root in shame, because her love and anxiety, so inflamed, were driving her to deeds which she could tell to none. They sent her wandering in the neighbourhood of Acacia Road in the hope that she might see Tom leaving or approaching his home. Now and again she adventured farther —along St. John's Wood Park, that avenue of huge grey Victorian mansions where this Charlie Dyson lived. She went past the doors of the Prince of Wales public house where Tom and Charlie had first met. But she never saw Tom. " One never does. I don't know why one does this sort of thing, but one does. It's so silly."

When at length she did see him, it was in the Wellington Road, and she saw only his back, for he was hurrying towards the cross roads. She stood arrested, and watched. And suddenly she saw him raise an arm to some figure in the distance. Which was it, which of the many walking this way ? It was a girl—and Susannah's hand leapt from her pocket to her breast that it might press against the anguish there. It was a girl ; she had raised her neat umbrella in laughing welcome ; a slim young creature in a large hat laden with roses and a white feather boa, her whole attire too bright and summery for this grey, dank autumn day.

They came together beneath the high east wall of Lord's and he gathered up her hand and led her like a protector through the people. He drew her towards the cross roads ; and Susannah followed, shamefully, but tied to them by a cable of pain. They turned into St. John's Wood Road and walked, hand in hand, the linked arms swinging joyously, beneath that south wall of Lord's which Susannah had once called the Rejoicing Wall. They turned into Grove End Road, and into Willow Road, and then she knew where they were going. "Oh, no, no!" she cried in a voiceless pain. "He can't be going to do that. He can't. Oh, no. They're not going there."

But they were. They were going to the old ruined house of the actor-manager where there was cover for an embrace. She was sure of it, and yes, she was right. Sometimes, it seemed, the mind could be so quickened that it knew of things ahead of their happening. They were standing opposite the dead house, looking up at its suppurating stucco, its tall eyeless windows, and the bones of its roof. With hands joined they looked at it : the place which Susannah had told him about, the place to which she had brought him, the place where they had kissed and made love and talked of their future together. Laughing at their trespass, the two stepped over the dwarf-wall into the jungle of undergrowth, the girl holding up her skirts and Tom helping her with a hand under her arm. Lightly she jumped down.

Susannah came towards her torment. She ran towards it. Through the yellow leaves of a sycamore she looked at the empty window-frames of the great drawing-room. She even stepped on to the dwarf-wall that she might see over the tall weeds. And she saw Tom and the girl walk into the room and glance around at its desolation. Doubtless he was telling her that this room had seen the merriment and dancing of famous men and lovely actresses—telling her all the things which she, Susannah, had told him, having heard them from her father. But not for long : soon Tom had his arms about the girl and was kissing her. Susannah saw the passion swell within him, just as it had done that first time he kissed her in the hansom—but this girl did not resist as Susannah had done. And after a time he took her by the hand as if to lead her to some place where he could gratify the passion. They went the way that he and she had gone ; along the passage to a back door and down the steps into that wilderness of weeds and sapling trees which had once been an elegant garden of roses and shadows. Susannah slipped to the side-gate and looked along the tradesmen's alley right to the foot of this back garden. Now she could see the old gipsy wagon in the corner veiled by the high weeds and the drooping leaves of the ash tree.

They came towards the steps of the caravan, the girl with

her free hand holding up her skirt as they plashed through the wet, dead leaves. Susannah heard the acorns crack beneath their feet. Laughing, they thrust aside the thronging weeds and, bending beneath the branches of the ash, climbed into the wagon. Leaves and branches closed behind them. Its door slammed shut.

Ten minutes, twenty minutes, thirty, Susannah waited. But they did not come out. She stood there remembering the stained and flocculating mattresses on the slatted bunks. She thought of her own hour there with Tom. And she came slowly away, walking home with her hands deep in her raincoat pockets and her head a little down.

CHAPTER SIXTEEN

THE KITCHEN EMBASSY

There were three in the kitchen to hear Mrs. Lawton's story. Mrs. Kenny, the cook, sat in her chair by the big kitchen range ; Collins, the parlour maid, stood with the tips of her fingers on the kitchen table ; Amy, the little housemaid, stood at a respectful distance away, between the table and the door. And all three stared and were quite still, because they were immobilized by the story.

" It's all along of that young Mr. Charlie Dyson who lives in St. John's Wood Park," said Mrs. Lawton. She should have been hanging her hat and coat and fur tippet on the hooks behind the kitchen door, but she did not do so. She had more urgent business to discharge. She stood between Collins and Amy, as still as they, with the tippet in her hand, the hat at rest upon her head, and the coat buttoned across her well-braced bosom. In the course of her tale, however, she did, almost unconsciously, unbutton the coat because it was wet with rain, and she breathless. She flung it open, and her breast protruded from it like a promontory. " It's that young Mr. Dyson what's put Mr. Tom up to it. Them Dysons have got all the money in the world, as you know ; and old Mr. Dyson's in the theatrical line, so Mr. Charlie can have free seats for all the shows and—if you take my meaning—he can have all the young actresses that are going free."

Mrs. Kenny nodded, to show that she had no difficulty in

taking her meaning ; but at the same time she slid an anxious eye towards Amy, the little housemaid, hoping that she was too young to take it.

"Mr. Lawton had the whole story from Mr. Stephens, their second coachman," continued Mrs. Lawton. "Mr. Stephens comes regularly into the Prince of Wales, where Mr. Lawton goes of an evening, and last night he come in and tell him."

Mrs. Lawton was the charwoman who came three days a week at nine in the morning, and this morning she had walked in with this splendid burden of news. They all knew that Miss Susannah and young Mr. Tom Budlier were " sweet on each other," so it was with some fervour that Mrs. Lawton had come upon them with the information that young Mr. Budlier was " carrying on, almost openly, as you might say, with a girl called Carolyn Eyre. An actress. But not an actress of any importance, as you might say. A beginner, because, law bless you, she's not above eighteen. She plays maids in them drawing-room comedies, and well she might, being as how her mother was a lady's maid and no better than you or me."

"Mr. Stephens tells him," continued Mrs. Lawton, looking now at Mrs. Kenny, now at Collins, but never Amy, " that he knows of at least three girls that his young master's going with regular. Three, mark you, all at once. He's a holy terror, that young gentleman : he just believes in taking anything that can be had for the ah'stin'. This here girl, this Carolyn Eyre or whatever she calls herself, is a friend of one of his young ladies, and I suppose, not wanting her hisself, he 'ands 'er over to Mr. Tom. The two girls lodge at Mrs. Connaught's in Alexandra Road who's been an actress herself, and quite well-known in her time, they say. She now runs a regular home for young lady theatricals and is quite a nice woman, they say— won't allow any goings-on in her house or any coming in at all hours—so their ma's think they're well looked after. But there you are : neither Mrs. Connaught nor their precious ma's knows what's going on of an afternoon and out o'doors. It's my firm belief that Mr. Charlie put Mr. Tom up to the fact that the Eyre girl was anybody's apple and that a nice-looking fellow like him, a famous cricketer and all, could have her for the ah'stin'—he's a regular Mephistopheles, that Charlie, a regular serpent in the garden. I've no doubt he told Mr. Tom that he wouldn't be the first she'd had, not by a long chalk. She may be a beginner on the stage, but she's no beginner at this game. I expect he said Mr. Tom'd be a fool not to take all that's offered him. And you know what Mr. Tom is, weak as water. I blame the little hussey far more than him. But poor Miss Susannah! Knowing nothing about it!"

"She did ought to know," Mrs. Kenny proclaimed from her chair. "She certainly ought. It's terrible. She don't understand the first thing about men, poor lamb."

"I think you ought to speak to the Master," Collins recommended. "Yes, I do, really."

Amy, the little housemaid, said nothing, but turned fascinated eyes from one speaker to the next.

"I don't know as it's my place to speak," said Mrs. Kenny, pretending a distaste for the task. "I don't really."

"I'm not at all sure that it isn't your duty," the charwoman argued, for she could not but desire to see this remarkable fat in the fire and an adequate blaze. "You been with them all these years. You're the one to speak."

"And she's got no mother now," added Collins, whose dramatic sense was no weaker than Mrs. Lawton's and demanded that an exciting situation should march to the adequate climax. "She's got no woman at her side, now that the Mistress is dead."

"Yes, there *is* that," Mrs. Kenny meditated on this point, which seemed to provide an excuse for that which she wanted to do, and to give it a colour of merit. "Yes, that's true."

"I reckon it'd be a kindness to everybody in the long run," Mrs. Lawton submitted. "These things ought to come out. And young men like Mr. Tom should be brought up smart, if you ah'st me. If you take my advice, Mrs. Kenny, you'll have a word with Sir Albany. Yes, have a word with him."

"No." Mrs. Kenny's meditation was over. "I shouldn't like to do that. I shouldn't like to go carrying tales to her father, who doesn't know one quarter of what's been going on between Miss Susannah and Mr. Tom. Not one quarter he doesn't. Give over now, Amy. It's no matter to be laughing about. Come to that, it's no matter you should know anything about, to my way of thinking. Perhaps the best thing would be to have a word with Miss Susannah herself."

"Yes . . . well . . . that's right: you have a little word with the girl," said Mrs. Lawton, quite satisfied with this solution, and going to the door to hang up her coat and hat. "I reckon it's your duty. I do, really."

Mrs. Kenny nodded two or three times, not so much in agreement as in consideration of this advice. "If you think I ought to . . ." She said it slowly, to persuade her audience, and herself, that her assent was unwilling because few tasks could be more disagreeable.

" I certainly do," Mrs. Lawton ; and Collins said the like.

So that same morning Mrs. Kenny walked into the dining-room where Susannah sat by the window, looking out at the rain. Susannah's elbow rested on a little writing-table, and her cheek lay bedded in her hand. She had been thinking in the seconds before Mrs. Kenny appeared in the room, " Maybe I shall one day love someone else," for she was now convinced —or nearly convinced—that she hated Tom, bitterly hated him. Never, never would she speak to him again—or, rather, once more only—and might the chance come soon—once more when she could unloose upon him her knowledge and her wrath. She might be looking through the rain-splashed window at a lawn darkened to its deepest green, and at croquet hoops rusty and fallen, but she was seeing only Tom and a girl going up the steps of the gipsy's wagon. And she was finding one small grain of alleviation in a couplet of Adelaide Procter's. The words of the couplet were, " In that one moment's anguish Your thousand years have passed."

They were the last words of a poem, " The Story of the Faithful Soul," which told of a bride who had died on her wedding eve and, joining the souls in Purgatory, suffered greater torments at the thought of her husband's misery than any the penal fires could inflict. In his compassion St. Michael (so the old French legend went) offered her one more moment at her husband's side, but only at the price of a thousand more years in Purgatory. So great was her pity for her husband, and so small her love for herself, that she accepted the Arch-angel's offer ; but when she approached her husband, " in the lime trees' shade at evening," she saw that he was courting and fondling another. And the poem ended—it had been Sus-annah's favourite poem in the treasured book long before that deathly moment at the gate of the ruined house, looking at the caravan :

> ' Near Purgatory's entrance
>   The radiant angels wait ;
> It was the great St. Michael
>   Who closed the gloomy gate
> When the poor wandering spirit
>   Came back to meet her fate.

> "Pass on," thus spoke the Angel :
> > "Heaven's joy is deep and vast ;
> Pass on, pass on, poor spirit,
> > For Heaven is yours at last ;
> In that one moment's anguish
> > Your thousand years have passed." '

Yes, there was some small alleviation in thinking that she too had suffered a similar anguish in that moment by the gate. At least one may take pride in the depths of one's pain.

And now she saw Mrs. Kenny standing at the door, tall and thin and grey and rather like her mother.

"Yes, Mrs. Kenny ? "

If it is possible to be both faltering and fluent, Mrs. Kenny was so now. " I hope you won't take it amiss what I'm going to say, I wouldn't wish to presume in any way ; I know it's not my business to interfere, and I never want to poke my nose in where it wouldn't be proper ; nor do I want to pass remarks about anyone, but I *have* known you since you were only so high, and I feel that I can't stand by and see you taken advantage of. If I'm wrong, I'm wrong."

" But what is it, Mrs. Kenny ? "

" Well . . . you see . . . it's about young Mr. Tom. Yes."

" What about him ? "

" You'll pardon me if I say that I know how you feel for him, and I'm sure I understand how you couldn't help taking to him. I took to him meself. But he isn't behaving straight by you now, miss, he isn't behaving at all nicely, not at all he isn't. He's getting hisself talked about ; they're passing remarks about him ; passing remarks everywhere ; Mrs. Lawton's been telling me this morning—— " and she repeated the charwoman's story, concluding, " I thought it my duty to tell you. Yes, I did really. If I'm wrong, I'm wrong."

Not a word answered Susannah, and Mrs. Kenny, wondering if the silence was a rebuke, and she *was* wrong, hurriedly continued, " I'm sure meself that it's all the fault of that young Mr. Charlie Dyson ; he's a young Limb, he is ; and the girl too, she's no more than a—well, you wouldn't understand what she is, miss. All I can say is that, if she was a daughter of mine I'd rather see her dead at my feet than being like what she is. But whoever's the fault, it's not right of Mr. Tom to behave like that, when he's almost as you might say, engaged to you. I don't know what your father'd say if he knew, but I thought at least I ought to tell you. At the very least."

Susannah, all this time, had been gazing up at Mrs. Kenny, and she now said, " It's kind of you, Mrs. Kenny, but it's no longer of any importance to me at all."

" Not of any importance ? "

" No. I no longer care for him. I've long ceased to."

" Oh, no, miss." Mrs. Kenny refused the statement, putting her head to one side, incredulous. " No, no. Please, no."

" Yes, it is so. He means nothing to me now, and hasn't for some time. We're friends no more. He can go out with anyone he likes. I'm only glad he's got someone to be happy with."

But as she said this the tears, unmanageable, flooded into her eyes, and she shook her head as if to shake them angrily away. At sight of the tears Mrs. Kenny began to weep too. " Oh, miss, miss . . ." she said, and stood there weeping.

And at sight of Mrs. Kenny's tears Susannah jumped up and rushed to the window, hiding her face from the figure at the door. " Please, please don't talk about it or sympathize with me. I need no sympathy. None of it matters at all to me. There's nothing to worry about, nothing at all. I'm not unhappy. I'm not really."

But as the door closed on Mrs. Kenny, copiously weeping, Susannah rushed back to her place at the table and flung her head on to her arms for a storm of sobbing.

CHAPTER SEVENTEEN

GHOSTS

" SHE's a physical medium, and that's rare," said Bait. Albany and he were walking home from a matinée performance of ' The Passing of the Third-Floor-Back ' and this play with its hint of a ghostly visitant had plunged them into a fascinating argument about the possibility of the dead reappearing to their friends on earth. And Bait, to support his contention that such manifestations were at least conceivable, had mentioned Mrs. Druce, the medium : Mrs. Druce who would be giving a séance the Sunday after next in Mrs. Repton-Wills's drawing-room.

" But what exactly is a physical medium ? " asked Albany

" A physical medium is a materialization medium."

" And what's a materialization medium ? "

" Well, the theory is that a materialization medium extrudes something from her body called ectoplasm which the spirits use to build themselves up before our eyes.   This Mrs. Druce is a most remarkable case of a very rare gift, I'm told : probably the most celebrated medium of her kind in England.   Mrs. Repton-Wills says that the phenomena she produces are astonishing.   People swear that she's produced for them their mothers or their fathers or their boys who were killed in South Africa."

" My God, Bait, I should like to go to this séance.   Could you get me in, d'you think ? "

" Old Colonel Budlier's going."   Bait avoided a direct answer. " He goes to all Mrs. Repton-Wills's séances in the hope of getting in touch with his wife.   I suppose that this time he's hoping actually to see her and talk with her."

A sudden alarm pricked at Albany's breast.   Delia ? He had loved Delia in a way, but . . . he certainly didn't want her to materialize before him and say that she was ever at his side. No, to put it bluntly, she was better where she was.   He remained silent for a few seconds.   But curiosity conquered fear, and, fortifying himself against any such phenomenon with the resolution to disbelieve in it, he repeated his request.   " Any chance of getting *me* in, d'you think, old chap ? "

" I don't know.   There'll be a crowd, I expect.   But I can try."

" Does one pay ? "

" Oh, yes.   We all contribute our half-guinea."

" And how many will be there ? "

" Thirty or forty, I dare say."

" It sounds a profitable business for Mrs. Druce."

" Not very.   Not if these physical mediums tell the truth when they say that they can only sit very seldom because it takes so much out of them."

" I see.   Well, do try to get me in."

" I'll do my best, but I can't promise."   Bait, as ready as a boy to magnify an event to which he had the privilege of access, did not want to sound too confident.   " I'll ask Mrs. Repton-Wills.   She may do it for me."

And two days later, pleased as any other man to demonstrate his influence at a court, he came round to Albany's house and told him, " It's all right, old man.   I've managed it.   Mrs.

Repton-Wills says she'll welcome you as a friend of mine. The Sunday after next at three o'clock."

Whereat Albany was almost as excited as a child who has been invited to a pantomime. Anticipation was a recurring sense of pleasure throughout the next eight days. And on the Sunday afternoon, a fine warm day of St. Luke's summer, he walked, with the excitement in his feet, towards Avenue Road and the big house of the Repton-Willses. As he turned into the shady Avenue Road he saw—and was further stimulated by the sight—a string of carriages before the house. There was a victoria with a pair of nodding and prancing bays, an electric brougham, a large motor cabriolet (the first he'd seen) and, just drawing away from the kerb, an old-fashioned closed barouche with a cockaded coachman and groom on its box, the groom sitting very erect with his arms folded. This last was like the carriage of an ambassador driving away from a royal levee. He walked the faster for the sight of this cavalcade. Besides these carriage people pedestrians were coming along the pavement who were obviously Mrs. Repton-Wills's guests because they were dressed for a party, the women in silk dresses and large hats, the men (like Albany himself) in their frock coats and silk hats. " A fashionable affair," he thought, " this appointment with the dead."

The door of the house was open, and a manservant stood in the hall, directing the guests into a large room that was clearly the Library. In the midst of it stood Mr. Repton-Wills, receiving the guests. He was almost as tall as Albany, but much portlier about the stomach and much ruddier in the cheek. A retired Indian merchant, everything about him, from his deep frock coat and black pearl tie-pin to his Chippendale chairs and massive mahogany bookshelves suggested that he had retired from his Indian trading with more than one lac of rupees. Smiling, exchanging jokes, laughing noisily, patting people amicably on the back, especially the ladies, he was explaining to them all that they must wait in this room till the Memsahib was ready.

Albany presented himself, stating that his name was Grahame and Mr. Bait was his sponsor.

" Delighted to see you, Mr. Grahame. Yes, old man Bait's not here yet, but he'll come. He's a regular worshipper— customer, I was going to say. This the first time you've been to one of our shows ? "

" Yes. First time I've ever been to a séance."

Mr. Repton-Wills lowered his voice. " Awful hokum, don't you think ? . . . Or are you a True Believer ? "

" No, not yet. I know nothing about it. I've just come to learn."

" Then you'll learn something to-day, my boy, if my dear wife's to be trusted. This Druce woman raises the dead, it seems. The devil only knows who's going to look in on us this afternoon in addition to those we've invited. Queen Elizabeth, perhaps. Or our late beloved Queen Victoria—and *then* we'll none of us know what to do. And you wouldn't believe the twaddle they all talk, whether they're Socrates or Napoleon or Nero's aunt. They all say exactly the same, and it sounds like a nonconformist padre's muck. *You* know : a lot of flapdoodle about the Infinite and the Astral and the Higher Life. If you learn nothing else, you'll learn something about human credulity."

" I gather you're a sceptic."

" Of course I am. Good afternoon, Mrs. Fowler. Do find a seat. The Memsahib won't be long. . . . I don't say that all of its trickery. Some of these mediums undoubtedly have a thought-reading faculty and so I daresay they come to believe in themselves but even these, I'm convinced, if they can't get going, put up a show rather than disappoint people who've paid them good money. They're all fraudulent to that extent. But what matter ? It amuses the wife. She needs something to amuse her now that the children are all gone. Besides, she's ever so much nicer to me since she got in tune with the Infinite. You married ? "

" Widower."

" Ah, here's old Bait coming in. And old Colonel Budlier too. Old man Bait imagines he comes purely as a scientist, but he's as ready to believe as any of the other old women. The old colonel comes again and again hoping to get a message from his dead wife. It's sad ; his boy plays for Middlesex. You've heard of Tom Budlier ? Afternoon, Bait. My wife's in the vestry with Mrs. Druce : they won't be long. Take a seat, Colonel. . . . Yes, the Memsahib has turned my house into a spiritualist church, and I'm the verger. You know old Budlier, you say. Poor old boy, no doubt he's hoping his wife'll materialize for him to-day. Perhaps she will. What we're going to see—God help us !—*I* don't know."

Again that prick of alarm, and a running for refuge into scepticism. And again the alarm was crowded into a corner by his interest in what they were going to see.

He had time for only a few words with Bait and the Colonel because just then Mrs. Repton-Wills signalled from the passage to her husband who promptly announced in a loud voice, "You can go into the room now, ladies and gentlemen. Please go very quietly and take your seats as silently as possible"; and in a side-whisper to Albany, "Awful hokum, isn't it?"

All flowed along the passage and into a large room with lofty bay windows. Here four rows of chairs were set in concentric arcs, tranversely, so that they faced a corner between chimney breast and outside wall. Across the corner heavy blue curtains hung from a rod but, not being closed as yet, they revealed a single elbow chair against a back-cloth of black velvet. All daylight was shut out from this place of assembly, the thick gold curtains being drawn across the bay windows, but the room for the present was brilliantly illuminated by the electric lamps on the walls. As bidden, the people went quietly to their chairs and sat there as silently as in church-pews. Albany found himself in the farthest chair of the second row, with Bait on his left and the Colonel beyond Bait.

A stirring of heads: Mrs. Druce had entered. Behind her came three other women, with Mrs. Repton-Wills at their tail. Mrs. Repton-Wills was a small brisk managing woman, a little black tube of energy, information, smiles and instruction, but Mrs. Druce was even smaller and as placid in her movement as Mrs. Repton-Wills was bustling and restless. Perhaps fifty years old and barely five feet high, she was so thin as to seem almost cadaverous. Her tiny attenuated body was draped from throat to feet in a black gown like the soutane of a Greek Orthodox priest. This enveloping robe was brightened only by a gold chain and pendant like the chain of a lady mayoress. The three attendant women diverged to chairs among the congregation, and on Albany inquiring, "Who the deuce are they?" Bait explained, "They've been examining her dress and her hair, at her request, to see that she's nothing concealed there. Somebody else has already searched the cabinet and the upholstery of that chair."

"I see," said Albany, and thought that while Bait might pretend to be judicially impartial, what he really wanted was to be an advocate for Mrs. Druce.

Mrs. Druce went to the chair in the 'cabinet' and sat in it, facing the audience with her arms on its elbows and her little black-slippered feet crossed. Her eyes closed ; a long uncomfortable wait—and then her head drooped, her right arm fell from its rest and hung down lifelessly, her head went back as she drew in a long raucous breath, it dropped sideways and came up again as she drew in another long asthmatic inhalation, her mouth twitched spasmodically, and she moaned. Then, sharply, she jerked herself upright, brought the lifeless arm back to its rest, and, keeping her eyes still closed, sat before them like a statue.

The trance was complete—or its simulation—and Mrs. Repton-Wills drew the curtains across that statuesque figure, carefully closing them.

" Why close the curtains ? " Albany inquired in a low mutter.

" *Tsh* . . ." warned Bait.

And at that instant Albany became aware of a woman standing in the aisle at his side and impending over him. As a crane impends over a cargo-boat to deliver its goods so she leaned over him to deliver an answer to his query. She was a tall, round-backed, flat-breasted woman of about forty, with grey hair, a long narrow nose that was now pointing straight down at him, and large, too large eyes that glistened like wet boiled sweets. His query had shown her that he was a novice, so she had bent down to lower information into his empty hold : " The spirit guides like the cabinet to be closed," she said, " so that they can accumulate the necessary power within it."

" Oh, I see," said Albany, looking up at the super-incumbent woman ; but, never wanting to offend any woman, he forbore to suggest that the power could easily escape upwards and over the curtain rod. Instead he turned to Bait and whispered, " Who is this creature ? "

" She is Miss Winser," said Bait. " Mrs. Druce's business manager who travels with her and sees that everything's in order."

" A kind of front-of-the-house manager ? " suggested Albany, in whom the overpowering silence and solemnity was provoking a desire to be frivolous.

" If you like," conceded Bait with a lifted nostril and an unamused shrug ; and Albany perceived that, wanting to believe in the forthcoming phenomena, he did not want their approach to be treated with levity.

The white lights in the room went out to a series of clicks, and only a sea-green, submarine light saved the room from darkness. Albany turned his head to learn the source of this strange illumination and saw at the back a single electric lamp swathed in a green silk handkerchief. Even as he considered it, a lamp wrapped in a red handkerchief came alight, the green lamp went out, and now the long lofty room had no light whatever except the dim radiation from this single red star.

" Good Lord ! " he muttered, and brought his eyes back to the cabinet. At first he could hardly see it, for the red glow barely touched its curtains.

Miss Winser bent forward from her waist to load some more information into his hold. " The spirits won't materialize in a strong light. They find a dim red light best on the whole. It isn't only Mrs. Druce who needs a red light," she explained apologetically. " They all do. This is just how Roley likes it."

" Roley ? "

But Mrs. Repton-Wills was now standing up in front and speaking. " Friends, shall we just say the prayer we always use ? It's so helpful to Roley." And she led them in a prayer. This prayer convinced him that Mrs. Repton-Wills and the women joining in it must believe in all this business because not one of them looked capable of what else must be an hypocrisy. Bait was mumbling the words with them.

They were only half way through the prayer when, suddenly, rather alarmingly, a deep voice from behind the curtains added itself to theirs : "—may obtain the promises which exceed all that we can desire. . . ."

Albany, startled, turned to Bait.

" That's Roley," said Bait. It was easy to speak aloud while so many voices were reciting in unison. " That's his voice."

But to Albany it sounded like a woman's voice pitched unnaturally low.

The prayer over, this deep voice said, " Good evening, friends. How d'you do ? " and Miss Winser, leaning her elevated frame against the wall, exclaimed cheerfully, " That's dear Roley. Good evening, Roley."

Other faithful women copied her. " Good evening, Roley."

" What d'you mean : ' evening,' " scoffed the voice. " It's three in the afternoon. There ! I caught you out there."

" Roley will always have his joke," said Miss Winser, exactly like Cornelia of Eddie.

" I suppose it's the darkness that's making you talk so silly," added Roley.

Slowly the curtains parted, with a rattling of their rings, and something which looked like a tall figure draped in a long white veil appeared in the opening. A dark patch at the top of the blurred whiteness might have been a face. Albany, aquiver with astonishment, stretched his neck to see more and saw that the white veiling, so thin and rare as to seem woven of spider-thread, fell almost to the floor, but not quite. It floated, and did not rest.

The voice, which might certainly be coming from the dark patch, said perkily, " Well, aren't any of you going to say how d'you do ? Come on ! Aren't you ? "

So perky was the question that Albany could only liken it to that of a marionette in a puppet show. But he did not say this to Bait since he had perceived now that Bait was disposed to give some credence to Roley. A pity to hurt old Bait.

Obediently the faithful ladies were saying, " How do you do, Roley ? " And, " Hallo, Roley."

" I'm glad to see so many familiar faces," Roley told them. " And one or two unfamiliar faces too. That is good. That's what we want. Now I hope you'll have some good manifestations this afternoon. Will you be so good as to wait a minute."

" Yes, Roley. That's all right, Roley."

" Okay," said Roley ; and the dark face and white veiling retired, backwards, into the curtains, which closed over them with a rattling of rings. Miss Winser lowered the upper half of her frame, like the crane's iron girder, towards Albany's eyes. " Dear Roley is Mrs. Druce's guide. He guides other mediums too. They're not tied to any one person ; they go and help people everywhere. They are wonderful helpers."

" But why is a guide necessary ? " he asked of this pendent woman.

" Well, in everything, even on the earth's plane, you need a master of the ceremonies, don't you ? "

" Do you ? " he began dubiously, but the curtains, rustling apart, stopped him. Roley's voice was saying. " Now then : there's Mrs. Druce for you to see, poor dear. There she is, in her trance."

Albany lifted his hindquarters an inch or two off his chair. Yes, Mrs. Druce was certainly in her chair, and the white blur seemed to be at her side.

" Show yourself, Mrs. Druce," said the voice. " Let the friends see you. Stand up. You're not very large, you know."

Automatically the figure of the medium obeyed, as if in hypnosis. It stood.

" Now can you all see Mrs. Druce ? "

" Yes, yes," declared the faithful.

" That's right. They can all see you, ducky. Sit down again, there's a good girl. We don't want to tire you. We want to get a lot out of you this afternoon."

Before she could recede towards her chair the curtains closed, covering her and Roley—if indeed he was an entity other than her.

Mrs. Winser appeared very ready to act as deputy master of ceremonies during the temporary absence of Roley, and she called out, " Shall we sing Roley a song, the one he likes ? " adding for the unitiated, " He likes one with a lilt. It helps the vibrations." And straightway she began to sing, in a high voice like the untrained treble of a child, ' Lily of Laguna.' The song didn't seem to surprise any of them, for the women sang it with her, a few confidently, others faintly and self-consciously. Apparently Bait couldn't persuade himself to sing such words as " She's the only rose Laguna knows, and Ah know she likes me " : he just sat there with nostrils unhappily elevated. As for Albany, he said, " Good God ! "

" That's nothing," Bait commented. " I've heard them sing stranger songs than that at séances. It's the tune that matters, not the words."

" Well, I don't know, but it seems rather rum to me."

Bait sniffed. After pretending that this was a show into which it would be difficult to introduce a friend, he did not want it ridiculed. " I see no particular reason," he began in his most sardonic tone, " why we should expect Reality to accord to our human tastes and desires."

Not liking the tone, Albany snapped back, " I can think of a good many reasons why it should " ; and he was wondering, warmly, if this was the opening bar to a fine quarrel when Roley's voice intervened. The vibrations of the song *had*, it seemed, helped him in his seclusion, for he now said, " I have here someone who passed over many years ago. A white-haired lady. She died after an operation. Would someone speak to her and call her out ? "

A man in front of Albany immediately exclaimed, " An operation ? Who is it ? Who are you ? "

But Miss Winser wasn't going to allow any such direct inquiry. The crane swung round from Albany and lowered itself to this new and empty vessel. " No, you mustn't say that. You must say ' Is it for me ? ' or ' Is it So-and-so ? ' "

" What ? " demanded the man of this overhanging face.

223

Miss Winser repeated her formulae.

The man obeyed. " Is it for me ? " he said to the curtains.

" Yes, that's the voice ; that's the vibration," said Roley, seemingly well pleased.

" Speak up, son," encouraged Miss Winser. " Call her out. Ask her to come out, whoever she is."

" Would you come out, please ? "

Through the curtains came a white form, much shorter than that of Roley, and Albany noticed that, as it came, the curtains bulged with it. He could just discern some features in the face, small features, like those of a woman.

" Speak to her, son," said Miss Winser. " Ask her questions."

Yes, thought Albany, for pity's sake give Mrs. Druce something to go on. He began to feel a kind of vicarious anxiety for Mrs. Druce, as if he didn't want her put to shame.

" Is it you, Mother ? " asked the man.

" Yes, my boy." A voice, low and breathless, came from the apparition. " I want you to know that I am happy and ever near you. I have no pain now since I passed into the world of spirit."

Having said which, the wraith withdrew with a sound very like the rustling of mundane textiles.

" They make very human noises, these spirits," muttered Albany to Bait.

" Ectoplasm, I imagine, is substantial," answered Bait in an offensively pitying tone.

" Do you ? " retorted Albany. " Well, I don't."

And down upon him came the crane, to unload any errors from his hold. " They are not human noises," it said. " Nor anything material. They are psychic winds."

Well, you can't both be right, thought Albany, projecting some of his irritation with Bait on to this beetling face, but he said nothing aloud ; and the crane, satisfied, swung upwards and rested.

Roley was speaking again. " I have another spirit form here. Is seems to be an elderly lady who passed over not long ago. Only some months ago."

Apprehension in one sitter, and a trembling of his heart. Delia ?

" She is very weary, but she seeks a friend in the second row."

Albany was in the second row. His heart thumped out the fact.

" I think her name is Mary . . . or Margaret . . . or perhaps Marion."

Marion ? Let's hope it's for old Bait. His woman was a Marion. Interesting if it's for old Bait. Amusing. His heart rested.

"Wait, friends. She—yes—she has a message for a lady in the middle of the second row. Her daughter, I fancy."

Ah, well . . . a relief on the whole . . . better so.

"Call the spirit friend out," urged Miss Winser.

Five seats away from Albany a woman said shyly, "Please come out," having to clear her voice to complete the sentence ; and in response to this broken call a form approached through the curtains, a form a little taller than the previous one, but not so tall as Roley. Again the dark oval at the top of the hanging white web might have been a face.

"Is it you, Mother ? " asked the woman.

"Yes," said the voice, very wearily.

"Could you come closer so that I could see you ? "

"No," answered the voice, "I'm too weary and tired for that."

Neat, thought Albany. A clever girl, Mrs. Druce.

"You have a message for me ? "

"Yes, your dear sister is with me. She is with me in the astral, and she sends all her love."

Evidently the woman was a believer, for she said, "It is sweet of you to come to me like this."

"I have often tried to get in touch with you." The weary voice was hardly audible. "Be good to the others." And the spirit faded—or it retreated soundlessly into the darkness behind the curtains. Did the robe sink to the floor ? Albany, who'd been craning his neck, could almost believe, not only that it had sunk to the floor, but that it had disappeared through the floor.

Or had it been drawn back under the curtains ?

"And you *had* a sister who's passed on ? " called Miss Winser to the woman.

"Oh, yes, yes."

"Well, there now," said Miss Winser in triumph to all. Let them not miss any success by her principal. "You see ? "

"I have someone else here," said Roley (or her principal), pleased by this success. "A young man who came over to us in the pride of his youth. He died on a battle-field. I can see a wound. He is very young, and his name, I think, is John. Or James. Jacob, perhaps. Does anyone claim him ? "

No one.

"He is very insistent to come out. Someone must know him.

225

Perhaps I've got the name wrong. I get also the impression of the name Henry. Or Harold. Does that convey anything to one of our friends ? He says his wife is here. Or is it his sweetheart ? He is very young. Please help him."

A voice behind Albany, a young woman's voice, said timidly, " Please come out."

" Speak up, dear," advised Miss Winser, but unnecessarily because a white shape, tall and a little different from that which had purported to be Roley, was standing—or floating—before the curtains. What had happened to his vision Albany did not know, but this shape certainly appeared to have materialized out of the darkness, without troubling the curtains.

" Is it you, Jamey ? Jamey, is it you ? "

" Yes," said the spirit and faded. There was nothing but darkness before the curtains.

" They're not exactly diffuse, these spirits," Albany whispered to Bait, sardonically, for in his irritation with Bait who'd been sardonic with him, he no longer cared to spare him. Rather the contrary. But he lowered his head to make this observation because by now he was as afraid of Miss Winser as he used to be of his teacher at school, and he didn't want her to know that he was talking in class.

" It's difficult for them to speak at all," Bait sniffed, jealous for the good name of this performance.

" That's very obvious," Albany rejoined. " It must be very difficult. Say a word too much, and you blow the gaff."

" Pfaw ! " That was all Bait said—or snorted.

" And I've noticed," continued the critic, to vex him further —but still keeping his head down and his lips nearly shut and only once casting a quick glance up at Miss Winser—" that if a masculine voice goes on too long, it changes back into Mrs. Druce's."

" And there's nothing strange in that," sneered Bait. " It's Mrs. Druce they're using. The power they draw from her may fail very quickly. I see nothing remarkable in that. Nothing at all. May I advise you not to argue from ignorance."

Albany, unable for the moment to debate this insolent advice (Teacher was at his side), said nothing but resolved to open fire on a wide front, when dismissed from school. Bait, however, that prince among arguers, *did* wish to continue the disputation and, since nothing was happening at the moment, he asked provocatively, " You don't believe then that they are genuine manifestations ? "

226

" I do not.   Certainly not."

" Then, pray, what are they ? "

" Butter muslin," suggested Albany.

" Butter muslin ! " Bait despised this interpretation so heartily that he echoed the words quite loudly.

" Yes ; or cheese cloth."

" Pshaw ! " Not worth an answer.

Miss Winser heard them and came down upon Albany—both metaphorically and literally, because she bent forward at an angle of sixty degrees.   " That is the spirit robe," she breathed into his ear, not, it seemed, without pain and pity.   " The ectoplastic shroud.   It's partly physical because some of Mrs. Druce's etheric body provides the ectoplasm."

Albany, interested, was staring up into her face.   It was not more than twelve inches above him.   " But how does it come from her body ? "

" Through the mouth or the pores of the skin—or indeed from anywhere.   There are many different grades of ectoplasm."

" Oh, I see," said Albany.

She nodded and smiled, glad that he saw.

And he, glad that she was glad, smiled too and said, " Thank you very much."

" I have here a spirit— " Roley's voice—" for a gentleman on the left as I stand here."

Oh, dear ! Albany started.   Sitting at the end of his row, he was well on the left as Roley stood there (wherever Roley stood).   No one was more on the left.

" It's for a sitter in the back row.   Would the gentleman speak ? There's a sailor here.   Call him out, please, and do the talking."

Someone at the back, a man with a strong, rich voice, asked, " Are you an officer or an ordinary rating ? "

The sailor behind the curtain didn't seem to know, so Roley spoke for him.   Somewhat sadly, he rebuked the questioner. " There is no rank and file, my dear sir, in the spirit world," he said.

" Ah !   Well   fielded ! "   thought   Albany.   " Saved   the boundary."

" Call him by name if you know him," Roley advised.

" Are you Solly, by any chance ? If so, come along and let's have a peep at you." Clearly the man at the back was a merry soul.

Something white, tall, and bulky came through the curtains. It said no word.

227

" Hullo, how are you ? " asked the merry soul at the back.

" Fine," said the spirit.

" What's my name, eh ? Tell me my name, and then I'll know if you're old Solly or not."

" Pardon ? " said the spirit.

The questioner repeated his question and its purpose.

" Oh, no," objected Miss Winser in a low pained voice.

But the questioner persisted. " Come along, cock. What's my name ? "

" Alfred. Your name is Alfred."

" Well, that's right enough. Great snakes ! " There was a considerable stir in the darkness. " Everything okay with you, is it ? I can't say that you're looking very well." Clearly this was a man who must make jokes before an audience. " You look a bit pale from here."

" Yes, but wait a mo, Alfred," interrupted the spirit. " Let *me* speak for a change. You were always one who wanted to do all the talking."

" The gentleman asked me to talk. Your Mr. Roley said Talk."

" Yes, but give me a chance, mate. I've got little Liz here. She's very anxious to see her father. I've told her I'd see what I can do. You get her old man to come along."

" Liz ? Little Liz ? . . . Oh yes, of course ! Good Lord, little Liz ! Right you are ! I'll tell him. Is that all, mate ? "

" Yes, but good luck to you. Keep your pecker up. Never say die while there's a shot in the locker."

" Good Christ ! " said the man, forgetting the ladies in the darkness.

This was quite the most impressive demonstration they'd had so far and, on the face of it, carried some evidential value. Miss Winser was so pleased with it that she bore down upon Albany's ear and said triumphantly, " It makes you think, doesn't it ? "

" It certainly does," he answered, but doubted if the woman saw any double meaning in the words. In fact, he was wondering if the man was an accomplice. But how get into Mrs. Repton-Wills's room ? And how explain the question " Are you an officer ? " which had plainly worried the spirit. By now he didn't know what was happening or what he must believe.

" Well friends." Roley's voice broke upon his musing. " I am going to leave you now, but someone you all know will take my place. Help her all you can."

A brief silence, loaded with expectancy—and then came a voice, high-pitched and childish—obviously, Albany thought, an adult's voice forced upwards to an unnatural height and given the accents of a child. "Hullo, everybody. Hullo."

Instantly Miss Winser cried, "Oh, here's our dear little Ethy! Good afternoon, Ethy"; and she drooped over Albany and explained, "This is Ethy, a little helper who comes to us sometimes."

Albany nodded his understanding, so as not to disappoint her. And waited with parted lips.

Through the curtains came a little white fluffy wraith, four feet high, which a credulous imagination might have construed as a little girl in a party frock, her hands joined shyly behind her.

"Hullo, Ethy," and "How are you Ethy?" said the faithful.

"Quite well, thank you." Her accents could not have been more babyish. "Shall I sing you a song?"

"Yes, do, Ethy, please."

And Ethy, with all the heavy stresses of the Infants' School, sang, "Lazy Mary, will *you* get up, will *you* get up?" and as she sang the ditty danced this way and that—as might a doll whose body was manipulated by a hand through the curtains. Albany dropped his eyes from the sight, in a sharp distaste. He cast one glance at Bait and was pleased to observe, from the present position of those expressive nostrils, that Bait was not quite happy about this, either. But Bait watched, with a thin mouth. Not Albany; not again could he offend his eyes with sight of that little tap-dancing spectre. He kept his eyes on his feet and longed, prayed, for the performance to end.

Ethy, having done her act, retreated backwards into the curtains and said, "There's a big, big man here. Ever so big. He wants to come out. He's for the big, big man by the window."

By the window? Albany was by the window.

"The big gentleman in the second row."

Albany himself. Miss Winser bent to tell him so. "That's you. It's someone manifesting for you."

"For me?" His heart protested, his knee shook.

"Yes. Please speak. Speak quickly or the friend may go."

A schoolboy fear of this oppressive woman, together with a gentleman's desire to oblige her, compelled him to say something. "Who are you?" he asked, feeling as nervous of this public utterance as ever he felt in his first days as a curate.

"No, *no*," she objected with something of a teacher's

229

impatience when a stupid child repeats a mistake. " You mustn't say—"

But before she could educate him further, a different voice commanded, " *Wait!* Our spirit friend here is anxious to speak but the power of this medium is nearly exhausted." It was Roley's voice. Roley had changed places with Ethy. Either he had come back after a quiet rest or Mrs. Druce had forgotten that she was little Ethy. " Speak quickly— " had Mrs. Druce heard Miss Winser? —" and the friend will try to answer."

The friend, however, spoke first. " I am your brother," he said—surely in the same voice as Roley's.

Your *brother*? Vick? Good heavens, he had feared that Delia might appear, but he had never thought of Vick. Was old Vick coming? He didn't feel at all afraid of old Vick. Rather pleased to see him, in fact. But a ' brother '—yes, a pretty safe guess about an elderly Victorian gentleman.

" Ask him, is it So-and-so ? " prodded the eager Miss Winser.

Oh, no : he wasn't going to give Mrs. Druce any clues so he snatched at the first name that leapt before him. " Are you Fred ? "

" I am your brother," said the voice, skilfully evading this direct lunge. " I am pleased to see you at last. I have been waiting for you." A white figure, just the same as the others who had proffered themselves as men, was now before the curtains. " I have been close to you very often, ever since I passed into the Beyond, as close as ever I was in our life together— "

And that wasn't so very close, thought Albany.

" —but I have never been able to convey any message to you. God bless you."

Doesn't sound like Vick. Albany's brain, at a standstill, provided him with nothing to say ; with nothing to do but stare.

" Speak, say something, ask him something," urged the damnable woman at his side. " *You* must do the talking ; you must help the vibrations."

Too timid to tell her to shut up, to say " Not I ! Damn the vibrations," too timid not to obey, he asked feebly, " What is the message ? "

" Our dear mother is with me on the Other Side, and we are waiting for you, till you shall join us. She sends you her undying love."

Albany was just thinking, " A mother with him—*that's* a safe

230

gambit for two old codgers like myself and—" when the spectre's voice (or so it seemed) began to breathe forth in a kind of broken and fading sigh, " Tell Ed . . . Ed . . . Ed . . ." And at once Albany's thoughts flew to Eddie Clapton. " Tell Ed. . . ."

" Help him, help him," besought Miss Winser.

And Albany, surprised and interested, was well inclined to hear more. He was ready to give a gentle push to this needle stuck in a groove. " Do you mean Edward ? " he asked.

" Yes, Eddie. Tell Eddie my son that I am alive and happy and helping him in all his struggles."

" My *son* "—was this spoken *of* Eddie *or to* Albany ? The ambiguity of the Delphic oracle. Possibly, when one had passed into the Higher Life, one could address even one's brother as ' my son.'

" Tell him, my dear Eddie, that love is greater than death. Tell him that I am continuing to watch over him and work for him as I did in life."

And a lot you did for him in life, thought Albany—a thought which instantly raised before his mind the figure of Jean.

And instantly the voice said, " And give my dear love to Jeanie. Give Jeanie my blessing."

This so shook Albany, plunging him into doubts whether all his ridicule was wrong, that he felt he must trap this spirit by some trick and so escape from this sudden belief. What name could he use ? A name came into view from a novel he'd been reading that morning, and he snatched at it and uttered it, though with trepidation, because he didn't know what force he was tampering with. " You say Mother is with you. Is Queenie there too ? "

" Yes, yes, she is here," the spirit assured him. " And she is longing to meet you again." The relief was like a sudden loosening of taut nerves ; a sweet relief ; relief that he need believe in nothing more disquieting, nothing more portentous, than strange symptoms of thought-transference. It was so great that it took the form within him of a tremulant hysterical giggle. He listened to hear more about Queenie, and the g ggle became a violent inner trembling as the spirit told him, " She sends you her love. She will come through to you one day. If you come again she will try to use this medium. She asks me to tell you this. So come again . . . come again. . . ."

Aye, a good method of securing a continuation of his custom. He would have liked to say, " I know no Queenie," but he lacked both the courage and the cruelty. He could not shame Mrs. Druce before them all. And he could not distress them all.

All were silent around him, waiting for him to speak further ; but he did not speak, and Roley, as if to fill an embarassing hiatus, said, " That is enough. That will do, my son." (Like Bait, Albany was quite pleased to be called ' my son '). " I cannot hold my medium any longer. I think her power is spent, so that no more spirit forms can be produced for you." Was it that Mrs. Druce, fee'd for an hour only, was informing them that they'd had their time ? " Good-bye, friends. Come again, and I will try to get better and stronger manifestations for you."

" Good-bye, Roley. Good-bye, dear Roley. Thank you so much."

" You will come again, friends, won't you ? "

" Yes we will come again."

There was a general stir and shifting in the room as of a congregation released from stillness by the departing of the priests. He heard footsteps and a click ; and white light filled the room. Mrs. Repton-Wills was going from light switch to the cabinet, where she drew the curtains apart. And there in her chair was Mrs. Druce, her body slumped forward and her right arm hanging lifelessly by her knees so that its curved fingers almost touched the floor. She flung back her head, groaned, opened her eyes, shut them, raised the dead hand to rub them, and, opening them again, smiled on the company like one who had reawakened into life.

Bait and Albany walked home side by side. Some way ahead of them, under the wayside trees, walked Colonel Budlier, alone, and looking like a disappointed man but one who had accepted with a soldier's obedience the order that there should be no communication for him. He had one gloved hand resting sadly on the small of his back as he walked slowly home.

Bait was ready for the battle, impatient for it. " Well, what did you think of it ? " he asked.

But Albany was no longer so eager to fight. Always his cholers cooled quickly, and just now he was looking at the little lonely figure of the Colonel and feeling some compassion for him. And envying him his love of a wife now dead.

So he said to Bait that he never liked to attack anyone's beliefs if they afforded happiness. A somewhat self-satisfied remark, to which Bait replied that he wasn't a silly girl who refused to listen to anything that might shake her faith. He wasn't quite such a fool as that, he said.

All right, thought Albany; if he wants it, let him have it. And he was now glad that he could proceed for he was eager to demonstrate his superiority to all those naïve and gullible people. This was a powerful emotion, and it caused him to utter, before he could arrest it, a comment that was more vigorous than discreet. " I was shocked beyond measure at the whole idiotic performance," he said.

" Oh, were you ? " The lust for battle warmed within Bait ; it lifted his nostrils, thinned his lips and lit a faint gleam in his eyes. " That is interesting."

" Yes." Albany, having slid a little way down the slippery slope of violent utterance, could not stop his descent. He shot rapidly down the steep escarpment, gathering momentum as he went. " The whole thing was an insult to one's intelligence. I don't know which was the more contemptible, the quackery of that woman in her ridiculous cabinet or the credulity of her dupes in the audience. I was ashamed to be among them. And, lord, to have paid a half-guinea for *that* ! Why, I could have got a better show for twopence at a fair. Good God, Bait : surely your spiritual perceptions suggest to you that it's beneath the dignity of Omnipotence to employ such cheap and silly methods, such paltry punch-and-judy tricks, in order to reveal to us the not unimportant fact of our survival after death. I thought the whole show the performance of a mountebank before a collection of fools." (Good. That was good).

" Fools ! " Bait didn't think it good. " Fools indeed. You might remember that I was one of them. You think you're mighty subtle, but if you were a shade *more* subtle you'd see that the very triviality of the phenomena might be a proof of their genuineness. If Mrs. Druce were just a conjuror she could easily learn from Messrs. Maskelyne and Cooke how to give us an apparently miraculous exhibition and she could mug up from books some far more impressive revelations for the spirits to deliver. But I take it she's honest and—— "

But Albany was less anxious to deal with this suggestion than to continue his attack. " Good lord, you could simply *see* the trickery at work. First she has that revolting Miss Winser in the front of the house to start the bidding, as it were, and to jump us into giving the right hints and to act as a claque when her principal produces something that sounds good. And then

233

all the names she tried out on us. Among forty people someone's bound to have known a " Mar—— " or a John or a James
She'd time to overlook us all before Mrs. Wills drew the curtains
and it was plain that some of us must have lost a white-haired
mother—— "

" Maybe, but how do you account for the fact that some of
the apparitions were twice as tall as poor little Mrs. Druce ? "

" What's wrong with an upstretched arm and some cheese
cloth ? And we were not to say, ' Who are you ? '—oh, no !
—according to the atrocious Miss Winser, we must say ' Is it
Margot ? ' or ' Is it Mum ? ' and so give Mrs. Druce something
to be getting on with. The whole thing is bilge from beginning
to end."

" I suggest that the bilge is in your remarks. Each is rather
more nonsensical than the last. How do you account for
' Eddie ' and ' Jean ' ? "

" And how do you account for Queenie ? There's no such
person, and she sent me her love. That damnable woman
prodded me to speak, and, okay, I spake with my tongue.
I invented Queenie, and I'm getting very fond of her."

" Never mind Queenie. Don't run away from the point.
It's the mark of good intelligence that it keeps to the point
and of poor intelligence—— "

" Poor intelligence, my *God* ! "

"— that it quickly leaves it. How do you account for ' Eddie '
and ' Jean ' ? "

" Everyone has known an ' Ed—something,' and as for
' Jean,' I have conceded all along a certain element of thought-
transference."

" And if you concede that, everything becomes possible. If
you concede direct communication between mind and mind,
all materialism falls to the ground. I don't suppose you know
the first thing about modern physics, but if you did, you'd
know that they now ask us to accept as an hypothesis that
material bodies can be affected by events in empty space which
are not discoverable by our finest scientific instruments and
are presumably non-material. Well, just as from the movements of magnetized objects we deduce a magnetic field, so
by the behaviour of these mediums we can infer the activity
of spiritual forces. But if you're going to monkey about with
a scientific investigation by throwing in a Queenie—— "

" Queenie was a perfectly legitimate check. And she did her
part splendidly. I was very pleased with her."

" —then of course everything in the experiment will go wrong. You will have jarred all the vibrations."

" Jarred all the hollyhocks! Merciful heavens, there are times when I don't understand you at all. You reject every orthodox God and are willing to accept any moonshine about vibrations and witches and diablerie and the Devil."

" If you knew anything about it, you'd know that God and the Devil are probably aspects of the same thing."

" And what in the name of Bosh that means I've no idea."

" I'm sure you haven't. It would need perceptions of far greater subtlety than yours—— "

" Great and holy saints above! "

" —and far greater knowledge of the old religions."

" Knowledge! I reckon I know rather more about the Devil than you do. You forget that I had a theological training."

" To be sure, I don't forget it. It's the source of all your pitiful myopia. A theological training is, by definition, designed to bind up a man's brain so that he's for ever incapable of unprejudiced and objective thought. A parson is vowed to believe and so can't practise any free inquiry. If you'd—— "

But Albany, hurt beyond bearing by several of these statements, by more than he could remember, announced with dignity, staring down the road, " I withdraw from this argument since it's only conducted with abuse. I'll say no more."

" Say all you want," encouraged Bait.

So he said a deal more. " I don't believe you really believe in any of it. You only pretend to, so that you can argue. Either that or you *want* to be deluded. Anything that suits your little human wish for survival you're ready to believe because you want to believe it. It's like a child that's determined to believe it'll be fine to-morrow because it's going to the Zoo. And I say that's infantile."

" Oh, I'm infantile, am I? Infantile in my examination of the evidence? I who've had a legal training! A legal training, let me suggest, is the one training that sharpens a man's mind into an instrument of more than usual clarity, precision and logical deduction."

" I disagree entirely. The logic of lawyers is almost always limited to their own little field. It's not at all uncommon for lawyers to talk the most clotted piffle—— "

" Tshaw! It's *your* mind that's lamentably limited in its field. You have the sort of closed mind that can't believe in the possibility of anything that doesn't cog in with its extremely limited sublunary experience. I speak under reproof, but I suggest that's the trouble with you. For my part, I have an open mind."

"And an open mind, you will allow me to suggest, speaking under reproof, can be so open that it's rather like a refuse pit into which any rubbish can be thrown."

"For which remark I thank you," said Bait. "Thank you indeed."

They were now so angry with one another that they walked along with fastened lips—their lips locking indoors a silence like the stillness of a hot day charged with storm. But it was difficult to maintain the silence because they had to walk side by side for some distance yet. And after forty or so paces Bait felt a compulsion to shock Albany further, and yielded to it.

"It may interest you to know," he said, "that Mrs. Grant in one of her trances assured me that in a previous incarnation I was a Franciscan friar of the name of Mario Elias, and I'm not at all disposed to deny the possibility."

Albany stepped off the pavement. "Great Powers above. I cannot stand any more of this. If you'll forgive me, I'll go my own way. Good-bye," and he began to cross the road.

"They run ! " said Bait.

Albany stopped in the middle of the road. "What do you mean : ' They run ' ? "

"That, I think," said Bait, "was what General Wolfe said when Montcalm and his host fled in rout before him."

"I run from no one," Albany affirmed, and stood still in the middle of Acacia Road, as a demonstration of this truth. "I merely know that some things are worth discussing ; others are not, and these I treat with the contempt they deserve ;" and he turned and continued his passage to the pavement opposite.

"They run," repeated Bait to his back, cheerfully.

CHAPTER EIGHTEEN

THE THRESHOLD OF HEAVEN

HE walked on towards his own Acacia Road, very hot, and very happy in his heat, though somewhere behind the heat a great sadness lurked. And, as always, when the coals of indignation dimmed into clinker and ash, there was little in his heart but the sadness. At home, in his study, as he walked around the room, twisting in his lips an unlit cigar, the heart within him was but a cold brazier, filled with clinker and ash. " Old Bait was my best friend, my one real friend ; who is there who means to me what old Bait meant ? No one. I loved old Bait —but I'll see him in hell before I apologize. He's quite impossible, sometimes, and I'm damned if I'll apologize. At least, I think I am. . . . "

Not the lightest of the clinkers in his heart was the feeling, the fear, the almost-certainty (which, desperate for the love of a friend, he so hated to entertain even for the moment) that Bait's affection for him was something very much less than his affection for Bait. It was nothing remarkable, really.

Always when Sir Albany Grahame was sad, Truth knocked at his door and came in. It did so now ; it came in through the closed door, and there followed a long interview with this austere guest. " Let me remind you," said the visitor, " that it is your egotism and vanity that shuts you away in a solitary cell. Shame on you that it should always be more important to you to show off your superiority than to refrain from wounding a friend. Your egotism and your vanity are an explosive mixture that detonate at a touch. You began with a cocky display of your superiority to all those poor people, and when old Bait was rather rude—when he was bloody rude, in fact— you went up in flames. You said he was like a child going to the Zoo. You implied that he talked clotted piffle. You likened him to a refuse pit."

A little more of this gazing into the clear, steady eyes of Truth, and he was possessed, temporarily, at any rate, by a haunting and rather sweet desire to return to—or, rather, to enter for the first time upon—a life of service and good works. There was no doubt, he thought as he trod his chamber round, that he had a great longing in him to be good. A longing to give himself to people. But one could only get the strength to do this out of a religion of complete self-sacrifice, and no—oh no. . . . He wanted to be good—but not as good as all that.

And just then he remembered that it was Sunday evening. And, though he didn't want to be as good as all that, he could not resist the temptation in his present low state (which was that of a man sadly split in places and aching to be mended) of going to church and learning if there was any comfort for him there. Not that it would be comforting if lesson or sermon made the old merciless demands. Still—listen, the bells were

237

even now ringing from under the white cupola of St. John's Wood Chapel. They were sending their clamour over the tree-tops around them, into the Sabbath calm. He would go. He would accept their invitation. And so mixed, so incongruous, were his motives that the thought that he was still in his party dress, and that in these garments he would cut a figure among the people, clinched his determination to go to church. He fetched his top-hat and grey gloves, and his neatly-rolled umbrella, and went forth. In a wedding garment, so to say, he went towards the ancient danger, fascinated.

As he walked by the green Burial Ground and came near the Doric temple at its southern end, he was surprised to see people almost as well dressed as he approaching it from all the five roads that flowed around this islanded chapel. Carriages too were driving up to its portico and discharged their furred ladies and opulent men. Odd; because Evening Prayer was usually regarded as the service for the maids and cooks and the families in the humbler streets. Masters and mistresses prayed and sang in the morning.

Albany, hat in hand, walked in with the streaming people, took a seat in the last pew of all, and approved of this humility. He bent forward and, according to custom, said a brief prayer into the lining of his hat. Then he sat back and waited, wondering whether God would arrange for psalm or sermon to speak privately and personally to him. The bells ceased, and now, as clergy and choir entered, he saw why this evening service had drawn such a large and socially important congregation. A bishop in his scarlet convocation robes and carrying his crozier was following behind the incumbent. Albany recognized him from of old; he'd met him sometimes in clerical assemblies. It was Arthur Chandler, Rector of Poplar some years since, and Bishop of Bloemfontein.

The service began; it was on its way. Nothing in Confession, Absolution, Versicles and Responses seemed specially designed for him. Their words were blunted by long familiarity, but he enjoyed singing the Responses because his voice was sounding well beneath this lofty vaulting and among these pillared aisles, and the people beside him must be hearing it. Also they must be observing that he was an expert, since he needed no book.

The Psalms were the traditional vehicle for God's personal messages to seeking souls and now Albany opened his prayer-book and wondered if he was to be vouchsafed such a favour.

There was nothing for him in the first two psalms, but the third—was the third intended for him ? ' My soul hath a desire and a longing to enter into the courts of the Lord '—curious, that ! Striking. ' Who going through the vale of misery use it for a well '—must he not use his unhappiness as a well-spring of good ? ' No good things shall he withold from them that lead a godly life '—that was encouraging—but no ; a ' godly life ? ' Impossible, he thought as the congregation sang the Gloria ; for ever impossible for him to do all that these words demanded.

The bishop in his scarlet and white entered the pulpit. Albany looked at him. Arthur Chandler was both scholar and saint. He was such as would demand, with gentleness and love, the utmost. He would never compromise ; he would say, with a scorching tenderness, the worst. Oh, no, keep away, all ye saints. Keep silence, Bishop. Or don't—don't ask too much.

But the bishop gave out as his text the very words the psalm which had set Albany wondering. " My soul hath a desire and a longing. . . " Disturbing, this. A little alarming. Not a light thing to sit in a London church, with the traffic clattering and jingling all round it, and to wonder if the Creator of all the worlds, whose name was Love, whose name was likewise Wrath, was speaking directly to him, Albany Grahame.

It was a terrible sermon ; terrible as truth is terrible, and holiness is terrible. Disillusionment with the world, said the bishop, was the proper threshold of Heaven—and Albany, listening fascinated, giving the preacher all his eyes and all his ears, wondered if he was now on the threshold of Heaven. Man was a temple of the Spirit which had fallen into decay, said the bishop, but fragments of the holy house were left, its foundations were intact, and its broken walls and echoing corridors still housed, like brief and fitful winds, all those vague aspirations and strange immortal longings that proved the high spiritual endowment of Man and his infinite possibilities. (That was himself exactly, thought Albany. Himself exactly). But sin and apostasy had wrecked the house with results that to mere human capabilities were irreparable ; it had broken down the unity of Man's nature into a chaos of incompatible and warring elements. (Himself exactly. A wreck. Irreparable in his own strength). Nevertheless within the wrecked soul there still remained this spark of Heaven which lit up, ever and anon, the darkened places and produced a restless dissatisfaction with all the things that the mere natural will could achieve. And this disillusion with all the things of this world was, or could be, the introduction to a spiritual life because it showed that down here in a world of merely sensuous things, there was nothing permanent, nothing wholly satisfying, nothing single, unified, complete and perfect. Only in that kingdom of Heaven, which was within every man as his potential home, could he find the permanence, the unity, the wholeness and perfection, which his immortal nature demanded. All else in the end was but vanity and vexation of spirit. The only alternatives before a man of vision, a man of fine and subtle perceptions (and that was himself exactly, in spite of what old Bait had said) were a religion of unqualified earnestness—or cynicism and despair.

Most unhappily Albany in his pew agreed with every word of it. He sat there listening steadfastly, and full of unwanted emotions.

When the bishop had finished, and the people were singing the last hymn, he could not sing too because that sermon had filled him, if only temporarily, with a hatred of all hypocrisy and self-display. He came out of the church into the lamp-lit darkness and walked homeward among the chattering people, a solitary figure, wishing he had stayed away from the danger ; from this fearful infection of good.

The bishop had been right, he thought next morning as he dressed in a dream and tended before the mirror his moustache and beard and felt rather pleased with both ; the bishop had been all too right : in face of the heart-sinking imperfections of this world there was no other choice but the full spiritual life or a cynical despair. But the spiritual life asked too much, asked more than he was able to give, now that he was old and habit-bound ; and, besides, try as he would, he could not believe sufficiently in the necessary dogmas (thank God) and you couldn't give yourself with devotion and self-sacrifice to the Unknown and possibly the Unexisting.

So he decided that there was nothing for it but to give himself to the cynicism and despair. And he found this quite enjoyable. He enjoyed feeling an intellectual superiority to those weaker souls who could not endure the harsh world without the consolation of a supernatural religion. He enjoyed his stoical acceptance of his loneliness in a hostile or indifferent universe. To be alone and self-sufficient among the indifferent stars—it was dignified. Eating his breakfast that morning he savoured his detachment from the common run of mankind, and from the stars.

In truth, he found this dignified intellectual despair almost as exciting as a new religion ; and after breakfast he went out for a walk with it, very pleasantly, behind an excellent cigar.

He had not gone many steps before he saw Commander Ludlow coming towards him ; Commander Ludlow looking very large and most personable in a thick, but open, overcoat with black astrakhan collar, brown fur lining and ornate frogged button-holes. The Commander recognized him, put up his monocle to make sure that he saw aright, and hove to before him.

" Albany ! The Great Sir Albany Grahame ! It's ages since we've met. There's nothing to do but celebrate this reunion with a drink." He laid a friendly hand on Albany's elbow. " I could do with a drink. Come along."

And for this admirable purpose he put about and convoyed Albany towards his home. They had gone perhaps a dozen paces when he halted to stare at a girl coming along the road towards them. He fumbled for his monocle, hoisted it aloft, and fixed it in his eye to study her better. Like a watcher at the races he leaned on his stick as she came close and passed by. " I often see that little piece," he said. " A shapely craft, you must say. I enjoy seeing her little round bottom dancing from side to side. And she likes us to see it too ; that's why she wears her skirts nice and taut around the stern. Yes, very pretty. Charming. It rolls like a dinghy in a nice choppy sea. Charming. I imagine even old Colonel Budlier'd want to take a second look at that."

Albany found something to admire in this frankness ; it blew like a cleansing wind, he thought, through the murk of men's normal hypocrisies ; but he was less confident of this, as the Commander, still gazing after the girl, went on, " A proper little ogling miss, she is, but then every woman's nine-tenths a whore. They all do everything they can to *enflammer les hommes*, but, good lord, the trouble with most of them is that they stick at the tenth part. My experience is that it's the very deuce of a jog to develop that tenth part for them. It's quite worn me out sometimes ; it has, really." The girl was gone round the curve of the road, and he said, " Ah, well," sadly, now that the entertainment was at an end, and, raising his eyebrows, scattered the monocle.

There was another halt twelve paces farther on, because two

dogs went by, in line ahead, a little terrier pursuing a large collie with interest and affection, and Ludlow must run up the monocle so as to give some consideration to their *pudenda*. But they too passed out of sight, and the monocle dropped to the Commander's breast, and he and Albany walked on in silence. As they passed into his garden they saw on his doorstep a little man in voluble and earnest parley with the housekeeper, Mrs. Tait. A little man with a bowler hat and a document.

" Who the devil . . . ? " began Ludlow, fiddling for the eye-glass again.

The man heard the ejaculation and turned towards them. Three steps sufficed to bring him opposite them because they too were approaching the door. He was a spare little grey-haired man in a dark suit with soft, earnest eyes and a long neck issuing from a turned-down collar like a dissenting minister's. He lifted the bowler hat and began to apologize for his intrusion in a voice that was soft and earnest too. Everything about his voice and his words suggested a visitor from a chapel. Commander Ludlow gave him one look, heard the first words of his exordium, and then fired at him, " In the name of the devil who are you, sir ? " The little man, standing opposite them, continued his fluent exposition, so Ludlow turned to his housekeeper. " Mrs. Tait, who is this ? Would you remove him out of my way ? "

" It's a gentleman from some Alliance, sir, about public houses and closing them down."

The man, in unctuous and forgiving tones, supplied some definition to this portrait, unrolling his document as he spoke. " As I said sir, I represent the United Kingdom Temperance Alliance, which is seeking signatures to its petition in support of the Government's Licensing Bill. You will know all about the bill, I am sure, and will wish to support it. Its aim is to reduce the number of licensed houses till they reach a statutory proportion of the population ; for example, one licence to every thousand persons where the population averages over two hundred to the acre—— "

The Commander was gazing into the speaker's eyes with a frown of incomprehension.

" You will admit, sir, that some such reduction is urgently necessary if the excessive drinking habits of so many of our people are to be discouraged—as we all desire—by lack of the present opportunities for indulgence. I'm sure you will think that the bill embodies a long overdue reform. We had a most successful meeting last week in the Marylebone Free Hall, with the Bishop of London in the chair."

Commander Ludlow turned to Albany. "What is he talking about?" he asked. "Who is this ordure?" at the sound of which word the housekeeper retired from her share in the colloquy and retreated into her kitchen.

"Ordure, sir?" There was a strong note of protest in the little man's soft voice. "I heard that word, sir, and I feel that some apology is due for it." He in his turn sought the sympathy of Albany. "You, sir, will agree that this gentleman has no right to apply such words to me. Never in my life has anyone spoken to me in such terms. You will agree that I am within my rights in asking him to apologize."

"Apologize my arse," said the Commander; and he weighed his anchor and walked straight past him.

The man continued to address Albany as the more promising listener. "It is regrettable that a gentleman should demean himself by using such language. Very, very regrettable. Perhaps you, sir, would care to sign our petition—— "

But the Commander, from his doorstep, turned round and told him where to shove his petition. And the effect of this recommendation was to cause the little man to abandon hope, roll up his document and retire towards the gate and the street. Ludlow shouted after him, "I hate all interfering teetotal cranks, who are less than five per cent. of the population and want to force all the rest of us to behave just as they think fit— damn their bloody eyes. Yes, put that in your bung-hole and sit on it awhile. Come on, Albany. Come along, Grahame. Forget that little bastard and come and have a drink."

In his small sitting-room, so like a naval museum, he poked up the fire, threw himself into a deep chair and said, "This is fine. This is very pleasant. Sit you down and drink. I'm afraid I was rude to that little man. Was I? You think so? Couldn't have been much ruder? Oh, yes, I could. I can do much better than that, but I always feel restrained in front of you, an old padre and all. I wasn't too coarse for you, was I? Can't stand these potty little tyrants who want to force us all to conform to their dreary little views. They make my blood boil. God sink 'em all to hell."

The whisky decanter and glasses stood on a low table at his side, and he poured out a measure for each of them with an angry hand. It was thus an exceedingly large measure, and he added but a trifle of soda water to it, unwillingly. Albany accepted his glass, and silence surrounded them both as Ludlow drank again and again to quiet his wrath.

After fifty years as a teetotaller Albany's head was still un-adapted to such brews as these, and soon the whisky was soften-ing the texture of his thoughts and preparing them for sentiment. He remembered his quarrel with Bait and his unhappiness after it. This grief came upon him again. It gradually pos-sessed him causing his lower lip to fall and his head to shake with a private sadness. One more drink from his second glass of whisky, and he felt he needed a confidant. He felt glad to have a suitable one sitting opposite him. " Ludlow," he began, lowering his glass to his knee, " I am very upset about some-thing."

" You are ? Have some more whisky. Hand over your glass. Yes, I thought you looked a bit under the weather. What is it ? "

Albany opened the matter by telling him all about the séance. He described, amusingly as he thought, all those tongue-tied apparitions who retired into the curtains, or into the Higher Life, whenever a question flummoxed them, and he fully ex-pected, from a hard-headed sailor, a lively contempt for such absurdities. Instead the Commander came forward in his chair as if weighted with interest, and even forgot to drink from the glass in his hand. It held less interest for him than Albany's tale. " My God ! " he affirmed, as Albany paused. " I must go along and see this. Any chance of getting me in ? "

" But you don't believe in any of it, do you ? "

" Oh, yes. I'm quite ready to believe in it all. I'm naturally a religious man. I firmly believe in ghosts. I could tell you some extraordinary stories about ghosts. I was in a ship once that quite certainly had a ghost on it and a curse on it. We all knew it. We could feel it."

" It's because I'm a religious man," interrupted Albany, forgetting that he was now a tough cynic, " that I was disgusted with the whole ridiculous pantomime."

" Well, some of it may be hogwash," Ludlow granted, " but not all. Not all, sir, by any means. I firmly believe that the dead go on living and that we shall meet our dear ones again. Fill up. Pass over your glass. They are in heaven, waiting for us. And probably doing their best for us, I'm sure of that. Say when. Nonsense, *that's* not strong ; hardly strong enough to make a fly drunk. A chap of your tonnage needs a good supply in his tanks. Yes, my beloved mother, for instance. She's watching over me and helping me."

"Maybe, but I can't begin to believe in any of this jiggery-spookery yesterday—though, to be honest, I did toy with the idea that my late wife might materialize."

"What? Who? Your wife?" Ludlow was suddenly alarmed. "But she didn't?"

"No. She did not."

"My God, I'd forgotten that possibility. Yes, perhaps I'd better keep away. I don't want any further truck with Isobel. She was a foul woman, if ever there was one."

To avoid this disconcerting side-issue Albany came quickly to his quarrel with Bait. "Old Bait believes in it all," he explained. "Or he pretends to, for the sake of an argument."

"Yes, he's a cantankerous old devil, Bait."

"We argued, and I'm afraid I was very rude."

"Good."

"He was rude first, of course, but that's no justification."

"It's every justification. If a man hits at you, slosh him one back. Every time. If he opens fire on you, sink him. Every time. That's only sense."

"Then you don't think I ought to apologize?"

"Hell, no! Apologize? Why apologize?"

"An apology is sometimes the action of a strong man."

"*Oh* no! *Oh* no!" The Commander was very confident about this. "Not if he was rude first. It's for him to lower his flag, not you. Yes, every time."

"But if he really believes in it, and it's like a religion to him, one shouldn't make fun of it. I called it bilge."

"You called it what?"

"Bilge."

"Bilge-water you mean. A bilge is only the bottom of a ship where the foul water collects. That reminds me: do you want to empty the bilge?—say if you do—it's only just round the corner. You don't? Well, have another glass. So you said it was all bilge-water. Good for you! He asked for it."

"I also called it a punch-and-judy show."

"Good. Fine."

"Yes, but never mind dignity, and who spoke first. I don't care a damn for that. Bait was my friend. He was my best friend." The whisky which he'd been sipping rapidly and unawares had now so moistened his thoughts as to make them slightly maudlin. He shook an unhappy head. "I haven't so many friends that I can afford to throw away the best. I don't make friends easily; I don't know why it is, Ludlow, but

I don't. There's you—I hope I can call you my friend. And old Budlier . . . Colonel Budlier. . . . And that's about all. Among men, I mean. There are women who are good enough to give me their love. What do I do, Ludlow? Tell me."

"Leave it, old son. He'll come round. Leave it, my dear sir, and have another sip of the old gruel. Next time you meet him he will have forgotten all about it."

"I don't know," sighed Albany, "If he doesn't say something, I think I shall. Pride can go hang, s'far's I'm concerned. Go hang. . . . Go hang."

They had been drinking together now for more than an hour, and Ludlow had filled his visitor's glass many times; too many times, so that Albany was feeling bewildered and a little, a very little, sick. Nay, if he was to be frank with himself, he was feeling rather drunk. Not completely drunk; not that his intelligence was completely submerged in that muddy pool, but that it was walking round and round it, so that his words slipped about on its circumjacent marges and sometimes slid to a fall in its shallows—which were oddly deeper than he thought. Luckily the Commander was noticing nothing, because he had drunk even more liberally and his eyes and his understanding were both a little filmed. Albany put his hands on his chair arms to rise, and drew in his legs, but he made the movements slowly lest he disturbed a stomach whose state was insecure. "Goo'bye, Commander. Goo'bye, Ludlow. I muss go now. Lunch time."

"Muss you go? Muss you really?"

"Yess . . . yess . . . Thank you for all your vice. I shall probably apologize. Goo'bye. Goo'bye."

The fresh air in the street made him feel better, but not much. He was not too sure that he wouldn't have to go into some secluded corner and there syphon up the contents of his stomach, if he was ever to feel right again. He hoped not. He felt he would like to get himself home and into his bed, there to conceal the fact that his mind was adrift and swimming in some luminous ichor; but he didn't dare to go home just yet, because Susannah was there, and he was not happy about this free and autonomous behaviour of his tongue, which seemed to be saying all manner of things before he instructed it to. Already it had addressed the Commander as "Commandment," which, fortunately, Ludlow's perceptions had been too blurred to observe; and more unaccountably, it had referred to Mrs. Kenny in her kitchen as "Mrs. Humphry Ward,"

possibly (but who could know ?) by way of ' Mrs. Henry Wood.'
Susannah with her quick eyes and ears must not observe this
holiday spirit in his tongue. So he walked slowly and carefully
towards the public garden behind the chapel, where he could
sit still and, if possible, avoid the eruption of his stomach. He
was glad when he arrived at an unoccupied seat among the
tombs and could end a walk that had not been empty of danger.
But the children on the paths were dancing and skipping, and
this ceaseless movement produced a situation that was much
the same as if he were himself in motion, and he had to hold
his eyes closed if he were to preserve a sense of stillness. Sometimes the children shouted, and each shout was a menace ; it
threatened a precipitation of the catastrophe.

He managed, however, to keep control of the upsurging
catastrophe ; he battened it tight down in the hold ; and it
did not, in fact, appear in public. Lips and eyes closed, he
told himself, " It will pass."

It passed ; and he rose with relief and went home.

CHAPTER NINETEEN

TOM IN REJECTION

IT was while he sat incapacitated in the public garden that
Tom Budlier knocked at the Grahames' door in Circus Road.
Mrs. Kenny opened to him. Had he been a less ingenuous lad,
and more conscious of his sins, he must have noticed the
hostility and the unwelcome in her face.

" Morning, Mrs. Kenny. How're things with you ? Could
I speak to Miss Susannah ? "

For a few seconds she did not even answer, and then said
grudgingly, " I'll see."

And she went along the passage to the drawing-room where
Susannah sat reading. " It's young Mr. Budlier, miss."

Susannah dropped her book and stared.

" You don't want to see him, do you, miss ? "

" No, *no* ! " Susannah jumped up and stood trembling.

" I thought not. Shall I say you're engaged ? " suggested
Mrs. Kenny, anxious to punish this wicked boy.

Susannah, still trembling, said, " Yes."

" Yes, that's best." And Mrs. Kenny went back to the door,

well pleased with her commission. "I'm sorry. Miss Susannah is engaged."

Tom who, quite unworried, had been dancing a broken tap-dance on the doorstone while he waited, started in surprise and stood still. "What do you mean, Kenny? She's in and can't see me? I can wait."

"She's engaged."

"I can wait."

"That's no good. She's engaged."

"But it's important."

"So is the young mistress's business."

"Nonsense, Kenny. What's the matter? Is something wrong?"

"Don't call me Kenny. I don't wish it."

"Good heavens, what's happened? What's gone wrong?"

"If the young mistress doesn't want to see you, you probably know what's happened."

"I know nothing. Please let me go to her. I've got to tell her something."

"Well, I've said you can't." She tried to shut the door and nearly succeeded, but Tom's powerful hand stopped it.

"Oh, but I *can.*" His hand, so much stronger than hers, pushed the door back. "I've got to know what's the matter. Susannah! Susannah!"

"Well, you've got a nerve, I'm bound to say." Mrs. Kenny, thus bound, said it.

"Susannah darling! Susannah!"

No answer from that room where Mrs. Kenny had certainly spoken with Susannah.

"Oh, hell! What in heaven's name——? Sorry. Kenny." And, gently putting her aside with a palm on her breast, he walked past her towards that room door.

"*Well!* Pushing past like that! Whoever heard the like? I mean to *say!* . . ."

"Sorry, Kenny," he said from the distance, amicably, but without turning his head. "Frightfully sorry." The palm that had pushed her aside now pushed open the door, and he saw Susannah standing by the window curtains, her hands locked before her breast, her body trembling. "Susannah! What's the matter? Has something happened?"

"Do please go away."

"But, darling! . . ."

"Do please go away. I never want to see you again."

He stood there, four feet from the door, without a clue to her anger. " Have I done something wrong ? "

" Something wrong ! " She echoed the words in contempt. He had left the door ajar behind him, and now Mrs. Kenny stood in its frame. " It's not my fault, Miss. He had the nerve to push past me. I told him you—— "

" Oh, go away, Kenny," Tom begged. " Please hop it. Yes, I've a nerve, I know, but there's a dear : hop it." And gently but powerfully, he shut the door in her face. Then opened it again and said, " Sorry, Kenny." She was still standing there like a statue of Indignation, and as motionless ; so he had no course but to shut it again in her face. No time just now to appease Mrs. Kenny. " Susannah, my beloved, what is it ? "

" Can you not go away when I ask you ? Go *away* ! "

The door opened. " That's no way to speak to me at all. No way to talk. And I don't care to have doors shut in my face. Pushing past and shutting doors ! It's no way to behave, and I don't care who hears me say it."

" I know it isn't, Kenny. I'm sorry. But good-bye. Good-bye for the present." And he shut the door a third time and turned the key. He heard Mrs. Kenny's voice saying " Upon my soul, I don't wonder Oxford and Cambridge wouldn't have him. Some people . . ." But he didn't remain to hear the rest. For all he knew, she was still talking through the door, as he went back to Susannah and pleaded. " Tell me, dearest."

" Go . . . go . . . go," she wailed.

" I'm not going till you tell me what all this is about. I've got to know."

" Isn't it enough that I don't want to see you any more ? Ever."

" Susannah, what are you saying ? I don't understand, I'm beaten. I came to ask you to come in a motor car with me for a drive in the country. Charlie Dyson has lent—— "

" Don't speak of that man to me."

" Charlie has lent me his car. I can drive it like anything now. I thought we'd go out and look at the farms and imagine ourselves owning one of our own. Charlie and I drove right out into the Essex countryside yesterday. It was perfectly lovely ; I've never seen anything like it. There's nothing to touch this autumn light. It seemed to be flushed through with gold because the leaves on the trees and the grass were all yellow and copper and gold. And some of the trees were so red that you could imagine they were on fire. And all the time

I was thinking I must bring Susannah to see this—*to-morrow, to-morrow*, as ever was ! Darling, I never see anything wonderful now without longing for you to share it with me."

" Share it with your actress friend."

He stared at her, speechless. The shot had emptied him of words. But at last he managed to say, " What do you mean ? "

" Everyone knows. Everyone's talking about it. You even took her—someone saw you taking her to that—to that caravan." She turned away and looked through the window, that he might not see the anguish tormenting her mouth. And not once did she turn her face to him again.

" Who saw me ? Who *could* have seen me ? "

" Never mind. Someone saw you. And those who knew about us are pitying me. Even the servants in the kitchen are pitying me. Oh, I do so hate you."

" You're talking of little Carolyn Eyre, I suppose ? "

" I don't care what her name is. Her name means nothing to me. And are there so many that you take to the caravan ? I did you a kindness when I showed it to you, didn't I ? "

Tom sighed, put his hands behind his back, and paced the floor in thought, while Susannah fiddled with the tassel of the blind cord. " I don't know how to explain, darling. Susannah darling, listen. She means nothing to me. You mean everything. Oh, the devil ! How does one explain this sort of thing to a girl like you ? You can't understand."

" I'm very sure I can't."

" She's just a friend of Charlie's. I'm fond of her in a way, and she doesn't mind if I——Look : I have no money, and I can't hope to marry for years. A man is a man—oh, hell ! " He threw himself on to the arm of an upholstered chair, laid his elbow on its back, and passed his hand many times over his brow and through his thick hair. " I can't explain. I promise, if you like, that I'll try never to do anything like that again. And when we are married—— "

" When we are married ! " she scoffed.

" Yes, I've always told myself that I'd be absolutely loyal to you, and I *will* be."

" You will not be, because that's all over."

" Oh no, no, Susannah my darling, *no*. You don't understand." He got up, went to her, and put beseeching hands on her arms, attempting to turn her towards him. But she snatched herself away ; and he, dropping his arms, went on, " You don't understand. It is possible to love one person only and yet do what I've done. I worship and reverence you. You are one thing. Carolyn is another. I wouldn't care if I never saw her again. I'd die if I lost you. Try to understand."

" I don't understand. I never shall. And I don't want to."

He now went to a window and looked out sadly. " I just took what was offered to me. That was all. I'm sorry about the caravan, but I had no money——"

" Oh, I don't know what you mean. It's all horrible. Wicked."

" Do you *really* think so ? "

" Yes. Who would not ? "

" Some people would try to understand. I think your father would understand."

" My father is a man of honour. How dare you mention him ? "

" Oh, well ... if you won't listen to anything I say ... I was only amusing myself with her."

" And you can go on amusing yourself. I have no desire to stop you. I have no interest one way or the other. Why should I mind what you do ? I don't love you any more. You killed my love for you stone dead. Now please go."

" But look, Susannah. I suppose you're right. I suppose I'm weak and a cad. I know I'm not good enough for you. I've always known it." She tossed her head in disdain, and he, wounded by the gesture, continued, irritably now, " Yes, I've admitted it. I can't do more. I've said I'm sorry. And I am. I'll try never to do it again. Don't say our engagement is over. Please don't say that."

" Of course it is. If ever I marry, it'll be a man of some decency."

At this stab Tom suddenly tired of being humble. Quick in temper, he lost all control and all contrition. " Oh well, God damn it, I'm not going to appeal for pity any more. I'm not going to bleat. I've said I was sorry. I've said I'm a beast. ' Some decency ' ! I haven't any, I suppose. Okay, find someone who has, and marry him and good luck to you. I'll find someone else too, don't you worry ! " He saw her whole body shiver and her shoulders hunch up in pain, but he didn't spare her ; she hadn't spared him. " And if I ever marry, dear lady, it'll be a woman of some understanding. She'll be able to forgive when one apologizes humbly. Good-bye. Good-bye, beloved. Marry someone who's worthy of you, *if you can find anyone*. And don't think I'm going to break my heart. I was in love with you—madly—but I can struggle out of it. I think I'm out of it already. Hurray! Just as well to be out of it, because there never was much chance of us marrying. I've no profession and damned little hope of ever having one. So it's all over, and that's fine. Who cares? I'm glad. I'm glad." And he rushed from the room and the house, letting doors close smartly behind him. Susannah, still at the window, with her heart battering against her ribs like a bird which has suffered the claw of a cat, saw him go from hall door to garden gate, whistling and humming in a show of ease.

" Who cares? " Tom might ask ; and the answer was Tom. Tom Budlier. Care? Why, his show of whistling indifference lasted only as far as the bend in Circus Road, and there it stopped, and his misery was allowed to come in and possess every corner of his heart. Almost he welcomed it in. " I shall marry a man of some decency." To think of her giving her love, and herself, to some other man, whether decent or indecent, was to put the bellows to his love and set the furnace aflame. Wandering home, with head down, mouth slackened and eyes dulled, he told himself that never till this moment had he known how terribly he loved her. Once in the house he rushed up the stairs to his study and shut himself in, that he might languish, and even luxuriate, in despair. He dropped on to the hard chair before his writing table and there, elbows on knees, hands loosely linked, he sat like a condemned man contemplating his life's calamity.

If he was really never to see her any more, he didn't care what became of him. Perhaps he'd ' go to rack and ruin ' so that she'd always know, to her lasting sorrow and self-reproach, that her heartlessness had broken him. Or, if this was a course too unmanly, perhaps he'd be a melancholy bachelor for the rest of his life—with a sad smile for all—so that she would know that he was loyal to her to the end. And at the end she would come hurrying to his bedside to hold his hand in the last sad moments, and he would tell her, " You were the only woman I ever loved." The farm ? Those fields mauve with clover, gold with stubble, pale with tall barley ; those slopes of down where the white sheep pastured among the travelling shadows—ah, the light of enchantment upon that landscape was out. Or, if he still felt a little love for it—and even in this abject hour he thought he did—why, then he would be a lonely bachelor-farmer ' making the good earth his wife ' and, because of his single-minded devotion to this new love, become one of the most successful farmers in the country. Yes, perhaps this was the best plan : a melancholy plan, but promising some comfort and a quiet peace.

He got up and, hands behind his back, went to the window. But, just as Albany had found in the chapel garden that it was a mistake to move suddenly if one's stomach was upset, so Tom found that it could be a mistake if one's heart was in a bad way. He no sooner got to the window than his burden swelled to such a load that he dreamed with some pleasure of assassinating himself or, better still, Charlie Dyson who had led him astray. He tried to feel angry with little Carolyn who had deliberately laid such an appetizing plate before him, but he found that he couldn't be as ungenerous as this. Carolyn, a little slut, had given him her easy and limited love, and he could feel some affection for her while not caring a hang about her. He felt some anger against—yes the more he dwelt on this, the surer he was of it—some anger against God who had made young men as they were, so that it was next to impossible for them to behave with decency.

" I wish I were dead . . . dead. . . ." But since one cannot die at will, he stood at the window and thought of the Foreign Legion . . .

He drifted back to the chair and sat there in woebegone thought ; and in the chair, brooding on questions of morality, he learned something that he decided was wisdom. This was the wisdom that percolated into his heart : any man who wanted a wife of such exquisite goodness as Susannah must pay the stiff price ; he must abandon all Carolyn Eyres, and live the austere life for her sake. Nothing else was an honest price. And was he ready to pay this price ? By God, he was, and would.

Much pleased with this influx of wisdom, because he had but a poor opinion of his brains, he suddenly saw how great a relief it would be to give it utterance in a passionate and penitent letter to Susannah. Tom Budlier was quick to sin, perhaps, but few among men, since these creatures felt the Creator's breath in their nostrils, had greater gifts for penitence or succumbed more readily to enormous purposes of amendment. He swung round to the table and with his shoulders bowed over the absorbing work, and his fingers sometimes scratching in his particoloured hair, he wrote and wrote, page after page. He wrote how he had seen the Light and would never do anything to hurt her again ; how he wanted to spend his life preventing anybody from hurting her ; how terribly, awfully, sorry he was, and what a beast he was, what a swine ; and how, if only she would let him come back and be engaged to her again, he would try to be everything she wanted him to be always.

Impatient for her to receive this surely admirable letter, and greatly hoping again, because he was a sanguine lad, he ran out and, speeding to Circus Road, thrust the letter furtively through her door.

He dared not expect an answer before the next morning and wondered how to endure the intervening hours. They limped by, and next morning he was hovering around his front door many minutes before there was hope of the postman's knock. Or he was wandering out to his gate to see if the postman was in the road. When the postman appeared and knocked, and the letters rattled to the mat, Tom was upon them like a bird upon crumbs. But they were all for his father : " Col. Budlier . . . Col. Budlier. . . Col. Budlier."

He went into breakfast with the letters in his hand and a smile on his face. " Here you are, Father. Your letters. How nice to have all those friends. Pass the paper. I want to see who won at Campdown Park."

Nor did any answer come that day or the next or the next. And he could do nothing but walk about the world with a death in his heart. Wilfully seeking knives to drive into that heart, he wandered to the places where they'd been happy together : to the entrance to the Underground station ; to the churchyard garden among the tombs ; to the garden wall of the mansion in Hall Road, behind which they'd attended the garden fêtes (Susannah in her large hat and with her fringed sunshade—oh, dear, oh dear !), and to the long, high wall of Lord's, this side of the towering stands—and here he stood upon the pavement and drove home the knives, the most terrible knives, one after another ; then turned and walked away.

In his room sometimes he mooned up and down, remembering for his pain the loveliest things she had written to him after they had first confessed their love, " I was dazed all the next day and walked about doing idiotic things. I put pepper on my pudding and everyone thought I was mad " ; after she had received her first love-letter, " I read it over and over and over again. I knew it by heart at last and was able to repeat it to myself a hundred times in bed " ; after he had told her all his dreams about the farm, " I'm so thrilled about it all. I want to be with you always and do everything for you."

Oh, Susannah, my beloved. . . .

But even in the midst of all this torment ; all this rack of love, he learned two disappointing and inglorious things ; and the first of these was that he could still look at a pretty face in the street and forget the storm till the face was gone. Once a girl with a foreign accent stopped him and asked the way to " the famous Lord's ", and he was quite shaken and troubled by her soft features and soft voice. The other disappointing thing was that after roaming the streets of London, for three or four hours, ministering to his misery, he could have so undoubted an appetite. Granted that he had eaten no lunch in his heartache, but still, this appetite at six-thirty was surely out of harmony with that sick heart and deplorably disloyal to Susannah. " I suppose I'm just horribly commonplace, really. I haven't the power to love that I thought I had." He said this to himself in the neighbourhood of Piccadilly Circus to which he had come in search of that café where they had first taken tea together. He didn't go into this café to assuage the appetite—at least he was above *that*—but he did find a cheap little restaurant in Lisle Street and here ate a large steak and chips, washing it down with an eighteenpenny bottle of Margaux. Nor was this all : he followed this with apple tart and cream, and biscuits and Camembert cheese ; and he had to admit, at the finish, that he'd seldom enjoyed a meal more. " I don't understand it," he said, as he wiped his mouth and was ashamed.

He was not ashamed when, comfortably replete, he went into a neighbouring tavern and spent an hour or so in solitary drinking, among trollops and probable thieves. This was harmonious ; this at least was in the right manner.

Days passed, and never a letter from that offended girl, that haughty pure lady. Every post had its stabs for him : " Col. Budlier . . . Col. Budlier . . . Col. Budlier." Each time he returned to the house and saw an empty letter tray, it was a spear-thrust in his heart. After ten days he wrote once again, four pages of appeal, and this time there *was* a letter for him on the mat in the morning. And a fat letter ! He rushed, three steps at a time, on wings of hope, to his secret room, and there with shaking fingers tore at the envelope. It contained his letter unopened with a note around it saying (in that beloved handwriting), " I wish you all success in life, but please, please, leave me alone."

Tom shut the door, kissed the letter as a man kisses the axe before putting his head on the block ; then laid his head upon his desk and surrendered to a tumult of tears.

When in control again he went down to breakfast with a smile for his father.

One more letter he wrote to her, a noble, self-sacrificing letter, assuring her that, since she wished it, he would trouble her no more ; enjoining her not to worry about him, but to be happy always ; and wishing her good-bye. It did seem a beautiful letter as he read it with tears, and he was much pleased with it. It would not be too much to say that his spiritual pride, after he had done this self-sacrificing thing, and done it in words so moving, had at times a colour of happiness.

He maintained a cheerful face before the world. Sometimes the good cheer was real enough because, like Sir Albany, he was subject to attacks of high spirits and hope. But usually at some stage in such an attack he became disappointingly conscious of it and plunged into the appropriate and desired gloom again. He went to parties and played in parlour games apparently as gaily as the rest ; and indeed it was only in moments when the game switched away from him that he remembered the heartache, welcomed it as a friend and suffered it anew. At none of these parties did he encounter Susannah, but at one the chattering company about the buffet table began to speak of her. One girl, with her mouth full, said Susannah Grahame was " fearfully attractive " ; a young man, a spotty idiot, said he was "in imminent danger of falling in love with her " ; the host (no danger from him, for he was fifty) said that she was "just about the sweetest girl he knew, and somebody was going to be a damned lucky man one day."

Oh Susannah, my beloved, my beloved. . . . Every word as he ate ice or wafer, was a sword piercing his heart and revived a mad wish to assassinate himself, or Charlie.

After a while he got an idea into his head that if he made strenuous efforts to be good, without telling anyone about it, or letting his right hand know what his left was doing, and just waited on the future, Susannah and he might yet come together again ; and with this idea rooting in his mind he began to go regularly, on Sunday mornings, to church with his father.

CHAPTER TWENTY

SUSANNAH IN DEJECTION

AND Susannah? She was not suffering less. Not less for her than for him did the memory of such words as " If I marry it'll be a woman of some understanding " work like bellows on her love and blow it into flames. And yet, despite this love—or because of it—she was driven to keep her flag of disdain at the very top of her mast and to continue his exile and punishment. She was the prisoner of this ache to punish him, and sometimes ashamed to be so, deciding that she was ' a rather contemptible creature.' That first letter, on the evening of his dismissal, in which he ' swore and vowed ' never to hurt her again, had come like a tide of pleasure, so that she exclaimed, " Oh, he's sweet ! He can be so sweet ! " but—no, she could not bring herself to announce the amnesty. They stayed sundered. And she, like Tom, would dream of her death-bed and of Tom at its side, to whom she would say, " There was only one man in my life, really "—though several other men had married her.

His second letter, ten days later, was also a great draught of joy, but unluckily it was a perhaps sharper pleasure to return it to him unopened, with good wishes for his success in life and a request that he should trouble her no more. " It is clear," she thought in momentary gleams of humour, " that to be in love is to be faintly mad. There's no sense in anything I'm doing : I'm merely tormenting myself and him too." But she couldn't stop this mad behaviour, this compulsion to remain on a sea-bottom of sadness and to keep him down among the dead men too. She would have liked to discuss their common misery with her father, but concluded that either he'd be so shocked at Tom's sin as to prohibit any further association with him—and she didn't really want that—or if she insisted that her love was unchanged he might recommend her to be sensible and tell Tom this cardinal fact—and she didn't want that either. And so day trod upon the heels of day, and none brought reconciliation.

Like Tom, she would escape from the house and stroll in the streets with her sorrow, but, unlike Tom, she could no longer go near the places where they had been happy together. Her favourite walk now was to hurry past these haunted places and enter the Park by Hanover Gate. In the Park she would wander along its pathways with her hands in the pockets of her overcoat and her present heaviness more than filling the pocket of her heart. She came here on a day in St. Martin's Summer which had forgotten to be November and was bright with sunlight, pink clouds and warm, soft air. She turned from the rattling highroad, losing the noise of hooves and wheels in a silence under the avenue of tall planes. The yellow leaves from these noble trees were either piling in the gutters or fluttering towards her as she came. A pale gold sheen between the blue-grey shadows on the roadway spoke of sunlight in the Park and lured her on. This shadowed avenue emitted her into the Park, and she saw that all its lawns and paths were untidy with leaves. Anxious to escape the nurse-maids and the shrill children, and even the old men dreaming on the seats, she crossed the first bridge over the lake and came to the second bridge, which was the most secluded bridge of all, a brief ornamental causeway almost lost among the trees. It spanned a narrow arm of the lake between steep embankments crowded with trees.

She leaned her elbow on its iron rail, her chin on her palm, and gazed at the prospect before her. The floors of those twin escarpments were littered with buff and russet leaves, but not all the branches of the crowding trees were bare ; and there was still a sound of leaves above her whenever the breeze stirred in its afternoon sleep. The narrow strait beneath her issued into the broad, still sheet of iron-grey reflections ; and this sheet widened into a shining lake whose long vista was closed by an island massed with trees. Beyond the shallow dome of this island, bronzed with its dying leaves, she saw nothing except the infinite apse of clean blue sky.

A single sail swept round the cape of the island ; and this seemed strange to her, because yonder, on a shelving bank below a boat-house, a swarm of pleasure skiffs slept on their sides, their summer outings done. What sounds came to her as she leaned on the rail in a chasm between the trees ? Only that occasional flutter of the leaves and the distant cries of children and the footsteps of people unseen.

" I am clearly being a beast to him—I see that—but it's so hard to be anything else. I love him terribly, and yet I haven't enough love to be generous and stop punishing him. Why can't I go straight home and write to him ? But that's the one thing I just *can't* do ; I *can't* take the first step and ask him to come back. If only he would write once more so that I could answer him nicely! But perhaps that letter which I refused to open said all that I could want—and I returned it to him. To hurt him. I am brutal. And it's too late now—too late to say anything nice. . . ."

Yes, impossible now to write a humble letter, beseeching him to come back; but it was pleasant to dream of such a letter, to compose it with one elbow resting on the rail. "Darling Tom, I am thinking of you always and wanting you so terribly. The pain is well-nigh unbearable. Come back and——"

No, impossible. Such surrender was impossible.

Perhaps, then, a calm and dignified letter in which she appeared to regard their severance as final but suggested that they might meet sometimes as friends. "I have given the subject much thought. . . . I feel we should approach the question calmly. . . . We who did love once can never be quite indifferent to each other. . . . I don't feel somehow that we should part altogether, and, at any rate, I want you to write to me if ever you are ill ——" but here the pathos of her words and this sudden undesired picture of Tom ill, shot a gush of tears from her eyes, so that she wept and wept over the bridge. The tears were almost dropping into the water. Tom ill—and she nowhere near him—the picture stayed all further composition that the real truth might clamour in her heart: "Oh, Tom, my heart's beloved, come back to me. Come back, please come back—come—come—but without my asking you."

At this moment, while she was weeping and "making an exhibition of herself," a sculler in an outrigged skiff slid slowly towards her privacy with perfect rhythm and soundless motion; and she fled from his intrusion. She shot from the bridge into the cover of the trees, and thence, her solitude broken, wandered slowly homeward, thinking, "Oh well. What will happen *will* happen."

But what happened was something beyond the wildest thought. As she opened her door with her key Mrs. Kenny came from her kitchen. "There's a gentleman to see you miss."

The leap of hope! A leap like an ecstasy. Tom? Had he heard her call from the bridge, miraculously, as Jane Eyre heard Mr. Rochester calling? "Yes? Who is it, Mrs. Kenny?"

"It's the Reverend Clapton, miss. Young Mr. Bakewell-Clapton."

Oh, sickening the fall. And with it came hate; irrational

hate of that fool. How dared he work a disappointment for her like this? " Oh, no . . . oh, darling Mrs. Kenny, no, I can't face him. Where's Father? Give him to Father."

" Sir Albany's not in miss. He went out just before tea."

" Went out? Will he be back soon? "

" No, he came to me and said he wouldn't be back till late. He said he wouldn't want any dinner."

" But this is something new! He never told me he'd be going out. Has anything happened? Did anyone call him away? "

" I don't think so. It seemed to come over him suddenly that he'd like to go out, if you see what I mean. It was all sudden."

" Curious. Did he say he was going to his club? "

" No, miss."

" Where can he have gone? Oh, well, I suppose I shall have to cope with Mr. Clapton myself. Has he been here long? "

" Yes, miss. He's very anxious to see you. He said he'd come all the way from Plaistow where he works. He told me all about his church—he's a very talkative gentleman, if I may say so; I could hardly get back to my work. He followed me into the passage with talk about the Bands of Hope and his I-don't-know-what."

" He would. I forgot: he's a full-fledged curate now. Is he dressed like a parson? Oh, I must see that! Is he? "

Mrs. Kenny grinned. " That's right miss, and—well, really, he does look rather a sketch."

" Oh, quick! " And she went into the drawing-room. Eddie rose from the sofa as she came in. Yes, he was the complete parson now—with some odd additions. His jacket and trousers were of pepper-and-salt serge; his waistcoat was of black silk, double-breasted, and square cut in front of his clerical collar; this collar was of abnormal height as though to emphasize his now reverend character; a gold chain swung across his convex stomach, with the emblem of the Church of England Men's Society hanging from it (and this seemed absurd because one hardly thought of him as a complete man); the untethered reversible cuffs, white and stiff, fell over his wrists, showing their half-way mark; above his lips the pale unclerical moustache was now rather more than incipient; and finally, and most unexpectedly, his square-toed shoes were almost extinguished by mouse-grey spats. A shovel hat rested on the swell of a cushion, as might a crown jewel.

He came forward to her with his usual excess of heartiness,

calling in a deep voice, " Ah, dear lady ! Ah, my fair cousin ! "
and holding a hand high that it might swoop like a cock-bird
on her smaller hand and grasp it with the strength of ten.
Perhaps his manner of greeting was even heartier than of old
because he now wore the uniform of his order and was determined to be numbered among the ' bright and brotherly '
clergymen. " This is indeed a pleasure," he boomed as he
shook her hand up and down and pressed its bones together,
while she set her teeth with the pain of it.

" So you're really a clergyman now ? " she said, secretly
rubbing the damaged hand against a buttock to comfort and
recover it, before sitting down on the chair facing his sofa.

" Yes, I'm a pale young curate now," he said, resuming his
seat on the sofa and splaying his hands over his knees, whereupon
the cuffs came down and curtained his wrists.

Eddie will have his joke, thought Susannah.

" Yes, no more wild oats for me, I'm afraid."

Dutifully she smiled at his second piece of humour, while
wondering what strain of wild oat he conceived himself to have
sown. She was wondering also how any vicar could have
offered a title to such a grotesque. Was it that curates were
hard to come by in Plaistow ? Did a vicar have to take what
he could get ? Presumably a loon like this could be of some
help to a hard-worked priest. He could baptize the babies,
bury the dead, read the services and give out the grocery tickets.
But one thing stared at her from his large bespectacled eyes :
he hadn't the least suspicion, in his splendid complacency,
that anybody could be other than impressed by his palpable
fitness for the ministry and his likely success therein.

" How do you like Plaistow ? " she inquired.

It was a polite question, and incumbent on a hostess, but
it was also an ill-starred one because it launched him on a long-
winded exposition of the spiritual backwardness of Plaistow
and the great opportunities for Christian work there. He
leaned forward and was fluent about the heathen ignorance
in the slums, the evil influence of the public-houses, and the
plans which ' the Vicar and he ' were making for some ' real
mission work.' He burbled on about the children who were
the ' chief hope ' and the success which, in his humble opinion,
he was achieving among them ; about the little mission church
in Dock Street and the services he conducted there ; and
he did not omit to mention certain compliments which had
been paid to his preaching. The whole verbose and polysyllabic

discourse was being jetted from sofa to chair with an enthusiasm that almost pulled him off the sofa's brink. Nor did it come towards Susannah without an occasional spitting.

She was leaning back in her chair to escape this occasional spray. She had long since suspended all listening and was giving her thoughts to Tom, when at last, and of a sudden, she became aware of a pause in the recitation. Hastily she inserted a word. " I'm so sorry Daddy isn't at home. I can't think where he's gone to, but I'm afraid he won't be back till late."

" That doesn't matter. Doesn't matter at all," he assured her. " It's you I came to see, dear lady."

Wish he wouldn't call me ' dear lady,' she thought. Aloud she said, " Me ? " with eyebrows uplifted.

" Yes." and " Yes," he said again : it seemed he needed to assure himself once more that this was the exact position. " Yes, and I do hope you will realize that it's only after great thought that I've decided to come to you with a very, very important question." He pushed his spectacles back on his nose, and his enlarged eyes gazed at her through the thick round lenses.

" What is the question, Eddie ? "

" You may think that I should have approached my good uncle first, but on the whole I'm of the opinion that in these modern days—and you as a modern young woman will probably agree with me—these formalities are not so necessary as of yore."

As of yore ; she repeated the phrase to herself delighted with it ; and she wondered what these formalities were, of yore.

" Anyhow, my uncle is not here," he laughed, " and that seems to settle it, doesn't it, haw, haw, haw. I have to get back to Plaistow for Evening Prayer. I take Evening Prayer regularly for the Vicar."

" You do ? " she said, for something to say.

" Yes. In the chapel. So I hope I shall have your pardon, if I speak first to you rather than your good father."

" But, Eddie, I'm afraid I don't know what you're talking about." She was now staring at him in bewilderment, not daring to suspect what, in fact, she *was* suspecting. Oh, no, not that !

" Let me come to it." He raised a bland hand as if to calm all fears. " The first time I got to know you, Susannah, I was —if you'll allow me to say so—attracted by your beauty and charm. Ah, yes, very much so. It was on that festive occasion when we all came to dinner here, and I had a little contretemps with my plate, haw, haw, haw . . . haw . . . haw. . . . You remember ? ''

" I remember, yes.''

" Naturally I had no immediate thought then of what I desire to propose to you now. These are serious matters that require long and earnest deliberation.'' And for a serious moment he paused. He paused and fingered his enlarging moustache, of which he was probably as proud as of his round collar, black waistcoat and spats. " You must unders and that I've long considered the advisability of taking to myself a wife as soon as I was settled in my profession. I have given the subject great thought, and I now envisage such a proceeding as almost a matter of duty. A good and dear wife could be of such untold help to a hard-worked parish priest.''

Oh, it couldn't be what she was fearing. No, he'd come to ask her advice about some girl or woman, some hatchet-faced church worker in Plaistow, some lonely spinster who'd marry anything—oh, God, say it was that.

" I need hardly tell you I had no clear idea in my mind as to who the young lady would be whom I would ask to become my partner in the work to which I have set my hand. A clear and definite idea only came to me the other day when I was taking a wedding. It seemed to come almost as a revelation from on high, if to say so is not profane, and I can assure you it was accompanied by a quite remarkable glow of happiness. I cannot remember when so happy a glow has suffused me. I thought, apart from her beauty and charm, there is no one more suitable ; she has been accustomed from childhood to a clergyman's household ; we are much of an age, I a year or two older ; she is alone now, having, alas, lost her dear mother——''

Oh, then it *was*—but it couldn't be. It couldn't be that in the midst of her pain this incomparable fool, this ludicrous figure in clerical garments, should come asking her to marry him. And how dare, dare, he suggest that she needed his comfort in loneliness, when she had her darling father ?

" Furthermore, we are of the same social status, and the fact that the blood of the same ancestors flows in our veins is, in my submission, an advantage rather than a disadvantage. It means that our tastes would be similar ; and *re* the Table of Kindred and Affinity—— ''

" But, Eddie—— ''

Again the bland hand came aloft and stayed all comment

263

till he should have completed his submission. So does the hand of a policeman stop the traffic in its tracks. " —the Church is willing to give its blessing on the marriage of cousins. I realize that I'm not offering you much of this world's goods, and that Plaistow is not the most salubrious spot in our our realm of England ; but as soon as I am priested my stipend will be advanced, and at a later date, no doubt, I shall be preferred to some living where the temporalities will not be wholly negligible—— "

A living ! Such cocksure hope. No perception at all that patron or bishop would have to be hard pressed indeed before handing over to him a cure of souls. " Eddie ! Please stop ! It's impossible what you're suggesting. Quite impossible."

" But why ? " His plump hands were back upon his knees, and he sat there, patently surprised, disappointed, at this early conviction on her part. " Why do you think that ? "

" Because—oh, because—— "

" Is it that you don't love me ? "

" Yes, it is that, of course. Exactly that."

" Well." He was quite cheerful about her answer. " I suspected that might be possible. I am not a fool ; and I fully realize that as yet we have seen but little of each other. But I know I could love you, and I imagine you could grow to love me. With time. I take it there's nothing about me to make me quite unacceptable to a serious-minded young woman. I am a man of sincere religious principles and—as I think I may say—of some abilities. *Re* my profession : it is one which carries with it a certain *kudos*, I think, and ensure that my wife will be received everywhere. And who knows : I might go far in it ; I might attain to high position in the Church, and then it would be a very great happiness to think I had carried my wife along with me."

He to carry *her* along. Oh, how endure this ?

" I admit I had thoughts of having my dear mother to live with me as soon as the Exchequer permitted of such luxuries, but I now think a wife would be better. One has to consider one's parish as well as oneself ; and you with your experience of church affairs —— "

" Oh, do *stop* ! " She had leapt to her feet and given way to a transport of furious tears. Furious, because she was seeing Tom. " Oh, do go away before I say something horrid. . . . Thank you, thank you for what you've suggested, but there's nothing more impossible—nothing in the whole wide world."

Eddie, who as a pleading lover had been leaning from his sofa towards her, swung back and sat upright. It was plain that he was aggrieved by these words. And indeed they were rude. " I don't see why. It can't be that I'm not good enough for you, I hope. We are of the same family. Perhaps it is that you're not yet quite used to the idea. You would like to think it over, I dare say. That I can well understand. Shall I leave my little proposition with you and——— "

" No, *no*, I tell you ! " She stamped her foot ; and the tears gushed. " Oh, can't you understand ? Won't you please go before I say something rude and hurt you ? "

Surprised by her refusal even to entertain his little proposition and shaken by this extraordinary outburst, he gathered his shovel hat from its cushion and rose. He just said, " Well, I don't understand quite, but still . . . if that is what you say . . ." and he went towards the door with his shoulders slightly bowed, his shovel hat hanging limply, and, as it were, disappointed, at his side, and an unattached cuff slowly approaching its rim. That bowed back and disappointed hat seemed so pathetic to her, or, as she would have phrased it, so ' heart-breaking,' that she ran towards him, touched his shoulder and said, " I do thank you for asking me—I do really—I think it's wonderful of you. I'm so sorry——— "

" Never mind, never mind," he said, forgiving her, but not looking at her in his grief ; " I only thought it would be a nice arrangement for us all ; " and he proceeded on his way out.

" I do feel most terribly honoured that you should have asked me, I do really, but I don't want to marry anyone—I don't think I shall ever want to marry anyone— " and then, overcome by the general falsity of her words and by the general loathsomeness of life, she rushed past him and up the stairs to her room, where she slammed the door and flung herself on the bed, that the whole of her tears might run free. That anyone should come bursting into the heart of her misery with a proposal of marriage ! Worse, that the blind intruder should be an imbecile like this. " Tom, Tom, come back, please come back . . . come back . . . but without my asking you."

CHAPTER TWENTY-ONE

SIR ALBANY COMES HOME

SIR ALBANY, when he suddenly left the house that afternoon, had not said that he was going to his club because Susannah had discovered the uses of a telephone and had once used the instrument next door to get in touch with the Savage when he wasn't in fact there but in the house of Miss Maddow. This had been an unpleasant experience because it had involved him, when he got home, in an abundance of lies, and he didn't like lies—at least not so many of them.

So nowadays he avoided, if possible, any statement as to where he was going ; if possible, he slipped from the house when no eyes were at the windows ; and it was only when he was safely returned that he made mention of his club.

He had spent the afternoon in his study, not reading, but thinking . . . thinking. Thinking continuously for two hours. While Susannah was leaning on the bridge under her cloud of grief, he had been engaged with a thought which, if it was by no means a pure and sustained exultation, did give him moments of excitement and sweet inward trembling. He had reclined in his chair with the thought ; stood before the fire with it ; walked the carpet with it ; and lingered by the window with it, gazing out at the autumn-rusted garden but seeing only a future that was, or might be, a bright and sunny prospect.

It was not eight months since Delia died, and for the first three of these months he had stayed away from the house in Waterloo Close, as seemed to him only decorous. He had enforced upon himself a Three Months' Court Mourning. And when at length he was free to return to Prudence Maddow for comfort, neither he nor she had said a word about any change in their relationship, and this silence of hers he had accounted as an example of excellent taste. He had now a very high opinion of Prudence Maddow and (he liked to think) a very real love for her. No one, he would tell himself, had ever shown him such overflowing affection ; no one before had made such a prodigious fuss over him ; no one had listened with such sympathy and intelligence to his talk (was she not a brilliant woman whose work was printed in journals ?) ;

no one else had made herself, at all times, so seductive and beautiful for him ; and certainly no one before (but even to himself he spoke of this only *sub rosa*) had shown what a woman's love could mean to a man in his bed.

He was now exceedingly sentimental about Prudence Maddow, and this feeling for her had been reinforced in these last days by the partial foundering of his affection for Bait. When Bait and he met again after that violent dissension in the road, not a word had Bait said about it : either he had forgotten all about it, or he was quite untroubled by it ; and, perceiving this, Albany had accepted at last, what he'd always fled from admitting before, that Bait's need of him was as nothing compared with his need of Bait. Then, and it was a sad hour, he let their friendship sink to its real level, which was one of neighbourly goodwill and no more. And as his affection for Bait decreased his love of Prudence increased. He needed her now as once he needed Bait.

And the question with him on this quiet afternoon, as he trod his carpet up and down, was, Did not both duty and pleasure suggest that he promoted her from mistress to wife ?

There was nothing insincere in his use of the word ' duty '. It would not be untrue to say that the idea of ' doing his duty by her ' was pleasing him quite as much as any thoughts of the pleasure and pride that would be his in having a woman of such distinction and beauty for wife. Sir Albany Grahame had not been thirty years in Orders without receiving a moral impress that nothing could erase ; and he was instructing himself now that there was, beyond question, a duty to be considered. She might, in her tact and taste, be maintaining a silence, but what was she thinking ? Was it not an insult to keep her as a mistress now that he was free to offer marriage ? Was he to be like the Earl of Clanbethry and use her for a while and then cast her aside ? No, he desired to think himself a better man than the Earl. A man of finer quality altogether. And then there was Vick. Vick who had cast out the Clapton woman and her children. Albany had a very strong desire to be better than Vick. " I am not a good man, but I am better than that. I do most firmly believe in honour and decency. And in charity and forgiveness." There was that in Prue's past which he must forgive.

He went to the window. And he found it very pleasant to think of himself as a man of charity who could understand and forgive. Pleasant to think of rebuilding a life that had been broken—broken by the Earl in his coarseness. The thought of asking Prue to marry him began to wear the fine look of a mission to rescue and restore. Something like the mission of Perseus who came from the skies to rescue Andromeda from the rock to which she was chained. Would it not be gratifying indeed to witness Prue's joy when he said, " Will you make me the happiest of men ? " And throughout his life would he not be conscious of her gratitude to him for his understanding and forgiveness and rescue ? What glow like the glow of doing a good deed ?

But—he returned to the fireplace and put a foot on the fender —let him not be thinking of it as a wholly unselfish act. The old moralist within him, like a stern prophet of old, reminded him that it was anything but that. How proud he would be of Prue in drawing-room and theatre ; proud as he had never been of Delia ! To tell the truth, he had sometimes been a little ashamed of Delia. And what a mate for his bed. And what a manager for his home—look at her own home.

But Susannah—Susannah who so enjoyed her position as the mistress of his home—Susannah the most beloved of all—what of her ? One thing was certain ; one thing admitted of no debate ; he would do nothing to hurt Susannah, Susannah was more to him than all the world ; yes, more than Prue. But why should it hurt her ? Soon now she would marry ; this was as sure as all the summers to come, because her beauty and charm were acclaimed by all. That young Tom. (Albany knew nothing, nothing at all, thanks to Susannah's silence, of the rift between her and Tom.) That young Tom. He might yet be the man to marry her. A lovable lad, and anyone could see that, since he'd fallen in love with Susannah, he'd turned over a new leaf and was behaving well and striving to make himself a profession and an income. He might yet prosper well enough to marry her. Love brought out all that was best in a man—as witness himself now.

And what of himself when Susannah was married ? His heart sank with leaden weights as he imagined Susannah gone from his home for ever. He would need comfort and companionship then.

Decided, was it ? " Do I act upon it ? " Back to the window again. " It is a very great step."

The sun on its afternoon journey helped him. It looked down from a clear blue sky and helped him. Perhaps if it had been blanketed by grey November cloud he would never

268

have gone forth that day. But it was the same sun that had entranced the sad heart of Susannah when she leaned her arm upon the bridge. It invited him out into the clean roads where that pale gold light checkered the shadows of the trees; and where the bright air looked warm and caressing. He decided to go out into the air and to think further as he strolled in the direction of Waterloo Close. He left the room abruptly, said a quick word to Mrs. Kenny, and when she inquired if he'd be back to dinner, answered that he didn't think so. But why had he said that? Did it mean that he was pretty sure he was going to do the deed; that he had a mind to do it before his resolution melted?

But when he was out in the streets he could not drive himself along a direct route to Waterloo Close. Instead he walked round and round the streets behind his dwindling cigar and its blue-grey smoke; round an Inner Circle of streets, and then round an Outer Circle; and it was tea-time when he came towards Waterloo Close. He was disobeying her injunction always to let her know if he was coming, but surely when a man brought such a question as this, he could bring it as a joyous surprise. He turned into the secret and gated close, his pace slowing, because this was a tremendous step that he was taking. The brief, blind avenue was shadowed like a woodland ride by its over-spreading trees, and it was a recess so quiet and enclosed, so sheltered from the winds, that its Viginia creepers still drooped in full red leaf over the garden walls.

He opened Miss Maddow's gate and walked up her hearth-stoned steps. Beneath the Ionic portico he stood for one more hesitant minute; then—what decisive action was this?—he pulled the bell.

It jangled in the basement; and his heart jangled too.

No one answered.

Again; and still no answer. The house was silent; oddly, oppressively, silent.

Now, since his ringing of the bell was the climax to an afternoon of deep thought, this unexpected silence was a sharply unacceptable disappointment. He was loth to go down those steps again without some further effort. So he came from under the portico and looked up at the house. And for a second he thought he saw a face at a first-floor window—a face he could not recognize—peeping through the lacework of the curtains. The window of Prue's room. It must have been a servant's face, and he felt very angry with the girl for shirking her duty and declining to answer his bell. At least she might tell him where Prue was to be found. He rang again. Almost violently.

And still no steps approached the door.

Devil fetch the girl! He came down the steps and walked round the house to look up at its back parts. All was silent there: the kitchens certainly empty. The french windows into the drawing-room were shut—those windows through which, two years ago, Prue had first led him into her house —but were they bolted? Much annoyed by that servant he walked up the three steps, opened the windows without difficulty and entered the pale and pastel-tinted room. He glanced around it. On the little coffee-table by the sofa stood two sherry glasses and a decanter. One of the glasses still held a portion of amber liquid. Cigarette stubs littered an ash-tray. Prue's cigarette holder lay beside it. Queer. He walked into the hall. On the hat-stand hung a man's black sombrero. Such a hat as the Wood's many actors wore to proclaim their difference from the inartistic multitude, and their genius. Albany's fear, pain, and anger were now clamant enough to demand instant answers. He snatched the hat from its peg and looked into its lining. " Geoffrey Allison " said the name-tab. Geoffrey Allison. Yes. Albany, holding the black sombrero, imagined the silver-grey locks and fine sharp features of Geoffrey Allison under its wide brim. Geoffrey Allison: one knew him well by sight: not in the First Eleven of the Wood's actors; say, rather, in its Second Eleven, or its A team: and perhaps that was why he dressed the part and wore his hair like Sir Henry Irving.

God! He put the hat back on its peg but kept his fingers on the brim. He turned his head and sniffed. Stale cigar smoke. He was now no more than a vessel for a racing heart. He must know more, he must know more. He tip-toed up the stairs, passing from twilight to dark because all doors on the landing above were shut. The scent of old cigar smoke seemed stronger in this unventilated darkness above. A stair creaked beneath him. Loudly. He stood still, one foot on a higher tread than the other. His hearing enhanced like a blind man's, he detected whispers in Prue's bedroom: her voice whispering, and a man's.

" But he came in, didn't he? Oh dear, oh dear: Geoffrey! He came in."

" *Tsh !* He will go again. Keep still."

" But I thought he was coming up."

" *Tsh !* "

" Why on earth didn't I lock those french windows ? He knows that way so well."

" Keep quiet. *Quiet !* He will go the way he came."

Then a hush complete.

Albany's thoughts were now a blend of swelling wrath and sickening humiliation, but, strange to say, there lurked in the bitter and boiling cup a faint sweet taste of relief. The need to know all quickened his ingenuity till it was feline in its slyness. He did not go the way he came. He trod heavily down the stairs, opened the hall door and, passing out, shut it loudly enough to be heard in that room above. He went slowly down the steps in case eyes watched him. He walked from such eyes, but returned and entered by the french windows. And softly, soundlessly, he ascended to the dark landing and the closed door. " I am not the fool she thinks." He turned an ear to the crack of the door.

" No, I don't know his name. Who is he, Prue ? "

The bed creaked. " A priceless old silly who comes after me. Surely you must know him by sight. An enormous man with a neat grey beard who wanders about the streets like a lost dog. He's generally smoking a cigar, but rather sadly, as if it were a substitute for all the things he's missed."

" Does he try to make love to you ? "

" In a way, yes. But he's such an old simpleton he doesn't know how to. I should think I'm the first woman he's ever attempted to be amorous with, except his old scaffold-pole of a wife ; and it couldn't have been much fun with her. She's dead now ; and he's trying to be a Don Juan. A Don Juan at nearly sixty ! "

" Hey, but *I'm* fifty-two ! "

" Yes, but you're different. You're so alive. Some men are at their best at fifty-two. My old Sir Albany has only just come alive."

" You don't give him anything, I trust ? "

" Of course not ; silly boy ! " Kisses. " Naturally I don't. You wouldn't like me to do that, would you, my pet ? What do you take me for ? What do you think I am ? "

" A filthy whore." Albany shouted it through the door—and was grateful to Ludlow for having set him free to use this word. He rattled the handle of the door, chiefly to terrify them, because he would not have liked to go in. " Don't you believe her, Geoffrey old boy," he called, " She's been my mistress whenever you were not around. And no doubt she's obliged a dozen others as well." He beat a diabolical tattoo on the door. Tatta-tat-tat ; thump, thump—the last thump like enough to crack the door. This moment must be paying her in full. That tattoo must have beaten its blows on her heart. Loud creaks and rustles as of people stirring, rising, in dismay—he spurred on the dismay. " All that stuff about being one's best at fifty. She said it all to me : the very same words, my dear chap." Three paces from the door he stepped, but thought of something else to say, and went back. " Did she tell you not to come and see her without first letting her know ? Eh ? Did she tell you that ? Well, take my advice, old son, and come one day uninvited. You'll probably find her in bed with someone." He beat another little parting tattoo, almost a friendly one this time and came away ; but again the storming memory flung up something more to say, and he went back. " As likely as not, it'll be her lawyer. Or the fellow she calls her lawyer. Stephens, Sons, and Someone, Bedford Row."

Now he heard their voices, his level and deep, hers shrill and angry. What sort of dog-fight must they begin now ? The bigger the better. " Let her have it, Geoffrey. Don't take it from him, Prue. Let him have it." He left them to it, after one last lunatic " Ha, ha, ha," at the door. He came down the stairs, humming merrily to himself, and shut the door with a sufficient bang.

Slowly he came homeward—even as Susannah had come home, some months before, after watching the door of a caravan. But his thoughts were not the same as Susannah's. His feeling for Prudence had been tenderness and affection rather than passionate love, and he was not suffering now an agony of loss like Susannah's, because all desire for that woman had changed at her chamber door into hate and recoil. And, never really confident that he wanted to marry her, he was savouring more and more that taste of relief in the cup he'd been made to drink.

The bitterest taste in the cup was humiliation : the knowledge that he'd been but a blind fool and a proper subject for ridicule. " He's trying to be a Don Juan." It had a sickening taste as he sipped his medicine again and again, walking home.

But he was not suffering only. Between these nauseating

sips he was giving himself to thought. He was considering the revelations that had come to him ever since he'd changed his clerical coat for a layman's livelier wear, and come to town. Much disillusion had been his; many sentimental beliefs about the natural goodness of mankind had been peppered with shot till they were sadly tattered. Ludlow and his women; Bait and his woman; Vick and Cornelia; Cornelia and her sacrifice of Jean behind pretty curtains of hypocrisy; and to-day the straightest, cleanest shot of all. Walking home slowly, he was accepting, as never before, the heavy truth that only a minority of men were not self-seekers and hypocrites. There was something of knavery, little or large, in most men of business and a measure of hypocrisy, often plentiful, in most men of the professions—lawyers, doctors, teachers, politicians and priests. Careerists, and therefore confidence tricksters, nearly all. And women—what women did not live their lives behind a veil of dissembling? What women were not lechers at heart? Of such knaves and hypocrites he accounted himself not the least, but certainly not the worst, which was comforting. It was a sad but penetrating vision at which he had arrived, and he was rather proud of it.

There was comfort, too, in the thought that the worse the majority of men seemed to be, the less he wanted to be like them. He very greatly wanted to be good. He wanted to be self-sacrificing—up to a point. And sincere. Of this desire he was far more confident, as he walked home, than he had been of his desire to marry Prue, as he walked out.

Thus it was a man not wholly miserable who opened his front door guiltily and shut it guiltily. He walked past the drawing-room door, and stopped. Surely he heard sobbing. Someone was sobbing in the drawing-room. Susannah? Now he was listening at the threshold of another door. Yes, Susannah. Sobbing like a punished child. He opened the door instantly and, going in, saw her thrown down like an old coat on the sofa, her arm along its back, and her head in the bend of the arm, shaking.

" Susannah darling ! My dearest ! "

She sprang to her feet, and he saw her flooded eyes and ravaged face.

" What is it, sweet ? What has happened ? "

" Nothing, nothing," she lamented. " There is nothing the matter."

" But yes, there is. Come. Tell me."

She rushed to his breast and flung her arms around him, and he was happy in this rush and this dependance. Happy to think, in this hour when he was so filled with a desire to be good, " I care only for her. She is the only person I have ever loved properly. I will do anything for her ; anything on earth." He patted her back and stroked her hair.

" Tell me all about it, my pet."

" Oh, Daddy, that fool—he asked me to marry him."

" Which fool, precisely ? " He turned up her chin that she might see him smile. " There are so many fools in this world."

" That fool. That unspeakable fool." And she told him of Mr. Bakewell-Clapton's ' little proposition ' ; and he at first was as indignant as she at that mooncalf's insolence and conceit. *He* to have Susannah ! Susannah, his beautiful daughter. Susannah, allowed by all to be one of the most attractive girls in the Wood and a great prize for whoso should win her.

But the indignation dissolved into humour. " But, darling, this is only something to laugh about. Not to cry about."

" It upset me."

" So I seem to notice. But there must be something more to such vehemence as this." With his silk handkerchief he wiped the tears from under her eyes. " There is something else."

" No, that is all . . . really."

" Is it something about Tom ? "

" Tom ? Good gracious, no. I don't love him any more. I'm not crying about Tom."

" You don't love him any more ? Is that so ? "

" Yes, I'm cured of all that. I'm never going to see him any more. It's a release—a wonderful release, and I'm very happy about it." And she burst into tears again. She sobbed there on his breast and said, " Really happy. It's the best thing that's happened for a long time."

When this paroxysm of happiness was over, he looked down on her, smiling. " Now suppose you tell me the truth instead of all these lies. You and Tom have quarrelled ? "

" Well . . . yes . . . we have. . . "

" Tell me. Come, we'd better sit down to this. I have a feeling this is going to be long." And he led her to the sofa and sat there beside her, holding her hand. And she, nervously squeezing his hand now and then, told him all about her following of Tom and the girl Carolyn, nor concealed the fact that she'd eavesdropped like a spy outside the caravan.

274

He covered her fingers with his spare hand to encourage her—and saw himself on a dark landing outside a bedroom door.

" He seemed to think, Daddy, that it wasn't so very dreadful, what he did ; but it was, wasn't it ? It was unpardonable. Do say it was unpardonable, and I was right to declare I'd have nothing more to do with him."

Albany saw himself going to the gate of Waterloo Close ; and did not immediately answer.

" You must agree with me that it was wicked. It was, wasn't it ? "

He shrugged beneath the burden of answering, and said at last, " Not as wicked as you think. Nature has filled young men with a force far too strong for most of them to manage, and I can only think them hardly done by, and pity them."

" Then was I wrong in saying that I'd have nothing more to do with him ? "

" Yes, I think you were, because he really loves you and probably longs to be better. Or shall I say, you *would* have been wrong, if you'd meant it, which you didn't."

" But I did . . . I did."

" No, you only wanted him to think you did. And probably it was good for him to think so. But, Susannah dear, *you* sin sometimes, don't you ? In other ways ? "

" Oh, yes, I'm awful sometimes. I know that."

" Then surely there's nothing to do but try to understand a young man's difficulties. He loves you and I think that, if you'd let it, his love could bring out the best in him. Love does . . . sometimes."

" Well, what am I to do ? Daddy, be nice to me and tell me what on earth I'm to do ? "

" How far do you love him ? "

" Love him ? "

" Yes."

" Oh, idiotically."

" But just now you said you were cured of your love and it was the best thing that had ever happened."

" Oh, but that only meant that I was furious with him."

" I see. Then I think we must get him back for you. You must tell him he can come back."

" Oh, no, that's out of the question. *I* can't ask him to come back. Certainly not . . . at least, I don't think so."

" Why ? "

" Becasue I just can't do it. How could I ? Do talk sense."

" Why not ? "

" Oh, don't ask why. I don't know why. How should I know why ? I just can't do it . . . ever. That's certain. Never, never. . . . Or not, at least, for a long while."

" But what," he expostulated, " do we do then ? "

" Something may happen. He may come of his own accord —no, I don't think he will now. No, nothing will happen. I'm sure it won't. It's all over—at least for years."

" Have you finished ? Never mind all this pretending. Let's see things exactly as they are. Do you want to marry him ? "

" Why, of course ! Naturally."

" Why ' naturally ' ? "

" Because if I don't marry him, I shall never marry anyone. I shall never love again."

He patted her hand and did not at once speak, because he was seeing the loneliness that stretched before him. " Still," he thought, " *I* don't matter ; it's she that matters ; let me begin now upon this business of self-sacrifice ; " and aloud he said, " Do you know what I wish ? If you've set your heart on marrying him, I'd like it to happen quite soon. It'd be best for both of you."

" Oh no, not just yet."

" Why not ? "

" Oh, we must wait for years. Years and years. Hundreds of years. He won't have any money till he's established himself on a farm."

" He really wants to be a farmer ? "

" Yes, he cares for nothing else. It's a dream that's got him by the throat."

" Well, just suppose that next year, or the year after, he was on the farm and able to keep a wife, would you marry him then ?"

" Oh, yes. Yes, I suppose so. Yes, perhaps. But he'll have to go to a theological college first—I mean an agricultural college—and it's take years and years. Two years at least before anything could happen."

Albany nodded understandingly ; and for the present said no more.

CHAPTER TWENTY-TWO

THE SECRET IDEA

NEXT day people on the pavements of the Wood saw Sir Albany, if they cared to look his way, walking along rather slowly, with mouth slightly open, eyes fixed in thought, hands joined behind his back, and a rolled umbrella dangling from them like a long but well-groomed black tail. The thoughts behind those remote eyes were such as he could publish to none ; not this time because they were selfish thoughts or mean, but because they were on the high places where a man deals in private with his aspiring soul.

Some said that he looked sad ; and sad he was—a little. Not only did he still feel the ache of that lash across the eyes which he'd received yesterday at a bedroom door, but he was also making himself sad by considering the prospect—a prospect which had suddenly come into close view—of living quite alone in his house with no Susannah. Before that moment of punishment on the dark landing, he had selfishly hoped that it would be years before Tom, or any other man, could take Susannah from him, but now—now it was different—now selfish no more (or so he hoped) he saw himself helping Susannah on her way to another and then dwelling alone in his empty home ; eating alone, reading alone, sleeping alone, and getting daily older, while the young people, far away, gave all their love to each other. Susannah would protest that she still loved him, but for nine-tenths of her days, nay, for ninety-nine hundredths of them, he would be forgotten. So it always was. Such was Life's pattern.

He would be left alone in Circus Road like an old stranded bark. Well, if this was right, it had to be. Let it be.

From the soil of his mind, broken up by that deep humiliation of yesterday, and further harrowed now by this prospect of loneliness, there was springing one pleasant bloom—and this was his very secret desire to be a better man. To do good things. Not to be holy—the Lord knew this was impossible because he no longer had the necessary beliefs or the necessary strength—but to be, well, quietly good. Old age was not so far off now; it was creeping apace towards him, and it seemed there was little choice, once this loathly infirmity settled upon you, but to be either an unpleasant old man, selfish and tetchy, or a nice gentle old man, universally loved. Say like old Colonel Budlier. Yes, he would very much like to be a nice old man like Colonel Budlier. He didn't want to be an old nuisance. He wanted to be kind and universally loved.

He must begin now. What could he begin by doing? He must begin with Susannah, because his love of her was a real thing and would give him the much-needed strength. What could he do for her? Let it be something big. For her and Tom. He loved Tom too (did he not love all young people?); and he was ready to believe in the boy despite that caravan. Had he not qualified himself, so recently, to forgive him the caravan? Tom was probably much like himself; a weak lad with one show for the drawing-room and the street, and something quite different within him—something full of unpublishable desires and vanities and self-seeking but housing further in, deep in his innermost cell, a poor, weak hunger to be good.

He compared the young Albany of thirty years ago with the young Tom of to-day. The young Albany, wanting a "gentleman's profession" had taken the road to Orders, and so erred. Tom had started on a similar track towards Law and the Bar, but had seen his mistake in time. He was diverging towards something for which he had a real vocation. Probably if he was given the work of his heart, and the woman of his heart, his life would run clean and straight. Or as clean and straight as any man's.

As he thought this, an idea sprang up in his mind. It burgeoned within him. It spread from bud to blossom and flower, like a plant in a quick-motion film for botanical students. When it was in full bloom he turned about and hastened home to talk with Susannah. Not to tell her of the idea—no, nothing was decided yet—but to get certain answers from her.

He sat down to lunch with Susannah and talked for a time of anything but Tom. Then he shepherded the talk towards him and casually asked, " About that farm? I wonder if he'll ever be able to have it. I suppose it's—" he got up to cut an innocent slice of bread—" it's a question of money."

" Yes, he hopes to make enough money somehow, but, Daddy, I can't see how he can. Everybody tells me it's a crazy idea that he can make any large sum out of selling cars."

278

"Yes, that's a young man's wild dream. One's all too sanguine at twenty-two. How much would he need? Don't you want some bread, my dear?"

"No, thanks, Daddy."

"What were we saying? I forget." He returned to the table. "Oh, yes: Tom. He'd have to make a lot, I suppose?"

"Oh, yes, a terrible sum. He did tell me. I think it was thousands."

"Thousands! Dear me! That's a packet."

"Yes, he'd have to get his training first. That wouldn't cost so much, but he wants to own his farm."

"And how much does a farm cost? I never bought one."

"I think he said fifteen pounds an acre."

"And how many acres are there in a farm? Dear me, this is all very interesting. I'm learning a lot."

"I think he wants at least five hundred."

"Great Scott!" Rapid calculation. "Seven thousand five hundred pounds! Well, that's far beyond him. Have another slice, my dear? No?—well, what were we talking about? Oh, Tom, yes . . . yes. But there's such a thing as renting a farm, isn't there?"

"Yes, and that's what he'll have to do."

"And how much does that cost? You seem to know all about it."

"He's always talking and talking about it—or he was." With a grim little smile, she reminded him that all that was over . . . "Was it fifteen shillings an acre he said? I think so."

"Three hundred and fifty a year. Well, that's not so terrible. With his tremendous enthusiasm he should make the place pay."

"Yes, he says farmers have been doing well ever since the war, but he'll never make enough to buy his farm. And it's certain his father can't leave him anything. He has nothing left but his pension, and that dies with him."

"Perhaps we'll have another war soon, and then he'll make a small fortune. You never know."

After the meal he went out into the streets again to walk round the houses and under the sky. He could always think better when he was walking round houses and dangling stick or umbrella against his back. He walked round and round a circle of streets, stopping sometimes at a corner and letting the dangling stick beat against his thighs. His idea was gaining in power and possession of him. It was filling him with delight. What inner splendour could equal this strong desire to do a good deed in a large way ? But he walked on after these halts with no final resolve as yet. . . .

And it was two more days before the resolve set firmly in its mould, and he walked to the house in Acacia Road, climbed its stone steps, and knocked.

The door opened to him ; and standing there was Tom : Tom with a face as grey-white as the stone steps. For a second Tom's eyes, staring as if punch-drunk with pain, seemed not to recognize who was on the threshold ; then he said, " Oh ! " and " It's you, sir," and no more. No more, as if his brain wouldn't function and tell him what to do. This staring silence put Albany's brain out of gear too ; he didn't know what to make of it or how to deal with it. Was it because he was Susannah's father that the boy stood stupefied ? Was the face of Susannah's father, like a Gorgon's head, turning him to stone ? If so, speak kindly ; put him at ease.

" You look worried, Tom, old man. Had some bad news ? "

" Bad news ! Haven't you heard, sir ? "

" Heard what? "

" About my father. He's very ill. I think he's dying. I— I know he is."

" Tom ! No ! I knew nothing of this. My dear boy, what can we do ? "

" Nothing." The boy's eyes looked helplessly into Albany's. " The doctor says it's only a matter of days. But come in, sir."

" No, I'll go, Tom. You want to be with him."

" The nurse is with him. Do please come in. I shall be glad to have someone to talk to."

" You mean it ? "

" Yes. No one's been near us since yesterday. And in any case they never come further than the step. They come and ask after Father and go. I suppose they're shy of death. I know I should be, but it's a pity ; one longs for someone to talk to. Do please come in for a little."

So Albany followed him into the front room : into that room which was like a palimpsest, where the careless hands of two lonely men had overwritten the delicate caligraphy of a dead lady. There was the piano and the bureau and the work-table littered with the masculine acquisitions, the pipes and cigarettes, the tobacco pouches and copies of *Punch*, which the Colonel was leaving. There was the roll-top desk, so out-of-place in this feminine salon, its surface littered with the bills and letters and business papers which he would attend to no more. And there on its top, in the place of honour, was the framed picture of the dead lady, a graceful, smiling creature in a princess gown.

" Sit down, sir."

Albany sat on the first chair he came to, a tall-back Caroline chair with carved rails and caned seat. Tom sat awkwardly on the long plump arm of his father's fireside chair. He seemed to have no more words, so Albany helped him. " Tell me, Tom."

" It happened some days ago. In the early evening. We were sitting here together, and suddenly he leaned forward and gasped and pressed his hands upon his heart. He looked as if he couldn't breathe. I thought something was suffocating him. He just said, " Tom, Tom, I need help, Tom," and I ran to help him, but he couldn't move for pain. He just gasped, " It'll be all right," but he couldn't stir. The doctor came and told me—told me to expect the end."

The boy's arms and hands and knees were trembling. He couldn't go on.

" And this was some days ago ? Why didn't we know ? "

" I haven't seen Susannah for a long while. She . . . we . . . she doesn't want to see me any more. She said so. She said she didn't want to have anything more to do with me. Besides, I haven't left the house for days in case he wanted me. He lies there so quiet till the next awful spasm of pain. He holds my hand, and I know by his grip what he's suffering. I press back—it's all I can do. I want him to die, sir, and stop suffering. I wish I could help him to die. Oh, sir. . . ."

Tom plunged his head into his grasping hands, and the taut shaking of his shoulders was the only evidence of his sobs. Albany rose and laid a hand on one of those shaking shoulders and gripped it tight. This both encouraged the boy to relieve his anguish in a complete breakdown and sustained him through it. But Albany's gripping hand trembled too because he, who wept easily, was having a task to keep his sympathy within the needful bounds. " He was the best father ever," said Tom, when he could speak. " And I always was a disappointment to him. He tried to do everything for me, he simply beggared himself for me, and I let him down, I let him down always. And it's too late to do anything now."

" Don't you believe it, Tom. You were the joy of his life, and his pride."

Still keeping his head down and his face from sight, Tom asked, " Do you think he knows how much I loved him ? It's so difficult to say anything to a father. I've never in all my life been able to say it. I cannot say it even now—even though I know he is dying. Why can't one say one loves to a father? But I want him to know it, sir, I so want him to know it, before he dies."

"He knows it every time you hold his hand and help him through his pain."

"Oh, I hope so, I do hope so. Do you think so?"

"I am sure of it."

Tom lifted his face. "How is Susannah?"

Albany smiled down at him and let the smile be his answer. It said perhaps, "She pretends she isn't longing for you, but she is."

"You know she's furious with me? And I suppose she was right. Yes, I'm sure she was right. You know all?"

Albany nodded and patted his shoulder. "We all stumble sometimes. Don't have two troubles at once, my boy. I know that she loves you as much as you love her. So give yourself to your father now."

For one second Tom brought an arm across his breast and touched with his fingers the hand gripping his shoulder. It was a simple touch of gratitude, but it pierced into the too soft heart of Albany, so hungry just now for affection. He squeezed the boy's shoulder again and said, "Look: I'm going now because there's something I think I can do for you. I shall come again."

He went home as fast as he could and told Susannah all. And she, all memory of the quarrel thrown aside, all pride burned up in a fire of sympathy, ran through the streets to Tom, to take, as her father said, one sorrow from his shoulders and to bear her part in the other.

For two days Susannah was hardly away from that house in Acacia Road. She was at Tom's side in the drawing-room, where little daily duties had to be transacted or the kindly callers welcomed, and in the sick room above, where the dying man seemed happy to see her, following her movements with his eyes. Thus it was that Death, waiting in that house, blessed the betrothal of Susannah and Tom, and announced it to the world, before he went hence, his business done.

On the evening of the second day Albany walked round to Acacia Road because he felt he'd like to be where these two children were. Acacia Road was very still that evening. For some twenty yards on either side of the white Gothic house thick straw had been laid on the roadway to deaden the noise of hooves and wheels, and the people on the pavements were moved by the sight of the straw to walk quietly and keep silence as they passed the house and looked up at its windows, thinking of death. Before their eyes Albany went through the gate and up the steps, feeling—with his usual shame at his egotism—a pride that they should see him and know he had the privilege of entry.

It was Susannah who opened the door to him. " Oh, Daddy, you're just in time," she said. " He's dying, we think."

" Shall I wait ? Shall I wait downstairs ? "

" No, I think he'll be glad to see you. He's conscious and I don't think he's suffering much. The doctor's given him something to ease the pain."

So Albany walked up the dark stairs behind her to the room on the first floor. His heart beat nervously, for all his life he had feared to come into the presence of death, even though his attendance, as the representative of the Church, had been commanded so often by that royal master.

The blinds of the room were down, for it was past twilight now, and the gas lamps were turned low within their pink shades. This was a woman's room with white-enamelled furniture, and the green carpet, pink curtains, and variously coloured cushions of her choice, all much faded and discoloured now. Flowers, sent by the Colonel's numberless friends in church and neighbouring street, brightened the room from a dozen stances—if they did not sadden it. They filled it with their sweet, green, poignant scent.

Tom was standing by the bed, and he turned and smiled at Albany as he came in. The nurse sat in a chair by the window curtains, with folded hands. Albany walked towards the bed, and Tom's side. It was a big double-bed of shining brass, the bed on which the Colonel had lain with his loved wife and Tom had been conceived.

Very wasted and frail did the Colonel look now. The round face had collapsed to its bones ; and within the grasp of the cropped grey side-whiskers and moustache an eight-days' growth of beard had whitened his chin. One hand, translucent as alabaster, emerged above the bed-clothes and, seeming all of him that could move, kept feeling for and gathering up the sheet. His gentle eyes stared dumbly at them all, because his

283

laboured breathing inhibited speech. They turned towards Albany as he approached; and the head tried to nod a courteous welcome, and the lips to smile and say the same thing. The shoulders too essayed a shrug as though to say, with a last effort at humour, "This is the end, Grahame. This is where we say our good-byes."

Albany laid his hand on that one fever-shrunk hand and pressed down on it; and the Colonel tried to nod a thank-you. Tom, turning to Albany, shook his head gently, as much as to say, "Not long now," and fastened his lips together to control, or try to control, their trembling. Susannah slipped her fingers into Tom's hand.

They waited. Albany's eyes, glancing around the room, dropped upon the objects of the old-fashioned pedestal-table by the bed's side. Two velvet-framed portraits stood there, one of the gracious lady in her princess gown, and the other of a boy in an Eton suit. Below these frames was the Colonel's worn Bible and a little manual of devotional passages to be read before sleep. Its title was 'Come Ye Apart.'

The Colonel's eyes had opened again and were staring up at Tom, and continuing to stare. Albany believed he knew the thought behind those fixed eyes. The father was thinking that his son would now be alone and uncared for, and that he, his father, could leave him nothing. Nothing at all. There was almost an apology in the eyes. They swung once or twice from Tom to Susannah and back again; their brows knitted in some unspoken thought; and then he faintly smiled in pleasure and a hope. Susannah trapped his thought on the wing, and putting her arms round Tom's shoulder possessively, drew him close to her. The gesture pleased the Colonel, and he lifted the eyebrows again and faintly smiled.

Albany had stayed back behind the young people, feeling that he had no such place in the room as they, or such power as theirs to comfort the dying man; but now the Colonel looked at him with the same half-humorous lift of his eyebrows; and he nodded from his place, and smiled back.

But now, suddenly, that thin, fluted, alabaster hand jerked upwards and pressed upon the breast so far as it had strength to do so; a look of agony gripped the Colonel's face; he made a momentary attempt to sit up, but failed, and fell back. Tom flung himself on to his knees by the bed, seized his father's hand in both of his, and held it saying, "Oh, Dad!" And he stretched his head forward and kissed his forehead.

The Colonel smiled happily and lifting up his son's hand a little way tried to shake it many times. The effort ceased, and he closed his eyes. Only once did he open them again, and then —with his pale opalescent hand still in his son's hand which was stroking and stroking it—sank away from them into un-consciousness and death.

It was the hovering nurse who touched Tom's shoulder to tell him that all was over, but he shook her hand away and, understanding its message, forced his face into the bed-clothes and sobbed. Susannah passed her arm around him and he, recognizing her hand, gripped it and hung on to it. It was a gesture like that with which he'd responded to Albany's comfort, but far quicker, easier and more passionate. In time she drew him to his feet, and he put his head into her breast and sobbed and sobbed there as if she had been a mother. " I did help him through his pain, didn't I ? " he asked. " I was all right at the end ? " " Yes, yes, my dear," she comforted him, like one who was twenty years older. Albany stood apart, sure that in this moment there was nothing he could do for Tom which Susan-nah could not do better. He was content to be forgotten for a while.

CHAPTER TWENTY-THREE

THE PLOT

THERE was a large congregation in the pews when the Colonel, for the last time, entered the church which he'd served so long as a sidesman ; but only a few friends, in three carriages, followed him up the steep slopes to the London Cemetery on Highgate Hill. In one of the carriages sat Albany and Susan-nah, both very silent, Susannah looking out of the window at the old grey houses of the Highgate Road, and Albany very erect and still beneath a top hat bound with a mourning band and behind two black-gloved hands which rested on the crook of his umbrella. Opposite them sat Bait and Ludlow ; for this was a carriage-load of old friends who'd evaded together all the strange faces assembled in the Colonel's honour. Bait, the ex-lawyer, was disposed to break the long, slow journey with some *obiter dicta*, but Ludlow, the ex-officer, was plainly convinced, behind a monocle as fixed and steady as the eyes of a sergeant on parade, that a funeral procession should be honoured with silence.

"That boy will have to turn and fend for himself," Bait was saying, either unaware of the Commander's disapproval or indifferent to it. "He'll have to come out of his dreams and turn to and earn a proper living. He's got no father to keep him warm now."

"How much money will there be for him?" asked Albany.

Ludlow tut-tutted in annoyance at this chatter about money on a church parade.

"None at all," proceeded Bait, cheerfully unconscious of this sibilant tut-tut, or indifferent to it, or rendered more contumaciously talkative by it. "Practically nothing, after the funeral expenses have been paid and the few debts settled. They don't drive us very fast, these coachmen, do they; but there: I rather hope they won't go posting along too gaily, when they've got *me* instead of the old Colonel in the front carriage. Yes, I remember the old Colonel saying he'd like to see the boy settled before he died, because he could leave him nothing."

"There's the furniture, isn't there?" suggested Albany.

"And what's that worth? It's all old-fashioned stuff and mostly worn out. It'll sell for a song."

"Then what'll the boy do?"

Bait shrugged. "He was reading for the Bar, but there's no sense in that now. He can't go on earning nothing for another two years, and then sit around, waiting for briefs."

"And in any case," Albany reminded him, "his heart was never in it. He wants to be a farmer."

Bait screwed up his nostrils at this mention of a farmer. "And of all the silly ideas," he said with a sniff, "that was the silliest."

"Oh, no!" Susannah breathed low.

"A boy born and bred in London streets who doesn't know a heifer from a haystack!" Bait scoffed. "Likely to make a farmer, isn't he? And where's the money coming from? He talks about selling cars and amassing capital. Flim-flam. I made some inquiries for him about this motor business and soon saw that there wasn't a chance of his making any money out of it. To begin with, there are far too many lads attracted to it, because they find some glamour in these disgusting machines." His nostrils stood pinched up at the very thought of these disgusting machines. "And they're mostly lads with money to play with, like that empty-headed young wastrel, Charlie Dyson. No, there's nothing in the motor trade for Tom."

" Then he'll have to put the farm out of his head ? " Albany concluded.

" Obviously," sniffed Bait.

" Well then, what *will* he do ? "

" There's one job, and one only for him. He can be an assistant master at a prep. school. Not that he knows anything about anything, but his Cambridge Blue and his Middlesex cap'll get him that any day of the week. It'll get him a hundred a year, resident. And lead him where ? Nowhere. There's no future in it for a man without a degree and, as you know, he came down with a flea in his ear instead of a degree."

" Can't you think of anything else for him ? "

" Here's the cemetery. A real white city of the dead—but why built on London's highest hill ? It's filled up since I was here last. Hope there's still room for us, Grahame. Won't be so long now before we both need a nice berth ; and the Commander too. Personally, I feel partially dead already, and, upon my soul, I never look in my glass nowadays without thinking I look like it. Can't think why any of us, Tom or anyone else, worries about what he's going to do with his life. It's only seventy years between one dismal blackness and the next."

" Can't you think of anything else for him than a schoolmaster's job ? "

" Nothing. Nothing, unless he becomes a professional cricketer."

" Oh, my God, no ! " Ludlow exclaimed. This had provoked even him to speak on parade. " Good Christ, no ! Tom's a gentleman. Excuse me, dear lady ; I forgot you were present. Tom can't be a professional. Never ! " It was as if Bait had suggested an impossibility in the realm of thought, as that a door should open and shut at the same time.

Albany and Susannah were also shocked at the suggestion, but attributed it to Bait's tart humour. After all, the position of his nostrils, as he offered the suggestion, and the sniff that accompanied it, implied that, to him also, it stank.

Ludlow, having been pricked by the appalling suggestion into breaking his irritated and reproachful silence, and having thereby lost his pleasant position of moral superiority, decided that he was free to lapse further into this unseemly behaviour of talking while in a funeral convoy. " By heaven," he said, " if I had any money, I'd help the boy. He's one of the best. But I'm only another useless old officer put out to grass, like his father. Not quite so far out to grass as we're putting the Colonel now, poor old boy, but, as Bait says, we'll all be coming this way soon. If I had a thousand or two I'd rejoice to establish that lad in some worthwhile job before I come feet-first up this hill."

It was as he said this that two things happened: the carriages turned through tall gates into that white city of the dead, and in Albany's mind a door seemed suddenly to open, disclosing a bright light behind it.

When the carriages, their mission discharged among those crowding tombs, their small lading unloaded from the hearse, came spanking down the hill towards the living world and that house in the heart of it, the white Gothic villa, Albany was carrying a happy notion in his heart. He did not speak of it in that house but took it with him to his own home and his study, where he prowled around with it for thirty minutes or so, before summoning Susannah to an interview.

" Yes, Daddy, dear ? " she inquired at the door.

" Come," he said, " and plot."

" Oh, delighted ! " she agreed, and sat herself on a chair's arm to plot. The curiosity in her eyes pleased him. What more pleasant than an audience taut with interest ?

" You heard all that old Bait said about Tom ? "

" Yes. And he annoyed me quite a lot. Silly old man."

" There was unfortunately truth in what he said. Don't you think we ought to help Tom ? Somehow ? In a little way ? "

" Oh, it'd be wonderful if we could. Oh, *do* let's. But how ? "

" You and he are back where you were ? "

" Exactly what do you mean ? "

" You are loving each other as much as ever ? "

" But *yes* ! Why not ? "

" Even after that prodigious row ? "

" Daddy, I love him more. I just know I do. I'll tell you why. The other morning he took me up with him to see the last of his father while the men were already at the door with the coffin. He lifted the sheet off his father's face, and his eyes were full of tears. I could only hold his hand and press it. And he bent down and kissed his father. And he said, " I've never done that since I was a baby ; and he was always too shy to kiss me. I only did at the end when he was dying." Then he broke down again and flung himself on his knees by the bed, crying out, ' Oh, Father ! ' and sobbing. I knew then how terribly I loved him, and I cried bitterly too. We both cried together."

" Bless you, dear ; you could have done nothing better."

" When he got up he came into my arms, and that finished me. I felt something bigger than I'd ever felt. I knew that I could never love anyone else as I love him."

" So I suppose you still think you'd like to marry him ? "

" Oh, of course, of course."

" You have no hankerings after Mr. Bakewell-Clapton ? "

" Who ? Oh, Eddie.   No, I fully intend to be unfaithful to him."

" But just how can you marry Tom ? You heard what Bait said."

" I'll marry him if I have to wait a dozen years."

" Perhaps, between us, we could make the wait rather less. I've been wondering for some time if I could help him, and now, with the loss of his father, I—Susannah, do you think he'd let me—as far as possible—step into the place of his father ? "

" Oh, Daddy, yes ! That'd be wonderful.   But how ? "

" If I could believe two things about him—— "

" Oh, but you *can*—— "

" First, that his dream about being a farmer is a real voca-tion—— "

" Oh, but, Daddy, that's certain ; absolutely certain.   You can see it in his eyes and hear it in his talk.   He's quite different when he talks about it.   You'd hardly know it was Tom.   He's like one inspired ; like a poet.   I'm not a fool, am I ? "

" Not wholly."

" No, and I just know that he'd make a success of it.   So that point's settled.   What was the other point you wanted to believe ? "

" That he'd be a good husband if he was married to some good and reliable woman—— "

" Oh, but, Daddy, he mustn't marry anybody but me."

" Well, let us say he marries Susannah.   Then, if he loves her properly—— "

" He does—— "

" —and if he owes a good deal to the woman's excellent old father. . . ."

" Yes, yes ? " she encouraged him.

" Well, I suppose we could make a good husband out of him as well as a good farmer."

" You mean ? Oh, darling, what do you mean ? "

" Do you think he'd let me advance the money for his training ? I could pretend it was a loan he could pay back. And
then, perhaps, I could buy a farm and put him in as a tenant,
and one day—who knows ?—if it was a success, and he married
some nice girl, I might give it to them both as a wedding
present."

She rushed from her chair to him, hung her arms on his
shoulders and leapt up to kiss him. " Do you *mean* it ? Oh,
how completely Albanian ! Oh, let me go and fetch him now !
He must be so alone and miserable in that house. Let me go
and say you've got something to tell him."

Never had he felt happier than in this moment, with her
hands on his shoulders ; her delight obscured the memory that
he was opening the door for her to go from him. But he did
say, since these were big decisions, " Not so fast, my pet. Not
to-night. Let me think a little longer. To-morrow, perhaps ;
to-morrow."

And to-morrow, in the early evening, he told her to go
and fetch him, making her promise that she would say nothing
of the plot they were concerting together. He might be making
a big effort to be self-sacrificing, but he couldn't deny himself
the pleasure of first disclosing his offer to Tom. So eager
was he for the disclosure, and so happy in the hope of seeing
their happiness, that he watched at his window for their
coming and at last, impatiently, walked across the garden to
the gate and peered round it to see if they were yet in the
road. Yes, there they were : coming through the sunset with
their fingers linked and swinging, and their eyes looking laugh-
ingly at each other. He was moved, much moved, by the
pathos and poetry of two young things, both with the freshness
of their springtime upon them, and a glow upon all their hopes,
because they were young. Youth might not have charity towards its fellows—that came only, if it came at all, after you'd
suffered many things and were growing old—but what a charity
towards life had all the young ! Believing all things, hoping
all things. God bless them, and let their disappointments be
not too great.

He was well pleased to find within himself, now that he was
growing old, this terrible deep feeling for the young. Unseen
of them, he slipped back into the house and waited in his study.

" Here's Tom, Daddy," called Susannah from the hallway.

" Oh, yes ? " Going to the door, he put something like surprise into the syllables, as if he'd been engaged with other and more important matters than two young people. " Come in, Tom. Come in and sit down."

" Susannah said you had something to say to me, sir."

" Yes, I have. Take a cigar."

" Do I stay or go ? " demanded Susannah, standing by the door.

" You go, woman."

" Oh, what a shame ! "

" We shall be much better off without you."

" That seems to me to be nonsense, but—as you say," and she went. Closing the door.

Albany lit a cigar to help himself through this embarrassing business of beneficence. He was surprised that his heart should beat with fear of what he was about to say. " I've been wondering," he said, as he threw the match into the fire and placed himself before it, " what you are going to do now."

" I really don't know," said Tom. He smiled as he said it, but his eyes looked full of unresolved doubts.

" This sudden death of your father leaves you high and dry, I imagine ? "

" It does rather. But I'll find something to do. Mr. Bait suggests that I should be a prep-school master."

" Are you keen on the idea ? "

" Not frightfully, I'm afraid, because it's a blind alley if you've neither money nor a degree. But I must earn something quickly and it seems the only opening anywhere."

" What about the farming ? "

" That's a goner. Gone for six. It was a pleasant dream, but . . . I've woken up."

" You were really keen on that, weren't you ? "

" My God, yes ! "

" Tom, you and Susannah are very fond of each other ? "

" Fond ! I dare say you think it impudence, sir, but I love her madly. I love her like—like heaven knows what."

" I believe you do. And I'll speak for her. I'll betray all her confidences to me. She loves you very much too."

Tom remained silent before this majestic fact, but his eyes were bright with it.

And Albany, beginning after his fashion to walk up and down, went on, " Susannah is everything to me, Tom. Her happiness means everything to me, just as yours did to your father."

" I'm sure it does, sir."

" And, that being so, I should like to think that you two could marry."

" Marry ? But I've got nothing to offer her, and I can't see that I ever shall have."

" Tom, it seems to me that the death of your father ends a chapter and provides the right moment to begin a new one. I want you to start your training. I want you to let me advance all the money you'll need for it, and you can pay it back if— or, let us say *when* your farm begins to show a profit. What's more, I should like you to find a farm of your choice and let me perhaps buy it and put you in as my tenant; and one day— who knows ?—always supposing you make a success of it— I might give it to you both as a belated wedding present."

" Sir ! . . ." The boy was speechless.

" Do you think there's anything in the idea ? Or is it all rubbish ? "

" Sir, I couldn't take all this from you."

" I don't see that I should be doing so much. I'm merely investing some money to secure my daughter's happiness. It's been done before, you know. You see, Tom, I do really believe in you, and I'm quite ready to gamble on you as a farmer and as a husband for Susannah—a good and *faithful* husband."

" I don't know what to say, sir. It's all too overwhelmingly wonderful."

" I don't know what I shall do without Susannah. I shall be very, very lonely." Pacing back and forth, he deplored that he was not strong enough to leave unmentioned his sacrifice. It was some comfort that this ingenuous lad would not perceive the weakness. " It'll be the end of a chapter for me—say, rather, the end of a book. But there you are : such is Life. It's you young people who matter now. Not us who are old."

" Couldn't you come and live with us ? " asked Tom, but even in this moment of gratitude he couldn't hide his doubt about this invitation and his hope that it would not be too readily accepted.

Albany detected the doubt and the hope, and was not angry, because he understood. Rather was he satisfied, perceiving that there was no worth in self-sacrifice unless it hurt a little. " No, no. Youth to youth, Tom. You won't want an old man about the place. I want you to be happy and live your own lives."

" But this is terrific, sir ! " declared Tom, and, bless the boy, his relief that they would not have a father-in-law permanently on the farm was but poorly concealed. Youth to youth. "How can I ever thank you?"

"There's not much to thank me for, Tom, because I don't think anything in my life has ever made me so happy."

CHAPTER TWENTY-FOUR

GEOMETRICAL PROGRESSION

IN the next days so high was his happiness in what he had done, and in the joy and gratitude of the young people, that the desire to sacrifice himself for their benefit increased. It increased by geometrical progression. He considered doing twice as much for them, and then twice that amount again. Having tasted the sweet drug of self-sacrifice, he craved it in larger quantities. He looked for other persons near at hand for whom he could sacrifice himself a little—persons for whom it would not be so easy to sacrifice oneself. These new muscles of unselfishness must be developed by progressively stiffer and longer exercises. Thus his benevolence began to extend beyond these two children and to spread over parts of St. John's Wood.

When he saw the two children together, in street or drawing-room, he would diverge away from them that their happiness in each other might not be diluted by his presence, and he would think, "Yes, there's no happiness like making other people happy." This thought, in a little while, set him wondering whether it wouldn't be right and good to help them to marry sooner; next year, perhaps, before Tom went up in the autumn to the Carter-Weyman's Agricultural College, which was the school of his choice. And casually sounding Tom one day, revealing nothing of what was in his mind, he learned that there were quite a few married students living in cottages around the College buildings.

So? Would it then be a good thing, perhaps, to enable Tom to be married soon instead of in some unnamed future? Must the lad wait for two years, three years, till he'd taken his diploma and established himself on a farm? If he wanted to be a real father to the boy (and he had secretly fallen in love with his idea of taking the Colonel's place), wouldn't it be a

293

very good thing to end his present solitude and strengthen his character by endowing him with the responsibilities of a wife and a home ? Young men, if left in their loneliness, became wanton in their thoughts and went often astray.

And for that matter, elderly men too.

But this was not a plan that he could welcome easily into his mind. Till now he had been enduring the thought of losing Susannah only by telling himself that there were still two years and more to go before she went from him for ever and left him quite alone.

No, not a plan that filled him with pleasure at first, but he was determined not to consider himself too much. He was sick of considering himself too much. For fifty years, for half a whole century, he'd been considering himself too much. Let him try not to consider himself at all.

Or hardly at all.

So he considered only Tom and Susannah ; and once again he found that his pleasure in contemplating the increase of nobility within him more than compensated for his sadness in contemplating the price he must pay for it. There was no doubt, he reflected, that he uttered no lie when he declared that he was more religious now than he ever was. " Indeed I really think that after thirty years in Orders I'm being Christian for the first time."

At which stage he began to feel a contempt for Mr. Bakewell-Clapton who certainly wasn't in sight of what Christianity was.

But what would he do when Susannah went ? Went for ever. That empty place at his table. That empty chair on the other side of his study fire. The silence in the house. Never a glimpse of her sitting happily at her desk and arranging the day's work with Mrs. Kenny. The silence in the garden. No slight figure cutting the flowers there and singing to herself as she walked along the borders. His lonely seat at Lord's.

But he might marry again. Perhaps ; but there was no one in sight, and it was a nervous business, this looking for a wife. Dangerous going. He was in no hurry to begin on it again after his late lee-shore grounding in Waterloo Close and the heavy damage sustained there. And never again would he run the risk of being lured to his humiliation by a—a common whore. Thanks be to Ludlow for his simple Tudor English. No, if he got married again, it would be to some good religious woman. They alone could be trusted, all said and done. But good religious women could be tedious. Very. Remember Delia.

Nothing to do but take these difficult thoughts out into the cool air and walk round the houses with them. And so he walked and walked in the usual circumambience—round Grove End Road, St. John's Wood Road, High Street, and Grove End Road again—trailing his cigar smoke behind him like a slow steamer in quiet weather. And it was just opposite the Eyre Arms at the corner of Grove End Road that an idea stood up before him so abruptly, and with such a light on it, that he stopped on the pavement to scan it with meeting brows. It was not so radiant as to expel all darker and sadder thoughts, but it had this light on it; and it was a light that steadily brightened. Yes, a possible idea . . . very possible. In sudden decision he turned round and walked speedily towards Park Road. Towards Park Road and its string of antique shops. And just as there had been happiness in the thought of visiting Prudence Maddow with an offer that would mean the rebuilding of her life, so there was joy in coming on a like mission to Jean Clapton. How pleasant to see a sudden surprised delight in those sad eyes, and (when you came to think of it) how right, how meet and fitting, to take Vick's child and, with some of the money he had left, build a happier life for her.

Here was the shop. ' Dorothy Dean. Antiques.' Silly name, Too flowery. He went up the three steps and pushed open the narrow door. As he trod on the mat the bell rang. It rang loudly—and to what future ? Summoning Jean to him. Would life be no longer the same because that bell had rung ? He stood amidst the cluttering bric-à-brac, the brass trays, glass inkpots, copper scuttles, drawer-cabinets of birds' eggs and moulting butterflies, all standing or lying upon the black oak dressers, the Jacobean settles, the gate-legged tables and the Tudor Gothic chests ; and as he looked round upon all these ancient pieces of furniture, wondering what scenes they had witnessed in long-dead homes, Jean came from her back parts, tall and formal and remote. But beyond doubt there leapt into her surprised eyes a gleam of affection for him. It was a gleam that would not have appeared there for anyone else.

" Uncle ! "

" How's our Jeanie ? " He took both her hands and just touched her brow with a kiss.

" Oh, Jeanie's dragging along." She returned his kiss.

" And how's Eddie ? How's the Reverend Mr. Bakewell-Clapton ? "

" Quite happy. Only waiting to be made a bishop."

" He's no longer huffed because Susannah was so misguided as to refuse his offer ? "

" My dear, he's forgotten all about that. He'd forgotten it in twenty-four hours. He's chasing one of his churchworkers now, a woman twelve years older than he. She's a good creature, no doubt, but I think she's rather like a camel. She has the same long, rather hairy face and the same apparent sneer for all who are not camels. She's got money, and because she's ugly she'll have him. Some women'll marry anything. Especially if it's a clergyman. Oh, our Eddie's providing for himself all right."

" I think Susannah may be marrying soon now."

" Good for her ! I'm *so* glad." She put a brightness into her eyes that her pleasure in this news might show no trace or shadow of personal pain. It was like the praise, or the show of praise, that an unsuccessful artist will give to a friend whose painting a salon has just chosen. " It's Tom Budlier, of course. They'll make a lovely couple. Oh, I'm so glad for both their sakes."

" I feel pretty happy about them too."

" But what will *you* do, Uncle ? "

" What'll I do ? That's rather something I'd come to discuss with you. May one sit on this settle or is it only for sale ? I may ? Thank you. Well now, say if there's nothing in this idea and send me away. It's just an idea that——— "

But someone *would* come into the shop at that point and engage Jean in prattle, leaving him to sit foolishly on the settle, with the idea still on his lap, still unpacked. This irrupting visitor was a little grey-coated garrulous woman, with a string bag and a fluttered umbrella. She was so small that she seemed a vessel incapable of holding all the gabble that now poured out from her—while the future waited. She prattled about a blue ornament that she needed for some room, about the problem of matching blues, about the price of everything since the war, about her ' passion ' for Wedgwood ware, about a cracked Sévres clock that had suddenly caught her eyes, and (though how she'd arrived in this channel who could say ?) about her boy at school who was a regular caution. She told Jean several of the comical things the caution had said. For twenty minutes or more (or so it seemed to Albany) she prattled on, and all the time she was quite unperturbed by the fact that another customer sat in the shop, tapping a toe on the ground, impatiently. She talked and talked, while a crisis stayed suspended and all the future waited. She let the jabber dwindle as she moved to the door, but turned and talked again about a pair of old Sheffield candlesticks in the window, which she pronounced cheap; then taking a step further, she trod on the bell-push under the mat, screamed at the sound of the bell, and talked about her nerves. These required no little explanation, but at last she went through the door, having bought nothing but leaving a smile for Jean, and strangely enough, one for the customer on the settle.

"Phew!" sighed Jean, as she shut the lady out. "They can never imagine that another woman may not be as keen on talking as they are. Now you see what a female shop assistant has to put up with."

"Jeanie dear, tell me: do you love your work here?"

"Love it? I loathe it. I might quite enjoy it if the business were my own and I could dash about like Molly Prendergast, my boss, buying quaint things and pasting a price on them that gives her a hundred per cent. But poor me: I just sit in a smell of dust for nine hours of the day. And all for thirty shillings a week. Did you know I'd had a rise of ten shillings?"

"You wouldn't like to try your hand at something else?"

"*What* else? A governess at thirty pounds a year? No, thank you. I can at least live alone here and think my own thoughts."

"Jeanie, I was just going to ask you a question when that cylinder of gas came in and somewhat stifled us."

"Yes, Uncle?"

"We were talking about Susannah getting married. I think it possible she may marry next year. Well, if she goes, do you think you could bear to take her place?"

Jean was standing quite still before him. Her eyes pierced into his; her face paled; then her throat and neck flushed and the red mounted into her cheeks. "Take her place?" she murmured in a voice hardly to be heard.

"Yes. I should want you to look after my home, but you do understand, don't you; you'd be no mere housekeeper; you'd be the daughter of the house. You'd be like—well, like my own daughter."

"Oh!" It was like a sigh of unbelief; of protest against something too pleasing to be possible.

"That's the idea. Say if there's nothing in it, my dear."

"Oh, Uncle! No, you mustn't do this. . . . No, we're

nothing to you. You've been much too kind to me already. You've been wonderful."

" But, my good child, it's not I who'll be doing the kindness. I'm asking you to do one to me. I'm asking you to save me from some awful old housekeeper in black bombazine, of whom I should certainly be terrified."

" What about your Mrs. Kenny ? "

" Yes, what about her ? That's a very important point. I must have a buffer between the Kenny and me. I may love her, within reason, but I really can't have her for a companion in my study and at my table ; and I want somebody sitting opposite me, Jean. I'm sure she's Righteousness Itself, but really, now that you've mentioned it, I see that it's Mrs. Kenny I shall want you to save me from. Would you think about it ? It might be only for a little while—till you married."

" *I* shall never marry. What's far more likely is that *you* will."

" What ? An old antique like me ? It's just occurred to me that I'm in my right place in this shop, a genuine antique, deposited with other junk on an old oak settle. Perhaps that was why the voluble and sociable lady didn't notice me here. Or only observed, just at the end, that I was alive."

" Don't be absurd. And don't fish for flattery. You know you're just about the handsomest person anywhere around. I often wonder if my father was like you. You know perfectly well that any woman'd give her eyes to get you. And some horrible scheming woman probably will."

" Well, then, that finally settles it. You must come and protect me. But there's one point, Jeanie : I love your mother very dearly but on the whole, and all things considered, I'd rather she didn't come too."

Jean laughed. " Ma ! Oh, there's no doubt what Ma would do. She'd go and live with Eddie. She's always talking about it."

" But I understood from Susannah that he'd pondered that question and decided that he preferred a wife about the house to a mother."

" Maybe, but he'll always do what his Ma wants rather than what his wife wants."

" But that—that camel you mentioned : would she put up with—I mean, would she welcome his mother as a dear mother should be welcomed ? "

" Oh yes, if she couldn't marry Eddie on any other terms. I

think if you saw the camel you'd agree that she'd marry a clergyman at any cost. Even Eddie."

" All right then. Ma's catered for. But there'd have to be another undertaking."

" And what's that ? "

" That if you didn't like it, if you found you couldn't put up with me at any price, then I should have to set you up in some little business of your own. After all, that would be only fair since I should have ruined your happy and promising job here."

" Happy and promising ! Oh, Uncle, do you think there's any chance of this happening ? "

" That's simply for you to say. We have two certainties to go on : one, that Susannah will marry sooner or later ; and the other, that I don't want anyone else but you."

Jean, Vick's daughter, in whom all effusive affection had long been clamped and closeted out of view, bent forward and gave him a nervous kiss. " How is it that you are so different from my father ? " she asked. " You're all goodness."

He repudiated this with the incumbent ridicule, but he went from the shop, and for a quarter of a mile along Park Road, swinging his stick in arcs and circles because he was happy. Or fairly happy. The heaviness in his heart when he thought of Susannah going for ever was certainly being lightened by the thought which accompanied him, as he walked along swinging the stick, that he would have the love of three children.

It was a large wedding at the church which had known old Colonel Budlier so long as a sidesman. Albany, so much in the giving vein, had told Susannah and Tom to invite everybody to the feast, and since in addition to the guests Tom was known to the whole congregation as the Colonel's son, and to a large pagan public without as a Middlesex cricketer, and since the news ran all over St. John's Wood that some of the most famous Middlesex amateurs, and some of the Gentlemen of England (Tom had played for the Gentlemen last season) including K. B. Glossop, the Surrey Idol, himself, would be there, why, the congregation—or should one say the spectators ?—stretched the pews to their uttermost and burst from them into the aisles. Perhaps half had been invited and the other half come to see.

The beauty of the day encouraged the crowds to assemble. Ten months had passed since the Colonel's death, and it was autumn again. In less than a fortnight, on the first Monday in October, Tom would enter upon his training at the

Carter-Weyman's Agricultural College, and Susannah and he would have the use of a furnished cottage not far from the College gates. Albany and Susannah, searching together, had found this cottage and secured it for two years. Now it was the twenty-second of September—and what a day ! If it was not St. Luke's Summer, or St. Martin's, it was clearly St. Matthew's. When in the early morning Albany awoke to the remembrance that before evening this silent house would know Susannah's voice no more, he rose and went to the window to see what manner of sky would bless or mar his child's wedding. He saw a pale blue sky and a sun so low that the shadows reached from wall to wall of the broad garden. A frost of silver and chinchilla grey powdered the grass, and the autumn leaves lay on this silver hoar in a dabbed pattern of yellow, apricot, and rusty gold. The big beech tree still kept its ruddy leaves and so heavy they were that its branches hung down like tresses. An acorn falling from an oak broke the silence—but was it silence, now that he was becoming aware of the capricious bird-song here and there and the uncertain wavering of the trees ? The dahlias by the path resembled the face of autumn with their proud blooms, and the bright red of their big rosettes answered the scarlet berries along the wall.

Albany had an eye this morning for all these things.

After breakfast—his last breakfast with Susannah—he went forth into the streets, partly because it was his everlasting habit to take his morning cigar round the houses, partly because it seemed best to leave Jean (who was already in residence) and the women to prepare the bride, and partly that he might visit the Assembly Rooms of the Eyre Arms and see that all was in train for the Reception. Walking glumly on, he found some small gratification in gazing upon the beauty of the day. Under the far trees the shadows made a mist of blue, chiffon-soft ; nearer at hand they lay blue on the roadway, their patterns broken everywhere by sunspots of gold ; and above, on the slate roofs still wet with dew, they rested in flung purple shafts —shawls of colour without substance and fugitive. The air was cold, but it was a cold that animated rather than depressed. Indeed the cold air seemed bright like the sunlight.

At noon, dressed in a new morning coat, since these garments were now more fashionable wear than the frock coats of yester-day, and with a gay white flower in his buttonhole that belied the heart behind it, he helped Susannah, in her gown of white slipper satin, into the carriage and sat himself at her side, where, pretending to laugh at their dress and situation, he picked up her hand and pressed it.

In some three hours' time that hand would be gone from him.

As the carriage turned out of Circus Road and went north towards the church, he saw a queue of strangers thronging through its west door, a chain of carriages and cars creeping up to its gates, and an accumulation of sightseers standing along both pavements. " Lord ! " he said, " The whole population of London is assembling. My dear, it might be a royal affair."

" It's Tom's cricketers they've come to see. It's just that the whole of Lord's is there."

" Don't you believe it. It's you they've come to see. Heaven knows why."

" Oh my God, support me, Daddy."

" The bridegroom on these occasions is an appendage of the bride, rather less important and less to be studied than her veil or her bouquet. Still, the sky's done handsomely by poor Tom. It's put on its best suit of Cambridge blue."

" Never mind the sky. I'm suffering."

" But you're happy ? " he asked, suddenly anxious.

Instantly she squeezed his hand—the hand that had provided so much happiness. " Daddy dearest, my happiness is just terrific but it'll be far more perfect in an hour's time when this scarifying business is over."

" Yes, of course," he agreed. " I understand."

Aye, but not more perfect for him in an hour's time. Ah well, and heigh-ho ; that was the way the world went : even the best of daughters found the end of dependence and her passage to a throne of her own more exciting than sad. For the parent left behind it was, or it could be, a small death. And no one in the world, not the best, not Susannah, could have a full share in the sadness of another. One must sit with it alone.

The coachman had a heart beneath his livery and slowed his horses that he might not unship the bride a second too soon and spoil her triumphant entry. And in the slow march of the carriage Albany found himself thinking of the parents who would have no place in this press of people : Delia and Colonel Budlier and Tom's mother. He imagined himself saying to Delia, " I hope, my dear, I've done everything you would have wished for your daughter ; " and to the old Colonel, " I hope I've helped your boy to find himself, sir. I think I have," and to the beautiful dead mother whom he'd never met, " I hope, Madam, that you are satisfied."

And since these were his dominant thoughts and, in the main, unselfish, he forgave himself for a smaller thought that was anything but unselfish, namely, that he and Susannah would make a pretty exciting pair when they entered the church. They should disappoint nobody. This thought at least he needed for his comfort. Never had Susannah looked so beautiful as in her veil and white low-breasted gown, with a double row of pearls about her throat and a sheaf of lilies in her hand. And her father : well, it was certain that he was dressed from crown to foot to create a pleasing impression. In all this well-dressed congregation there would hardly be a more dignified figure than he.

Not a very large comfort, but something.

He was not wrong in his surmise that Susannah's advance up the nave would create a stir. Sighs of admiration followed her all the way to the chancel step ; and not only followed, because they came to greet her from in front as shameless ladies put up their long-handled lorgnettes to scrutinize her or actually stood on the hassocks to get a deeper view.

It was disgraceful in this sacred place, and pleasant.

There in a front pew was Tom, dressed and garnished like a tailor's window-model and waiting for her. At his side, likewise in festival dress and white carnation, towered his best man, the enormous Bill Judd, his Cambridge and farming friend, who'd recently attended his funeral. Bill Judd, looking round and seeing Tom's bride getting so close, hastily poked his charge in the ribs and directed him towards her.

As Tom slid from his pew to join her, and the two children smiled at each other, Albany felt joy in their mutual happiness, which was of his making, but a joy that could not compete with his sadness. Two hours or three, and Susannah would have gone. For ever. A good wine, the best wine of his life, was very near the bottom of the bottle and the dregs.

Standing up there before the packed sightseers, he allowed himself one look round at his guests and at the mass of strangers behind. There was Ludlow, monocle up in the mast-head lookout so that he could see everything ahead, and everything to port and starboard as well ; and old Bait bending forward and peering with a slightly pinched-up nose ; and Cornelia Clapton arrayed in astonishing glory, all frills and flounces and flowers, so that she reminded him of one of his larger dahlias ; and the Reverend Mr. Bakewell-Clapton reading his hymn book through his huge thick spectacles and rendering the hymn with a powerful deep gusto, in that voice which always seemed so surprisingly masculine in such a half-baked figure of a man. There was Jeanie—Jeanie looking wonderfully different already from what she had looked in that crowded, dusty shop, looking brighter of eye, fuller in cheek, less pale of countenance, more erect in carriage—Jeanie changed already by her happier place in the world, which was of his making too. There were Mrs. Kenny and all his maids, God bless them, all in their best and brightest clothes : and yes, there at the back, surely, was Prudence Maddow—Prudence Maddow in a large black hat with an ostrich feather like a breaking wave—yes, he was certain it was she, and he hoped he looked to her like something it was a pity to have thrown away.

But he turned round quickly and faced the Vicar.

Now came the question, " Who giveth this woman ? " and he put Susannah's hand into the priest's, who gave it to Tom ; whereupon Albany put both hands behind his back.

" For as much as Thomas and Susannah have consented together in holy wedlock and have witnessed the same before God and his company . . . I pronounce that they be man and wife together . . ."

How many hundreds of weddings had he taken, how many hundred times had he said these words over the heads of two young people, and only to-day, when his beard was whitening, had his heart really opened to the full beauty of this moment— and of paternity.

What a hubbub of voices in the ballroom ! He alone seemed a little centre of silence among the shrill women, the loud-laughing men, and the scampering children. He wandered among them with his silence ; he stood still at times with hands joined behind his back or a finger and thumb touching his moustaches ; he watched them rather than spoke with them because he'd never been able to mix easily with convivial groups ; and at last he put himself beside Jeanie, where alone now he felt at home and at ease. Together, two solitaries, they surveyed the seething assembly.

" There's one person perfectly at ease," said Jean. " Our Eddie. Just look at him."

Albany looked. There was the Reverend Mr. Bakewell-Clapton ponderously satisfied with his social gifts and his poly-syllabic vocabulary and his haw-hawing humour, fatter than ever, and following after his unfortunate victims, who were obviously trying to shake him off. He would thread after a man, two steps behind, buffeting through the crowd with a continuation of the topic on which he'd been enlarging or with a further specimen of his humour. Now, a victim having escaped him, he had lassoed the Vicar with his rope of talk and was trailing after him, probably with a discursus on some ecclesiastical matter about which he accounted himself an expert, after being a parson for a year. The Vicar moved away, but Mr. Bakewell-Clapton, not having concluded his allocution, went with him.

He was not in the least unhappy to be celebrating the marriage of a cousin to whom he'd offered himself less than a year before ; had he not since then acquired someone else for wife, this tall woman who trailed after him from one victim to the next, and always in silence, because there was no opening for her voice while his was in full flood ; this tall, well-meaning but ill-favoured woman, with whom he was as satisfied as with his priestly collar, his pale moustache, and his conversational talents. Or with his grey spats. Mr. Bakewell-Clapton was surely the only parson in England who enlivened his sable garments with a pair of dove-grey spats. Did he wear them perhaps because, to his simple mind, they felt like junior episcopal gaiters ?

Unhappy ? Not a trace of it. Why, when he first greeted Tom at the Reception he had held his hand high, to smack it down on the bridegroom's and press it even unto torture, while he declared in loud voice, " I salute the Lucky Man, haw, haw, haw. The Happy Benedick caught in the snare. She's inveigled you into it, has she, but never mind, my dear chap ; believe me, there's no life like it. I speak as an old married man, haw, haw, haw . . . haw . . . haw."

" Who is the fool ? " inquired Tom of Susannah, as Eddie and his lady passed on.

" That, my pet," said Susannah, " is the Reverend Mr. Bakewell-Clapton, and he is now your cousin."

" Good God ! "

" Never mind," said Susannah. " We shall soon be in Suffolk."

Not once that afternoon did their cousin pass them, as he chased through the mob after a victim, but he discharged another jest in their direction or briefly patted the happy bridegroom on the shoulder in fraternal felicitation—nay, in paternal benediction since he was now a father-in-God.

Now Jean and Albany were watching him as he chased after the Vicar, attached to him by a leash of talk, and holding his end of the leash securely.

" He fully imagines he's the life and soul of the party," said Jean. " And *is* the lad enjoying himself ? "

" In spite of the fact that he's the rejected suitor at the wedding ? "

" My dear, he's forgotten that he ever proposed to her."

" Couldn't you extricate the poor old Vicar from his clutches ? "

" Oh, must I ? If I do, he'll tack himself on to me. He'll follow me back here, talking all the way."

" I think you should sacrifice yourself for the Vicar's sake. After all, you're Mr. Clapton's sister."

" But, my dear, the one thing I don't want anyone to know is that I'm his sister. That's why I keep a safe distance away. No, I'm sure the Vicar teaches his people to suffer fools gladly. Let him have a little practice at it himself."

The gay gabbling and general bavardage turned to humorous cheering as Tom and Susannah approached the buffet table and the tall tiered cake. Directly behind them marched Commander Ludlow, glass in hand, and singing for their comfort (with some recollection of an earlier party at these Grahames) " There'll be no war So long as we've a king like good King Edward." Behind him came Bait, his nostrils registering a slight distaste because he had to make the chief speech. He raised a thin hand for silence. The crowd condensed around the young couple and the cake and the speaker ; but Albany stood well back from this lively crush, a solitary figure temporarily forgotten because all eyes were on Bait.

Bait coughed and cleared his throat. He had no voice for speaking to a crowd, nor any gift for platform oratory. He who could talk so amusingly to a single listener was as nervous as a cat when he had to address a field of staring faces. His jokes which came naturally on his private carpet sounded unspontaneous and effortful now ; and indeed they were laboured things, and elicited only the dutiful and uncomfortable laughter of good-hearted people who wanted to save a speech from failure.

It was only, he began in stilted and hesitating fashion, because he was Sir Albany's oldest friend that he had been entrusted with the great honour of proposing the health and happiness of these two young people, and he was sure there were others far better qualified to do this——

Commander Ludlow, to help him in his manifest difficulties, shouted " No, no ! " but unfortunately this did not help ; it only drove Bait off his course, so that he looked in some dismay at the interrupter and had to clear his throat once and again before he could recover his bearings. Back on his course he worked his way towards certain jokes about women and wives which he'd sought for diligently and unhappily, all last night, in jest books, novels, and manuals on public speaking. As always, when a speech is prepared in this way, there was insufficient justification for the borrowed epigram or anecdote, and he delivered the point with too much emphasis.

But then, all of a sudden, and to the people's great relief, he really did score a boundary or two off his own bat. " I understand," he said, " that Tom is some sort of priest or hierophant in that shocking cult down the road at the place called Lord's. What kind of heathen mysteries are performed there I fortunately have no knowledge. For all I know they may resemble the famous Eleusinian mysteries in Greece, where, we are told, strange and appalling happenings were witnessed by the spectators and horrible noises and howlings heard, what time the ground quaked and the Shrine itself was alternately resplendent with brilliant fire or covered with darkness and gloom." This seemed so admirable a summary of any afternoon's entertainment on an English cricket field that the Gentlemen of England and the Cambridge Blues bellowed loud and heartily and applauded so stylish a stroke. Much encouraged, Bait went on, " So in my ignorance I do not know whether I am right in suggesting that Susannah, who's now an initiate in these mysteries, has clean bowled Tom or Tom has claimed Susannah's wicket—— " at which Ludlow, as delighted as the rest with the happy metaphor, called out, " Why, it's Susannah of course ! Susannah who's caught and bowled him. Susannah every time ! The umpire's finger's gone up for you, Tom. Caught and bowled Grahame." And he clapped Susannah's achievement. Others clapped too and cheered.

Lastly, and to his surprise—and pleasure—Bait scored a further six with a remark that he'd not intended as a joke at all ; it was when he turned to Susannah and began, " I raise my glass to you, Mrs. Budlier—— "

He could not continue the toast, for all cheered this new title, and laughed in surprise at it, and raised their glasses to it, repeating, " Mrs. Budlier : Mrs. Thomas Budlier " ; and deep from the body of the hall came Mr. Bakewell-Clapton's

" Mrs. Thomas Budlier, haw, haw, haw," the last haw a laggard which had a silent room to itself.

There was one only who did not laugh at this new name, but he smiled fittingly and continuously that he might not spoil the fun.

When at last the taxicab was at the Assembly Room doors, and the whole company had poured on to the pavement for the high-jinks and horseplay with confetti and rice, Albany stood behind them all, not wanting, once again, to spoil with his silence their noisy fun. He stood there with the required smile, looking at the motor taxicab, which was a vehicle new enough on the streets to be worth a study. He stretched his neck to examine it better.

Now an excited rustling and ebullition among the people, and a tight-lipped smile on the faces of most as they kept their confetti-laden hands out of sight, showed that Susannah had appeared in her going-away dress, with Tom in his overcoat at her side. The cries rose, " God bless you, dear," " All the best, Tom, old man," " Every blessing on you both," " Good-bye," " Good-bye," and from Ludlow, " Good-bye, Summer, good-bye, good-bye : The swallows are making them ready to fly " ; Susannah and Tom perceived the grins and the hidden hands ; they appeared to bend their heads as if to charge through a hail-storm ; and for a heart-stopping moment Albany thought that in the *mêlée* they would dash to the cab without a last good-bye to him.

But it was not so. Susannah, holding Tom's hand, looked about her, saying, " Where's Daddy ? " and when she saw his head at the back above all the others, she pushed her way towards him, bringing Tom like a longboat in tow. She threw her arms around his neck and dragged down his face to kiss. " There's never been any father like you," she said ; and when, unable to speak, he shook his head, she insisted, " Oh but yes ! It's no good being silly about it ; the plain fact is that in all history there's never been a father like you."

Many times she kissed him and, between kisses said, " Jeanie's promised me that she'll look after you. She will ; I know she will ; she's bound to because she loves you almost as much as I do. You do, don't you, Jeanie ? Yes, of course : how could she do anything else ? "

He only patted her back with locked lips, and then unlocked them to say, " You must go now, dear. Mustn't miss your train."

Susannah pulled forward the longboat. " Come, husband mine, say good-bye to your father."

Tom put out his hand shyly. " Good-bye and thank you for everything, Father," he said, and this word on the boy's lips gave Albany an unexpected and sharp pleasure.

He nodded gratefully and patted him also on the shoulder. Then, waving to him, the two children ran through the riot to the cab, and the cab carried them, still waving in acknowledgment of the cheers, to the nearby corner of the street. Albany and Jean walked to the corner to watch the cab as it dwindled down the long straight stretch of Wellington Road towards the high wall of Lord's and the five-branched crossroads which would swallow it up. In that dwindling cab, thought Albany, are Susannah and Tom, speeding towards the enchanted garden of love and mutual possession. Oh, might they be of the few for whom the enchantment, though it must surely fade, would never wholly pass. The cab swept round the corner of the crossroads and was lost. A moment of very great pain as he thought, " That is all. Save for a visit now and again they will come no more "—and then he turned to Jean with a smile, saying, " Come, my dear, we must go back to our guests. You are my hostess now."

CHAPTER TWENTY-FIVE

THE RESIDUE

Now that Susannah was gone Sir Albany indulged more than ever his habit of wandering round the houses with his stick dangling behind him and his head full of thoughts that he could never open to anyone. Nearly always he followed the same route—Grove End Road, St. John's Wood Road, the wall of Lord's—and thus there was no more familiar figure in this small section of London's multitudinous streets ; nor, for that matter, one more admired by the women. " He has such a kind smile," they would say.

Sometimes he was thinking of the past ; of Delia ; of Susannah ; or of days before he'd known either of these ; days when he and Vick were boys together on Richmond Hill with all their larger sins ahead of them. Brooding thus, with lips pouting forward between moustaches and beard, or with his cigar sending up a blue smoke like the very substance of these transient dreams, he would recreate many a scene of childhood and early manhood and draw some pleasure from the melancholy beauty that bathed them now. At other times he was considering the vision, the philosophy of life, the religion (if you will) at which he had arrived, and of which he was proud. To Tom Hood, we may remember, it gave little joy to think he was 'farther off from heaven than when he was a boy;' Sir Albany Grahame's most secret thought, it must be confessed, was of the opposite colour: he felt some small joy in thinking that he was much better now than ten years ago. More religious than ever he was.

Most men, he was now convinced, were slightly or greatly knavish in their businesses, and all, yea verily all except the saints, were hypocrites of larger or smaller degree, hiding their self-seeking behind pleasant masks that would be acceptable to the world. He, alas, had been one of the larger kind for his first half-century, but he had now diminished, thank God, into something rather smaller. Something less unamiable, he felt; something even perhaps (as men went) rather admirable.

And the most of mankind were fools, and the knaves, for all their pride in their smartness, were perhaps the biggest fools of all, because they were blind to where true happiness lay. Himself was less of a fool now, and content to live in quiet, as he liked to think, apart from the rascality and folly of the world.

Good, then. This was the residue after the old hypocrisy was shed; this the vision. He no longer pretended to know anything about the Awful Power behind the world, but he could bow before it in wonder and hope, trusting that it was benevolent and worked its little growth within a man, if he would let it do so. Oh, yes, there were all those bewildering incompatibilities, Good and Evil, Love and Hate, Joy and Pain, and there was no explaining them yet; but a man must accept them, knowing it presumptuous to think that because their explanation was not yet obvious to human intelligence, it was not there, somewhere behind the sun.

"No denying," thought Sir Albany, swinging his stick, "that since those Mosgrove days I've changed into something quite different from anything I pretended to be then. I am really religious now. Far more truly religious than ever I was."

Only a wonder and a hope about God and the Eternities, but a certainty, a final certainty, about Man in Time: that kindness and service and judging oneself before others were the rudder by which to steer one's prow.

A narrow vision, but sure ; and repaying one with happiness when one tried to be loyal to it. Such the residue.

Thinking such thoughts, he would sometimes see little of the houses and gardens he was passing, and much of the pavement at his feet ; but one afternoon he really did apprehend, and for the first time, an enormous block of mansion flats that now stood in Grove End Road. It must have been standing there for some months now ; he must have passed it many times while it was climbing towards the sky behind its thicket of scaffold poles ; but he had never properly considered it. He halted in his stroll to do so now. He took his cigar from his mouth, exhaled its last draught of smoke, and surveyed the massive block from base to cornice.

Nine storeys high, all red brick and white paint, it rose like a crimson, many-windowed mountain above the little square houses in their walled gardens. It made them look like the homes of a different world. It thrust them into a past time. And suddenly he saw all the little individual houses, including his own, as existing fifty years in the past. Soon more and more of these mansion flats would tower like islanded cliffs above the low slate roofs of the villas and the swelling foliage of their trees. The roadways and pavements would remain, and perhaps too some of the garden walls, because they had been well and truly built in their day and would serve as fences for the buildings of a new age. He saw these winding, bosky roads as they would be then ; streets of long-spent sorrows and joys long dead ; the streets where two young people in old-time clothes, Susannah and Tom, had walked as lovers or lingered to embrace ; the streets where he himself had walked with his shames and hungers, and with his aspirations (more shameful than the shames) after love and self-improvement. They were not famous people, he and Susannah and Tom ; their lives had touched nothing of importance ; and no one would know of them in this distant to-morrow. They would be like faded figures in a picture of no value and long cast out. Or, let him say, like leaves of the Wood that had had their summer and been long ago swept away for mould.

The Wood. Change ; ever change. He looked yet farther into the future—into some future beyond easy imagining. What would this timbered suburb in which he now stood be like then ? Once, not so very long ago, it had been a dripping wildwood ; one day, perhaps, when Man was dead, or gone from the old London site, it would be jungle and forest again.

A rueful thought this should have been, quenching men's pride and hope and struggle; but it wasn't; somehow it wasn't; it seemed to inspire rather than depress; he got more satisfaction than sadness from it, as he contemplated his power to deal with thoughts so profound and the measure of poetry that must undoubtedly be within him. He turned about and walked homeward along the serpentine twist of his own Circus Road, dangling his stick, and continuing to think with pleasure of himself as a figure everywhere forgotten and walking in a time long past.